FORGOTTEN

P.C. & KRISTIN CAST

First published in the US in 2019 by Blackstone Publishing

This paperback edition first published in the United Kingdom
in 2020 by Head of Zeus Ltd

9 7 5 3 1 2 4 6 8

A catalogue record for this book is available from
the British Library.

ISBN (PBO): 9781838933869
ISBN (E): 9781838933852

Typeset by Adrian McLaughlin

Printed and bound in Great Britain by
CPI Group (UK) Ltd, Croydon CR0 4YY

Head of Zeus Ltd
First Floor East
5–8 Hardwick Street
London EC1R 4RG

WWW.HEADOFZEUS.COM

To my good friend Bridget Pilloud,
who shined a light in the middle of darkness.
Thank you, girlfriend.

Prologue

Once upon a time, long, long ago, there was only the Divine Energy of the universe. Energy was neither good nor bad, light nor dark, male nor female—it simply existed, a maelstrom of possibilities, clashing, joining, and growing. As Energy grew, it evolved. As it evolved, it created.

Energy first created the many realms of the Otherworld, filling them with beauty and magick. Those incredible realms inspired more creations. From the womb of each of the Otherworld realms great solar systems were born, tangible reflections of the Otherworld Old Magick filled with countless celestial bodies. Energy divided and evolved, reflecting the infinite aspects of the Divine. Some Energy was content and rested, eternally existing in a swirling orbit of stars, moons, suns, and beautiful, but empty, planets.

Some Energy destroyed its creations, more content with itself than with possibilities.

And some Energy continued to change, evolve, and *create*.

In one Otherworld realm, the Divine Energy was particularly restless and precocious because it desired companionship. So, from the magnificence that was the Otherworld, the Divine fashioned fabulous beings. It then breathed immortal life into the beings, and thus were born the goddesses, gods, and the sprites that made up the many magickal species called fey. The Divine granted the gods and goddesses dominion over all the Otherworld realms and tasked the fey with being their servants and helpers.

Many of these immortal beings scattered throughout the endless Otherworld realms never to return, but for those who remained at their birthplace, the Divine had a gift. They were given an additional dominion over all other immortals, that of the stewardship of one spectacular planet in their system and all of its mirror worlds—a planet that intrigued the Divine Energy because it reflected the emerald and azure beauty of the Otherworld. The Divine named the planet Earth.

The Divine adored Earth, so much so that it stroked Earth's surface and became her lover. Alas, Energy cannot long be contained, and it eventually moved on from Earth, but not before it granted to its lover Earth the Divine's most precious gift—the magick that is the power of creation.

Young Earth, fertile and curious, began to create.

The goddesses and gods were intrigued by Earth and her mirrored images. They and their fey visited often, and Earth welcomed the immortals, children of her beloved Divine. She loved them so fondly that she was inspired to design a very special creation. From her bosom, she formed and then breathed life into beings that she fashioned in the very image of the goddesses and gods, naming them humans. Though Mother Earth was not able to give her children immortality— that was a gift only Divine Energy could bestow—she placed within each of them a spark of the Divinity that had been shared with her, ensuring that even though their bodies must always return to the Earth from which they had been made, their consciousness would continue eternally in the form of spirit, so that they could be reborn again and again to Mother Earth.

Created in their image, Earth's children enchanted the goddesses and gods, and the immortals vowed to watch over them when the inevitable happened and their mortal bodies died.

All was well for many generations as humans prospered and multiplied. They were grateful to Mother Earth, each culture holding her sacred. The goddesses and gods visited Earth's children often, and humans revered them as Divine.

Well satisfied, Mother Earth retreated within herself to rest from the strain of creation. When next she awakened, eons later, she looked for the children of the Divine and was hardly able to sense their presence at all. Concerned, Mother Earth called to Air, commanding the element to send out a message to the Otherworld, asking the children of her beloved to remember their vow and return to her.

Only one immortal responded. The Goddess Nyx, in her many forms, had remained true and faithful, even after her brothers and sisters had become bored and restless and deserted Earth.

Mother Earth was moved by Nyx's fidelity. Grateful for her loyalty, Mother Earth granted Nyx dominion over the five elements, and she gifted the young Goddess with her heart's desire—two beings created especially for her.

The first of the winged immortals was the son of Mother Earth and the Moon, fashioned to be Nyx's warrior and lover. Earth named him Kalona and gave him silver-white wings.

Kalona's brother came next, created from the union of the

Earth and the Sun to be Nyx's playmate and friend. Earth named him Erebus and gave him golden wings.

To test the strength, intelligence, and loyalty of her new creations, and to be sure they were worthy to be companions to her precious Nyx, Mother Earth fashioned three tests the brothers were required to pass before they could join their Goddess in her Otherworld.

In one of Mother Earth's realms, Kalona became incensed with jealousy during the testing process, misunderstanding his golden brother's relationship with Nyx, and the winged immortal allowed Darkness to taint his spirit so completely that not even the Goddess's love could save him.

But through Kalona's jealous mistakes, and the violence they caused, came about the creation of Nyx's most special children, her vampyres. The day of their creation was so tragic for Nyx that the Goddess made Kalona and Erebus swear an oath that they would never speak of the events of that day. Our young Goddess did not understand then that by silencing the truth, she was setting into motion a series of disastrous events. Though Erebus and Nyx tried to mend Kalona's spirit—tried to make him understand that anger and jealousy beget only despair and disaster, Kalona refused to soften. So, to save the Otherworld from encroaching Darkness, Nyx broke her own heart and banished Kalona from her realm. As he Fell to Earth—as he tumbled to his exile—the color of his wings changed from silver to black.

In his grief and anger at being separated from his Goddess, Kalona became completely consumed by Darkness. He terrorized Nyx's human children until finally the Wise Women of the Cherokee people created a maiden to draw Kalona into a trap, where Mother Earth imprisoned him for generations until the vampyre High Priestess Neferet, another fallen follower of Nyx, released him.

Though Kalona eventually evolved enough to earn forgiveness from Nyx and was able to rejoin his Goddess as her Consort in the Otherworld again, he left in his past a trail of violence, destruction, and despair that would haunt him for eternity.

But what if…?

What would have happened if Erebus had somehow gotten through to his brother? What if Erebus broke his word to Nyx and spoke to his brother about the events that had changed them all so tragically? What if that very sacrifice of his oath, and something much, much deeper, managed to make Kalona understand there was no need for his jealousy and rage?

What if Kalona of the Silver Wings had never Fallen?

Well, dear readers, in a mirrored realm of Mother Earth, that is exactly what happened. Turn the page and learn of Erebus's choice. A choice that saved himself, his brother, and—ultimately—two worlds.

Nyx's Realm
in the Other World

I

Other Erebus

Erebus couldn't stand to watch Nyx suffer—especially as he was coming to believe more and more that a simple misunderstanding was the cause. *It would be so easy to fix this if we could just explain to Kalona that he misunderstood what he had witnessed.* The golden-winged immortal pondered silently as he stood in the arched doorway to Nyx's suite of chambers. Within, the Goddess sat lethargically on her balcony, looking out over a crystal lake so blue it hurt Erebus's eyes if he gazed at it too long. Water sprites frolicked in the waves, doing impossible flips and spins and dives as they tried to amuse their Goddess, and though they sparkled like precious jewels, Nyx barely glanced at them. She reclined on a cloud-like chaise lounge, looking at the beauty of her Otherworld but seeing nothing except her own sadness.

Erebus wasn't surprised. He'd seen his brother's moonlight-colored wings flash as he flew away from the Goddess's balcony. The dark look on Kalona's face and Nyx's melancholy told Erebus everything he needed to know.

"Blessed morning to you, my Goddess!" Erebus greeted Nyx as he entered her chamber.

At the sound of his voice, Nyx sat up and smoothed back her mass of thick, dark curls, turning to smile at Erebus, though the winged immortal saw that the Goddess's lovely smile did not reach her eyes.

Today she had chosen to appear in skin the color of the fertile earth she loved so well. She wore sheer sunset-colored silk that alluringly draped her athletic body. Around her neck was strand after strand of maroon beads that glistened magickally like they held secrets.

"Blessed morning, my Erebus," Nyx greeted him as he bent to kiss her smooth cheek.

"Ah, today you are lovely Oya! Are we going to visit the earth felines you're calling Golden Cats, or are you simply going to run with the antelopes again?" He pulled a strand of her springy curls playfully.

"You know me so well, sweet Erebus. You are correct. I had thought to visit the Niger River and perhaps frolic with my Golden Cats before racing some antelope." Her gaze slid from Erebus to stare from her balcony up, up as she obviously searched for a glimpse of moonlight wings and passionate, amber eyes.

"Have you and Kalona argued again?" Erebus asked softly as he sat beside Nyx.

"You already know the answer to that question, my friend," said the Goddess.

"What was it this time?"

She sighed. "I mentioned the Golden Cats."

"Ah, his jealousy. Again." Erebus had introduced Nyx to the wildcats that delighted her so and had gifted the first vampyre maiden ever created with a magickally domesticated version of those kittens, earning his Goddess's sincere appreciation. Since that day Kalona hated even the mention of felines.

Nyx nodded in weary agreement. "Again." Then she shook back her mass of ebony curls and waved dismissively at the sky, saying, "No matter. You and I shall frolic with the Golden Cats and race the antelope. We will have a wonderful day. Perhaps we will visit one of the tribes that hold Oya's image dear and I will invoke water to bless their planting. That will cause a joyous celebration."

"It certainly will, and I think it is a nice idea. Your people will be grateful." Erebus paused and took her hand in his. "But before we go, please talk to me. You do not have to carry your sadness alone."

Nyx met his gaze. "Speaking of it feels as if I am a naive maiden pining for…" Her words faded as her gaze lifted again.

"Pining for the moon?" Erebus offered.

Her melancholy gaze found him again. "I don't suppose I have to speak of it to be the pining maiden. You do know me, my friend. And so you know my sadness. I am sorry."

He held her hand gently. "You have nothing to be sorry for."

"I do. Somehow I have caused—"

"My Goddess, forgive me, but I must interrupt you. *You* have not caused anything. May I speak plainly?"

"Of course."

In a rush of words Erebus told her what he'd been silent about for far too long. "You did not cause Kalona's jealousy. I did not cause Kalona's jealousy. Nor did we cause the anger that is festering within him and—" Erebus paused, suddenly not sure he should speak quite so plainly to his Goddess.

"Festering within him and what? I granted you leave to speak your mind, Erebus. Please do so," the Goddess commanded.

"And destroying his capacity for love," Erebus said slowly and distinctly, realizing at that moment just how true his words were. Kalona should be completely content to live an eternity as Consort to Nyx. He was created to be her warrior and lover, yet as each day went by it seemed the winged immortal became more withdrawn and angry—always angry. If something didn't change soon, Kalona's anger would, indeed, eventually destroy everything of Light within him, including his ability to love.

Nyx stood abruptly, pulling her hand from his. She walked to the edge of the balcony. Erebus followed her.

"Forgive me," he said.

She shook her head. "I think you and I must stop apologizing to each other about your brother. He is not here—he is rarely here—but his anger still feels present, and I believe that is because you and I apologize our way around the wounds his anger causes and do not speak of it."

"Then let us speak of it. I was created to be your friend. Let me share this sadness with you—as a friend."

"Erebus, recently I have often wondered if…" Her words faded as she stared miserably into the sky.

"If what, my Goddess, my friend?"

Nyx turned to Erebus. "I have been thinking that perhaps Kalona was flawed from his creation."

"You will have to explain that," said Erebus.

"He was destined to be my warrior and lover. Perhaps he wasn't given the inherent joy you were given as my playmate and friend. You find joy so easily—so naturally. It is one of the things I love most about you."

Erebus drew a deep breath and released it slowly before speaking, choosing his words carefully. "Joy isn't easy or inherent. It is a choice, and not always an easy one—not at first. I've wanted to retaliate against Kalona's sarcasm and anger and just general grumpy meanness, but I *choose* not to. Though I do understand your meaning. We were created to fulfill different purposes, and though we are brothers we are definitely not similar."

"You do not have his rage. You never have. Nor do you have his despair," said the Goddess. "His rage baffles me, but it is Kalona's sadness that hurts my heart." Nyx cocked her head, studying Erebus. "You still love him too."

She didn't frame it as a question, but Erebus answered. "Yes. I love him. Now he is almost always brooding and unapproachable, but he was not always like this. When Mother Earth first created us, Kalona was surly, and his sense of humor tended to be rather dark, but he used to be able to set aside the jealousy he was beginning to feel for me. And when we arrived here in your magnificent Otherworld, he and I used to spend easy days fishing together or simply roaming your groves and talking of the silliness of humans and the strangeness of some of their animals. Have you ever seen a creature called an anteater? Or a blowfish?"

The Goddess's smooth brow furrowed. "I have not."

"Well, Kalona and I have seen them. We had *fun* observing them. We laughed together." Erebus shook his head. "Those were good days. I wish they had not ended."

"You miss him too."

"I miss who he used to be, and the Consort and brother

he could have chosen to grow into. When he isn't here now, I do not miss him. At all," Erebus said firmly.

"I understand exactly what you mean. I love him well, but I am beginning to believe—for the first time in my eons of existence—that love might not be enough."

"Oh, my Goddess! No! I cannot bear even the thought that you might become cynical—might turn away from love."

"I do not turn from love in general—not for my earthly children, not for you. But Kalona was created to be my love, so if he cannot love me then I fear, perhaps, I was not meant to have a Consort." Her gaze went skyward again. "And if Kalona continues to reject all that is offered here…" The Goddess made a sweeping motion that took in the glistening Otherworld, her palace of wonders, and finally herself. "Then I must consider whether or not this should be his home. Mother Earth warned of Darkness encroaching on this place through Kalona's anger, and I will not have my Otherworld, or myself, tainted by evil."

Erebus drew a deep breath, as if he was readying himself to leap from the balcony and dive into the bottomless crystal lake before them. Then he spoke quickly, before his words could stop themselves. "Perhaps we should speak of it. Perhaps we should explain to my brother that he was mistaken in what he saw that day—in what he has assumed since the night that—"

"No!" Nyx's countenance changed. Her eyes sparked with anger and her voice shook the palace around them. She grabbed Erebus's hand and pulled him from the balcony into her chamber and away from the prying eyes and listening ears of the fey. "You gave me your oath! We speak of the events of that day and the sprites will eventually overhear us.

You know how they are! Their gossip will spread to earth and my children, my vampyres, will hear of it. I will *never* have my precious children of the night know that they were born of tragedy. Humans already vilify them because they are different, special, *spectacular*. It would devastate my night-dwelling children to know that their beginning was a bloody accident I corrected by creating them."

"Even if your silence causes your heart to break?"

"I am a goddess. My children often break my heart."

"Your children, yes. One expects that from the young and the mortal, but I was not speaking of them. I was speaking of your lover, your warrior, your true—"

Nyx pressed her finger against his lips. "I know of whom you were speaking, and my answer is the same. You know me well enough by now that you understand I am not changeable or prone to fickle fancies. I asked for your oath of silence and I will keep that oath—heartbreak or not."

Erebus bowed his head to her. "I meant no disrespect."

Nyx took his hand in both of hers. "Oh, Erebus, I know that. You are my true friend and you brighten my days like the light of your father, the Sun. Ignore my melancholy. I am being ridiculously self-indulgent. Let us put aside Kalona and his sadness today. As your brother decided not to accompany me to Earth, would you do me the honor?"

Erebus grinned. "Will we race antelope?"

"As many as you'd like, but be forewarned—I do not intend to lose!" Nyx stood and clapped her hands together, disappearing in a shower of diamond dust.

Erebus followed his Goddess, but more slowly, as if he was burdened by heavy thoughts and weighty decisions—because truly, he was. For that was the day he decided that he could no longer remain silent, even if his words cost him Nyx's friendship and love.

I cannot watch them break each other's hearts for eternity. I must end this, and Nyx's own words have given me an idea—a sliver of hope. I am going to help my brother understand the truth and know joy. If that condemns me—then so be it.

2

Other Erebus

The next day, while Nyx visited Greece in the form of Demeter to preside over the annual Rites of Eleusis, Erebus took action.

Kalona wasn't difficult for Erebus to find. They were brothers, created together by Mother Earth and bound by blood and spirit. Erebus had only to concentrate and he would get an image of his brother, wherever he was in this realm. He often wondered if his moon-touched brother had ever used their connection. But Erebus would not ask him. He did not want to hear that yes, Kalona did use their connection—to stay *away* from Erebus.

On this day, Erebus was drawn to Kalona in one of the most distant of Nyx's Otherworld groves. The grove wasn't particularly large and, though beautiful enough not to be out of place in Nyx's realm, it was also not as exquisitely designed as the places where Nyx usually chose to spend her time.

Erebus entered the grove, ducking under low-hanging hawthorn and rowan boughs. Wan light filtered through the canopy as he picked his way around glistening crystal-embedded boulders. Kalona was sitting on one of those marble boulders. Its carpet of verdant moss caressed his legs while he silently whittled a long, narrow stick.

"Brother! I didn't know you liked to carve." Erebus clapped him on the shoulder and sat on a boulder across from Kalona.

Kalona barely glanced at him. "It keeps my hands and my mind busy."

"What are you carving?"

"Arrows."

Erebus laughed. "Can't you just conjure those?"

"I can. I choose not to. As I already said—this keeps my hands and mind busy." He finally looked at Erebus. "Why are you here?"

"I wanted to talk. Why are *you* here? Nyx's palace is a lot nicer."

"Nyx's palace is also a lot more crowded." Kalona gave his brother a pointed look. "I like solitude."

"Do you really?"

"What kind of question is that?" Kalona asked, returning to his carving.

"An honest one. I'd like an honest answer in return."

"I'm not playing this game with you. What do you really want? And why aren't you with Nyx? I'm sure she misses you already."

"STOP IT!" The words exploded from Erebus.

Kalona looked up from his carving, a half smile playing at the corner of his full lips. "Be careful. That sounded angry. I didn't think you could get angry."

Erebus ran his hand through his long blond hair and sighed. "I can get angry. I just try not to."

"Why?"

"I could spout a bunch of platitudes like, 'Anger doesn't solve anything,' or 'Anger isn't the loving choice,' but I'm speaking with complete honesty today and the truth is that being angry isn't fun." Erebus shrugged and chuckled. "I don't think I've ever even admitted that to myself until now."

"Huh. Not the reason I expected," said Kalona.

"Well, it's the truth. Your turn. Tell me why you so often embrace anger."

Erebus waited, though he didn't believe his brother would answer him, so he was pleasantly surprised when Kalona spoke.

"I do not embrace anger."

"But you're usually angry."

"Not because I want to be."

Erebus leaned forward and steepled his fingers as he met his brother's amber gaze. "*Then stop choosing it!*"

"Do you not think I've tried! I don't want this—this unending jealousy and burning, festering anger. I want to choose Nyx—choose us. But I cannot seem to sustain the choice—the happiness. One look at you—one thought about you and her, together, in each other's arms—" Kalona's jaw clenched and he looked away from Erebus. "And the jealousy creeps back and then anger follows. Sometimes I feel like there must be something missing inside me."

"Interesting to hear you say that. I've been wondering the same thing recently, and I may have a solution, but first I want you to know something."

"If I sit here and listen will you go away?"

"I hope if you sit and truly listen, after you hear me out you won't want me to."

Kalona snorted. "Not likely, but speak anyway."

Erebus met and held his brother's gaze. "The night of the spirit test when you found Nyx in my arms and then—"

"We have sworn to never speak of that!"

"Then keep your oath. Do not speak. Only listen."

"Wait," Kalona put the half-whittled arrow down and focused his entire attention on his brother. "Are you actually going to break your oath to Nyx?"

"I am."

"But if the Goddess finds out, she will not trust you as she does now," Kalona said.

"Yes. I understand that."

"Why are you giving me the power to harm your relationship with Nyx?"

"Because I cannot spend eternity watching you and the Goddess break each other's hearts, especially when there is no reason for it. Now, will you listen while I speak?"

Kalona nodded slowly, and Erebus realized that for the first time in a very long time his brother was truly listening to him, so he continued.

"Before the spirit test and the horrible death of the maiden, before Nyx breathed life back into her and named her vampyre, when you came upon us laughing in each other's arms as she told me how happy I make her—*the reason she was so very happy is because we were speaking of you and of her love for you.*"

"What? That cannot be true. She was in your bed."

Erebus laughed. "She was sitting with me beside a geyser, pretending she did not mind the foul smell. I was showing her a litter of wild kittens that I'd found."

Kalona snorted. "You and those damn cats."

"It's not *me* and those damn cats. It's Nyx. She loves them, and I enjoy seeing her smile, and not because she and I are lovers. Because she and I are *friends*. That day she was telling me how difficult it was for her to be away from you, but that she wanted to allow you time to prepare for the last test so that you could finally join her in the Otherworld."

"She said that? Truly?"

"Yes. Truly. She also told me she was sad that you never called for her, but that she understood because you were busy preparing for the test."

"But I did call for her. Many times!" Kalona stood and began to pace.

"That's strange, brother. I know Nyx would come should ever you call her. She admitted to me that she was *waiting* for your call—*hoping* for your call. That she'd sent her little servant, L'ota, to stay near you so that you had a way to contact her."

"Of course! I should have known there was something wrong with that damned skeeaed! Especially after the old Shaman killed her—or whatever he did to her. He told me she—" The winged immortal paused, thinking back. "He said she was a demon in league with Darkness."

"So that's what happened to the sprite. Why didn't you say anything about it, especially when Nyx asked about her absence?" asked Erebus.

"I had my reasons!" Kalona snapped.

"Fine." Erebus raised his hands as if in surrender. "Keep your secrets, but you should ask Nyx if the skeeaed ever relayed a message to her from you. I would bet my golden wings the Goddess tells you no."

"And if I asked Nyx if she and you were lovers that day?"

"You would be breaking your oath to never speak of it,

so I will answer you. Brother, Nyx and I have *never* been lovers."

Kalona frowned and opened his mouth to speak, but Erebus stopped him.

"No. Let me tell you exactly what I said to Nyx when she asked me, that very day, if I ever feel jealous that you and she are lovers, and she and I are not. I told her clearly that I would most willingly and happily come to her bed should she desire me, but that I have no burning need to be her lover. My only wish is for her happiness, and I believed then—and now—that she would be happiest with *you* at her side for eternity, brother. *You* as lover and warrior. Not me. That is not my destiny. And that is when she threw her arms around me and told me how happy I make her. *All because I'd acknowledged her adoration for you.*"

Kalona blinked as if he was trying to clear his vision, and for an instant Erebus saw tears pooling in his brother's amber eyes. "It is *me* she loves with desire."

"Yes. It is. But you're ruining that."

Kalona's eyes flashed. "Then leave! Go to Earth and let me spend eternity with my Goddess!"

"And you think that would make Nyx happy? She loves me too! Not like you, but she and I are friends, companions, playmates. Can you not find it within you to share even a small piece of her love with me?"

At this Kalona softened, and Erebus could see hopelessness in his eyes. "I want to. Truly I do. But I do not know how to combat the dark thoughts within me. Brother, I can feel it. Even now, even after you have told me how baseless my imaginings have been, I can still feel my jealousy brewing, waiting to boil over into anger." Kalona's broad shoulders slumped and he shook his head. "I should leave—not you. I should take my jealous rage and retreat to Earth."

Erebus went to his brother and stood before him. "If you could have your heart's desire, what would that be?"

"That Nyx and I spend eternity together, of course," he said. When Erebus said nothing, Kalona sighed and added. "And I would like to overcome my jealousy. I would like to know what it would be to feel like you do—joyful, free, playful, *happy*."

"Without me leaving the Otherworld?"

"If I could overcome my jealousy, there would be no reason for you to leave. And you are right. It would sadden Nyx if her playmate went away," Kalona quipped dryly.

"Well, then, I can help you with that," said Erebus.

"How?"

"To overcome jealousy and anger you only need joy."

"Great. Like I didn't know that already? I told you. I have *tried*, but for me holding joy is like carrying water with a sieve. It always leaks away," said Kalona miserably.

"I think that's because something is missing within you," said Erebus.

"Are you trying to insult me?"

Erebus grinned. "Not at the moment. I only want to speak the truth. We were created together. I think when Mother Earth and the Moon joined to make you warrior and lover, they were far too focused on the warrior part— and perhaps, they also didn't believe a lover needed to be given joy."

"Why wouldn't a lover need joy?" asked Kalona, seeming honestly curious.

"Because if you're a goddess's lover, why would you need

to be *given* joy? Being Nyx's Consort should be joyous enough."

"That's what I have been trying to convince myself for centuries, and I can tell you it is a misconception," said Kalona.

"I agree. How can you feel joy if you've never really known it? So, let's fix that now. Today."

"Sounds good *and* impossible. Where am I going to get joy? Mother Earth sleeps, and the Moon hasn't stirred since the night I was created."

"We don't need them. I'm going to give you some of my joy," Erebus told his brother.

Kalona's eyes widened in shock. "You would do that? For me?"

"Yes."

"But why? I have treated you terribly."

"Because you are my brother. My family. I love you and want the best for you, as well as for our Goddess." Erebus spoke simply and honestly—and he was surprised to see tears pool in his brother's eyes again.

"Thank you, Erebus. Brother. I will gladly accept whatever joy you can share with me."

"That makes me very happy!" Erebus started forward, arms open as if he would hug his brother, but Kalona frowned and moved back a step. Erebus smiled sheepishly. "Guess I should wait until after you have the joy to try a hug?"

"That would probably be for the best," said Kalona.

3

Other Kalona

"Are you sure this is going to work?" Kalona asked Erebus, who stood silently, head bowed and eyes closed, in the middle of the sunny clearing just outside the grove where his brother had found him.

Erebus opened one eye and lifted his head. "Yes. Well, I'm sure I'm going to give you some of my joy. What you do with it is up to you."

"I will remain by my Goddess's side—true to her and loyal!" Kalona responded quickly.

"Good. Then be quiet so I can concentrate. It's not easy for a playmate and friend to conjure a weapon of war."

"Huh?" Kalona shook his head, completely confused. "How are you going to give me joy with a—"

Kalona's words broke off as a short sword, which appeared to be made entirely of gold, manifested with a startling *POP* just above Erebus's head.

"Yes! I knew I could do it!" Erebus cheered as his hand closed on the glistening grip and he plucked it out of the air.

"Brother, gold is a weak metal. It isn't a good choice for a sw—"

"I know that!" Erebus frowned at Kalona. "It isn't gold.

It's golden, as in made from the power of the sun. You touch this and your hand melts."

"Oh. Good to know. Carry on."

"Okay. You need to take off your shirt." Erebus explained as he pulled off his own shirt.

"What are you going to do?" Kalona watched his brother with narrowed eyes, not liking the golden sword, which was now back in Erebus's hand, and the command to bare his chest and be weaponless, vulnerable, before him.

Erebus sighed. "For this to work you're going to have to trust me."

"Can that sword kill me?"

"Definitely. Take your shirt off."

"If it can kill me why should I stand here weaponless waiting for you to stab me with it?"

"I'm going to cut myself first. Here, over my heart." Erebus pointed to the spot on his bared chest. "And draw out a drop of joy. Then I'm going to take that drop of joy and put it into you."

"Does that mean you're cutting over my heart too?"

"It does. Unless you'd rather have a joyful butt. Then I'll stick you there. Or wherever else you'd like joy inserted." The tip of the golden sword wavered as Erebus pointed it between his brother's legs. "I prefer feeling it in my heart, but…"

"Okay—okay," Kalona interrupted him, pulling off his shirt and tossing it aside. "Now what?"

"Just stand there and get ready to accept joy. I'll do the rest."

Kalona pressed his lips together to keep more questions—and sarcastic comments—from escaping. He watched Erebus bow his golden head and close his eyes. He could see his brother's lips move, and he heard some of what he was whispering.

"Blue skies... a feather bed... earth's songbirds... spring rain... Nyx in all of her forms."

Then Erebus lifted his head and the sword. He shifted his handhold so that it covered the grip and the pommel, and then rested the point of the sword against his chest. His voice was strong and sure as he shouted, "Joy! Come forth!" With one quick motion he drew the blade down.

Kalona expected blood to well along the cut, but instead the sword acted like a sponge, soaking the crimson drops up into it so that the blade changed color from glimmering gold to a burnished rose. Then Erebus strode to stand directly in front of Kalona.

"This is probably going to hurt. A lot," said Erebus.

"No doubt. Go on. I promise not to cry."

"Don't be an ass. You're getting joy. Be happy about it."

Kalona lifted one brow. "But I don't *have* it yet, brother."

In reply, Erebus tilted his head up and looked directly into the sun and spoke the invocation, *"As was meant to be, brother, I share my joy with thee!"* Then Erebus pressed the blood-filled tip of the sword against the smooth bronze skin over his brother's heart.

Pain exploded across Kalona's chest. He gasped and grunted with the effort it took to remain standing, remain still, as heat flowed into his heart and then surged throughout his body in time with his pumping blood.

At the same moment, Kalona felt a great outpouring of coldness. He gasped as something he hadn't realized was there loosened its frigid grip on his heart and rushed from his body.

Erebus suddenly mirrored his gasp. His brother staggered, but somehow managed to hold the sword steady against Kalona's chest until it had drained completely into the immortal's heart and returned to a shining golden color before disappearing with the sound of a snuffed flame.

Both brothers fell to their knees, breathing hard. Kalona's hand went to his chest, but there was no slash to mark his perfect flesh.

And then it hit Kalona—*joy*.

It was like a great infilling of warmth, but it wasn't just warmth. It was a lightness that bubbled through his blood. Kalona blinked and then drew a long, deep breath—releasing it in a full-body laugh that shook the trees in the nearby grove.

"It is gone!" Kalona shouted as he jumped to his feet. "The constant stress—the tension—the anger and jealousy. Gone!" He turned to Erebus, who was still kneeling and gasping as he tried to find his breath. "Brother! You did it!" Kalona reached out his hand, offering it to his brother so he could help him rise.

The unexpected gesture made Erebus glance abruptly up at his brother—and in that look Kalona saw raw pain, and something darker, more intense.

"What is it? What happened to you?" Kalona asked.

Erebus shook himself like a horse plagued by biting flies. His lips tilted up—at first in a wan shadow of the golden immortal's usual joy-filled smile—but soon the shadow passed and he reached up, grasping Kalona's hand and rising to his feet.

"Nothing. It is nothing."

Kalona continued to grip Erebus's hand when his brother

tried to release his. "No more hidden things. We must always tell each other the truth now, brother."

Erebus sighed again and nodded wearily. "You are right. I felt anger. Your anger. It entered my heart."

Panic and fear filled Kalona. "No! I did not mean for that to happen!"

"I know. This isn't of your doing. Remember the invocation I used: *As was meant to be, brother, I share my joy with thee.* Well, it seems you weren't the only one flawed. Apparently I was unbalanced as well."

"And now will you struggle with jealousy and anger as I did?" Kalona felt a terrible stab of regret. Now that his heart was free of the hold of anger he could appreciate Erebus's childlike ability to find joy in everything.

"I believe I probably will, but no more—or less—than you. And now that you have joy, do you feel you can keep anger at bay?"

Kalona thought about it, testing that place within him where he used to nurture the image of Nyx laughing in Erebus's arms and telling him he made her so, so happy…

His gaze shot to his brother's. "It is gone!"

"It?"

"The biting, nagging, never-ending jealousy that I used to worry daily like a sore tooth. *It is gone!*" Kalona laughed again as he pulled his brother into a bear hug. "Yes, Erebus! Thanks to you I can keep anger at bay!"

"And I will be able to keep it at bay as well. *If* you release me before you break me in half."

"Oh. Sorry." Kalona hadn't realized he'd picked up Erebus until he released his brother, who then dropped several feet to the mossy ground.

Erebus smiled at him. "You need brotherly hug lessons."

Kalona snorted.

"Am I going too far too soon?" Erebus asked—still grinning.

"Yes, but I find that I suddenly do not mind." He paused and then added. "Brother, let us swear an oath right now."

"Not to give in to anger?" Erebus asked.

"Yes, and more. Are you with me?"

"I am."

Kalona lifted his arm, opening his hand, and his deadly onyx lance instantly manifested. He plucked the lance from the air and sliced the pointed tip across his palm, drawing a line of scarlet. His gaze went to his brother expectantly.

"I suppose it is your turn to cut me." Erebus held his hand out to Kalona, palm open.

Kalona's lance cut a narrow trail of red across it. The brothers gripped one another's hand, mixing their blood.

"I vow not to allow anger to win," said Erebus solemnly.

"And I vow not to allow anger to win. Darkness will not use me to enter Nyx's realm," said Kalona, slowly as if each word was a great weight he was lifting to release. Then he continued. "The reason I didn't tell anyone about L'ota's death is because she was killed after leading me to the White Bull."

"The White Bull! Kalona, that creature isn't a bull! He isn't even a creature. He's the embodiment of evil, just as the Black Bull is the embodiment of good."

"Yes. I realize that. And that is why I did not tell anyone that the sprite died—because she was in league with Darkness, which I only knew because Darkness had tainted me—though I refused to see that as the truth it was."

"We should not tell Nyx of this," Erebus said. "Do you agree?"

"I do, and gladly. It would only hurt her, as well as worry her," said Kalona. "She has had hurt and worry enough from me for an eternity. And with us both swearing not to give into anger, Darkness will have no way to seep into our Goddess's realm—so she need never know her favorite fey betrayed her."

"Let us go to Nyx!" Erebus spoke, and then he quickly added, "Unless you would prefer to see her alone first. I would understand if you—"

"No, brother. You are responsible for the brightness of our future. I want you to come with me."

Erebus looked away, taking a moment to gain control of his emotions. Then he wiped his eyes and grinned at his brother. "That makes me very happy." Erebus spread his wings, ready to fly to Nyx's palace, but his brother touched his shoulder.

Kalona met his gaze. "Thank you, little brother. For not giving up on me. For knowing I could be more. For being a good brother, even when I did not deserve you."

"You are most welcome, big brother. Now I'm going to show you how to give a proper hug!"

Other Nyx

"I'm going to call you Princess, little one." Nyx kissed the tip of the spotted kitten's nose and the baby wriggled playfully, trying to lick the Goddess and burrow closer to her at the same time. Nyx laughed musically. "Oh, sweet Princess, let me untangle you from my hair and then we can—"

Laughter boomed from the sky and interrupted Nyx. Confused, she looked up to see Kalona and Erebus, golden and silver wings catching the morning sunlight, flying toward her balcony *as they laughed together.*

Nyx's stomach did a strange flip-flop—something she hadn't felt since the two immortals had been created for her and Kalona had first looked into her eyes. She placed the kitten in the little round bed one of the sprites had fashioned for her and stood, shielding her eyes with her hand as first Kalona and then Erebus dropped lightly to her balcony.

"I won!" Kalona shouted as his smile radiated good humor.

"Because you cheated! There were no songbirds in that tree you pointed at." Erebus was frowning at his brother, but Nyx saw the laughter dancing in his eyes and pulling at the corners of his lips.

"Guess you should have set the rules before you said *go!*" Kalona said.

As Nyx stood there speechlessly staring at the brothers, Kalona clapped Erebus on the back. Not in a gesture meant to hurt him or knock him aside, but with what appeared to be real affection.

"I'll definitely remember that next time," said Erebus. Then he turned to face Nyx and bowed with an exaggerated flourish. "Beautiful Goddess! Good day to you. I see that you've added another kitten to your collection." Erebus went to the baby's bed and reached down to pet her, but the cat hissed and spit at him.

"They never like anyone but our Nyx," Kalona said before turning to the Goddess. "And I cannot blame them. Once you've known the beauty and majesty that is the Goddess of Night, everyone else pales in comparison." He also bowed to Nyx, though he held her gaze as he did so. "Good day, my beloved."

"Good day," Nyx said slowly as she looked from Kalona to Erebus. Both immortals grinned at her with expressions that suddenly reminded the Goddess of precocious little boys. There was a feeling spreading over her skin that was very much like standing on a field during an electrical storm. "What has happened?"

Erebus looked at Kalona. "You should tell her."

"But it was your idea, and you did it," said Kalona.

"True, but I think she'd like to hear it from you."

"That's kind of you, little brother."

"Not at all, big bro."

"Bro?"

"I just made it up. I like it shortened," said Erebus, scratching his chin in contemplation.

"By all the lost gods and goddesses! Will one of you

please tell me what is going on?" Nyx rested her fists on her hips and narrowed her eyes at the brothers.

"Sorry about this. In my defense, I am new to this feeling and it is making me rather…" Kalona paused, searching for the correct word.

"Giddy?" Erebus offered.

Kalona nodded and grinned. "Good word. Giddy. The feeling is making me giddy."

"*What feeling?*" The Goddess didn't exactly shout, but the intensity in her voice had the air around them swirling in response.

"Joy!" Erebus said. "My big brother now has joy within him."

Nyx's smooth brow furrowed. "I do not understand."

Kalona moved closer to Nyx. Taking her hand in both of his, he kissed it gently. "I was flawed at my creation. Erebus figured out how to correct the flaw."

"Not just you, big bro," Erebus said. "I was flawed as well, Nyx. Kalona wasn't given a capacity for joy, and I was given *too much* capacity for it. It tainted my life, though not as obviously as the lack of it did my brother's life. So I fixed it."

"You fixed it?" Nyx felt dizzy with the beginnings of a great, swelling happiness that caught her completely unawares. Her gaze flew from Erebus's smiling, familiar face to Kalona's. He too was smiling—and the expression reached and filled his eyes, blazing joy and love. "You *are* joyful!"

"I am indeed," said Kalona. "Thanks to Erebus."

"And you are no longer jealous of him."

Nyx didn't speak it as a question, but Kalona answered readily.

"I am not jealous of my brother's relationship with you. I never will be again. That I promise you. I also promise that from this day forth I will do everything I can to make up for the sadness and hurt I caused you *and* my brother. Can you forgive me, Great Goddess?" Kalona went to his knees and bowed his head.

Nyx stared from Kalona to Erebus. The golden-winged immortal nodded.

"He's telling you the truth. Joy has replaced anger, just as love has replaced jealousy," said Erebus.

"Oh! I can hardly breathe with happiness!" Nyx pulled Kalona to his feet and threw her arms around him, laughing as he held her tightly.

Then the son of the moon opened one of his arms, motioning to Erebus. "What kind of hug did you call this?" Kalona asked.

Erebus's smiled blazed like the sun. "Group hug!" And he too stepped into his brother's embrace while Nyx laughed and cried tears of joy. Then he kissed Nyx softly on the cheek and clapped his brother's shoulder. "And now I am going to make a trip to Earth. Mangoes are in season on the island where the people call our Goddess Pele. I intend to collect a basketful."

"I adore mangoes!" Nyx said, clapping her hands like a girl.

"And that, my Goddess, is why I am going to bring you back a basketful." Erebus paused and waggled his brows suggestively. "But not until much, *much* later tonight."

Nyx put her arms around Erebus and held him close. "Thank you is not enough, but those are the only words I have."

"And they are the only words I have too," said Kalona. "You gave me my life back. Thank you doesn't seem enough."

"Oh, it isn't, big bro. But what is enough is you loving Nyx and filling this realm and our little family with joy and Light."

"Now, I can do that," Kalona said.

"Then that is thanks enough."

Erebus unfurled his wings and lifted into the cerulean sky, leaving Nyx alone with her lover.

The Goddess looked up at Kalona. She touched his face intimately, cupping his cheek in her hand. "I can feel the lightness within you."

His hand covered hers. "As can I. It's as if, until now, I've not been able to draw a deep breath in all the centuries I have been alive."

"But now you can breathe freely," she whispered, tilting her head up invitingly.

"Yes, my beloved. Now and forevermore." Kalona kissed her as he picked her up and carried her within to her curtained bed while outside the fey frolicked in Nyx's lake, mirroring the joy that radiated from their Goddess and spread, like spring rain, throughout her realm.

4

Other Kalona

Years uncounted passed, lengthening to decades and then centuries—and joy ruled this realm of Nyx's Otherworld. Kalona, Erebus, and Nyx were the best of friends—a family that wasn't just content with one another. They were truly happy and enjoyed the company of one another.

Before Erebus gifted Kalona with joy, the son of the Moon had disdained Earth, especially avoiding the vampyres his mistake had created. And so, for many years Nyx's vampyres saw only Erebus at their Goddess's side. Naturally, they concluded that he was Nyx's Consort and Warrior—and they named the best and most courageous of their Warriors the Sons of Erebus.

Erebus sought to correct that misperception quickly, but Kalona was adamant. "Brother, when I was self-absorbed and filled with anger I let our Goddess down, but you remained at her side, visiting her favorite children and supporting her. The bravest of the House of Night Warriors *should* carry your golden image and your name. I will not take that honor from you."

Kalona could see that his acquiescence moved Erebus deeply, so he made certain that he often found excuses not to join Nyx and Erebus when they visited the growing number of House of Night groupings of vampyres. He understood his presence would only call into question Erebus's place at the Goddess's side—and now that there was no need for him to struggle with jealousy, he was glad to gift his brother and his lover special moments with Nyx's vampyres.

When Kalona visited earth, he often did so alone. Not because he wanted to be away from Nyx or Erebus, but because he discovered how very much he enjoyed interacting with another group of Nyx's special children—those who called themselves Tsalagi, and would eventually become known to the world as the seven tribes of the Cherokee peoples.

It began by accident—the way so many things in Kalona's long life had begun. He'd come to earth to surprise Nyx by gathering a basket of her favorite spring berries and come upon a young Tsalagi hunter who was attempting to bring down a bison bull—by himself. The hunter was moments from being gored by the bull when Kalona swooped down from the sky, landing between the huge charging creature and the frightened, doomed youth. Kalona easily turned the bison aside, saving the boy.

He'd tried to fly away, but the youth had fallen to the ground, prostrating himself to the "Great Winged God." With a sigh, Kalona told the boy to rise and then explained patiently to him that he wasn't a god. He was only Kalona, the Consort of their Mother Goddess.

The young hunter had insisted that his father, who was chief of his tribe of the Tsalagi, must repay his kindness, so Kalona reluctantly went with the boy to his village.

Thus began one of the most satisfying relationships in

Kalona's existence. The tribe welcomed him, naming him Kalona of the Silver Wings. Though he did not allow them to worship him as a god, the Tsalagi revered the winged immortal and he often joined their storytelling circles. The artists of the tribe created images of him, and their homes, horses, and even the great headdresses of their warriors were decorated with silver-white wings and amber eyes. Kalona wasn't their god, but any member of the tribe would say that Kalona of the Silver Wings was their beloved protector and friend.

And that made the mighty Kalona joyful.

The years passed peacefully for the three immortals. Erebus and Nyx appeared to vampyres frequently, encouraging them to establish their society as a matriarchal one that revered the arts and sciences and respected their Warrior protectors, who were trained in the art of hand-to-hand combat as well as ancient battle strategies—the best of whom were accepted into the ranks of the elite Sons of Erebus Warriors.

Kalona and the Cherokee tribes developed a close relationship. The winged immortal visited often, watching as the decades passed and one chief took over from another. He wept with the tribe when lives ended and celebrated with them when crops were plentiful and babies were born healthy and happy. And every time he visited the tribes, ravens flocked to him. It happened so often that the Cherokee celebrated when a flock of the intelligent black birds gathered, as they knew Kalona of the Silver Wings must be near.

All was well for many decades, and then Kalona realized something was wrong.

At first it was barely noticeable. Filled with joy and utterly content with his life, Kalona would not have recognized that anything was amiss if *he* had never known his own sadness—never kept his own secrets from Erebus and Nyx.

But Kalona had known sadness, anger, jealousy, and heartache—and so he recognized shadows of those old, base feelings beginning within his brother as Erebus slowly and quietly withdrew.

It didn't happen when Nyx and Kalona were being overtly affectionate—kissing and laughing in each other's arms—but rather in moments when either he or his Goddess lover were still.

The first time Kalona had to face the fact that there was something wrong with Erebus happened when Kalona had been watching Nyx as she swam with the water sprites in her crystal lake. The Goddess was as naked as the little sprites, and her loveliness shined so brightly that the magnificent fey looked like wan shadows beside her glory. The warm breeze lifted Nyx's laughter up to the balcony the brothers reclined on as they sipped ambrosia and enjoyed the magickal view of their Goddess frolicking, childlike, with the sprites. Kalona remembered he had been staring at Nyx, thinking how very grateful he was to be her Consort, her lover, her friend. He'd turned to smile at his brother and thank him once again for sharing his joy—and he'd caught Erebus unawares. Kalona's brother had turned away from the lake and was staring down at nothing in particular, but the look on his face stopped Kalona's breath.

He is sad! Miserable, actually! How did this happen? When did this happen? And how did I not know?

Kalona had opened his mouth to speak to Erebus—to ask him what had upset him, but his brother had abruptly stood, made a quick excuse about forgetting something he'd intended to do, and left the balcony.

Nyx had chosen then to reappear beside Kalona, soaking wet and laughing as she wrapped her arms around him, saying, "Come swim with me, my love!"

Kalona could not—would not—tell his Goddess no, but he made a mental note to observe his brother more closely. And observe Erebus he did. Kalona tapped into his innate warrior skills and covertly studied his brother. He didn't exactly stalk Erebus. Instead, he thought of it as a reconnaissance mission with his brother's mental health as the target.

What Kalona discovered troubled him greatly.

Erebus had become so good at withdrawing that he'd mastered the ability to make it seem as if he was present when he was not. He would make plans with Nyx and Kalona—he would even be with the two immortals at the beginning of whatever adventure the three of them had decided to embark upon, seemingly enthusiastic and joyful. But more often than not, Erebus would make an excuse and leave Nyx and Kalona alone to complete the adventure.

"Have you noticed that Erebus seems withdrawn and quieter than usual?" Kalona asked Nyx one warm, beautiful day when the three of them were supposed to be in disguise to attend and bless the Celts Beltane celebration, but somehow in the revelry Erebus had slipped away.

Nyx was laughing in Kalona's arms as they danced around one of the big bonfires. She was wearing an elaborate headdress made of vines and flowers and ribbons, with the image of a full moon resting in the center of it all. Kalona's wings were tucked carefully against his back, concealed by a long white cloak. His headdress featured antlers and ferns.

The two of them moved with the crowd, but many of the Celts recognized that there was something special about the couple, and they were frequently given gifts of golden jewelry and beaded leather belts. Nyx tilted her face up, smiling.

"What did you say, my beloved? Did you ask something about Erebus?"

"I did." Kalona twirled Nyx around, drawing her closer within his arms so that he could speak more intimately with her. "I do not see him anywhere, and I wondered if you'd noticed that he has been withdrawn lately."

Nyx searched the crowd with her sharp eyes. "I did not realize he left. Now that you mention it, I believe he has been disappearing often." Her looked turned contemplative, and then she smiled brilliantly. "He has probably taken a lover! Oh, I hope it is someone he has a passionate affair with, and that he even fathers children here on Earth!"

Kalona was taken aback. "That's possible?"

"Of course." Nyx tilted her head to the side, studying her Consort. "Would you like a child, my love?"

"Your child?"

Nyx's musical laughter caused several couples near them to smile in response.

"Oh, no! I have children aplenty here on Earth." She swept out an arm in a graceful gesture that took in the celebrating Celts. "But you could take a human lover. You would father children with her. I am quite sure they would be spectacular."

"And you would not be jealous of my human lover?"

Nyx's smile was slow and seductive. "Would I need to be?"

"Never. No woman—human or immortal—could ever take me from your side."

"Then, no. I would not be jealous. And I would shower your children with a multitude of blessings."

Kalona twirled his Goddess around again. "I will keep that in mind should I feel the need to be a father. Right now, I'm more concerned about being a brother."

"You are a wonderful brother. It is one of the great joys in my life that you and Erebus have grown so close," said Nyx.

"That is why I'm concerned. I worry when he withdraws."

"Do not worry, my love. Our Erebus is one of the happiest beings in my realm. If he doesn't have a secret love, then he is probably planning a surprise for us."

"I'm sure that's all it is," said Kalona as he and Nyx moved to the pulse of the music again.

But the son of the Moon couldn't stop thinking about the sadness he'd seen so clearly in his brother's face. He'd recognized the despair of loneliness all too well, and he was determined that he would not let his brother suffer in silence. So, on a day when Nyx was on Earth blessing the opening of a new House of Night Temple, Kalona went in search of his brother.

Erebus wasn't difficult to find. The brothers were connected, and Kalona often used that connection to find him, but he also knew Erebus's favorite spots. That day the golden-winged immortal was sitting silently beside the geyser he'd created for Nyx during their water test so many centuries before. Kalona circled overhead, gliding on silent wings, watching his brother. Completely unguarded, Erebus looked miserable. His shoulders were slumped and his wings loose—as if he hadn't the energy to tuck them against his back. He sat staring at nothing, face propped up by his fist, his expression filled with a sadness that was all too heart-breakingly familiar to Kalona.

"What I don't understand is why you created that thing with this smell," Kalona said as he landed beside his brother. "You made it. Couldn't you also make it smell good?"

Erebus's look changed, brightened, as he motioned for his brother to sit beside him on the log he'd felled many years before and placed perfectly for viewing his faithful geyser. "Ah, brother! Would you be offended if I told you that I purposefully did not remove the smell all those centuries ago *because* I knew it would annoy you?"

Kalona snorted. "Offend me? No. You used to pretend to be perfect, but I've always known you're incorrigible." He softened the remark with a warm smile. "Just as you've always known my true nature."

"Arrogant? Proud? And too ready to use your sword instead of your wits?" Erebus teased.

"Exactly! But of course you left out that I am also rakishly handsome and exceedingly generous."

"I'll try to remember that next time I'm asked about your true nature. Good thing we understand each other."

"Yes. Good thing. I think it's part of being brothers," Kalona said.

"I think you're right," Erebus said.

Kalona cleared his throat. "So. What is wrong?"

Erebus blinked in surprise. "Wrong? With whom?"

"You."

Erebus's brow went up sardonically. "I thought you just said I was perfect."

"I said you used to *pretend* to be perfect. We already established that I know better. And I also know there's something wrong." Kalona reached out and tapped Erebus's chest over his heart. "There." And then he tapped his brother's temple. "And there."

His brother swatted his hand away and made a show of laughing. "Big bro, my heart and head are fine."

Instead of laughing with him, Kalona simply shook his head. "Little brother, we made a promise to each other to always tell the truth. I hold you to that promise now. What is wrong?"

Erebus opened his mouth to give a flippant answer, but the expression on his brother's face had him sighing and looking away instead.

"You can tell me. You've seen me at my worst and you were there for me. Little brother, let me be there for you too."

Erebus stared at the faithful geyser that was spewing hot, sulphuric water and steam into the air. He spoke slowly, softly, as if he had to coax each word to leave him.

"I am lonely."

Kalona nodded. "I can see that. And I owe you an apology. You've been withdrawn. You disappear suddenly when you accompany Nyx and me to Earth. I've known it for some time now, and I should have spoken to you earlier. I should have gone after you—brought you back to us."

"I do appreciate your care for me, but bringing me back to continue watching Nyx and you fall more and more in love every day—every year—every decade—does not help my loneliness."

"Then tell me what will help."

Erebus's laugh lacked any humor. "Could you conjure another goddess? This time for me."

"Ah, *that* kind of loneliness. But Nyx and I thought you've been taking frequent human lovers," said Kalona.

"I have. Well, I did." Erebus finally met his brother's gaze. "Have you ever taken a human lover?"

"No. How could I? Who could possibly compare to Nyx…" Kalona's words ran out as he understood. "No one. No human could compare to our Goddess."

"Exactly," Erebus said. "Humans can be delightful. They are enthusiastic, giving lovers. But they are not divine and they are not immortal." He gazed at the geyser as the huge plume of water and steam sputtered and died. "At first I didn't mind not having a mate. Nyx's realm is a place of beauty and wonder, and I love to explore it. The earth too, fascinates me. I've spent centuries exploring it—with Nyx and you, and also alone. But it has been centuries uncounted, and I grow weary of being alone."

"And yet here you are—alone," Kalona said gently.

Erebus nodded. "It is a paradox. I am lonely, and yet it is worse when I'm with Nyx and you. Big bro, I'm not sure what to do."

Kalona clapped Erebus on his shoulder. "I know exactly what to do."

Erebus sat straighter. "You do?"

"Absolutely."

"Are you going to tell me?"

"I think it would be better if I showed you," Kalona said cryptically.

"Can you give me a hint?" Erebus asked.

"I can. What I'm going to do is the right thing—just as you did for me so long ago."

"But what exactly does that mean?"

"Well," Kalona said as he stood and readied himself to fly away. "First it means I'm going to put things right with our mother."

Erebus's eyes opened wide in surprise. "After all this time? But she sleeps."

"She certainly does, but one of the things I have learned from years of observing the Tsalagi peoples is that mothers always hear the cries of their children."

Erebus's brows met his hairline. "You're going to *cry*?"

Kalona grinned. "Something like that. It's my turn, little brother. And I won't let you down." He crouched, ready to spring into the sky, but paused first. "This might take some time. Would you tell Nyx that there is something I must do, and that I will return to her realm afterward?"

"Of course, but she's going to want to know where you are."

"Tell her I am repaying the debt I owe my little brother. Our Goddess will understand. Also tell her I love her with every breath I draw."

With that, Kalona spread his mighty moonlight-colored wings and flew into the sky, heading east. His wings beat against the wind as he rode the air currents up so high that the boundaries of nations were indecipherable and the earth below him blurred into soft shades of azure, jade, and white. On and on he flew until the ocean stretched below him, at first turquoise, then changing as it deepened to navy and sapphire—and finally turning the familiar blue-gray of the waters surrounding the island on which he and his brother had been birthed.

He circled the island, searching for the perfect spot, and when he finally found a thick, verdant grove overlooking the sea, Kalona landed. It was a sunny morning, but the warmth of Erebus's father didn't penetrate the grove and Kalona was glad of his wings, which hugged his back, warming him. He moved through the grove until he came to the heart of it, the center of which held two rowan trees that had grown twined together, their red berries seeming to crown their joining.

In front of the rowans was a boulder of white marble carpeted with moss. Kalona sat on the rock, drew a deep breath, and began calling.

"Great Earth Mother, it is your son, Kalona. Erebus and I need you. Please awaken." Kalona paused and listened.

Nothing.

The immortal sighed, shrugged, and repeated, "Great Earth Mother, it is your son, Kalona. Erebus and I need you. Please awaken."

All through the day, Kalona sat in that isolated grove, calling to his mother. Huge, shaggy cows were drawn to him. They circled the spot, from which he did not move, chewing silently and watching the immortal with gentle brown eyes. Over and over Kalona spoke the same words until the sun set and the moon lifted, shedding silver-white light that trickled through the leaves, turning the grove into a fantasy landscape and the highland cows to the creatures of dreams.

Kalona called until his voice was gravel. And still he called. The moon sank into the ocean and the sun lifted above the horizon, exchanging silver light for golden—and that is when the entwined rowan trees shivered. The cows snorted, coming fully awake after their long vigilance of watching over the winged immortal. As one, they turned their shaggy, horned heads toward the two trees just as the moss that blanketed the ground around them stirred and then lifted, forming the shape of a reclining woman. Her hair was made of delicate rowan leaves, and red berries crowned her head. Her skin was moss and clothed with maidenhair ferns. Her body was lush and full. She blinked open her earth-colored eyes slowly, stretched, and yawned before focusing on Kalona.

He'd stopped calling as he watched her form, and when her gaze turned to him, Kalona left his marble seat to kneel before her.

"Great Earth Mother! Thank you for answering my call."

"Kalona? It is you, child. Have I slept long?"

"Yes, Mother, centuries," said the immortal.

Earth yawned again sleepily. "And yet I am still weary. I must sleep longer. I will speak to you when I awaken, son of the moon and—"

"No! Wait! You cannot sleep yet. I need to say something to you, and I also need your help."

She frowned at him. "Kalona, what have you done? Has Darkness entered the realm of my lovely friend, Nyx?"

"No! With Erebus's help I was able to defeat my jealousy, and because I was no longer angry, Darkness was not able to gain entrance to the Otherworld."

"Nyx is well?" asked Mother Earth.

"She is."

"And my other son, Erebus? He is well?"

"Well, yes, but—"

"Excellent. I must say that I am pleased that you have defeated your jealous nature. I feared that you would not, and that Nyx would eventually have to banish you to keep Darkness from her realm."

"I was wrong before—during the tests you devised for Erebus and me. You were right to test me. I was not worthy of Nyx's love. Mother, I apologize that I was so difficult—that I seemed uncaring and arrogant."

Mother Earth studied her son. "You *have* changed. I can see it. Your eyes are no longer shadowed. I accept your apology—gladly." She glanced around the clearing. As she noticed the raptly watching cows, she made a slight gesture with one hand, and tufts of impossibly sweet alfalfa materialized in piles before them. "Thank you for watching over my son," she told them.

The cows lowed softly before they buried their muzzles in the alfalfa.

Mother Earth returned her attention to Kalona. "I do not see my other son. Is he not with you?"

"No, but he is the reason I called you."

Her dark gaze sharpened. "But you said he was well."

"He is, but he will not continue to be if you and I do not help him."

Mother Earth sat up, resting her verdant back against the trunk of the rowan trees. "What is wrong with him?"

"He is lonely," said Kalona simply.

"Are you not his friend? And what of my Goddess? Is Nyx also not Erebus's faithful friend?"

"Yes! We love Erebus. We are family, but it isn't a friend or a brother, or even a sister that Erebus needs. He longs for a mate—for the kind of love Nyx and I share," said Kalona.

"Ah, I see. I assumed he would content himself with human lovers, and that his sense of fun and joy would enable him to move from lover to lover gracefully."

"And I believe he would have been content with that

life—had he not gifted me with some of his magnificent joy. And though I did not mean for it to happen, in return he received a measure of my anger."

"And that sliver of anger allowed loneliness to enter him and to grow," said Mother Earth. "I see. And has he turned to anger as well?"

Kalona shook his head. "It is not his way. I do not believe my brother will ever embrace anger. Instead sadness fills him, moving him to despair."

"Yes, despair is more in your brother's nature—anger is more in yours," Mother Earth agreed. "You should know that both emotions are allies of Darkness. Both will eventually destroy Light if left unchecked."

"I agree, and with your help we can stop that from happening."

"What is it you propose?"

"It's really quite simple. I only ask that you create one more immortal—a being brought to life especially for Erebus, who will live eternity at my brother's side and save him from a life of loneliness," said Kalona.

"I can do that, Kalona, but in order to create this incredible being I need an equally incredible sacrifice as I am too weary to seduce the sun or the moon again."

"Could I be the sacrifice?" Kalona asked with no hesitation.

"Child, I said that I need an *incredible* sacrifice. You are immortal, so it is not your life's essence that I can take. You need to understand that means what I take from you—what must be done—will be long and difficult."

"He's my brother. He's worth it."

Mother Earth's eyes softened with warmth. "Then your

sacrifice will be enough. I will help you. I am proud of who you have become."

Kalona's eyes filled with unexpected tears and his breath caught in his throat. He bowed his head. "Thank you, Mother. There was a time when I believed I would never hear those words from you."

When Mother Earth made no response, Kalona lifted his head and his gaze to see that she was standing before him, her arms open. And then for the first time in his very long life, Kalona stepped into his mother's embrace, rested his head against her bosom, and wept with relief and joy.

5

Other Kalona

"I do not understand why we couldn't do this on the isle. This place does not hold good memories for me." Kalona spoke as he looked around the area. Mother Earth had insisted he leave the grove and the island and meet her exactly where his last test had gone so very wrong and Nyx had had to create the first vampyre from a dead maiden.

"This is a place of special power. It is why you were drawn here for your last test," said Mother Earth as she walked to the eastern section of the space, with Kalona following closely. "Ah, this is exactly what I need." She paused before a huge east-facing oak that grew straight and proud. Mother Earth sat in front of the tree and began rhythmically beating her hands against the thick bark so that a sonorous pulse vibrated from the center of the trunk and spread through the ground around them.

"Is there anything I can do?" Kalona asked. "Maybe I should keep watch. The last time I was here a crazed Shaman did the unexpected. I wouldn't want that to happen again."

Mother Earth's smile bloomed. "That old Shaman did nothing unexpected. He was following my command exactly."

Kalona felt a lightning bolt of shock. "But he killed an innocent girl!"

Mother Earth nodded, still beating rhythmically against the tree. "Then you and Nyx saved her, creating the first vampyre."

"I do not understand."

"Kalona, my firstborn, I knew from the first moment you gazed on Nyx that your nature was going to be a problem. Instead of letting that make me sad, or instead of waiting until worse happened and your anger allowed Darkness entrance to the realms of the Goddess, I acted. I knew that the making of the race of vampyres would be your salvation."

"But that doesn't make sense. Erebus saved me."

One of Mother Earth's graceful, verdant brows lifted sardonically. "And who will save you from your plan to save him?"

"Vampyres?" Kalona said hesitantly.

"Yes, vampyres," Mother Earth said firmly. "Now, shush. I need to call the Wise Women."

Kalona wanted to ask his mother how vampyres were going to save him and from what—and also, he badly wanted to know what she was up to. Why she was drumming on the tree and singing in… He cocked his head, listening, and realized *she is singing in Tsalagi! She is calling Tsalagi Wise Women.* Kalona relaxed a little then. The Tsalagi revered him. Whatever the Wise Women were going to concoct with Mother Earth would be fantastical—of that the immortal was sure. He was also pretty sure that the Tsalagi wouldn't require too terrible of a sacrifice from him. He was, after all, Kalona of the Silver Wings—their protector.

The gloaming that heralded dusk had softened the day

when the women began to appear. They arrived alone and in pairs. They each had a determined look that changed to adoration and welcome when they saw Kalona, and then awe as their gazes shifted to the incredible being who played the mighty oak like a bison-hide drum. Each Wise Woman nodded respectfully to Kalona before going to the Earth Mother and bowing low to her.

"Osiyu, children!" Mother Earth welcomed them. "I have a task that I would ask you to witness. Are you willing to do that for me?"

"Uh, E-`tsi!" they chorused. *Yes, Mother!*

"Wa-do." Mother Earth thanked the Wise Women, and her smile was so beatific that their eyes filled with tears.

The oldest of the women stepped forward. Her long, thick hair was completely white and dressed in bluebird feathers—as was her fringed tunic and skirt. She bowed low. "Great Earth Mother, as long as we draw breath your Tsalagi Wise Women will answer your call. Ask what you will of us. We are in your service."

"Your fidelity moves me," said Mother Earth. Long-stemmed wildflowers with bright red and yellow cuplike petals appeared about her feet. "Form a circle around this tree of power and sit until everyone joins us."

The women eagerly did as Earth asked, forming a growing circle around Kalona and Mother Earth in the midst of fragrant wildflowers. He wondered how she would know when everyone had arrived, and then understood when the last Wise Woman appeared from the growing shadows, taking the one remaining spot in their circle.

Mother Earth finally stopped drumming against the skin of the oak. She stood and shook back the cascade of rowan leaves that was her hair. She moved languidly, as if she walked in her sleep, until she stood beside Kalona where he sat in front of the oak tree. She rested her hand on his shoulder and addressed the raptly listening Wise Women.

"It is good to see you my children. Though I have slept long I have watched you in my dreams. A mother should not have favorites, but I admit that you are mine."

The women beamed smiles at their Earth Mother.

"So, it is to you I come to ask for help for my eldest son, Kalona."

The ancient woman spoke again. "Great Earth Mother, we have long been friends of Kalona of the Silver Wings. Even were we not dedicated to serving you, we would gladly come to his aid."

Overwhelmed by their affection, Kalona bowed his head and pressed his hand over his heart.

"It fills me with joy that the Tsalagi and my son are friends. There was a time when I was concerned for Kalona's future. After hearing your affection for him I shall no longer be concerned."

"Command us, Great Earth Mother." The old woman bowed again.

"Wa-do, wa-do, my children." The Earth Mother's voice was filled with love. Her dark eyes gleamed with pleasure. "Then, if my son agrees, this is what we shall do. From my own bosom I will fashion a new being, one formed specifically to be the perfect immortal Consort for my youngest son, Erebus."

Kalona opened his mouth to agree, but his mother squeezed his shoulder and spoke for his ears alone, "Shh, do not agree until you have heard the cost."

Kalona closed his mouth and waited.

"I would have you sing this being into existence and fill her with joy and beauty, wisdom and kindness."

"And a sense of youthful fun," Kalona added.

His mother nodded. Her lips tilted up. "Ah, you do know your brother. Yes, his Consort must also be a playmate for him and share his youthful exuberance and excellent sense of humor. Can you do that, my children?"

"Uh, E-`tsi!" The women instantly responded as one.

The Great Earth Mother turned her gaze to her son. "I will give Erebus's mate a body fashioned from my bosom and breathe life into her, but in order for this new person to be more than an empty vessel she must be filled with spirit. She needs an immortal spirit to be an immortal's Consort."

Kalona's mouth went dry. He cleared his throat. "Do you mean I must give my life for the creation of Erebus's Consort?"

"No, but only because you are immortal and cannot be killed. What you must give is an essence of your immortal spirit. It will not kill you, but it will utterly drain you."

"I understand. So, I will be tired. How long must I rest?"

His mother stroked his hair gently and in a lovely sing-song voice she recited:

"Ancient one sleeping, waiting to arise,
When the dead joins with fire and water red
Son who is not—his word is key; the raven will devise
He shall hear the call from his sacrificial bed.

By the blood of she who is neither foe nor friend he is
*   free.*

57

Behold a terrible sacrifice to come—a beautiful sight,
Ruled by love they shall be.
The future will not kneel to her dark might.

Kalona's return is not bittersweet
As he will be welcomed with love and heat."

There was no sound from the group after the Earth Mother finished the recitation. Into that pregnant silence Kalona spoke. "That sounds like I am going to be *resting* until the prophecy is fulfilled." He paused. His gut turned upside down and for an instant he actually thought he was going to be sick. Kalona cleared his throat again and clung to his mother's gaze, hoping she would tell him he was wrong.

Instead she told him the truth. "You will be resting below, within the earth, cradled by me as you recover, though after you give away some of the essence of your divinity, you will be forever changed."

"You mean I will age and die?" he asked, feeling numb and thinking, Well, at least when I die Nyx will welcome me home to her realm and I will be by her side forever.

"No. You still will not age. You will not sicken. But should you be wounded too badly—or away from me too long—you will weaken. You will not die. You will never die. You may fall into a weak, fugue state—much like a mortal suffering from dementia. To revitalize you must simply return to me—to Earth. My world will always succor you, strengthen you, and return you to yourself."

"I can live with that." He smiled bravely at his mother. "Actually, I like knowing that my mother's world is the source of my strength."

She touched his cheek. "Such a warrior. My darling eldest child, understand that your sacrifice must be great so that your brother's Consort is a perfect creation. That means you will have to rest a very long time."

"You mean a decade or so?"

"Much more, my precious son," she said. "You will rest so long that your name will be forgotten by everyone except Nyx, Erebus, and the Tsalagi Wise Women who remain true to the old ways. Through the fidelity of the great-grandchildren of these women someday in the distant future there will be one Wise Woman who will remember your name and the prophecy that must be fulfilled, and she will set into motion the actions that will free you from your sacrifice."

Kalona felt cold. "But Nyx will worry. She will come looking for me."

"I know that, my son. And that is why I spoke the words I did. Should you agree, my spell will bind the prophecy and no one, not even your Goddess, can awaken you until it is fulfilled."

"Then I have to say goodbye to—" He broke off his words and shook his head. "No. I cannot see Nyx. If I do I will never leave her, and my brother will fade to a shadow of himself." He met his mother's gaze. "I agree. I will do it. Today. Now. My brother has already told Nyx that I am making right a wrong. My Goddess trusts me. She will know that I only left her because I had to. Go ahead. The sooner you do it—the sooner I can awaken and return to Nyx."

His mother held Kalona's gaze. "You are showing a depth of compassion and maturity that I admit surprises me."

Kalona managed to make the corners of his numb lips tilt up. "Erebus has influenced me well these many years."

"But you had to be open to his influence, which is not an easy thing for a warrior." She turned her focus from Kalona to the Wise Women circled around them. "My children! I task you with teaching the prophecy I recited to your daughters. Tell them that they alone are responsible for my immortal son returning to his life and his Goddess, so they must be fertile and faithful! They must repeat my words, passing from generation to generation. Can you promise to do that for me, Wise Women?"

As one the group cried, "Yes, Mother!"

"Excellent. I would like you to stand and begin to move around the circle to the rhythm of that beautiful morning song you so often greet the day with, but I ask that you change the lyrics. Sing these words instead, my children."

Then the Great Earth Mother began to sing in a voice that was so lovely Kalona's eyes filled with tears. Her moss-covered feet beat out a rhythm that the Wise Women immediately took up as their circle began to move clockwise while she sang.

"He is of our Great Earth Mother, it is so.
He is of our Great Earth Mother, it is so.
He is of our Earth Mother.
He is of our Earth Mother.
It is so, it is so, it is so, it is so,
Earth Mother, it is so. Earth Mother, it is so
Earth Mother, Earth Mother, Earth Mother!"

As the Wise Women sang and danced, Kalona's mother offered her son her hand. He took it and stood, walking with her to the base of the big oak. She motioned for him to sit again, this time with his back resting against the rough bark of the tree.

"What do you want me to do?" Kalona asked.

"Simply relax. I shall do the rest," said his mother.

"Will it be painful?" he blurted before he could stop himself.

She stroked his cheek. "Not at all. You will feel tired and you will sleep—secure in my bosom—protected and cherished."

"I'll just sleep for all those years?"

"Yes, and while you sleep I will send you dreams of your beloved Goddess."

"Mother, might I ask a favor?"

"Of course."

"Send Nyx dreams of me as well, so that she will not forget me." His voice roughened, tripping over the end of the sentence.

"My precious child, your Goddess could *never* forget you. You are her truest love—her only Consort. But I will honor your request and send your Goddess dreams of you."

Kalona felt the knot of tension in his chest begin to unravel. "Thank you. It makes me worry less."

"Are you ready, my son?"

Kalona couldn't find his voice, so he simply nodded.

"Then I need your hands," she said.

The request confused Kalona, but he lifted his hands, offering them palms up to his mother, who stood in front of him. With a movement so swift that Kalona's vision couldn't follow it, Mother Earth reached down and drew the tips of her fingers across each of his wrists. He felt no pain—only a slight pull, and then the warmth of blood as her fingernails, which had suddenly hardened to diamond-tipped claws, sliced two narrow scarlet paths across his wrists.

Oh-so gently, Mother Earth bent, guiding his wrists so that they rested on the ground beside him while Kalona's immortal blood soaked into the ground.

"Now, my precious son, I am going to call forth your brother's mate from this fertile land around you. As I do that you will weaken. Do not fight it. You must share your spirit willingly or the creation will be flawed."

"I understand, Mother."

"Remember that you have nothing to fear. I will hold you close until the day you are awakened."

"I will remember."

Mother Earth bent and kissed him gently on his forehead. "You have made your mother very proud."

Her words gave Kalona a feeling of lightness and joy he'd never before experienced, and he realized that the final missing puzzle piece within his heart had been his mother's love. Erebus had been close to Mother Earth all during the time she was testing them, and after she slept and they'd joined Nyx in the Otherworld, Erebus continued to return to Earth to leave small, special offerings to their mother. He even talked to her, which Kalona had found really strange. But now he understood. Mother Earth's love was warmth and softness and light, and he would miss it when he awoke.

Never again. After I awaken I will leave our mother gifts and speak to her like Erebus does.

"I won't forget you when I awaken." Kalona was surprised that his voice sounded so weak. "I will leave you offerings and pray to you—until next you rise."

"Thank you, my son. I do so love it when Erebus brings me gifts and tells me of his day."

"I will do the same. I love you, Mother," Kalona said to his mother for the first time.

"And I love you too, my Kalona of the Silver Wings."

Then Mother Earth spread her arms wide and commanded, "Spirit of immortality—essence divine—come forth to me!"

Kalona felt a terrible tug begin at his wrists. He glanced down as dizziness washed over him to see a ruby light lifting like smoke from the bleeding wounds on his wrists and begin to drift up to his mother's hands.

Automatically, he fought the pull. The warrior in him surged, trying to protect him—to hold on to every bit of his immortality.

No, I surrender. This is not a battle. Warrior, stand down!

With that last thought, a suffocating weariness settled over Kalona. His eyelids felt as if they were weighted. He struggled to keep them open while his mother gathered the glowing smoke of his immortality between her hands and began to speak the creation spell.

"I am She,
Loved so well by
The Divine.
Creation is my gift.

I am She,
Who cherishes her sons
So well.
To their aid I come, strong and swift.

I am She,
Beloved of the Divine—Beloved of my sons.
I call Essence
of my immortal one,
Given by Kalona to lift
Form from my body one whose joy, beauty,
    wisdom, kindness, and humor
is so great,
That thee must and always be golden
    Erebus's mate!"

Mother Earth completed her incantation, and Kalona felt a weariness he had never before known. The women's song raised around him until it seemed that the red smoke his mother had drained from his wounds began to swirl in time with the rhythm of their song. And then the smoke congealed to form the shape of a person. Kalona blinked fast, trying to see through his fading vision. There was a flash of scarlet light that left a naked form crouching inside the circle.

As the person stood, Kalona felt his own body begin to sink. At first he thought it was just a symptom of his weariness, but as he shifted his gaze around, Kalona could see that he was literally sinking—as if the earth was opening gently to embrace him more fully.

But I want to see her! Erebus's mate!

As if hearing his thoughts, Mother Earth's newest creation turned to face Kalona and his mother. And Kalona thought that *he* was, truly, beautiful. A perfectly formed man stood before them. He was tall and lean, and his skin was the color of a fertile field. His eyes were a striking green that reminded Kalona of the moss in the grove on the island from where he'd called Mother Earth.

"Ah! Well, this is a small surprise," said Mother Earth as she studied the young man. "I shall call you Eros, which means love."

Eros bowed low to Mother Earth. When he straightened his curious gaze met Kalona's.

Kalona wished he could have spoken—wished he could have welcomed Eros to their family—or at the very least laugh and shout, *Nyx, you were right again!* Nyx had always told Kalona that Erebus would be more content with a male lover than a female. *She was right... my beloved is always right...*

Suddenly Kalona was sinking faster. He looked up—feeling a flutter of panic. Mother Earth smiled kindly down.

"Close your eyes, my precious son. You must rest so that you may one day awaken. I shall join you as soon as I introduce Erebus to his love."

But I want to stay! I want to see how happy Erebus is!

"Shh, my son. Sleep. Just sleep. Sleep, my son. Sleep, my precious firstborn, sleep..."

Mother Earth's words became waves rocking Kalona gently, gently, until his eyelids closed and the light in his amber eyes went out.

Then, deep in the earth, under a sentinel oak in the heart of what would one day become Tulsa, Oklahoma, Kalona slept.

6

Other Neferet

The day Stark betrayed her and usurped from her the position of High Priestess and leader of the vampyre army was the second worst day of Neferet's long life. Somehow a High Priestess—more than likely one she had showed mercy to and left alive—had masqueraded as that Redbird bitch and managed to poison Stark against her, as well as the strange red vampyre named Kevin *and* her army. And then they manipulated the Old Magick sprites to join their side. Neferet had been forced to flee from her place of power by hurling herself from the football stadium window. Thankfully, her dark ones—the tendrils Neferet had begun to think of with a depth of affection most people reserve for children—were more loyal than her generals or her armies. They broke her fall and shielded her from prying eyes as she fled Skelly Field with the keening of her suddenly emasculated Red Army filling the cold Tulsa night.

Across the street from the stadium, Neferet limped into the first welcoming establishment she came to—Ed's Hurricane Lounge. The instant Neferet opened the door, stepped inside, and breathed the urine- and beer-soaked ambiance, she knew the place was no "lounge." It was a bar. A disgusting, seedy bar located next to a dirty laundromat. Ed's Hurricane Lounge was so far beneath an establishment Neferet would usually patronize that for an instant she felt dizzy and utterly out of sorts.

Then a thick, smooth tendril curled up her leg to twine around her waist. Automatically, Neferet stroked the creature's flawless skin, instantly bolstered by the touch of her loyal child.

"What is it, my darling? What do you need?" Neferet spoke softly, intimately to the tendril—and in return she was washed with a voracious need for blood and flesh. "Ah, I understand perfectly. Yes, saving me was difficult work. It *is* time for you to feed." Other tendrils slithered up Neferet's body, wrapping around her waist, arms, and even around her neck like macabre living jewelry. She'd never felt them so fully until the moment they'd broken her fall and aided her escape from the stadium—and she'd also believed that they'd never been visible to anyone else, but when Neferet finally looked up from the tendrils, every man and woman in the crowded bar stared at her in open horror.

"H-high P-p-priestess?" The fat man behind the bar spoke in a trembling voice as he wiped sweat from his forehead with a bar towel, his eyes riveted on the pulsing tendril that draped around her neck. "W-what can I g-get you?"

Neferet looked from the ridiculous, tacky bumper stickers that "decorated" the walls behind the dreary bar to the cooler that held cheap beer and even cheaper wine. But before she could speak—could tell the bartender that there was *absolutely* nothing she desired in this miserable establishment except a place to hide and think—a rotund woman with bleached-blond hair, fire-engine-red cowboy boots, and short-shorts that left no cellulite to the imagination emerged from a dark hallway that said RESTROOMS. She took one look at Neferet and her eyes widened.

"OHMYGOD, are them snakes?" When the tendrils turned eyeless faces in her direction she opened her mouth, screamed "SNAKES!" and then bolted for the door.

"Stop her," Neferet told the tendril that hung around her neck like a fat rope.

Instantly it detached from her and rushed down the priestess's body to slither with preternatural speed, beating the screaming woman to the exit door she was attempting to escape through. The tendril lifted so that its head was at about the level of the doorknob, opened its fanged mouth, and hissed.

"Oh, Jesus! Oh, lord! Snake! Snake! Snake!" the woman shrieked in hysteria.

"Shut her up," Neferet commanded in a calm voice.

Perhaps her reasonable tone was why the couple dozen or so other people in the bar didn't panic. Instead, like Neferet, they watched the tendril that blocked the door speed forward to the woman. Her mouth, open with hysterical screams, became the serpent's target. It hurled its body up, between the woman's lips, filling her mouth, sliding down into her throat, choking her screams. The woman clawed helplessly and staggered. She finally fell to the floor as the tendril burst from her neck in a bloody explosion. Her dying body convulsed and then was still as the tendril began feeding noisily.

"Well, isn't that interesting?" Neferet spoke above the biting and slurping sounds her tendril was making. The other creatures had remained wrapped round her body, but she could feel their tension and their need. Neferet looked from the bloody body of the dead woman to the slack-jawed, terror-filled stares of the humans. She stroked the heads of the tendrils that writhed around her. "This is going to be much simpler than I imagined." Neferet walked quickly to the door of the bar, being careful to step around the expanding pool of blood and gore that surrounded the dead woman. She smiled to herself as she heard the relieved sighs of the bar patrons who erroneously believed she was leaving. Neferet clicked the lock on the door, turned off the switch that illuminated the tacky neon ED'S HURRICANE LOUNGE sign, and then faced the humans. She smiled and continued to stroke the tendrils that were trembling with anticipation. "Kill them all, my darlings."

Neferet leaned her back against the locked door and observed the tendrils as they did her bidding—enthusiastically, efficiently, and except for the brief, terror-filled screams of the doomed humans, almost soundlessly.

She was amazed at how quickly it was over. Several of the tendrils paused in their feeding and dragged one of the fresh kills to Neferet. They bowed their eyeless heads, clearly offering the treat of the very fat, very bloody bartender to her.

"Oh, my darlings! How extraordinarily considerate of you! But this is your meal. I fed earlier, and I shall feed again later. Now it is *your* time to enjoy." The tendrils wriggled in delight, reminding her suddenly of kittens as they returned their attention to the body and continued slurping and tearing.

Neferet pressed the back of her hand against her mouth, utterly disgusted and trying not to gag at the sight of the offal that used to be a slovenly bartender. Neferet had killed before, of course, but she never fed from any human who hadn't been carefully chosen by her. The High Priestess insisted on beautiful or handsome donors who were made ready for her—meticulously washed, dressed, and prepared. She often restricted donors' diets for weeks before she fed. Neferet most enjoyed the subtle nuances in the delicious taste of blood that came from a controlled source. Feeding would help her heal from her fall quicker, but the dead bartender did not meet her standards. One more glance around the bar told her that no one there met her standards. Thus, she could not bring herself to taste their below-average blood, though she did very much enjoy watching her children drain the bar patrons and tear their flesh from their bodies.

"Darlings!" Neferet clapped her hands to get their attention as she moved around the scavenged carcasses and made her way to the bar. "We will not be safe here long, so eat swiftly. I'll look for keys. One of these," she paused and shuddered, "*humans* must have a decent vehicle we can use."

The tendrils paused in their feeding to listen, wriggled in response, and then returned to their bloody meals, ripping, tearing, and lapping with renewed focus as she searched behind the bar where she did find a hook in the shape of a big bronze breast that held several sets of keys dangling from its grotesquely long nipple. Grimacing with distaste, she spread the keys out on the bar and then began to look through the subpar alcohol selection until she found an unopened bottle of twelve-year-old Macallan single malt scotch.

"Average. Completely average, but at least palatable." Neferet held a highball glass up to the light to be sure it was clean before pouring herself a double. She drank it in one gulp and then poured herself another. There was a stool behind the bar, which she sat on as she sipped her second mediocre drink and considered the future.

"Now I can think." Neferet sighed and flicked a piece of dirt from her red silk jumpsuit. She grimaced as she finally had time to notice the horrid state of her clothes—and only then realized that she was shoeless and had lost one large diamond earring. "This is unconscionable. I need a decent meal, a long bath, and a change of clothes." She tapped the cheap glass highball with one pointed, red fingernail. "It isn't safe to return to the House of Night. Nor can we go to my penthouse suite at the Mayo. Not until I know who is in charge and who is coming after me," Neferet ruminated aloud. Her tendril children continued to feed, though they did often turn their adorable dark heads in her direction and hiss agreement. "Artus's death is definitely inconvenient." Neferet's lips lifted at the corners in more of a sneer than a smile. "But I rid myself of all High Priestesses, either killing, banishing, or demoting them, which means the House of Night will be desperately lacking in leadership. Isn't that a shame?" She laughed sarcastically, pleased to note several of the larger tendrils paused in their feeding to hiss their own version of amusement. "Oh, darlings, I adore you more and more—" She stopped short when the far wall of the bar drew her attention. It appeared to move, shift, change. It reminded Neferet of heat waves rising from a pot of lobsters being boiled alive. Her tendrils noticed as well. As one they turned their heads toward the wall and opened their bloody mouths in angry hisses.

There was the sound of thunder—a great cracking that shook the bar—and through the wall strode an enormous bull. Its head and chest were huge—its horns scraped the ceiling. The bull's breath was a cloud of foulness that seemed oddly familiar to Neferet until she placed it—*death, the bull's breath smells of death.*

His coat was white, but not the color of milk or snow or anything as innocuous. The creature's coat brought to mind one thing above all others—the color a person's eyes turn just after death claims them—the white of an absence of life and an unfathomable depth of nothingness.

"Ah, Neferet, it has been many, many years." The bull's voice rumbled with barely controlled violence—a harbinger of danger just as thunder is lightning's precursor to destruction.

"Children, to me." The High Priestess stood and made a slight gesture with her hands. The tendrils stopped hissing and instantly slithered to her, wrapping around her as they kept their heads turned in the direction of the bull. Newly engorged with blood and meat, they comforted her with the thickness and strength of their snakelike bodies. She stroked them soothingly before she returned her attention to the bull.

Neferet knew who he was—any priestess of power knew the story of the White Bull who personified Darkness, just as the Black Bull personified Light. She knew the two creatures were eternally locked in the struggle between good and evil, always trying to tip the scales to one or the other.

But she'd never spoken with the White Bull. Until that moment she'd only paid cursory attention to the warnings about him, as well as the aggrandizements of the Black Bull. With a sense of shock she easily concealed, Neferet heard the impostor Zoey Redbird's voice lift from her memory, replaying the vile things she'd said to her in the TU press box not long ago, *I also know that you're playing with the*

idea of being Consort to pure Darkness—the White Bull.
Well, she hadn't been—at least not then. Neferet collected
herself. She understood she would have to be wise in her
dealings with the creature, especially until she discovered
exactly what he wanted from her.

"Forgive me—I do so loathe rudeness," Neferet said. "Of
course I recognize you, mighty White Bull. It is an honor
to meet you." Neferet pressed her hand against her heart
and bowed—gracefully and slightly. "I have heard stories of
you, but I do not recall meeting you before now."

*The bull's laughter filled the bloody bar. "Ah, my heartless
one, I have known you since you were a child. How do you
think the tendrils found you?"*

Neferet's emerald eyes narrowed. "The tendrils are mani-
festations of my power."

"Your power?" The bull chuckled again. *"Eventually
several of them remained with you because of your insatiable
quest for power, but they originated with me. Behold!"* The
air around them changed, darkened, and became frigid.
Countless thick and eyeless tendrils exploded from around
the bull. They writhed together in seething nests of reptilian
blackness relieved only by a flash of sharp fangs.

Neferet's hands continued to stroke the tendrils that
remained wrapped around her body. Though they hadn't
originated with her, she did not believe her children would
leave her—not after all they'd been through that day. As
if reading her mind, they clung more tightly to Neferet,
quivering under her caressing hands.

"I drew the tendrils to you long ago," the White Bull continued, and as he spoke the air around them normalized and
the mass of new tendrils dissipated. *"Do you not remember*

the fountain in the garden of your childhood home? The garden where Emily Wheiler knew her only peace."

Neferet's gaze turned hard. She did remember the garden, and with a sense of shocked realization she also recalled the huge fountain. It had been adorned with a centerpiece of a white bull spouting water from his mouth, and it stood in the center of the sanctuary and was often her only companion. But Neferet had closed her mind to her past long ago and she had no intention of opening it. "Emily Wheiler died more than a century ago. I killed her."

"Well, that is certainly one way of looking at it."

"It is the *only* way of looking at it. Mighty Bull, I do acknowledge that my tendrils originated with you." She bowed her head slightly again. "I thank you for gifting me with such perfect companions—but they are now *my* companions and have been mine for many, many years."

"They do show incredible loyalty to you," said the bull.

Neferet shook back her thick auburn hair, wishing she looked presentable—and then an idea came to her and she met the bull's bottomless gaze. "They do, indeed. Especially today, when I have been so cruelly betrayed and usurped."

"I have followed your life's path eagerly and with much interest, especially after you declared war on humans—a war that was, for quite some time, even successful." He nodded his massive head, causing the tips of his horns to gouge the ceiling.

"My war will be successful again as soon as I remove the traitors in my army and regain my proper place as their High Priestess and leader."

The bull's head cocked to the side as he studied her. "And is that all you desire? To be High Priestess and hold dominion over mortals as well as vampyres for your long, but still finite, lifespan?"

Neferet's response was immediate. She observed the bull carefully as she spoke. "What is it that *you* desire, Mighty One?"

The White Bull went very still. Neferet saw the depth of intelligence and cruelty in his gaze—saw it, understood it, and appreciated it. So, she waited, silently, while she stroked the tendrils that clung to her.

"I desire a Consort worthy of me," the White Bull said.

Neferet felt a rush of relief. He may be the personification of evil, but he is also male, and their desires always make fools of them.

"And what makes a Consort worthy of you?"

"Intelligence, preternatural beauty, and insatiability." The White Bull spoke quickly, eagerly.

"I have those things in abundance."

"Ah, my heartless one, as I said, I have been watching you carefully, and I agree that you do indeed." The creature took a step closer and the tendrils cringed away from him, clinging to her even more closely.

Neferet didn't cringe away. She was intrigued by his power. He wore it like his skin. It pervaded everything about him. It radiated from him to pulse against her body. Like all males, he'd already forgotten that he'd asked what *she* desired. Neferet had learned early that men liked to mouth words that said they cared about how women felt, but their actions always spoke louder—always shouted that their true compassion and concern was only for themselves.

Had the White Bull—or any man—listened, he would have found her answer unchanging and simple; Neferet had had the same desire since she was a child. *I want limitless power. I want to control the world around me. There is nothing as safe as absolute power.* Staring into the bull's bottomless gaze, stoked by the immensity of his power, Neferet began to form a new plan.

She lifted a hand from her tendrils and let one delicate finger trace a slow line from her smooth neck to the deep V of her bodice, holding his gaze boldly. When she reached the fabric of her torn and stained jumpsuit, Neferet glanced down suggestively, and then gasped in horror and crossed her arms over her chest to cover herself. She shook her head and looked away. "No, this is not how your Consort should present herself to you, Mighty Bull! Forgive me. I am not myself." She half turned from him. "I am not worthy of you—not now. Not yet. Not until I have regained my place and hold dominion over my people."

Suddenly the bull was there, his mighty head towering over the bar, his nose nuzzling her shoulder with his fetid, freezing touch. Neferet easily kept herself from moving away in disgust. She only allowed others to see what she wished them to see, and this bull—this creature of pure evil—was no different than the others who for her entire life had tried to mold her into *their* ideal of what she should be.

None of them had ever been successful—nor would the White Bull be.

"Let me return you to your rightful position and give you more—so much more."

The bull's voice had deepened with lust and Neferet had to force herself not to smile in victory.

Instead she turned to him and rested her soft hands against his slick, white head. "What more is there?"

"*Divinity.*"

"Alas, unlike you, Mighty Bull, I was not created. I was born—thus, I am mortal."

His moist muzzle nuzzled her, leaving more stains on her torn and dirty clothing. Neferet ignored her distaste and leaned into him.

"*You are correct in one aspect. Immortals are created, not born. But there are still remnants of creation magick on this earth. You need only know where to look.*"

Her slender finger stroked the bull's white horn as she hid the rush of excitement his words caused. "I do not know where to look."

"*I do. You need only be willing to do anything, and immortality—as well as an eternity as my beloved Consort—could be yours,*" said the bull.

Neferet met his gaze steadily and did not hesitate. "There is nothing I would not do to gain the power of a goddess."

"*Excellent! This is most excellent.*" The bull's pleasure rumbled through the bar causing the tiny hairs on Neferet's arms to lift. "*Creation magick can only be found where Old Magick exists. The largest concentration of Old Magick is on the Isle of Skye.*"

"Skye is Queen Sgiach's domain." Irritation pricked at Neferet. All vampyres knew of Queen Sgiach, the Great Taker of Heads, and her ferocious Highland Warriors. No one entered or left the Isle of Skye without her permission.

"*Yes, it is.*"

"She will not grant me entry. When I called on her to join me in my war against humans she refused! Instead the Great Taker of Heads made a public statement condemning me." Neferet's lip lifted in a sneer. "A *statement*. I expected the warrior queen to join me, but she is obviously more interested in comfort and safety than regaining the power humans stole from our people."

"*Sgiach and I are not allies, but I have observed her for more than five hundred years. I assure you, it is not comfort or safety that keeps her on her island.*"

"Then what is it?"

"*She is obsessed with maintaining the balance of good and evil. Old Magick, and the limitless power it controls, could tip that balance. Should Sgiach fall and be replaced by someone who is less concerned with archaic ideals of right and wrong, this world—perhaps many worlds—would be vastly different.*" The White Bull dipped his massive head and nuzzled Neferet again.

"Then why don't you kill her?" Neferet asked.

The White Bull chuckled. "*Ah, my heartless one, I already enjoy you so. Old Magick is powerful enough to bar me from the island—just as it also bars the Black Bull. Our presence amidst such power would cause chaos.*"

"And that's a bad thing?" Neferet stroked his muzzle.

"*Only if it destroys a world.*"

Neferet nodded thoughtfully. "You want me to lure her off the island so you can kill her, and then I will control Old Magick and become your immortal Consort."

"*Sgiach is not so foolish. She's aware that I watch—that I wait. No, if the queen is to be killed it needs to happen on her island and you must do it.*"

"Me? I would be happy to, but I cannot. We've already established that I am mortal. Only an immortal can destroy another immortal."

"*The Great Taker of Heads is not immortal. She is not*

vampyre or human—she is something more and less," explained the bull.

Neferet's eyes narrowed. *What kind of game is he playing?* "But why isn't Sgiach immortal if she lives on the island where immortality can be attained?"

"Because she rejected the power. Queen Sgiach said those born mortal are always corrupted by immortality."

Neferet scoffed softly. "Foolish idealism."

"Indeed, but it means she can be killed. I will aid you. Together we will destroy Sgiach and take control of her warriors and the Old Magick that fills her island. Once we have control of that you will become my immortal Consort."

"What an intriguing idea." Neferet ceased caressing the bull. Her thoughts whirred. She had no intention of ever being anyone's Consort. The bull had already proven extremely useful, and she was quite sure he would be invaluable in the future as an ally, but she would not allow herself to become so beholden to him that she lost her freedom. She would never again lose her freedom. Neferet was quite certain she was capable of destroying a mortal queen who hadn't bothered to leave her castle in centuries, and he'd already given her the information she needed to attain the power she craved.

"Mount me, my heartless one. I will carry you through the night to the Isle of Skye. There, I will hide you in luxury as I coach you on how to enter the island."

"What more is there to know than the fact that I must get Sgiach's permission?"

"There is one other way to enter the island. Gain the permission of elemental sprites. They are pure Old Magick and can be bribed to allow you entrance."

Neferet listened closely, appalled at what a simple thing it was to talk the bull into divulging information. Her sharp mind moved quickly, reminding her of the rules she'd learned so long ago about Old Magick and its elementals. "Sprites always insist on a sacrifice to perform a task, and the sacrifice must hold as much value to them as the task does to the person making the request. I shall have to tempt them with something extraordinary to get them to allow me to enter Skye."

"So mortals believe. Typically, sprites are capricious and can be vicious destroyers one moment and strangely childlike the next. They are curious, though, and often inquisitive and precocious. They truly love scavenger hunts, riddles, and quests. With the exception of Sgiach, today's mortals have forgotten more than they ever understood about sprites. But I have not forgotten. So, instead of offering a sacrifice for entry, ask the sprites to set a task for you to complete. But first you must pique their interest. Show them respect, but in a unique way. If you intrigue them enough, they will agree. The task will be difficult, but I will remain close by. I will aid you in completing whatever it is they set before you."

Neferet knew what she must do. It was a gamble. She might anger the bull so much that he turned from her, or far worse, considered her an enemy and destroyed her. But Neferet would always prefer destruction to servitude. She drew a sharp breath and stepped back.

"My lord, I desire nothing more than to attain immortality and become your eternal Consort." Neferet told her half lie smoothly. "But would I be worthy of you if you had to help me, like a pathetic child, to attain my power?" She didn't pause long enough to allow him to answer, but quickly answered herself. "No! Of course I would not be worthy of you! My lord, my Mighty White Bull, I will go to Skye. I will gain entrance and defeat Sgiach. I will become immortal. When I do all of that *myself*, only then shall I be worthy to call myself your Consort. You must not carry me to Skye, and you must not wait close by with aid. I have to do this alone, and if I am not successful then that will mean that I am not worthy to be your lover, no matter how much I wish to be." She bowed her head and slid gracefully into an elegant curtsy, which she held, keeping her head submissively bowed and her eyes lowered.

The White Bull waited long enough that Neferet's thighs ached and sweat had begun to drip from her neck to pool between her breasts. Finally, his deep voice washed over her.

"I see now what my mistake has been these uncounted eons of existence. Before you I chose Consorts who so lusted for power that they always accepted my aid. And always I found them lacking."

Still holding her curtsy, Neferet was very sure what had happened to his discarded Consorts. The White Bull did not know mercy. Those ignorant women had met with entirely unpleasant ends. Neferet almost laughed. She would never allow her lust for anything or anyone to cloud her judgment.

"Rise, Neferet. You have surprised me, and I am rarely surprised."

Neferet rose. "Thank you, my lord."

"Now, is there some small thing you will allow me to do to aid you? Are your resources in order?"

"My funds are secure. My money cannot be frozen. Nor can it be accessed by anyone except me." She tapped her fingernails against the sticky bar contemplatively. She kept the bulk of her fortune in offshore accounts that were hidden. Neferet could easily replace her clothes, her jewels, even her property. But she needed to get out of this country and disappear into the highlands of Scotland—where neither Stark nor the Resistance would think to look for her—and that meant that she needed to get to her private jet before the House of Night thought to seize it. "There is one thing you can do for me."

"*Name it.*"

"Carry me to the airport."

"*Surely you want more than that? Why not let me carry you to Scotland?*"

"Because, my lord, carrying me a short distance to Tulsa's private airport is a simple thing—a thing I ask you out of convenience and not because I could not make my way there myself. From there I will strive to prove myself worthy of being your true Consort *without* your aid. You must allow me this freedom—this proving time—without your interference. Compared to an eternity by your side, it is a small thing to ask."

The bull's cold eyes skewered Neferet and she felt her blood chill with a terror so intense she had to ball her fists and gouge bloody half-moons into her palms to stop trembling.

"*Very well. I shall carry you to the airport and then I will stay away. For now, I shall wait. But do not test my patience, my heartless one. I am not a patient being.*"

Neferet forced herself to breathe deeply and steadily. She unclenched her hands and quickly wiped the blood on her clothes before wrapping her arms around his neck and whispering into his ear. "Oh, do not fret. I won't be long, as I too have little patience…"

7

Other Neferet

Being carried across the sky by the White Bull was not a pleasant experience. It was not like flying at all. It was more like being caught in a cold, dark void with only the bull's eerie coat to illuminate the nothingness. Neferet clung to the bull's back, taking comfort from her children, who twined around her body and one another. They trailed after her like a living veil. Swathed in Darkness, Neferet ignored her discomfort and brought the formidable focus of her intelligence on her future. There, as she was being magickally carried by the creature who symbolized Darkness, Neferet began making a mental list of what she would immediately need. The trip was not a long one and soon there was solid ground beneath the bull's cloven hooves, but even in that short time Neferet had outlined her plan and made her mental list.

She sat up and brushed back her mass of hair. The bull was standing in the tidy parking lot located beside the main building of the private airfield that ran adjacent to Tulsa International Airport. She quickly slid from his back. Her loyal tendrils followed her, flowing around her like a stream of tar.

"Thank you, my lord." Neferet curtsied deeply and

gracefully. "I eagerly look forward to the day I present my-self to you—filled with power and clothed only in immor-tality and desire."

The White Bull nuzzled her, leaving long strings of cold saliva dripping from her breasts. His deep voice pressed against her skin like another, more insistent caress, and she had to force herself to remain still and compliant.

"You will show yourself to those within as you are?" The bull's gaze roamed over her lush body, focusing on her filthy, disheveled state.

Neferet smiled coldly. "There are naught within but humans. I will not leave any of them alive, though their opin-ion matters not at all to me. Tell me, Mighty Bull, how do I find you when I have completed my tasks and am worthy of you?"

"You need only call my name aloud—ask me to come to you—and no matter where you are I shall respond. Eternally."

Neferet bowed her head. "Thank you, my lord." She put her arms around his massive head and gently pressed her lips against his forehead. "Until we meet again," she whis-pered and then turned to cross the parking lot and head into the hangar.

"Until we meet again, my heartless one." His words *rumbled after her.*

She didn't watch him leave, but she knew the instant he was gone. The air felt different—easier to breathe. And her children relaxed. One slithered up to wind around her waist. She petted it gently. "*His* heartless one? I am not *his* anything. I am my own person—controlled by my own will. Heartless or not, I will never belong to anyone except myself."

With the same decisiveness, Neferet strode to the airport hangar. She'd been there many times. One of the first things she'd done when she gained power over the House of Night was to purchase several private jets and a flight crew for each. They were human, and therefore unbothered by jetting through the sky in the daylight. And, since the vampyre/human war, they also were completely under the control of the House of Night and were required to do her bidding without asking questions, even when she broke human law.

Neferet understood she was gambling—that Stark might be smarter than she'd anticipated and ordered the Sons of Erebus to be inside watching for her. She paused outside the entrance to the main hangar and gathered her children close to her.

"My darlings, if there are Sons of Erebus within," Neferet murmured to the tendrils that clung to her, "you must be prepared. I will not call on the bull—not for something as mundane as freeing me from Warriors. It will be your job to slay them."

Her children trembled with excitement at the possibility she would loose them on the Sons of Erebus, and Neferet filed that knowledge away. *My children are eager to kill— even vampyres. Interesting...*

"Prepare yourselves, children, but do not allow yourselves to be visible unless I command it. We wouldn't want to give them warning, would we?"

She smiled fondly and stroked the tendrils as they wriggled enthusiastically. As soon as they disappeared from sight, she went to the entrance of the main hangar. The automatic doors opened with a soft *whoosh* and Neferet stepped into the tastefully decorated waiting room. She glanced at the wall of worldwide clocks. It was a little before three a.m., Tulsa time. She could hardly believe how much her life had changed in less than five hours.

A moderately attractive middle-aged woman in a tastefully tailored suit began to walk around the counter behind which she'd been working at a computer station. "Good evening, how may I—" When she got a good look at Neferet her words ran out and she stared, slack-jawed.

But only for the briefest of moments.

Neferet watched the woman control her shock and fear. She picked up an iPad and literally shook herself. Then, with her face held carefully neutral, she continued. "Welcome, High Priestess Neferet. How may I serve you?"

"First, I will need the Bombardier Global 6000 made ready for an overseas trip. I require privacy and secrecy. No flight attendants will join me."

"Of course, High Priestess. When do you wish to depart and where—" Her words broke off as the door to the rear of the building began to open. Neferet caught a glimpse of a blue pilot's uniform before the woman rushed to the door and stopped it with her solidly planted foot. She moved so that her body blocked the pilot's view of Neferet and spoke in a curt, no-nonsense voice. "Captain Sturdyvin, the High Priestess requires you to ready the Bombardier Global 6000 for an overseas trip. She demands privacy now and on the trip. No flight crew will be required and please be sure that they know to remain clear of this building until after take-off. I will contact you with more information as the High Priestess provides it to me."

"But where are we going, and when does she want to—"

"Captain Sturdyvin!" the woman snapped. "I have given

you all of the information Neferet has provided me. Would you like me to tell her that you're questioning her orders?"

"No! I'm not really *questioning* them. I just..."

"Good. Ready the jet. As I said, I will contact you with additional information when I have it." She shoved—hard—against the door, slamming it in the captain's face. She turned to Neferet with a polite smile stretching her lips. "High Priestess, I assumed you would want to freshen up in private."

The woman immediately impressed Neferet, and humans almost never impressed her. She spoke as if it was not out of the ordinary for Neferet to have appeared shoeless, wearing torn and stained clothes, unannounced and unaccompanied. She hadn't hesitated to block the pilot from entering the room and discovering Neferet's unkempt state. She'd commanded him as if telling men what to do came naturally to her—a skill too few human females understood the importance of *or* attained. Neferet studied her carefully.

"You look familiar. What is your name?"

"Lynette Witherspoon, High Priestess. I have served as your flight concierge often in the past."

"Ah, I do remember. You always wear such lovely suits. It's a shame you're more a size eight than a size four. But, no matter. I have clothes aplenty stored here and on the jet." And Neferet did. Not because she'd thought she would ever have to flee Tulsa, but because she hated to be inconvenienced. "And you are correct. I do prefer to freshen and depart in private."

"Very good, High Priestess. How else may I be of service to you?"

"Follow me to my locker room. I have a list of things I need you to make available to me when I land." Neferet spoke as she headed toward the rear of the building, where the private shower and fully stocked wardrobe room were located. She walked quickly, not glancing back, though she could hear Lynette's heels tapping against the floor almost as fast as her fingers flitted across the iPad. "I will be flying to whatever private airport is most convenient to Inverness, but tell the pilots we're going to London. They are to file a ghost flight plan with a cover story that one of the European High Council members has come from a secret visit to the Tulsa House of Night and is returning to San Clemente Island via a London shopping spree. I want no one to know where I have gone. No one—the pilots won't even know that we're heading to Scotland instead of England until we're airborne. Upon landing, I will decide where in Europe they should fly the jet to store it and standby. I may need them again, though no one is to know that it is High Priestess Neferet for whom they are on standby."

"A ghost flight plan. Very good, High Priestess." Lynette tapped against the iPad as Neferet continued.

"I will need a car and a driver to take me to Skye, but I will not enter the island. I wish to have time alone—to meditate and study—no one, not vampyre nor human, is to know I am there. Use the High Council member cover story."

"Shall I book you a room in a B&B, High Priestess?"

Neferet stopped so that she could turn to meet Lynette's gaze. "Only if you can book the entire B&B."

"For how long, High Priestess?"

Neferet shrugged. "A month. If I need more time, I'll arrange that with the owner. But my presence must be kept completely secret. How will you be sure of that, Lynette?"

Lynette didn't hesitate. "I will find an owner who cares more about money than gossip and pay him enough to buy his confidence."

"Very good."

"High Priestess, is there a budget I should work within?"

"None. Lynette, if needs be, buy the property. But do remember that I will require a small staff—sworn to secrecy—at least one housekeeper, a cook, and a general maid to serve and do whatever else maids do that I do not."

"I understand. With no budgetary restrictions I should have no problem staffing your temporary home."

"Try not to hire people who are too terribly unattractive."

"Of course not, High Priestess."

"I shall also require new clothes—different than I normally wear. Something rustic that will make me appear to fit in if I'm seen, though I cannot be too unfashionable." Neferet shuddered delicately. "No jeans. Ever."

Lynette nodded. "Jeans are inappropriate for someone of your social standing. Would you consider wearing local plaid?"

"Yes, Lynette. That is an excellent idea. In skirts or dresses, no slacks. And be sure you purchase several travel cloaks—each with cowls that can be pulled up to hide my face."

"Very good, High Priestess. Do you have a preference as to which clan plaid you wear—or would you like a mixture of several different fabrics from which to choose?"

Neferet considered. Her full lips lifted in an almost smile as she thought back to what she knew about Sgiach and her Warriors. "Yes, I do have a preference. Have them all made in Wallace plaid—the ancient version that is muted oranges and browns with the black." Neferet opened the door marked LADIES and entered her private locker room.

"Yes, High Priestess." Her heels tapped steadily on the marble floor as she hurried after Neferet.

Neferet shed her ruined clothes as she walked. "I will require meals to be procured for me. Fresh, young, attractive meals. They too must be sworn to secrecy in case I happen to be recognized." She turned on the rain showerhead and faced Lynette, who was already taking a thick robe and two bath-sheet towels from a cabinet and laying them across the heated towel rack beside the walk-in shower.

"Of course, High Priestess. Do you prefer your meals to be male or female?" Lynette didn't look up from her iPad, but tapped quickly, her well-manicured fingers flying across the face of the device.

Neferet didn't answer her but studied her silently for several minutes. She appreciated that Lynette did not get nervous. She did glance up at the High Priestess, but when Neferet made no response she then went back to tapping away on her iPad. When Neferet finally spoke, it was to ask her own questions. "Lynette, have you ever been to Great Britain?"

"Yes, High Priestess. London, often on shopping trips for my old business, and Edinburgh frequently as well."

"Are you competent to drive there?"

"Well, yes, I have driven in the UK, though roundabouts give me a headache."

"Lynette, I have changed my mind."

"Yes, High Priestess?"

"You will accompany me on my journey. I have need of someone with your skill set."

Lynette did look up at Neferet then—her shock only

reflected by two pink circles that suddenly appeared on her cheeks. "Accompany you?"

"Yes. Is that a problem?"

Lynette blinked quickly several times. "No! Not at all. I do not keep toiletries or clothes here, High Priestess. Will I have time to go home to—"

Neferet waved away Lynette's words. "You may purchase whatever you need in Scotland. Now, as you so appropriately put it, I am going to freshen. In thirty minutes, the jet must be ready to take off. Be sure you are on board. Remind the pilot that he is posting a ghost flight plan. I want no one to know where I am, and that includes the flight crew we leave behind."

"Do you require a meal for the flight?"

"I do, indeed, but stored blood and several bottles of wine from my private collection will suffice. And be sure the caviar service is packed as well. Again, I am traveling in secrecy. Any feeder from this area would recognize me, and then I would have to dispose of its body in the air, which would be quite inconvenient. Oh, and I assume you have access to the security cameras in and around this hangar?"

"I do, High Priestess. It is part of my responsibilities to be sure they are serviced regularly and in proper working order."

"Then you know how to erase and disconnect them?"

"Well, yes, I suppose I do."

"Good. Do it. Now. Secrecy, Lynette. Do I make myself quite clear?"

"Yes, High Priestess."

"Excellent. That is all for now. Close the door on your way out."

Other Lynette

Lynette paced the length of the Bombardier as she spoke firmly into her cell. "Yes, ma'am. You did understand me correctly. My employer wishes to book Balmacara Mains, the bed and breakfast—every room—arriving in the next twenty-four hours, for one month. Yes, that is the amount she is willing to pay for your entire establishment."

Lynette paused as the gruff Scotswoman who had identified herself as Mrs. Muir, owner of Balmacara Mains, sputtered and huffed.

"It cannae be done!"

"Very well, Mrs. Muir. Might you recommend an establishment in the area that would be more amenable to receiving an obscene amount of money for a month's privacy?"

"Ach, well, dinnae be so hasty. Did ya say you'd also be needin' the household staff?"

"Only the bare minimum—cook, housekeeper, and a maid to run errands, shop, etcetera. But, Mrs. Muir, my employer insists on privacy. If the staff cannot be trusted to be absolutely silent, I will handle what needs to be done until others can be hired."

Mrs. Muir made a rude noise through her nose. "Are ye aff yer heid? How will ye be doin' that?"

Lynette rolled her eyes to the heavens. "Mrs. Muir, do we have a deal or shall I stop wasting our time?"

"Aye, we have a deal. I'll be your employer's cook. One of my housekeepers is simple. She can clean, but isnea much for blethering. My Noreen will be the maid. She minds her own business and has three wee bairns to feed, thanks to the no-account man she merrit. I'll tell the current boarders a tall tale and relocate 'em in the village. Bedbugs, mind."

Lynette shuddered and almost said that it was asinine to start a rumor about bedbugs, but she held her tongue. Let Muir make her own mistakes. With what Neferet was paying her she could have the entire place fumigated and refurnished, and still have plenty of cash to spare.

"Excellent. You said you do have internet access?"

"Aye, this isnae the Dark Ages. You can email me through the information address on our website."

"Then from the air I will send you a list of items my employer must have upon arrival, and a second list for later in the week. Keep your receipts. We will reimburse everything you purchase with an additional payment for time and travel expenses. Expect to see the two of us in the next twenty-four hours. And, Mrs. Muir, the one piece of personal information I will give about my employer is that she is a vampyre. She is powerful and rich and dangerous. Keep your word. Show her loyalty and discretion and you will profit from her visit—greatly. If you do not you will suffer as greatly as you would have profited. Do you understand?"

"Och, aye. Well enuf, that's for sure. Tell yur mistress dinnea fash hersel. All will be ready."

Lynette stifled a sigh. The longer she talked to the old woman the thicker and more confusing her Scots accent became.

"Um, yes. Very good. My employer is counting on you.

You have my number and shortly you will have my email address. If you have a question—*any* question—ask. Thank you and goodbye."

She tapped the END button as she slid into one of the bench seats in the cabin. Her fingers flew across the iPad while she began the lists she'd send to Muir.

The pilot entered the cabin from the cockpit. "There you are. Okay, let's talk flight plans since Nefere—"

"No! We're not using her name!" Lynette raised her hand and cut off Captain Sturdyvin. "She wants you to file a ghost flight plan that says we're going to London. The High Priestess will tell you where she's actually going when we're airborne."

"These fucking ghost flight plans are not my favorite," grumbled the captain.

"If your job was easy, anyone could do it and you wouldn't be making seven figures a year in the middle of a vampyre-human war where humans are expendable." Sturdyvin glared at her, but Lynette continued to meet his surly gaze steadily. Her lips even lifted in the hint of a smile as she asked pleasantly, "Would you like to keep your job?"

"Of course."

"Then do as she orders without complaint. Though I do not know her well, I can already tell the High Priestess doesn't tolerate complainers."

"Who died and left you boss?"

After a lifetime living in the Midwest, Lynette knew this kind of man entirely too well—white, affluent, well-educated, and until not long ago entitled to basically whatever he wanted for a lot less effort or talent than any woman or person of color would have to expend. Captain Sturdyvin did not understand that the world had shifted, permanently and drastically, for humans. Men and women like him would not adapt, but Lynette had. Lynette would *always* adapt—and more. She didn't simply survive. Lynette flourished. Her tenacity, brains, and decent good looks had taken her from a squalid single-wide trailer in Camino Villa, Broken Arrow, to the million-dollar historical mansion she'd renovated in the exclusive Midtown Tulsa neighborhood of Swan Lake. And when the war started she was the *only* human to keep her home in Swan Lake. She'd anticipated the signs. Lynette had known the vampyres were taking charge and before the official beginning of the war she'd closed her personal-assistant business—let her entire staff of fifty-five employees go—liquidated everything except her home and her S Class Mercedes Benz, and successfully presented herself at the House of Night to apply for reemployment. Her organizational skills and her intimate knowledge of the Tulsa area had landed the airport concierge job when other humans were being designated as "feeders" and "refrigerators."

Now this pilot—this idiot of a man—was too arrogant to remember that it had been Lynette who had found him and offered him this posh job.

"Currently, no one has died. The High Priestess is boss. I am her mouthpiece. Were I you, I would treat me as you treat her, but if you'd rather test me go ahead. It'd probably be wise to first file your ghost flight plan and be ready to take off in—" Lynette paused and checked the time on her iPad, "Seven minutes." She stared at the captain until he scoffed and retreated to the cockpit to join his more silent copilot there.

Lynette gave Sturdyvin no more thought. He'd hang

himself with Neferet, of that she was sure, and Lynette would happily provide him the rope.

Five minutes later the copilot, a shy man named First Officer Schmidt, stepped from the cockpit, calling to her. "Lynette? Ma'am? Ed is calling from the main building. He says that Nef—uh, I mean the High Priestess is requesting you join her."

"In the main hangar?"

"Yes, the waiting room is what she said."

Lynette's stomach tightened with worry as she stood and hurried to the front of the plane.

"But I told the captain that *all* crew members were to stay out of the main hangar until after the High Priestess departed."

"It's just Ed! The watermelon-headed kid who details the cars. He's no rocket scientist. What is the big fucking deal?" grumbled Captain Sturdyvin from the cockpit.

Lynette didn't answer him. She was hoping it wouldn't be a big fucking deal, but her intuition told her differently—and Lynette always paid attention to her intuition.

She hurried down the stairs of the jet and jogged to the automatic door that opened from the flight line to the main hangar. Lynette paused for a moment to collect herself. She straightened her clothes, patted her chignon into place, drew a deep breath, and breezed into the hangar.

Neferet was standing in the middle of the waiting room. Her mass of auburn hair was newly washed and dried, and formed a tawny mane around her face. She was wearing black silk slacks and an exquisite emerald cashmere sweater—and she was staring at Ed, who was sitting behind the counter grinning with star-struck brilliance at the High Priestess.

"All is ready, High Priestess." Lynette spoke quickly as she entered the room. "Ed, you may return to the other hangar now."

"Will do, Lynette." He stood and made an awkward bow to Neferet. "Didn't mean no disrespect, but when Captain Sturdyvin said it was Neferet who was here I couldn't help myself." He turned from Lynette to Neferet, his face alight with delight. "My ma and dad don't get it, but I've been a fan of yours since I was a kid. I wanted to be Marked bad. Never happened, though."

"Ed, you may return to the—" Lynette began to repeat firmly, but the clueless teenager just grinned and cut her off.

"Hey, Lynette! I was just talkin' to the High Priestess about what people are tweeting from the Bedlam game. Somethin' real crazy happened out there tonight and I was wonderin' if she—"

"Ed, please stop speaking," Neferet said.

"Yeah. Will do. Not sayin' a word more. Can't wait to tell my friends that I saw the High Priestess again, though."

Lynette's heart was beating so hard she was afraid the vampyre would notice. She spoke fast, silently hoping the idiot boy, who had just turned eighteen last weekend, would listen and get the hell out of there. "Ed, return to your hangar. Now."

He nodded, grinned once more at Neferet, and then turned for the side door.

"Actually, young man, carry my bag and follow us to the jet." Neferet spoke as she moved past him and dropped her Louis Vuitton travel bag at his feet before she exited to the flight line through the door Lynette was still standing near.

Ed continued to grin at Lynette.

"Just pick up the bag and follow us—*and don't say anything else*," she told the kid.

"No problem-o! Hey, do you think she likes me?" he said.

"No. I do not. Now shut up and do as you're told." Lynette ignored the kid's crestfallen look and rushed after Neferet.

The vampyre was already standing at the bottom of the jet's stairway. The wind had picked up and gotten colder. It was lifting Neferet's hair so that she looked like a silver screen–era star modeling for a cover shoot beside the jet.

"Captain Sturdyvin!" Neferet called up at the jet as soon as Lynette and Ed had joined her.

The captain appeared at the top of the stairs, looking annoyed and confused. "Yes, ma'am? I'm tryin' to get us off the ground like you wanted, but that's tough to do if I have to keep leaving the cockpit."

Neferet ignored him and spoke to the boy instead. "Ed, carry my bag up and give it to the captain."

"Sure thing, Neferet!" Ed climbed the stairs three at a time, handing the expensive bag to Sturdyvin who took it and tossed it into the plane behind him as the boy scampered down the stairs again.

"Captain Sturdyvin, Ed says that you told him I was here. Is that true?" Neferet's tone was pleasant, but Lynette was watching her eyes carefully and she saw steel and anger in their emerald depths.

"Yeah, I know the kid has a crush on you."

"And yet you also heard Lynette tell you to keep everyone away from the hangar because I do not wish it to be known that I was ever here."

The pilot shrugged and grinned. "Didn't think it would do any harm. It's just the kid. Plus, I figured you'd be flattered."

Neferet's brow lifted. "Flattered. By a boy's attention."

She didn't speak it as a question, but when Sturdyvin opened his mouth to answer, Neferet cut him off.

"No. Not one more word. All you will do is stand there and watch, and know that your disobedience caused this." Neferet glanced down, as if speaking to someone crouching around her at about waist level. "Ah, yes, you will do nicely. Silence the boy. Permanently. Do it quickly. There is no need for him to suffer unduly for the captain's mistake. Lynette, join me in the cabin."

Two things happened simultaneously. First, from around Neferet's slim waist a thick, snakelike creature suddenly became visible. It slithered down her body and hurled itself at Ed's open mouth, boring down his throat to explode in a rain of gore from the center of his stomach. The boy made the most awful sounds as he fell to the ground, writhing in his death throes.

At the same time, Captain Sturdyvin began to scream—like a young girl.

Lynette forced herself not to look. She kept her gaze on Neferet and tried to shut her ears, mind, and heart to the sounds of Ed's gruesome death.

Neferet climbed the stairway to the jet. When she reached the captain, she backhanded him across the face, shutting off his screams like she'd flipped a switch.

"Do not ever be confused about who is in charge here, Captain Sturdyvin." Neferet almost spat the words at him. "The archaic ideal that says you are superior because of that insignificant appendage that dangles between your legs does not apply here—nor will it ever again. Do you understand me?"

The captain was breathing hard and staring in glassy-eyed shock at the boy's body. Lynette didn't look, but she could hear the snakelike creature tearing and eating Ed's flesh.

"Do. You. Understand. Me?" Neferet repeated slowly.

The captain blinked. He managed to pull his gaze from the teen to Neferet. His face had gone an odd color between white and green. Lynette thought he looked as if he was going to be violently ill, and for a moment she wondered what would happen if he vomited on Neferet.

"Y-you killed him."

"Well, *I* didn't. My child did. But, as I said, you're responsible for his death. Now, can you do better? Can you swear to obey my orders without fail?"

"I don't understand."

Neferet sighed and turned to face Lynette, who was directly behind her. "He seems especially thick, even for a human. Can you explain it to him?"

Lynette made an instant decision. She'd understood Neferet was ruthless but seeing her command Ed's death had changed things permanently. Lynette knew one thing beyond all else—unlike Captain Sturdyvin she would survive and thrive, and to do so she would ally herself with the person who could kill them all with a single command. "I can, High Priestess, but I don't think it would do any good. Men like our good captain tend to hear only what their lives have prepared them for—and he is ill prepared to be loyal to you, which he has already proven."

Neferet cocked her head to the side and studied Lynette. "I believe you and I have more in common than I originally thought. And I agree with your assessment of the captain."

The High Priestess touched Lynette's shoulder gently. "Go inside. I will only be a moment more."

Feeling intense relief, Lynette squeezed past Sturdyvin, who had returned to staring at the boy's body.

"Captain, it seems there is a mess at the bottom of the stairs that needs to be cleared away. Do that. Now," Neferet commanded.

"But I—"

"Oh, never mind!" Neferet stepped past him to enter the plane, and as she did she pushed him. Hard.

Completely off balance, the captain fell forward down the steep steps, crying out as he tried to catch himself.

"Children, kill him. Quickly. But no need to be gentle. *He* doesn't deserve it." Neferet stepped into the jet as Sturdyvin's shrieks went on and on and on.

Lynette pulled her gaze from the round window and faced Neferet as the copilot was coming out of the cockpit, looking pale and confused.

"Are we ready to depart, *Captain* Schmidt?" Neferet greeted him.

His gaze drifted out the open door to widen as he saw the bloody bodies that were currently seething with terrible black creatures. Sturdyvin suddenly stopped screaming, though his body was still twitching convulsively. The first officer went very still. He pulled his eyes from the gruesome scene to look directly at Neferet.

"You are captain now. Can you or can you not pilot this jet overseas?"

"I can."

"Then do it. And, *Captain* Schmidt, your pay has doubled. If you are loyal to me, this will be just the beginning of a very lucrative time in your life." She paused and added, "That is, unless you are the kind of man who believes he has to be in charge."

"I am not, ma'am," he assured her quickly.

"Excellent!" Neferet smiled before calling down the stairs, "Children! That's enough for now. You have had plenty to eat today, greedy things. Come to me."

Lynette couldn't help it. She looked. Again. In time to see several creatures leave the destroyed bodies and slither up the stairs to wrap around Neferet like living strands of ebony. "Now, please close this door, Captain. I cannot abide distastefulness."

Neferet strode into the cabin to lounge in one of the sumptuous leather chairs as Captain Schmidt closed the door and disappeared into the cockpit.

"Now, dear Lynette, pour me a drink—half blood, half red wine—and let's chat whilst our good captain gets us airborne."

8

Other Neferet

"It is really rather simple," Neferet understated purposefully as she sipped her bloody wine. "As the unfortunate boy mentioned, this evening during the Bedlam game, I was usurped by fools and ingrates."

Neferet watched Lynette's reaction closely, but the human woman was adept at controlling her expressions—just one thing that Neferet already appreciated about her—and the only sign of shock she exhibited was to gulp the goblet of red wine Neferet had insisted she pour for herself. Lynette dabbed her perfectly rouged lips before responding.

"High Priestess, I assume we are traveling to the Isle of Skye so that you may attain the forces you require to take back your rightful position."

"How delightfully competent you are! Your intuition and intelligence please me, Lynette."

"Thank you, High Priestess."

"There is no need to be so formal. For now, you may call me 'my lady.'"

"Very good, my lady."

"And you are correct, though you misunderstand—which is not surprising. You *are* only human." Neferet tucked her legs under her and smiled sublimely at Lynette. "Skye is an island of great and ancient magick. There I will become immortal. When I am a living goddess, I will return to this place that scorned and betrayed me, and as surely as I will reward those who have been loyal to me, I shall wreak vengeance upon each and every one of those traitors."

Lynette stared at her. Neferet watched her usually placid face shift with emotions she could not hide—fear, shock, and finally acceptance.

"I will always be loyal to you, my lady."

"And unless you give me reason to distrust you, I shall believe that." Neferet paused and tapped her fingernail against the crystal goblet as she considered Lynette. "My dear, if you could have *anything*, what is it you would desire?"

Lynette blinked in surprise at the question but didn't hesitate with her answer. "If I could have anything I would want a villa on the Amalfi Coast, preferably in the old town of Sorrento, staffed and furnished to perfection. I want enough money to be philanthropic, as well as an active businesswoman."

"What business would you wish to be in?" Neferet asked, intrigued that the human had a ready answer and wasn't afraid to speak it.

"Real estate." Lynette's eyes gleamed with shrewdness. "It is something I have been thinking of since the start of the war. I would purchase large amounts of property in the US— in places people, especially humans, think are dead because of the war. But you will be victorious, and when you are I will own prime vampyre real estate in the heart of the land you control."

"But you have no intention of living on any of that real estate?" Neferet asked, honestly curious.

"My only intention is to serve you, my lady," she said quickly.

"Yes, yes, of course. I am simply curious. If I gave you leave to live anywhere you would not choose to return to Tulsa? To perhaps build your Italian villa here?"

"If you gave me leave to live anywhere I would never return to Tulsa," Lynette said firmly.

"Have you no husband? No lover?"

"I have learned that men require a lot of time. I prefer to spend that time on myself, my businesses, things that bring me pleasure—and taking care of the male ego does not bring me pleasure."

Midsip, Neferet almost choked on her laughter. Lynette rushed to her with a fine linen napkin and the mixed bottle of bloody wine to freshen her drink.

"Forgive me, my lady. I did not mean to—"

"Do not apologize for speaking your mind. As long as you have something interesting to say, I wish to hear it. Tell me, my dear, what man hurt you?"

Lynette held the vampyre's gaze. "What man didn't?"

Neferet lifted her newly filled glass in a salute to the human. "I like you."

Lynette stood very still. Neferet could see that she was making a decision, and she allowed the woman to take her time—to think through the complexities of how the day had suddenly unfolded. Finally she nodded, as if agreeing with herself, and then she dropped to her knees before Neferet, but instead of bowing her head she kept her face lifted, meeting the High Priestess's emerald gaze.

"My lady, I ask that I be the first person to swear into your *divine* service. If you accept me, I give you my promise that I will always be loyal to you. I will always obey you. And I will always, *always* worship you. Do you accept me, my lady, my goddess?"

Neferet felt shock at the thrill Lynette's oath brought to her. She stood and bent so that she cupped the human's face between her hands.

"I have wealth beyond measure. Soon I will be immortal, a living goddess walking the earth. I will *literally* be able to have anything I desire—except for one thing. True fealty. I cannot buy that. I cannot command that. It must be granted freely, as you have just granted it to me.

"I accept your oath of service, and in return your goddess will protect you, keep you, and eventually grant you your heart's desire." Neferet kissed Lynette gently on the lips. "Rise, Lynette. You are no longer concierge or assistant. You are handmaid to the goddess—my first and my most trusted confidant."

Lynette stood, but only to drop into a deep curtsy. "Thank you, my lady, my goddess."

"For now, 'my lady' will do. The day you call me your goddess will be a glorious one."

"Yes, my lady."

"Now, please be quite sure that all who are in my service in Scotland understand, if I am betrayed—if any of them breathes one word about me—my children will be loosed on them. Tell them, my dear, so that we might avoid unpleasantness such as what just happened at the airport. Describe to them what it is you witnessed back in Tulsa. *In detail*.

"But also tell them if they keep their word and are loyal

to me, I will pay them handsomely *and* remember their good service. Whether it is through greed or fear, I will be obeyed."

"I'll be sure every one of them knows." Lynette paused and cleared her throat. "My lady, may I ask a question?"

"My dear, you may ask as many questions as you'd like."

"Thank you. The beings that appear and disappear that you call children. I do not understand what they are."

"Of course you don't. How could you? Vampyres do not even understand what they are; it takes divinity to comprehend something so magickal, but I shall simplify for my beloved handmaid." Neferet lifted one shapely arm and extended her hand, palm cupped. "My darling, make yourself visible."

Instantly, Neferet's hand was filled with the thick, eyeless head of a black creature that twined around her wrist and up her arm to drape around her shoulder.

"They are my familiars—my loyal children. They have been with me since before I was Marked. They will be with me for eternity." Neferet caressed the creature's slick head.

"I thought vampyres had cats," said Lynette.

Neferet laughed. "Are you not afraid of them?"

"I am, but not because they're snakelike. I've never been afraid of snakes. I fear them because of what they did back there—at the airfield."

Neferet leaned across the aisle and gently draped the tendril around Lynette's arm. "Show our dear handmaid Lynette she has no need to fear my children."

The creature slithered around Lynette's arm, gliding up to her shoulders where it draped itself like a living scarf around her neck. Lynette very slowly turned her head so she could meet Neferet's eyes. What the vampyre saw there pleased her immensely. The woman was obviously wary, but there was no fear in her gaze.

"May I touch her?" Lynette asked.

"Her?"

Lynette's lips lifted at the corner. "When you described their eternal loyalty, I inferred that they must be female."

"Precisely. I do love how delightfully competent you are, my dear. Yes, you may touch her."

Lynette stroked the tendril. "Soft—she's softer than I imagined. And she's warm to the touch. I hadn't thought that either." When the handmaid turned her gaze to Neferet, her eyes were alight. "She's really beautiful. More unique than a cat—more suited to a goddess."

Neferet felt a rush of pleasure. She hadn't realized how enjoyable it would be to have a companion who understood her—and her children.

"Exactly! Perhaps that is why no cat has ever chosen me. I never thought of that until now."

"That has to be it, my lady. No cat chose you because they were not worthy familiars for a goddess. A cat could not perform the service you required of your children today."

Neferet scoffed. "Not even many cats! And felines have their own ideas about things. My children's ideas only reflect my wishes."

"Then they are definitely perfect," said Lynette.

"As is my handmaid," said Neferet, ending the word on a yawn.

Lynette was on her feet instantly. As if she'd performed the task every day, she unwrapped the clinging tendril from around her shoulders and gently returned her to Neferet. "My lady, I made sure your sleeping area was made ready for you. We are heading into the east, and I knew that would tire you. Would you like me to turn down your linens and put out your nightgown?"

"No, my dear." Neferet stood and stretched. "I can manage myself. I would that you remain here, setting our stay in order. I have decided to change things slightly. In a few hours inform Captain Schmidt that we will truly be flying to London. While he refuels we will deplane. He is going to file a true flight plan with a continuance to Venice. He will say that his guests, vampyres from the High Council, deplaned to shop and returned to depart for Venice and San Clemente Island."

"But really you and I will be driving to the B&B just off the coast of Skye?"

"Indeed, we shall. It will take us longer to get there than if we fly to Inverness, but I want secrecy. Hire a limo in London—one that is blacked out and has a privacy partition. Insist on paying cash. The driver should never see me."

"Yes, my lady. I specified to the B&B that we would also be paying cash." Lynette's fingers flew across the surface of her iPad. "And the extra travel time will give Mrs. Muir longer to prepare for your arrival. I assume you will want new linens and blackout curtains?"

"Yes, of course. Who is Mrs. Muir?"

"The owner of the B&B. She will be your cook. In addition, she is providing a housekeeper and a maid."

"Excellent. All sworn to uphold my privacy?"

"Yes, my lady."

"Very well. Keep Mrs. Muir informed on our arrival time. I expect the staff to be awake and there to greet me no matter when that is."

"Yes, my lady." Lynette curtsied before her deeply.

Neferet surprised herself by lifting the handmaid to her feet and kissing her softly again. "Your goddess appreciates you."

Then with her children trailing her, Neferet retired to the rear of the plane where the windows were blackened and there was a richly appointed bed ready for her, with a cashmere robe draped across it.

Neferet changed into the robe as she thought about the surprise that was Lynette. The woman had given her pause—made her think she might need to reevaluate her attitude about humans, or at least some of them.

Since the volatile day she'd been Marked more than one hundred years before, Neferet rarely spent time with humans unless she was feeding or fornicating—and she'd learned early that humans rarely made good lovers. In her lifetime humans had either been cruel or ignorant—cowards or incompetent fools. But Lynette had shown more loyalty than any vampyre had that day—and more intelligence and instinct than even her longtime Sword Master and protector, Artus, who had stupidly gotten himself killed just when she'd needed him most.

Perhaps humans could be good for more than food or servants. Perhaps, like Lynette, *they* would truly know how to worship her properly.

Neferet fell asleep wrapped within her beloved children with the sound of Lynette's fingers tapping on her iPad creating a very human kind of magick.

9

Other Kevin

Kevin wiped his hand across his face and shook his head like a dog coming in out of the rain. *Snap the hell out of it! You gotta get it together for the meeting.* Kevin scolded himself as he made his way groggily from the wing of the House of Night that housed the professors' quarters to the main building where the School Council Meeting was set to begin—he glanced at a wall clock he'd passed—exactly *now*.

He sighed heavily and gave his fingers a half-hearted crack. It wasn't like him to be so muddy-minded, but Aphrodite's death had changed him—changed everything.

"Oh, Kevin! There you are!" A blue fledgling he only half recognized as a girl named Becky rushed up to him. "There's someone at the front door asking for you. Um, a *human* someone." Her blue eyes were big and round like she'd never seen a human before, and Kevin had to stifle the urge to point out that she'd probably only been Marked for a few months.

"No problem. I was heading that way to a Council Meeting. Could you run up to the conference room and let them know why I'll be a little late?"

"Will do!"

She started to rush away, and Kevin opened his mouth to ask her the name of the visitor—and then found he couldn't summon the energy. His body felt super heavy as he made his way slowly along the main corridor that fed into the foyer of the school and the administrative offices located there. As he took a left to the front entrance he saw a guy standing with his back to Kevin. Hands in his pockets, he was talking with the Son of Erebus Warrior whose shift it was to guard the front doors—and it appeared the Warrior was actually laughing. Then Kevin recognized the broad shoulders and the shaggy blond hair and he understood the Warrior's demeanor.

"Heath!" Kevin called, hurrying forward.

Heath spun around, a grin splitting his handsome face. "Kev! Dude! Look at you! You're, like, a real vampyre!"

"And you kinda sorta look like a real football player," Kevin teased as the two young men embraced warmly. "It's good to see you."

"Yeah, especially without death and destruction happening all around us," said Heath—his expression sobering.

"Seriously," Kevin said.

"Hey, uh, can we go somewhere to talk. I know you're busy vampyre-ing and all, and I gotta get back and catch some sleep before school tomorrow, so I just need a sec."

"Yeah, of course. I always have time for you. Come on into the auditorium. No one should be using it right now." Kevin led the way across the foyer to one of the multiple doors to the large auditorium. Except for the lights on the end of each row of velvet chairs, the room was dark and had a strange, undersea quality to it. They sat in two of the back-row seats. "So, what's up?" Kevin asked.

Heath spoke abruptly with no preamble. "Was she a ghost or for real?"

Kevin started at him. What the hell can I tell him? What the hell can't I tell him? What the hell? What the hell?

"Hey, don't stress. I know there's secret shit you can't tell me, what with me being human and all. But I saw her. And I wanta know if I'm gonna see her again. I figured you'd know."

Kevin cracked his knuckles. "Would it be good or bad if she was a ghost?"

Heath turned so that he met Kevin's gaze directly. "Neither, little bro. What would be good is the truth."

Kevin drew a deep breath. He knew what he *should* say. He should make some shit up and let Heath be good with half-truths and superstitious lies. But sometimes what you *should* do isn't the same as the right thing to do—and this was one of those times.

"Zoey isn't a ghost."

Heath's expression didn't change, but a tremor of emotion shivered through him. Kevin could even see the little blond hairs lift all along Heath's arm.

"That's what my gut said. So, she's alive?"

"Yes and no."

"You gotta explain that, Kev."

Kevin ran his fingers through his hair. "I'll tell you what I can and you'll just have to trust me for the rest of it."

"Hey, who didn't even tell Zo that time when you were a freshmen and you snuck out to hook up with that little dark-haired girl—what was her name?"

"Karla," Kevin said, unable to stop his embarrassed chuckle.

"Yeah, that was it. And she dared you to spray paint the school's gym doors and make it look like guys from the Union football team did it."

"And the Union football team caught me at Sonic getting a burger with her afterward with red paint all over my hands."

"They were gonna kill you dead, little bro."

"Yeah, you stopped 'em *and* didn't tell on me. I would've gotten suspended," Kevin said.

"Worse, dude. Your step-loser would've sent you to some kind of conversion therapy camp or somethin'."

"I don't think that's the right kind of camp for vandals," Kevin said.

"Whatever. My point is that we have a superlong history of trusting each other. So, I know you'll tell me what you can—and you know I'll keep my mouth shut."

"Okay, Zo isn't alive. Not in this version of reality. But there are a lot of different worlds—and more versions of our reality than we can ever understand. And sometimes someone who is very special can move between them. If the reason is important enough, world-changing enough."

Heath nodded slowly. A tear leaked from the corner of his eye and he brushed it away. "That's what happened during the Bedlam game. Another Zo showed up to save us, like some epic Captain Marvel *Endgame* shit, right?"

"That's actually not a bad explanation."

Heath blew out a long breath. "That's our Zoey. She's always been my superhero." He wiped away another tear. "Will she come back?"

"I don't know. She shouldn't. In order to get here, she has to use forces that can be very dangerous."

"Makes sense. I'll bet the Dark Side would love to turn her. You talked to her, though, right?"

"Yeah."

"She's—she's okay? Wherever she is?" Heath stared at Kevin like he was searching for a lifeline.

"She's good. Great even. She loves you, Heath. No matter what reality she's in. Zo would want you to know that." Kevin's stomach clenched as he tried to figure out what the hell he could say that wouldn't make things worse for Heath.

"I wish she could've stayed. At least long enough to see me—just one more time." Heath had stopped wiping at his tears. Instead they rained steadily down his face, dripping from his cheeks to soak his OU T-shirt.

"She wanted to," Kevin admitted.

"The, um, universe or whatever wouldn't let her?"

"No. She wouldn't let herself. Zo loves you too much to screw up your life like that. She knew she couldn't stay—and shouldn't come back. She thought it'd be easier for you if you didn't see her."

Heath's breath hitched on a sob, but he nodded. "I can see that, but if you ever talk to her again would you give her a message for me?"

"Absolutely."

"Zo and me—we never got to say goodbye, you know, before she died."

Kevin nodded. "I know. Me either."

"So, tell her I just want a goodbye. That wouldn't screw things up—not now that I know she's Super Zoey and has to go save the universe or whatever. But a goodbye would help. Didn't it help you to see her one more time?"

Unable to speak, Kevin could only nod again.

"'Kay, well, that's it." Heath stood. He reached into his pocket and pulled out a wad of tissues. He blew his nose noisily and wiped his face—then shoved the damp mess back into his pocket before grinning at Kevin. "I got into a habit of carrying Kleenex around 'cause Zo was so damn snotty every time she bawled." He shrugged. "Old habits are super hard to break."

"Nothing wrong with that." Kevin led the way from the auditorium. "Hey, how'd you get in the school without being skewered by a Warrior?"

Heath grinned. "Dude, even Sons of Erebus Warriors are OU football fans."

They hugged again and Kevin said, "When this crap between vamps and humans is over—don't be a stranger. Let's go fishing or something."

"Dude, I'm totally up for night fishing! Wanta gig some frogs?"

"Only if there's beer," Kevin said.

"There's always beer," Heath said. He clapped Kevin on the shoulder, gave the Son of Erebus Warrior at the door a high five, and left the House of Night.

"That kid's going to be a great quarterback," said the Warrior.

"That kid is already great," said Kevin.

Kevin hurried into the conference room and took a seat as he whispered an apology to Anastasia. She nodded in return saying, "Becky explained that you would be late. The meeting has just begun. Our Sword Master was updating us. Dragon, please continue."

Kevin smiled a thank-you to Anastasia before settling in his seat and exhaling a long sigh. Heath's visit had been a surprise. He had no way of knowing if he'd ever see Zoey again, but he did understand Heath's grief and his need for closure all too well. *At least Aphrodite and I got to say goodbye. Aphrodite... damn, I miss her so much it's a physical pain...*

Dragon's deep voice barely penetrated Kevin's inner dialogue as he answered his mate's question about the status of the red vampyres: "Well, it's bad. Even though Nyx washed the Red Army of their guilt for the things they did while their humanity was missing, they're just not coping. We lost over a dozen more this morning. They just walk out into the sunlight. Short of locking them up, there doesn't seem to be anything we can do to stop them from killing themselves. Do you have any insight that could help us, Kev?" Dragon Lankford stared across the conference table at the young vampyre who took no notice of him. "Kevin?"

"Huh? Yeah. I mean, what?" Kevin blinked and brought himself out of his own head and back to the present. He took in the new House of Night High Council members— the few left alive. Dragon Lankford and his mate, Anastasia; Professor Nolan, the drama teacher; and Professor Penthesilea—the literature teacher. Also Loren Blake, who was there because before the war he'd been named Vampyre Poet Laureate, which gave him an automatic seat on the School Council. Kevin thought it was a mistake to include him, though. During the war he'd proven himself to be a pain-in-the-ass pretty boy who only looked out for himself. But Anastasia was the new High Priestess, and with Dragon named her Sword Master, it was their mistake to make, not his to correct. And, of course, James Stark was also on the Council—though he was late joining them too, as usual. But no matter what, Kevin decided that six awesome vampyres and one pretty-boy dickhead was a definite improvement over one insane High Priestess and a gaggle of her sycophants.

"Honey, Bryan was commenting about the state of the poor red vampyres," said Anastasia. "Do you need a moment to collect your thoughts?"

"Oh. Sorry. No, I'm okay." Kevin cracked his knuckles and rubbed a hand across his face. "It's not good. One of them pried open a window in the boys' dorm and at sunrise seventeen of them crawled out and walked into the sun—right in front of a group of newly Marked Third Formers who were just heading to bed." Kevin shook his head. "It was truly awful."

"So, we do need to keep them locked up," Dragon said. "Only we need to do a better job of it."

Anastasia's smooth brow furrowed with worry. "Yes, because we're hoping after intensive therapy they can learn to forgive themselves and have normal lives."

"The tunnels are disgusting," Kevin said with a shudder. "No one with any humanity would live down there, but that's where we can contain them best."

"Then our priority needs to be cleaning out that tunnel mess and making it habitable. Fast," said Anastasia.

Loren Blake grunted. "I'd think our priority would be figuring out how we're going to keep this truce with the humans going—or are we? Why aren't we even discussing continuing the war? Neferet wasn't wrong about everything. Humans *have* segregated and abused us for centuries."

"Are you out of your fucking mind?" The words exploded from Kevin's mouth and he had to force himself not to leap across the big, round table and punch the asshole in his throat.

Loren scoffed at him. "What are you? Sixteen? Are you even old enough to be on this Council?"

"You—" Kevin surged out of his chair as Dragon grabbed the back of his shirt.

Anastasia stood. "Stop this at once!" Everyone froze.

She looked from Loren to Kevin and shook her head. "We do not meet violence and hatred and ignorance with violence, hatred, and ignorance. And this display of aggression and testosterone is exactly why Nyx created our matriarchy. Neferet is an abomination—a female who allowed Darkness to steal her compassion, empathy, and wisdom. I am High Priestess here. I am determined to lead this House of Night back to Nyx—back to our roots of wisdom and compassion. I do not know all of the answers. I do know we will defend ourselves, but we will *not* make war on humans. If any of you disagree, you will leave this Council and this school. Is that understood?"

Kevin bowed his head in shame. Anastasia had barely raised her voice, but the Council Chamber had gone gravely silent. "Yes. Understood. I apologize. I'm—this isn't how I usually act."

"You are forgiven," Anastasia said. She turned her attention to Loren. "And you?"

"I apologize as well. I fear Neferet's Darkness may have

tainted my attitude." Loren smiled sheepishly and bowed his head.

Kevin had to force himself not to call bullshit. Blake was slimy. But he didn't need to worry. It took one look at Anastasia, magnificent and filled with righteous anger, to know that she wouldn't be led astray by a handsome smile and charming but empty words.

"Realizing you've allowed Darkness to enter your spirit is the first step. Now you must return to Nyx and the Light. Until you do your voice does not belong on this Council. My suggestion is that you spend time in Nyx's Temple, apologizing to and recommitting yourself to her."

Blake blinked in confusion.

"Now," Anastasia added.

"You mean you want me to leave?"

"What I mean is exactly what I said. You admit to being tainted by Darkness, which makes you unfit to sit on our governing Council. You need to recommit yourself to the Goddess, which you should do with mediation and prayerful self-observation. Nyx's Temple is the proper place for both. Farewell, Loren Blake. Come see me when you have found yourself and our Goddess again."

Looking shocked, confused, and—Kevin thought—more than a little angry, Loren Blake stood, bowed mechanically to Anastasia, and headed to the door. But before he exited the Council Chamber, he paused and turned back to address them.

"It isn't just me. There are others who are also tired of living apologetically under the thumb of beings who are weaker and less talented than we are."

Anastasia shot to her feet. "These weaker, less-talented

beings also *outnumber us by the millions!* But forget that. Forget how cruel, violent, and heartbreaking this war has been. Remember one thing, if one thing is all your mind can grasp: Those beings are humans. Just as we were once humans. And it is inhumane to wage war simply because we are not all the same."

Blake tried to speak, but Anastasia's raised hand silenced him.

"Loren Blake, I officially relieve you of your title as Vampyre Poet Laureate, as well as your duties, which include teaching any classes. I expect to see you in Nyx's Temple for the foreseeable future, beseeching her help in finding your center again. You are dismissed."

Blake left the room, slamming the door behind him.

"Anyone else here who believes we should move forward with violence and hatred?" the High Priestess of the Tulsa House of Night asked.

The remaining Council Members were silent, watching Anastasia attentively.

"Good." She sat and smoothed her long, straight hair back. "Then let us proceed. Oh, and Sword Master," she addressed her longtime mate, Dragon Lankford. "Keep an eye on Loren. I have always suspected his looks and charm were concealing a lack in character—and now I am sure they are. We cannot allow the cancer of hatred to continue to spread. Cutting it out of our governing body is the first step. The second is to watch and be sure it doesn't metastasize outside this body."

"Yes, High Priestess." Dragon bowed his head respectfully and pressed his fist over his heart.

"Um, High Priestess?" Kevin raised his hand.

Anastasia smiled. "Yes, Kevin?"

"Blake's a douche, but he's not the only one who needs watching. Maybe it's because blue vampyres are used to saying whatever they want around red vamps and fledglings with no consequences, but I've overheard things that I don't like."

"Things?" Anastasia asked.

"Yeah, like the crap Blake said. There is a group of young Warriors who have been basically acting any way they want to act for the past year or so, and some of them aren't happy about having to give up their power."

"*Their* power?" Dragon almost elevated off his chair. "A House of Night Warrior doesn't hoard power selfishly. He uses it in the service of his High Priestess and his Goddess."

"Try telling that to guys like Dallas and his buddies. Their level of assholeness is a lot higher than Blake's."

Dragon's look reminded Kevin of a storm. "With our High Priestess's permission I will do a lot more than *try* to tell them. Anastasia, I would like to meet with all the officers and sergeants. I'll call it a debriefing. In truth what I will do is give them a reality check they won't soon forget."

"You have my permission. Make a list of the names of the vampyres you believe need to be temporarily removed from any type of Warrior duty. Perhaps we should create a retreat for them where they can reconnect with Nyx."

"That sounds like an excellent idea. I'll get on it immediately," Dragon said. "Kevin, I'd appreciate your help. Do you have other names besides Dallas?"

"Yeah, there's a whole group of them. I'll help you out with it."

Anastasia bowed her head slightly and said, "Thank you,

Kevin. Sword Master, please let me know if it would help if I spoke to the Warriors. It sounds naïve to say it aloud, but I am shocked that there are factions within our people who *want* war. We have much more work to do as a people than I anticipated. But we will get it done, and the House of Night will return to Nyx's path—a path that does not lead to senseless bloodshed and a war that only benefits bullies." Anastasia expelled a long breath. "I think that's enough for one meeting. I'm going to visit with as many of the Red Army members as possible. I'll see if I can comfort and reassure them."

Professor P spoke up. "I would like to come with you, High Priestess. Many of those vampyres were once my English students. Perhaps seeing my familiar face will be some comfort to them too."

"Excellent idea. We all have much to do. Let us reconvene in three days. Merry meet, merry part, and merry meet again. And may we all blessed be."

10

Other Lynette

Lynette had steeled herself for a nightmare eleven-hour drive from London to Balmacara Mains but was pleasantly surprised. Once they were out of London and the smooth-riding limo was eating up the miles to the highlands, Neferet curled up and seemed to be asleep for almost the entire way, leaving Lynette to coordinate the B&B's preparations and then to stress about how the hell she was going to get Mrs. Muir and her small staff to understand the danger they were in if they betrayed Neferet *without* the vampyre making an example out of another Ed.

The vampyre...

But was Neferet truly just a vampyre? Lynette was smart and apt. She'd educated herself about vampyres. She'd observed. She'd researched. She had never once heard of anything even remotely like the snaky children that were completely loyal to Neferet. Vampyres loved cats. Sometimes horses. But always cats. And Neferet had said no cat had ever chosen her, yet snakelike tendrils swarmed to her.

What did it all mean? Could she truly be powerful enough to become immortal? A living goddess?

Lynette stared at Neferet as she slept. The tendrils winked in and out of sight. They appeared to sleep wrapped around the vampyre, as if she rested in the center of a nest made especially for her. Lynette wasn't disgusted by them. Snakes had never bothered her—just like mice and rats and bugs had never frightened her. She'd always thought being squeamish about such things was a pathetic affect some women put on hoping to be saved by a knight in shining armor.

She'd learned early there was no such thing as a knight or a savior—in shining armor or a halo. Lynette saved herself— and that's how she preferred it. That was why she'd made the decision on the jet that she would pledge herself into the service of Neferet. Yes, she'd been defeated by other vampyres and was obviously on the run—and still Neferet commanded more power and more money than anyone Lynette had ever known. So, Lynette had gone all in. She'd chosen a side— and that side was firmly with Neferet.

Of course if the vampyre proved to be insane or deluded, or simply less powerful than she appeared, and was over- thrown—well, then Lynette would reevaluate and figure out a plan B. Hopefully, plan B wouldn't have to be invoked— and if it did it would be *after* Neferet had gifted her with her villa and wealth, but until then Lynette had every intention of serving Neferet with the loyalty, intelligence, and respect the vampyre deserved.

They arrived at Balmacara Mains a little after 2 a.m. Lynette was pleased to see that the B&B was as secluded as her swift research had led her to believe. The single-lane road that wrapped past the entrance was framed by an old Scotts pine forest on the land side, and Loch Alsh and what she'd read would be a majestic view during daylight of the Isle of Skye on the other. The B&B had a few outbuildings but seemed self-contained and perfectly private.

"This is a good beginning," Neferet said as she peered out the tinted window to the B&B. "It's all lit up. They're obviously awake, just as you instructed them to be."

"So far Mrs. Muir has proven to be highly competent," Lynette said, though her stomach was a pit of nerves because she'd also proven to be highly stubborn and opinionated.

"Ah, look! They're lining up outside to greet me. That is a lovely old-world touch." Neferet stroked several of the tendrils as she spoke. Then the car slid to a smooth halt and she added, "Children, do keep yourselves well hidden unless I command otherwise. Frightening the help is not necessary. Yet."

Lynette had texted Muir just a few minutes before, letting her know that she and the two staff members must be outside and lined up for their arrival. She allowed herself a small sigh of relief as she exited the limo and nodded to the gray-haired, thick-waisted woman who stood first in line before two much younger girls. "Mrs. Muir?"

"Aye, 'tis myself."

"I assume all is ready?"

"Weel, as ready as we could manage in the short—"

"Good." Lynette cut her off as she walked around the limo to open Neferet's door. "Remember that 'my lady' is the correct form of address." She didn't wait for a response but opened Neferet's door.

The vampyre emerged gracefully from the limo while Lynette retrieved her travel bag from the trunk and waved the limo driver away, then she trailed behind Neferet as she approached the entrance and the staff waiting to greet her.

Mrs. Muir bobbed an arthritic curtsy. "Me lady, welcome to Balmacara Mains. I am Mrs. Muir—owner and cook.

This is yer housekeep, Noreen, and yer maid, wee Denise."
The girls curtsied, keeping their eyes turned down.

"What a lovely greeting. Thank you, Mrs. Muir. I am going
to freshen." Neferet paused and met Lynette's gaze. They
shared a secret smile before she turned back to the staff.
"Then there is something I must do. Whilst I freshen, which
will take no longer than one hour, I need you to pour wine,
honey, and salt into three different bowls. Add a fourth
bowl, but it should be empty. Something earthy and quaint
will do nicely. Oh, and do add a loaf of fresh bread as well.
You bake all of your own bread, do you not?"

"Aye, we do," said the old woman.

"Perfect. I will need a lovely tray covered by expensive lace
to place the bowls on. I will also require a meal."

Lynette watched Neferet consider the two girls as possible
feeders and saw the moment she rejected them both. Relieved
she'd planned ahead, Lynette spoke up.

"My lady, I need only make a call and a proper feeder
will be here within the hour."

"How very competent of you, my dear. An hour is perfect.
Have—" Neferet paused, considered, then continued. "Have
him wait out of the way until I am ready. And now I would
like to go to my suite."

"Wee Denise, take Herself to the grand suite."

Denise bobbed another nervous curtsy and then led them
into the manor. Lynette fixed her face into a pleasant but
mostly expressionless mask. She decided quickly that the
house, which had obviously once been considered the great
house of a country estate, had been overenthusiastically
decorated in what some might call quaint country.

Lynette called it threadbare and cluttered, and she was

immensely relieved when wee Denise opened the door to a suite that, though modestly sized and decorated in homespun, was tidy and smelled of lavender. The new blackout drapes had been pulled aside and the little maid was quick to rush to them and point out that the grand suite overlooked the Isle of Skye.

"Adequate," Neferet said, waving the maid away. Looking relieved, the girl scurried from the room.

"I want you to choose a room close, but not adjoining. I was not exaggerating when I said I insist on privacy."

"Of course, my lady. This thing you must do—should I be sure a car is made ready for our use?"

"Oh, no, my dear. I need only walk to the water, but you may join me. I believe you will find it quite interesting. Now, where is my bathroom suite?"

The room wasn't large enough to make it much of a search, but the bathroom was surprisingly well appointed. The tub was oversized and there was a separate, modern shower.

"Well, I suppose it will do." Neferet frowned at the room. "You may go now, Lynette. I know you must procure my feeder. I will freshen and then meet you downstairs in that little drawing room we passed on the way up here—the one with the fireplace."

"Yes, my lady. Do you need anything else at this time?"

"No, but I can tell you that I will be ravenous after I finish my errand, so be sure the feeder is here—and be quite sure he is young and attractive."

"I would never consider any less for you."

"Thank you. And, Lynette, you did well to set all of this in order in such a short time. You should know that I never forget a service well done—just as I never forget a slight."

"I would expect no less from a goddess."

Neferet's smile was so beautiful Lynette couldn't help but stare.

The vampyre went to her and touched her cheek gently before kissing her softly on the lips. "Lynette, you are a jewel discovered exactly when I needed to be dazzled."

Lynette felt an unexpected rush of emotion and she had to blink back tears. "I am your devoted handmaid, my lady." She curtsied and hurried from the room, pausing outside the door to collect herself before she went back into the main part of the manor to call the feeder and be sure Mrs. Muir didn't screw up Neferet's requests.

Why did she want bowls with wine, honey, and salt in them? What was Neferet planning?

Better not to think about it. Better to focus on making everything as perfect as possible—keep her head down—survive and thrive...

Other Neferet

During most of the drive from London to the B&B, Neferet had been in a deep, meditative state where she had been focusing on lifting from her memory everything she'd ever learned about Old Magick and the sprites that were so closely allied with it. Her remembrance had made her decision. Neferet would not hesitate. She would not prevaricate or procrastinate. The sprites needed to be wooed, and she would begin her courtship of them immediately.

Neferet readied herself carefully. She bathed, anointing herself with the essence of heather—one of the items Lynette had made certain waited in her boudoir. Neferet left her hair loose so that it cascaded around her waist. She chose to wear a long, sheer nightgown that was really more a diaphanous version of a Victorian chemise—sleeveless, with a low neckline and volumes of sheer silk that pooled around her ankles. She chose her single piece of jewelry even more carefully, finally draping a fat, blood-colored ruby set in platinum around her neck. It nestled between her breasts. She pressed her hand over it in a fond farewell, remembering Loren Blake, the vapid but handsome vampyre lover who had gifted it to her many years ago when he'd first become smitten with her.

"I wonder if you spoke out for me." The ruby felt warm against her palm. "Or did you follow the traitor Stark's lead and betray me too?" Neferet shrugged and made the final applications to her dramatic makeup. She'd painted her eyes as the ancient Egyptians used to—heavy with kohl—so that they appeared even larger and more jewel-like. Studying herself in the floor-to-ceiling bathroom mirror, Neferet decided she was ready.

"Children! Make yourselves visible to me."

Instantly the nest of ebony tendrils appeared. They covered her king-size bed and dripped off the sides of it to cascade onto the floor. Each of them turned their eyeless faces to her as she spoke lovingly to them.

"Darlings, it begins this night. We court power—and that means we must woo the sprites so that I gain them as allies and win access to Old Magick and immortality. The White Bull said that sprites are curious—that they like to be intrigued. Then let us put on a show for them like nothing they have ever before witnessed because I am like nothing that has ever been—nor ever will be again. Come with me, children, but remain invisible until I command you appear."

Neferet slid on cashmere slippers and swept from the suite. She could feel her children all about her and knew they would not fail. Lynette was in the drawing room, sitting before a cheery fire with a tea service set out for her, though she wasn't sipping from the porcelain cup or nibbling on the biscuits. Instead she was tapping away—this time on her laptop and not her iPad. The instant she saw Neferet she stood and curtsied quickly. Neferet saw her take in the fact that she was practically naked, though the human woman maintained what Neferet had come to think of as her stoic expression.

"My lady! How may I serve you?"

"I need the tray that I asked the cook to fill with the offerings."

"Mrs. Muir!" Lynette called.

Neferet frowned as the old woman ambled into the room. "Aye?" She bobbled a quick curtsy.

"My lady needs the tray she asked you prepare for her," said Lynette.

Mrs. Muir nodded, threw Neferet a baffled glance that took in her loose hair and sheer nightgown, and then disappeared back through the swinging door that obviously led to the kitchen area.

"Get a bell. Something you can ring to call her. I cannot abide shouting," said Neferet.

"Yes, my lady."

Mrs. Muir returned with the tray, covered in fine lace and

laden with three filled bowls and one that was empty. "Shall I put this in the dining room for ye, my—"

"Give it to Lynette," Neferet said. "I'll need a lantern or candle."

"We have a torch I can get ye."

"Torch? That would be lovely! Much better than a candle and so much more authentic."

When Muir said nothing, but only looked confused, Lynette spoke up. "Mrs. Muir, do you truly mean a torch—with a live flame?"

The old woman chortled, her thick stomach wobbling. "No! 'Tis a flashlight I be meaning!" She laughed some more.

"Do you have a lantern or a covered candle?" Lynette's no-nonsense voice cut through Muir's merriment.

"Aye. I have an auld thing in the cellar."

Neferet spoke in short, clipped sentences. "Get it. Light it. Bring it to the front of the manor. Be sure the girls are with you. You will not come with us, but there is something I want all of you to witness." She motioned, and Lynette took the tray and followed her to the front door where the vampyre paused, waiting for the two girls to join the cook.

The night was cold. The low-hanging fog had cleared and the moon had risen. It was waning, but the sky was filled with stars so brilliant that they illuminated the water that stretched beyond the road, turning it to mercury. Mounds of more shadow lurked beyond the liquid silver, relieved by only a few lights that did little to lift the darkness. As the three women joined them, Neferet asked, "Mrs. Muir, I assume that darkness across the water is the Isle of Skye."

"Och, aye." She handed a rusty lantern to Neferet. Its flame burned brightly within the dusty glass jail.

"Excellent. Remain here on the porch. You need do nothing more than observe. When I am finished you may retire. I will not require your services until after sunset tomorrow." Neferet didn't wait for a response but turned to Lynette. "Come with me, my dear."

Ignoring the cold and what Neferet decided already would be the perpetual dampness of this wretched country, the vampyre strode across the small parking lot to the narrow blacktop that passed for a highland road. She crossed it quickly, navigating down a small ditch that emptied to a rocky shoreline. Neferet slowed then, picking carefully around and over rocks and sea debris. The night smelled of fish and mud and salt. By the time Neferet reached the water, she had decided she was unimpressed. She much preferred a coastline that was more civilized.

She paused at the edge of the water, setting down the lantern. She stepped out of her cashmere slippers, kicking them behind her where Lynette stood quietly holding the tray. "Please keep my slippers with you and dry. I abhor damp feet." Neferet shrugged out of the nightgown, stepping delicately from the silk. "And my chemise as well." Naked except for the ruby, Neferet lifted the lantern with one hand and held out the other to take the tray from Lynette.

"My lady, would it be easier if I came with you and carried the tray?"

"Dear Lynette, that is kind of you, but this is something you cannot help me with. It begins now—my quest for divinity. Await me here."

Holding the lantern high with her right hand and balancing the tray on her left hip, Neferet walked to the waterline, halting only when the cold, dark loch lapped around her ankles. She stood perfectly still as she concentrated, opening herself to the night.

Instantly she felt the pulse of power. It was rich, thick, and hidden—like a vein of gold nestled beneath the surface. It undulated from the tenebrous mound of land that obscured the distant horizon. It reminded her of the power she felt when she cast a circle, but so much *more*. As she would have during a circle-casting, Neferet gathered the power, calling it to her with the force of her will. When she felt a tiny spark—an electric thrill that said the energy acknowledged and responded to her, no matter how sluggishly, Neferet began.

"Children! Create for me a walkway—a raft to carry me nearer the magick that answers me there!" She lifted the lantern even higher, gesturing out at the silent water and the hulk of land beyond. "And be visible! Let *all* witness the glory that is my beloved children!"

From the night around her, the dark tendrils became visible. They slithered forward, laying themselves along the surface of the water and creating a living raft she stepped carefully onto.

"Steady me, children! Keep your mother above the darkened waves!" The tendrils flowed around and above her ankles, supporting and anchoring her. "Now, forward! Carry me to the center of the loch!"

The tendrils did as she commanded. The vampyre briefly wished she'd thought to have Lynette take pictures, for surely the night had never seen such a sight as Neferet, buoyed by magick, naked and glorious and seeming to walk on water to the middle of the loch. The whistling wind lifted her mane of auburn hair so that it flew madly around her. The flame in the lantern flickered as if it danced in partnership with the wind, sending playful, licking shadows over her perfect, porcelain skin.

Her children moved with preternatural speed. Impossibly swift and strong, they reached the center of the loch quickly—slowed and then stopped. Neferet placed the lantern beside her on her living raft. Then, from around her neck she lifted the platinum chain that held the fat ruby, placing it in the empty bowl where it glistened with trapped starlight. Neferet held the tray before her, raising it as if she offered it to the highest peak of the dark isle.

> *"Sprites of olde! Spirits of earth, sea, fire, and air!*
> *I greet you and gift you with libations rich and jewels fair.*
> *I ask nothing in return; I only honor your past*
> *And hold to the ancient ways true and steadfast.*
> *Accept what is freely given with love and respect*
> *As too often the present does the past neglect.*
> *So, I cleave to the olde ways and shall never forget*
> *Hear me—see me—know me! I am Neferet!"*

Neferet bent then and carefully placed the tray on the water in front of her living raft, where it floated and bobbed gently while it drifted away—the tide carrying it toward the darkness that was the Isle of Skye. Neferet did not turn away. She did not begin back. Instead she watched and listened—and was duly rewarded when a wave that appeared to be a watery arm ending in webbed fingers closed over the tray, pulling it and the bowls into the depths.

Neferet's smile was fierce. "Now, children, return me to land!"

Other Lynette

Lynette had been fearful at first. She'd never been a fan of deep water—especially deep, dark water—and standing on the bank of the loch in the middle of the night with little light in the company of a vampyre and her supernatural children had been a creepy experience—especially when those children carried the naked vampyre out onto the silent loch.

But something changed when Neferet began speaking the invocation—or at least an invocation was what Lynette assumed it was, and she made a mental note to research vampyre spellwork and rituals. Whatever Neferet's intention had been, the result was that from the middle of the loch she blazed with passion and power—like Aphrodite newly born from the sea. *No,* Lynette shook her head as she watched Neferet place the offering tray on the loch, *Aphrodite was too tame a goddess. Neferet was a more powerful force. Something untamed and as yet unnamed. More than vampyre—more than divine—she seemed the personification of strength, confidence, and beauty. She is everything I ever wished to be, and if she becomes immortal I will worship her for the rest of my life,* Lynette vowed.

Neferet stepped from her living raft and, smiling victoriously, returned to Lynette, who offered the slippers and the sheer chemise.

"My lady, next time I will bring your robe. It is far too cold out here!"

"Dear Lynette, you need not worry for me. I do not feel the cold as do humans. Did you see? They accepted my offering—immediately and the first time."

"Did you doubt that they would, my lady?"

"Of course! Sprites are beings created by Old Magick. They are mysterious, powerful, and capricious. Never forget that. Never underestimate anything linked to Old Magick."

"Yes, my lady."

Neferet peered back at Balmacara Mains, her smile returning. "I see the staff has already retreated within. Did you watch to be sure they observed everything?"

Lynette's stomach tightened. *Why the hell didn't I think to look behind me?* "I apologize, my lady, but I was mesmerized by you. I—I have never seen anything like what you just did. You are so powerful—so beautiful. I wasn't thinking of anything else."

Neferet's expression softened and she touched Lynette's shoulder gently. "Of course you could not look away. I was quite a sight, was I not?"

"Oh, my lady! You were magnificent!"

"Yes. Yes, I was. And you are forgiven. We should know soon if the staff did as I commanded, and if not, they will be reprimanded. Now, hurry ahead and be certain my feeder has arrived. I am famished. Make quite sure he is washed. I cannot abide a sweaty, filthy human. Give him drink—something strong. And then bring him to my suite."

"Of course, my lady. How else may I serve you tonight?"

She didn't answer right away. Instead Neferet studied Lynette so closely that she had to force herself not to fidget nervously. But when the vampyre spoke, her voice and her expression were filled with concern and kindness.

"My dear, tonight you may serve me by resting. You have done well—very well. But I see that you are exhausted. Eat something nourishing. Sleep. I will send the feeder on his way when I am finished with him." Neferet paused and then added, "He *is* one I must return, is he not?"

Lynette swallowed past the ball of tension that had suddenly risen in her throat. "He's local, my lady. Registered as a willing feeder. I believe if you drained him it would call attention to you."

"Well, that wouldn't do. Not at all. But in the future consider that there are times I enjoy finishing a meal—completely. Tonight I shall show self-restraint. Now, go ahead and prepare him for me. As soon as you deliver my feeder you may retire—with my blessing."

"Thank you, my lady." Lynette curtsied and began picking her way back across the slick rocks and muddy bank, and as she did, Neferet's voice drifted on the cold night air to her, turning her blood to ice.

"My children! You have done so well tonight that I grant you a boon. You may choose one home—out there somewhere—be sure it is not close enough to us to draw human attention here. Feast on whomever lives there. Finish them completely. Leave no trace. Bon appétit, my darlings..."

Don't think about it except to be glad it's them and not you, Lynette told herself firmly as she reentered the B&B. She assumed the feeder would be waiting in the drawing room, which is where she was headed when Mrs. Muir, face the color of spoiled milk, stepped from a dark alcove to stop her.

"I ask that you give the brollachan a message." Mrs. Muir spoke breathlessly, as if she'd run a marathon and not been waiting silently in a shadowy corner.

"Brollachan?" Lynette asked with some hesitation.

"Herself." Mrs. Muir jutted her hairy chin in the direction of the loch. "She is welcome here to bide as long as she will. We willnae speak a word of her—ever. I only ask she not steal our souls—not a one from this household."

Lynette sucked in a breath. The old woman was clearly terrified, and Lynette realized she could answer Neferet easily about whether the staff had observed as she'd commanded—just as she understood the vampyre's intention had been exactly that—to terrify Muir and the others into obeying her. A wave of relief washed over her, making her legs feel wobbly. *This means Neferet doesn't have to make an example of another Ed!*

"My lady protects those who are loyal to her. Be true and you will only know her generosity and support. Betray her—even in the smallest thing—and she will—"

"Gonnae no' dae that!" Mrs. Muir blurted, her accent as thick as her fear.

"Good. Then you have nothing to worry about. Is the feeder here?"

"Aye, in the sitting room."

"I'll see to him. You may retire."

Mrs. Muir bobbed an awkward curtsy before hastily retreating. Lynette walked briskly into the drawing room. The young man was seated before the fireplace. He stood quickly as she entered.

"Missus, good day," he said.

"Hello, what is your name?" Lynette studied him quickly. He was tall, young, muscular, and handsome—just as she'd specified to the local network of feeders.

"Robby, missus," he said.

"Robby, when did you last bathe?" she asked as she went to the silver tray on which Mrs. Muir kept a decanter of scotch and several glasses. Lynette filled one of them with the amber liquid and handed it to the boy.

"Just before I came, missus. Vampyres don't like us mingin'." He grinned.

"Well, this particular vampyre wants you clean and a little drunk. Is that fine with you?"

"Och, aye!" his blue eyes sparkled as he drained the glass. Lynette refilled it. "Another."

"Sláinte mhath!" Robby raised his glass again.

Lynette refilled it a third time, but touched his hand, stopping him before he drained it. "Take that one with you. I'm going to show you to her suite. Listen carefully to me. Call her only 'my lady.' Do not speak unless she begins a conversation or asks a question. This vampyre is not like any other. She is powerful and she is dangerous. If you speak a single word about her—if you describe her to anyone or tell anyone there is a vampyre High Priestess staying at Balmacara Mains she will know, and—make no mistake—*this vampyre will kill you.* Do you understand, Robby?"

The glint of humor and mischief extinguished instantly, and the boy nodded. "Aye."

"How old are you?" she couldn't help but ask.

"Eighteen, missus."

"Be smart and you'll make it to nineteen. Be stupid or reckless or arrogant and you will die."

"I willnae be clyping."

"I hope that means you'll keep your mouth shut."

"Aye, fur sure."

"Good, now close your mouth and come with me."

Lynette led him to Neferet's suite and knocked twice on her door. The vampyre opened it standing in a pool of light cast only by candles she'd lit around the room. Lynette heard Robby suck in his breath, and she couldn't blame the boy. Neferet had to be the most beautiful thing he'd ever seen.

"Come in and take off your clothes," Neferet said after barely glancing at the boy. As he entered the room she met Lynette's gaze, smiled, and nodded before closing the door firmly.

Lynette made her way slowly to the parlor to pour herself a generous glass of single malt before she retired to her own room and began googling "brollachan" and "vampyre spellwork."

Other Kevin

Kevin made sure he was early to the next Council Meeting, and he was rewarded with a special smile from Anastasia, but then she was all business, calling the meeting to order even though Stark hadn't arrived yet.

"Professor Penthesilea," Anastasia began. "You've been leading the tunnel renovation. How is that coming?"

"The construction crews are working as quickly as possible," said Professor P. "I decided to enlist to help of the red vampyres who are most lucid. It gives them purpose and keeps them busy and out of their own heads. It seems to be working—at least for some of them."

"May Nyx continue to help them heal," said Anastasia.

Professor P cleared her throat and continued. "For the record, I'd like to say how good it is to have a High Priestess who truly follows the path of Nyx again."

Anastasia's smile was wise, but more than a little sad. "As Priestesses of Nyx we should never have allowed Neferet so much control, especially as we began to see the warning signs. We are all culpable for the chaos and war and hatred she loosed on this world. We must all take responsibly for repairing the damage she has done to our reputation. I will never stay silent again. Now, what is our next priority?"

Dragon straightened in his chair. "We need to be sure the Zoey ghost story is buried so Neferet, wherever the hell she's hiding, doesn't put two and two together and get curious about where a fully Changed, living Zoey Redbird could have come from," said Dragon. "Kevin, how is our IT team coming along with that?"

Kevin spoke up immediately. "I've been working with them, and they're having some pretty good luck in buying the images of Z and taking them offline, and/or disseminating confusing alternative ghost stories so that my sister isn't the only weird thing that happened that night."

Professor Nolan gestured in animated frustration as she added, "I don't think we have much to worry about, though I do agree that we need to take down as many of the images of Zoey as possible. The truth is that there are a lot more images of Nyx swirling around out there on the internet than Zoey anyway."

Professor P chimed in. "And don't forget that video of Neferet falling from the stadium press box and then skittering away like she was boneless," she shuddered. "Most of the attention is focused on her, especially after we announced the one-hundred-thousand-dollar reward for anyone who brings us information that leads to her capture."

"Actually, I have word on that," Stark said as he entered the school conference room, looking grim. He nodded at everyone before he took a seat. "Sorry, I got held up dealing with the funeral plans for the red vampyres who committed suicide earlier today."

Anastasia shook her head sadly. "It is such a tragedy that

we cannot reach all of them." Then she stiffened. "We found Neferet?" The High Priestess sounded equal parts excited and frightened.

Stark ran a hand through his hair as he took a seat. "No. But we did finally track down the jet. It's in a hangar just outside Venice."

"Did the pilot admit that she's alive? That she was his passenger to Venice?" Anastasia asked.

"Absolutely not. He made up some crazy story about being ordered—by a phone call from someone who claimed to be Neferet—to fly a roundabout ghost flight from Tulsa to Venice via London, and then he said he was told to wait with the jet in Venice for further instructions. He's young. Just promoted to captain for that flight, and he was borderline hysterical when the Sons of Erebus Warriors were questioning him," Stark said.

"Did they torture him?" Anastasia asked, her tone making it clear that she disapproved.

"No. Not at all," Stark assured her.

Dragon leaned forward in his chair. "So, his fear level tells us Neferet is definitely alive and that she chartered the jet after she had her creatures—what is it Zoey called them?" he asked Kevin.

"Tendrils of Darkness. Zo said *her* Neferet began manifesting them as she gained more and more power," said Kevin.

Stark nodded. "Yes, that's it—tendrils of Darkness. Apparently, they are what ate the humans that night at the bar across from the stadium, *and* the pilot *and* a teenage human who worked at the private airport," said Stark. "Neferet left no witnesses. The high-definition security cameras were all wiped clean. We can't find the human woman who was the flight concierge. So, she either escaped or Neferet killed her too but did away with her body. The bottom line is, if Neferet wasn't behind what happened, the pilot wouldn't be so terrified. I agree with Dragon. She is definitely still alive."

"And we have no idea where she is." Kevin rubbed his forehead. For the past four days, it seemed he always had a headache. It felt like there was sand in his eyes. He couldn't remember the last time he'd eaten. He could remember the last time he'd felt happy—felt whole. It had been four days ago in Aphrodite's arms. Since then nothing had been the same. They were calling Zoey a ghost, but he wanted to shout, *It's me! I'm the ghost! I'm only half here without Aphrodite!*

"And the High Council hasn't spoken with her?" Anastasia was asking.

"No," Stark said. "They're prepared to place her under arrest the instant she shows herself, and that's all the information I can get out of them. They hold us responsible for Neferet *and* her war."

"They should. We are responsible," Anastasia said. "We allowed Neferet to have too much power. No one questioned her, even though many of us felt increasingly uneasy about her motives."

"You're right. I should've done something sooner," said Stark.

Dragon nodded. "We all should have. And now we all are paying the consequences for our apathy."

Anastasia lifted one hand, silencing the room. "On the positive side, we understand Neferet. She's smart enough to know that the High Council is not her ally, and no one here on the School Council will be her ally ever again. She won't show herself until she's powerful enough to take on all of us." She squared her shoulders, as if preparing for a battle. "We should have one of our people watch San Clemente Island. She may follow the plan Zoey's Neferet concocted and try to convince the High Council that she is Nyx come to earth. If she gets them on her side, she has all of Europe behind her."

Stark spoke up. "It's definitely what I'd do if I'd become a twisted immortal who wanted to rule the world."

"I agree. We need to know the moment Neferet reveals herself," said Anastasia. "If the High Council won't work with us, we need to work *around* them."

"I'll send a Son of Erebus to secretly keep watch over San Clemente Island." Dragon turned to Stark. "You had them confiscate the jet, right?"

Before Stark could respond, Kevin said, "No! Leave it where it is. Take the pilot's cell and place guards around the plane—but be sure it doesn't look like they're guards. Neferet told the pilot to go there—told him to wait. She might be planning on returning to the jet. And the Sons of Erebus need to be there to take her into custody."

"Yes, that makes sense," said Anastasia.

Stark took out his phone. "I'll make the call." He moved to the side of the conference room as he gave the Warriors guarding the jet their new orders.

"So, we have no idea where Neferet is or what she's up to," said Anastasia. "And that is very, very bad."

"Actually, that's only half right," said Kevin. "From what I learned from my sister and my short time in her world, I can tell you that their Neferet—who is very much like our

Neferet—had one main focus. To become immortal. After she attained immortality, she was obsessed with commanding the humans in the modern world to be her sycophants and slaves, and the vampyres to be her accomplices—willing or not. So my guess is that wherever she is, Neferet is trying to attain immortality, and after she does we will definitely hear from her again."

Professor Penthesilea's face blanched to the color of chalk. "She'll return to enslave or kill us all," she whispered.

Stark slipped his phone into his pocket as he returned to the table. "No. We'll stop her."

Dragon frowned. "How the hell do we defeat an immortal?" he grumbled.

"Zo did it with the help of another immortal being," Kevin said, sitting up straighter and wiping a hand across his face. Since Aphrodite's death, he'd felt as if he was moving through a fog. Desperate to latch onto something that would force him to focus—force him to see beyond the loss that had broken his heart—he concentrated on everything Zoey and her circle of friends had taught him. "They had the help of Rephaim's father, a winged immortal named Kalona. Remember? Zo told us about it in the cave on the ridge. They were able to trap their Neferet in the grotto in Woodward Park for eternity."

Dragon clapped his hands. "That's right. I spoke with Rephaim about his father. But he said that the Kalona from their world Fell from Nyx's side and was a monster for centuries, preying on humans—most especially Native American people—until he was entrapped."

"Yeah, Neferet freed him to legitimize her claim of being Nyx incarnate," said Kevin. "Kalona was supposed to pretend that he was Erebus and name Neferet as his living goddess. The bad news is that it took some doing to get Kalona to change sides from Darkness to Light. The good news is he *did* change."

"But he *didn't* defeat Neferet, correct?" Dragon said.

"Correct. She killed him, but only because he'd given part of his immortality to the Stark who is in my sister's world." Kevin paused and nodded at Stark, who he thought looked like he too was having trouble sleeping.

"So, what you're thinking is that we need to figure out how to free our version of Kalona, who definitely has *not* shared any of his immortality with me, and then hope like hell he'll join us against Neferet," said Stark.

"That's about it," said Kevin. He pulled out his phone and tapped a quick text. "And I know who can help us with that."

"Good. I want to hear all about your plan, but that doesn't tell us where Neferet is hiding," said Dragon.

Anastasia drummed her fingernails on the table contemplatively. "Kevin, did Zoey tell you *how* her Neferet attained immortality?" she asked.

"No. I don't think she fully understood how she did it. She called Neferet a Tsi Sgili—which is basically an evil being from Cherokee legend. But we have to keep in mind that even though the two Neferets share a lot of the same characteristics, especially when you talk about who they are at their core, there are differences," reminded Kevin. "An example would be that Zo's Neferet could read minds." He met Stark's gaze. "Ours can't, right?"

"Not as far as I know," said Stark.

"If she could, she hid it from everyone," said Anastasia, "from the time she Changed. And I do not believe Neferet would hide such a thing. She would use it—exploit it—but never pretend she didn't have that power."

Kevin nodded. "So, there *are* differences. And unless Neferet is hiding somewhere on tribal lands, she isn't going to attain immortality as a Tsi Sgili."

"Did you mention tribal lands?" Grandma Redbird backed into the conference room, holding her picnic basket from which the aroma of warm lavender chocolate chip cookies wafted.

"I'll get that for you, G-ma!" Kevin was up out of his seat to help his grandma, taking the picnic basket from her and helping her into a chair. "How'd you get here so fast?"

"Thank you, u-we-tsi. I was already on my way here when I got your text. I have something to show you. But first, what's this about our lands?" she asked as she took a plate of freshly baked cookies from the basket and put them in the middle of the table.

"We were talking about how Zoey's Neferet became immortal," said Kevin.

"By embracing the Darkness of the Tsi Sgili." Grandma Redbird shuddered delicately. "Awful, awful creatures."

Kevin snagged a cookie. "Yeah, and we figured that our Neferet is trying to become immortal here too."

Disgust filled Sylvia Redbird's voice. "And were she becoming Tsi Sgili she would be gravitating to our people. I see. I will put out a call to the Wise Women of the Tribes. If Neferet is hiding on our lands we will discover her—have no doubt about that."

"Sylvia, have you had any luck understanding that poem Zoey left with us?" Anastasia asked. "The one that freed her Kalona from his earthly imprisonment?"

"Ah, that is why I planned to join you today, even had Kevin not texted and asked me to," said Grandma. "Here is the poem she left with us." Sylvia Redbird reached into a leather bag slung over her shoulder and smoothed out a piece of paper that had what looked like a poem printed in the center of it. "I have read this over and over the past several days. I have shared it with my sister Wise Women—they have shared it within their tribes. No one recognizes it."

Kevin sighed heavily. "Maybe in this world Kalona isn't even trapped in the earth. He could be with Nyx living happily all these eons as her Consort."

"One would think if that were true, your Warriors would be called Sons of Kalona—and not of Erebus," reasoned Grandma. "I do have some information, though. I was going through sketchbooks kept by my great-grandmother." The old woman smiled, her dark eyes twinkling. "She was quite the artist. I noticed that she dedicated many of her sketches to an immortal she called Silver Wings. She drew him several times, and in the margins of the journal she'd copied a rather strange poem that I gave little thought to until I read the piece Zoey left behind for us. The two are oddly similar." Grandma took a plain white sheet of paper from her bag and held it so the rest of them could see that it was a copy of a very old pencil drawing of a massive winged man. In the margins was a poem written in Tsalagi.

"G-ma, you're gonna have to translate that for us," said Kevin.

"Oh, of course u-we-tsi. I already did." She turned the paper over and on the back, in her bold handwriting, was a poem that was roughly the same length as the one on the purple paper. "But first, this is the poem Zoeybird left with us from her world." Grandma Redbird cleared her throat and read:

"Ancient one sleeping, waiting to arise
when earth's power bleeds sacred red
The mark strikes true; Queen Tsi Sgili will devise
He shall be washed from his entombing bed

Through the hand of the dead he is free
Terrible beauty, monstrous sight
Ruled again they shall be
Women shall kneel to his dark might

Kalona's song sounds sweet
As we slaughter with cold heat."

Professor P clutched her hands together to stop them from trembling. "There's something about that poem that terrifies me."

"I am in agreement with you," said Grandma Redbird. "Now, the one I found in my great-grandmother's sketchbook."

She read:

"Ancient one sleeping, waiting to arise
When the dead joins with fire and water red
Son who is not—his word is key; the raven will devise
He shall hear the call from his sacrificial bed.

By the blood of she who is neither foe nor friend he is free.
Behold a terrible sacrifice to come—a beautiful sight,

Ruled by love they shall be.
The future will not kneel to her dark might.

Kalona's return is not bittersweet
As he will be welcomed with love and heat."

Kevin felt a rush of excitement. "The '*son who is not*' has to be Rephaim!"

"Exactly what I thought, u-we-tsi," said Grandma Redbird. "I also thought that the line, '*When the dead joins with fire and water red*' could be referring to a red vampyre who can call on fire and water."

"Could be Kevin, though I'm not sure about the fire and water parts," said Anastasia.

"Yes, exactly," said Grandma. "And even understanding part of it is a great help. Especially as the next stanza is baffling. Neither friend nor foe? A terrible sacrifice that is a beautiful sight? Does anyone have any idea to whom that could be referring?"

No one spoke.

Anastasia sighed. "But you truly believe this being called Silver Wings is our Kalona?"

"I do. I also believe he did not Fall as the Other Kalona did."

"Why do you say that?" asked Dragon.

"Because of the lack of terrifying stories. Zoeybird said that their Kalona Fell—that his wings turned from light to dark—and that he so terrorized our people, enslaving our men and raping our women, who in turn gave birth to Raven Mockers—nightmarish creatures that are half bird, half human. Our people have a few tales of such creatures, but they are different than the stories from Zoey's world. Our ancestors tell of dark spirits that swarm when one of the Tsalagi is near death, but they are easily banished by the simple burning of sage and the evocation of the Great Goddess. They were never considered half human, and as far as the other Wise Women and I can tell, they have never taken physical form. Basically, they're nothing more than a tale to frighten children, like the boogie monster."

"So, if there were no Raven Mockers that means our Kalona didn't rape and enslave anyone," said Kevin.

"Or at least he didn't rape and enslave any of the Native American peoples," said Anastasia. "Sylvia, have you looked beyond the Tsalagi's legends to see if our Kalona might have terrorized others?"

"I have, and so far no one recognizes the name Kalona at all."

Stark leaned forward. "But if he didn't do anything wrong, why would he be imprisoned?"

"There is no evidence in this poem that he is imprisoned," said Grandma Redbird. "Look, Zoey's poem calls it '*his entombing bed*.' But my great grandmother's poem names it '*his sacrificial bed*.' In addition, though there aren't many, any reference I find to the immortal Silver Wings is positive. He seems to have been a friend to our ancestors."

"Zoey did say Kalona's wings were silver-white *before* he Fell from Nyx's Otherworld. Then they turned black."

"And they returned to white again after he died, and Nyx welcomed him to her realm," agreed Grandma Redbird.

"Maybe I should go back to Zo's world and ask Rephaim to return here with me," said Kevin.

Grandma Redbird cleared her throat before speaking in a

strong, clear voice. "I have something to say. I hope you will hear my words, even though I am not a Council Member."

Anastasia gestured magnanimously. "We will hear you, Sylvia Redbird. You have proved yourself a valuable ally."

"Wado," Grandma said. "These words are difficult for me. I love Zoey—in any world—and I miss her desperately. So, my heart says Kevin should return to that world, as I am certain if Rephaim comes here again, my darling u-we-tsi-a-ge-ya would accompany him. But it is best to listen to the heart *with* wisdom from the mind, and my mind says that this mingling of our worlds is not a good thing. What ramifications will come to pass—in both worlds—if we do not each solve our own problems? It gives me an uneasy feeling that has moved from my mind to my heart, especially as we must use Old Magick to open the boundaries between worlds. We already know Old Magick is dangerous. We learned that lesson when we lost our precious Aphrodite. What more might we lose, *who* might we lose, if we continue to traffic with ancient powers none of us truly understand?"

Into the silence Kevin spoke softly. "It is a risk I am willing to take."

"But not one I am willing to have you take," said Anastasia firmly. "At least not yet. We will only need Kalona if Neferet becomes immortal. So, let us find that fallen High Priestess and end this nightmare before it costs us more of our loved ones."

Professor P spoke in the no-nonsense voice of an experienced teacher. "Council, I believe the next logical step is to research how a vampyre—or any mortal—can attain immortality. Once we isolate the *how*s we should be able to figure out where she might be."

"Agreed," said Anastasia. "Penthesilea, I task you with leading the research. Choose anyone you wish for your team, but hurry."

"Could you use my help?" asked Grandma Redbird.

"Absolutely," said Professor P. "I would also like to task a few of my most advanced fledglings to help us with the research, though it would mean telling them more than is generally known about Neferet."

"That's fine with me, but be careful not to tell them anything about the Other World," said Anastasia. "We cannot allow that information to leak."

"Of course not, High Priestess."

The High Priestess continued, turning to her mate. "Speaking of information leaks, are you still keeping an eye on Loren Blake?"

Dragon snorted with irritation. "Yes. He sleeps late. Has meals brought to his chamber. Then he puts in a lackluster appearance at Nyx's Temple where my Warriors tell me he spends most of his time either napping, whining, or on his phone. He is a waste of time and an embarrassment to vampyres everywhere."

"I will consider where Blake should be sent, as he serves no purpose here," said Anastasia.

Through a mouthful of cookie Stark said, "Send him to the High Council. They're so pissed at Neferet that they'll slap his pro-war crap down in a heartbeat."

Anastasia's brow went up. "That's not a bad idea. I'll give him another couple days to straighten up, and then put him on a one-way flight to San Clemente."

Dragon muttered, "Be sure he flies coach."

That made Anastasia smile. "Another good idea. So, Blake

will be dealt with. Now, where are we in our negotiations with the humans?"

"Not far. The truce holds, but it could fail at any moment," said Dragon. "The humans are hardly speaking to us, and when we can get their representatives to come to the treaty table they continue to reiterate that their only solution is segregation."

"Which puts us back to where we were before the war," said Anastasia grimly.

Stark used his cookie to gesture. "Worse, actually. Before humans were obviously bigoted against us, but their violence was limited to what amounted to sneak attacks and hate crimes. If we allow our borders to reopen to humans, the violence will no longer be isolated and hidden. Neferet's war has given human hatred and bigotry a platform. Too much of the country is calling us illegals—saying we don't belong here and that we need to return to Europe where we came from."

"We didn't come from Europe! It is clear in our history that the first vampyre was created here, in the Midwestern United States," said Dragon.

Grandma Redbird spoke softly, but her voice filled the room. "History is being rewritten by fear and hatred."

"Then we must combat it with love and truth," said Anastasia.

"How?" asked Kevin. "It's insane out there. Are you guys watching the internet? Do you see all the lies being spread?"

"I have. It's like a forest fire," said Stark. "One small lie, like vampyres being foreign, has caused a blaze of hatred. I'm sorry, High Priestess, but I cannot recommend withdrawing any of our Warriors from the DMZ at this time."

"I must agree with Stark," said Dragon. "Our continued show of force is the only way we're holding on right now."

"It feels like the entire world has turned against us," Kevin spoke slowly, staring down at his hands.

Grandma Redbird reached across the table and covered his hands with hers. "No, u-we-tsi, it is not the entire world. Neferet's cruelness has caused much damage, but there is still love, always love."

"And there is our Goddess," said Anastasia. "She is on the side of Light, and now that the House of Night is once more following her path, I believe goodness will prevail. So, let us begin with a show of goodwill. Sword Master, I want you to announce that our Warriors will be pulling back from boundaries Neferet created." When Dragon opened his mouth to protest, her raised hand silenced him. She continued. "I am not being foolish. I do not mean that the Warriors return to their usual posts at their schools. I only ask that they fall back under a white flag of peace—if only a few miles. Announce that we willingly stand down so that the peace talks can continue. Then let us see what our human neighbors do in response."

"Yes, High Priestess," Dragon said, though Kevin thought he sounded reluctant.

"Splendid. I look forward to receiving good news soon," said Anastasia. "Is there anything else we need to discuss today?"

Professor Nolan cleared her throat, drawing the Council's attention. "I had an idea about helping the red vampyres."

"Please, share," said Anastasia.

"I know that the majority of them are fully Changed vampyres, but they were never given a proper education.

I believe they should *all* return to school, and that we should tailor special classes for them."

"I like that idea," said Professor P. "Writing and art classes would be an excellent way for them to begin working through their feelings."

"Red fledglings learn nothing about our history. We also weren't allowed to worship Nyx," said Kevin. "It made me feel isolated and really just lost."

"Neferet did that on purpose," Stark said. "She commanded that the red fledglings be kept from Nyx's Temple and only be taught Warrior skills. I confronted her about it, and she said they were too animalistic to be educated—and that the Goddess understood and approved." He shook his head. "I will forever regret that I justified her cruelty as truth."

"We all did at first," said Dragon.

Stark's voice was gravelly with regret. "But you realized your mistake. I didn't before it was almost too late."

"*Almost* is the most important word there," said Anastasia.

"Yeah. Had you not realized your mistake and taken action to fix it, that football game at TU would've had a very different ending," Kevin added.

Stark nodded but avoided meeting anyone's eyes. Kevin thought he knew a little of how he felt. Had his own actions been different—had he realized what was happening earlier, he might have saved Aphrodite.

"I very much like this idea of returning the red vampyres to school," said Anastasia. "Professor Nolan, I give you charge of that. Create five new classes, specifically for the red vampyres, including an hour of temple time and ritual instruction. And be sure you get them interacting with the rest of the blue fledglings. I think it's important they don't feel segregated, and it would do them good to be around the others. Kevin, would you aid Professor Nolan? You have more insight into the red vampyres than any of us."

"Yeah, of course."

"Then let us get to work," said Anastasia. "This Council Meeting is adjourned."

As the Council slowly followed their High Priestess from the room, Kevin found himself face-to-face with James Stark.

"If you go, I'm going with you." Stark spoke low. His expression was so fierce and so familiar that Kevin almost smiled.

"Dude, it's freaky how similar you are to the other you. And hell no, you're not going with me."

"Gentlemen, I need to speak with you." Grandma Redbird's voice sounded from behind them.

Together, Kevin and Stark jumped guiltily.

"You mean me too?" Stark asked.

"Gentlemen is plural. Yes, James Stark, I mean you too. Sit, please." Grandma Redbird gestured at the large round table. The boys sat.

"I want the two of you to hear me. Will you do that?"

"Of course, G-ma," Kevin spoke quickly.

"Yes, I'll listen, Mrs. Redbird."

"Call me Sylvia or Grandma Redbird."

"Yes, ma'am," Stark nodded.

The old woman folded her hands in her lap. "I will not allow either of you to waste the vast amount of love and potential for happiness you both have *and deserve to have in your lives* longing for women neither of you will attain in this lifetime." She met Kevin's gaze and he felt his stomach drop.

"My darling u-we-tsi, Zoey's Aphrodite has found her love, and in that world, it is not you."

Kevin nodded and cracked his knuckles. "But doesn't she have the capacity to love more than one person at a time?" He knew he sounded desperate, and he did not care one tiny bit.

Grandma reached forward and covered his restless hands with hers. "That isn't the question. Ask yourself this—is *your* love big enough, strong enough, mature enough to share?"

Kevin stared at his grandma. He hadn't actually thought past the fact that one version of Aphrodite was still alive—and he could get to her. He'd mostly, conveniently, forgotten about Darius.

Grandma Redbird squeezed his hands before releasing them and facing Stark. "James Stark, I have no doubt that my Zoeybird could love you and your double—the Other Stark—at the same time. Again, that is not the question. What I want you to consider is this—could you bear to see Zoey with a version of yourself and know every sweet, intimate touch they would share when you weren't with her? Would you wonder if she laughed and sighed and smiled like that with Other Stark too, or just with you? And what would that wondering do to your heart, your soul, and your relationship with Zoey?"

Stark hesitated, then opened his mouth and began with, "I think—" But he couldn't continue. Instead he closed his mouth and stared at the top of the table.

"James, look at me."

Stark lifted his head and met her gaze.

"You will find love."

"In the press box at TU, Zoey said she'd be under the

Hanging Tree in the Goddess Grove." Stark sounded like he expected to enter Nyx's grove any second.

"She also told you not to be in a rush to get there. She wants you to live a long life, and to love passionately," Kevin chimed in. "I was there too remember? And she's my sister—in any world. I know her. G-ma's right. She could love you and Other Stark at the same time. Her heart is that big. But is yours? And if you question it, know that your double will question it as well."

"So, in this lifetime I've missed my soul mate." Stark's voice broke and he had to clear his throat before he continued. "Guess that's a good thing to know so I don't get my expectations too high."

"Do you think our souls are so shallow?" Grandma Redbird asked.

"I haven't ever really thought about it," Stark said.

"Well, do think about it."

"What do you think, G-ma?" Kevin asked.

"I *know* we are many-faceted. There is no *one* person and *only one* person for each of us. Why would the Great Goddess be so cruel?"

"Cruel?" Stark said.

"What else would you call it? If we were fashioned with the capacity to love only once, I call that divine cruelty." Grandma Redbird smiled kindly at Kevin. "U-we-tsi, you have met your Goddess. Did she seem cruel?"

Kevin jerked with surprise. "Absolutely not!"

Grandma's smile shined on Stark. "Then that is your answer. If you allow it—if you open yourself to it—you will love again, James Stark. It will not be the same love you would have found with Zoey Redbird, but you will know love."

"It might even be better." At the shocked look in his grandma's eyes, Kevin hurried to explain. "Um, I just mean that Zo totally causes Other Stark a lot of stress. Maybe Stark will find someone less High Priestess-y who doesn't have to save worlds, that's all."

"Ah, I see what you mean," said G-ma. "And I have to agree."

"I'll think about what you've said. It's been weird. I'd just met Zoey a day or so before she was killed, and I really didn't know the Other Zoey at all, but I can't stop thinking about her. I close my eyes and I see her. I hear her voice in my dreams. It makes me feel…" Stark's words trailed off.

"It makes you feel sad," said Grandma Redbird. "Of course it does. But the sadness will fade, and as it does so will your obsession—*if you let it*."

"I get that. Yeah. Thanks for this. Thanks for understanding, Grandma."

"I'm going to be staying here at the House of Night for awhile, so I want you to know you can come to me anytime you need to talk."

"I'll remember that," said Stark.

Then he surprised Kevin by walking around the table, bending, and kissing the old woman on her forehead. Grandma Redbird stood and reached up, wrapping Stark in the mother of all bear hugs. When she released him, the young vampyre wiped his eyes, nodded goodbye to Kevin, and then quickly left the room.

"Wow. He really needed that," said Kevin. "So, I was going to go check on the red vampyres. Do you want to come—"

"I am not finished with you, u-we-tsi. Follow me."

Grandma Redbird picked up her picnic basket, leaving the half-eaten plate of lavender chocolate chip cookies on the table, and headed to the door.

"You're just going to leave all those cookies out here for anyone to take?" Kevin peered over his shoulder at them.

"That is the point of making cookies—for anyone to take. And I saved a dozen just for you." She patted the side of the basket. "Now open the door for me and let us go."

Kevin opened the door for her with a flourish. "Where are we going?"

"To speak to Nyx."

"Am I in trouble?"

"Have you done something terrible?"

"I don't think so," he said.

Grandma looked up at him. "U-we-tsi, if you'd done something terrible I believe you would remember it."

"Good point."

He followed his g-ma down the stairs to the main floor of the school, and then out the door that led to the rear schoolyard, which held the huge statue of Nyx that stood before her Temple. Grandma went directly to the statue. From her picnic basket she took out a lavender pillar candle, a box of wooden matches, and a fat smudge stick made of white sage and lavender twined together and wrapped with turquoise-colored thread. Grandma lit the candle, bowed respectfully to the statue of Nyx, and then placed it at her feet with the other offerings that were always there. Today Kevin saw several other candles—some lit, some burned out—as well as a few crystals, a beaded necklace, and a bowl of what looked like honey.

"You're not sleeping."

Her voice drew his gaze from the statue. He opened his mouth to lie—to say that he was fine, but the words wouldn't come. Not in front of Nyx's statue. Instead he drew a long, exhausted breath and as he let it out said, "I can't sleep. I lay there and think about her."

"Aphrodite."

"Yeah, of course. *Her*."

"There is great power in a name. Claim that power, u-we-tsi."

He drew another breath and then whispered. "Aphrodite."

"That's a start." Grandma took the smudge stick and held it to the flame of the purple candle. As it lit she moved around Kevin, walking slowly clockwise, wafting the sweet-smelling, fog-like smoke over him. "Say it again."

Kevin cleared his throat. "Aphrodite." This time he spoke the name aloud.

"And again."

"Aphrodite."

"Louder, u-we-tsi."

"Aphrodite!"

"Yes! Who is it you miss so desperately?"

"Aphrodite!"

"Who is it you love so dearly?"

"*My* Aphrodite." His voice had begun to shake as tears flowed down his cheeks, dripping from his jawline and dampening his shirt. Kevin tried to stop them as he wiped angrily at his face.

"No, my sweet boy. Do not hide your grief. There is no shame in showing your tears. Kevin, being a man means claiming *all* your power. Strength without honest emotion is toxic—to yourself, and eventually it makes you toxic to others. How can you truly love without showing sadness, acknowledging loss, dealing openly with despair?"

"I—I don't know G-ma. I've never felt like this before." He stared through the smoke at her. "It hurts too much to lose her. I don't think I'll ever be okay again."

"Yes, that is what grief does if you allow it to isolate you. It leads to depression and worse. Weep for Aphrodite. Speak her name. Talk about her—the things about her you love—the things that made you laugh. You cannot recover if you do not allow yourself to grieve."

"It's okay to cry."

"Yes, u-we-tsi. It's not just okay. It is a necessary part of the grieving process."

Kevin sobbed and as he did he spoke her name—over and over. Grandma Redbird finally put the still-smoking smudge stick among the offerings at the feet of the marble statue before taking out a carefully pressed linen handkerchief from her seemingly bottomless picnic basket. She handed it to Kevin. He blew his nose and wiped his face, surprised to realize that he'd stopped crying.

She took both of his hands in hers. "I want you to breathe with me. In and out through your nose to a count of four: one... two... three... four. Now out: one... two... three... four."

He breathed with his grandma for several minutes, losing time as he drank in the thinning smoke and the scent of the lavender candle.

"Now as you breathe in, I want you to think about the parts of you that hurt—and send breath *to those parts of you*. As you release the breath, concentrate on releasing the pain. Do you understand?"

It was difficult for Kevin to speak, so he just nodded. Then he breathed in, focusing first on his head, which had dully ached for days and days. Next, he sent breath to his gut. He couldn't remember the last time he'd eaten a real meal. He hadn't been able to—his stomach hurt too much. He drew healing breath to his arms that missed holding Aphrodite so badly that they ached constantly. And finally, he breathed into his ravaged heart.

"Good. Yes, that's it," Grandma said, squeezing his hands reassuringly. "I want you to do two more things. One—ask for comfort."

"From Nyx?"

"Yes, but also from Aphrodite."

"Do you think she's here?" Hope fluttered in his chest.

"I do not know, but I wouldn't know. She wouldn't be here for me."

Kevin cleared his throat again, then spoke in a soft, trembly voice. "Aphrodite, I—I need you." His voice broke and he clung to Grandma Redbird's hands as his lifeline.

She nodded encouragement. "You can do it. Just talk to her like she's really here—that's all."

"I feel like I lost myself when you died, and I can't find myself again without you." He paused and steadied himself. "If you could help I'd appreciate it. This pain is so bad, Aphrodite. Mind-numbing and soul-sucking. But I'm afraid to let it go because if I do, I'm afraid that means I'm letting you go too. And if I had my choice, I would never, ever let you go." His voice broke again, and he had to swallow several times before he could finish. "Please, help me. Please."

"Well done, u-we-tsi. I am so proud of you. When you acknowledge your grief you also acknowledge your love.

And when you ask for help and are willing to accept it—that is when your broken heart can begin to heal. We are done now." Grandma pulled him into her embrace and held him, singing softly, while he sobbed against her shoulder.

Kevin didn't know how long they stayed there like that. It seemed forever happened in just a few minutes, but his tears slowed and stopped—and he was able to step out of his grandmother's embrace.

"I feel a little better," he surprised himself by speaking the words, and by the truth of them.

"Tears are cleansing. Now you need to eat a real meal. You must ground yourself. And how many days has it been since you've fed?"

"I don't remember."

"That's what I thought. Feed. *Then* eat a meal. And tonight, if you cannot sleep, repeat the breathing exercises. I am going to spend a few more minutes here with Nyx, but then I will join you in the cafeteria."

Kevin kissed her gently. "Thank you, G-ma."

"You are most welcome, sweet boy."

Kevin began to walk away, but her voice stopped him. "Oh, u-we-tsi, I almost forgot the second thing. Expect a sign."

He stared over his shoulder at her. "A sign? You mean from Aphrodite?"

Grandma smiled. "Perhaps. I will let you tell me when you recognize the sign. Now, go on—feed. You look pale as milk."

Kevin made his way slowly to the cafeteria. Classes were in session, but it was still early—just before sunset—and the halls were empty—thankfully. He understood what G-ma had said about allowing his emotions to show. He even agreed with her, which was just smart. G-ma was always right. But that didn't mean he wanted to be gawked at by fledglings who would definitely gawk. He bypassed the student cafeteria, grateful that Anastasia had given him permission to eat in the Professors' Lounge. As he entered the posh dining room, he passed a wall display of wine bottles—and then almost jumped out of his skin when one of the bottles suddenly exploded with a deafening *POP!*

Kevin automatically ducked. His rational mind knew that it wasn't a gunshot, but his war-weary senses reacted differently. From the kitchen area two vampyres, a cook and a server, rushed out looking completely panicked.

"Hey, it's okay," Kevin explained as he pointed to the wall of wine. "It was just a bottle of champagne that—" *It was a bottle of champagne. IT WAS A BOTTLE OF VEUVE CLICQUOT PINK CHAMPAGNE!* Kevin's mind shouted as a smile spread across his face. "What brand of champagne did the Prophetess Aphrodite like best?"

He asked the server the question, but he already knew the answer.

"Veuve Clicquot—and she always preferred—"

"Pink!" Kevin finished with the server. "Yes, I remember. I'll always remember. Thank you. Thank you so much."

But the server had already begun cleaning the spilled champagne and she didn't hear him. That was okay with Kevin. It wasn't the server he was thanking…

12

Other Lynette

The days and nights that Lynette spent with Neferet at the modest B&B in the shadow of the Isle of Skye were the most interesting and enjoyable of Lynette's life. Neferet set the tone—and they all followed her lead. It was a surprisingly serene, intimate time that fell into an easy pattern.

Neferet woke moments after sunset. She would emerge from her suite, face completely free of makeup, wrapped in a thick bathrobe with her hair pulled back and her cashmere slippers on, to join Lynette in the drawing room, which the vampyre had commandeered as her own. Their first full day at Balmacara, Neferet supervised Noreen and wee Denise in a quick redecoration of the room—which meant they decluttered it, found a chair that looked like a throne for Neferet, and added several velvet throws in rich jewel tones that Denise had materialized, whispering self-consciously about her sister sewing them for a boutique in Edinburgh—and that she'd much rather sell them to Herself than tourists. Neferet's sincere delight with the beautiful pieces caused the girl to blush happily, winning the vampyre a new devotee—and a surprisingly capable one at that.

Lynette rose several hours before the vampyre—time enough for her to be sure that night's feeder—or feeder*s* (one night, Neferet wanted both a male *and* a female feeder at the same time)—were procured. She went through the daily news, focusing on what was happening in Tulsa so that she could update Neferet.

Lynette had never been so glad she wasn't in Tulsa. A cruder woman would call what was going on in T-Town a clusterfuck. When she'd read the Oklahoma news to Neferet, with all the details of the chaos that had been caused by what the media was calling the "rehumanization of the red vampyres," the High Priestess commented, in a voice of ice, "Anarchy and chaos and a lack of the proper order of things. That is what happens when betrayers and men rule. Is the war still being won by vampyres?"

"James Stark of the Tulsa House of Night is quoted as saying there is a truce—that vampyres and humans are attempting a treaty."

"James Stark! That traitor! Did they quote *only* a male vampyre? Males never speak for us." Neferet scoffed. "Are they forcing the priestesses to be mute?"

Lynette flipped through several news articles until she found a female name. "It says here that Anastasia and her mate, Dragon Lankford, have returned to their residence at the House of Night. Oh…" Lynette's words trailed off as she quickly scanned the rest of the article.

"What is it?" Neferet prodded.

"My lady, it says that Anastasia has been named High Priestess of the Tulsa House of Night, and her mate has reclaimed his title of Sword Master." Lynette held her breath as she waited for the explosion to follow.

But Neferet had surprised her. She had laughed! Genuine laughter, and not a show of malicious glee.

"They make it too easy for me! I defeated and banished those two simpletons once. I shall do it again, only this time I will not make the mistake of allowing them to live. And now I understand why a male is representing the House of Night. Anastasia is a weak, milquetoast version of a High Priestess. Of course she would allow a male to speak in her place. I will set it all to right, dear Lynette. All to right."

As the days passed and the news from Tulsa got no better, Neferet had Lynette make careful notes of every vampyre's name that was mentioned. What they were quoted as saying, what they were doing as the Tulsa House of Night—and every House of Night in the US—was trying to rediscover its place in a world that both feared and loathed them now more than ever before. Each day the list of names became longer, but Neferet repeated it, slowly and solemnly, reminding Lynette of a vampyre version of Arya Stark.

Once what Lynette thought of as the breakfast news was over, Neferet disappeared into her suite to shed her bathrobe and slippers for long, wool skirts of homespun Wallace plaid and comfortable cotton blouses. It seemed the vampyre also shed the stresses of Tulsa and the world in general. Wrapped in the muted colors of the ancient plaid, with her hair tied back and a shawl around her shoulders, Neferet youthened. Her beauty shifted from that of a carved statue—impossibly beautiful and completely unattainable—to that of a young, carefree girl. She was no less stunning but seemed more human.

No matter the weather, and it was always wet and cold,

every night Neferet would walk the bank of Loch Alsh, the body of water that separated their section of the mainland from the Isle of Skye.

Lynette wasn't entirely sure what the vampyre did during her walkabouts, but she always returned around midnight. Sometimes she would have collected smooth white pebbles of sea-worn Skye marble. Another day she found a whole handful of sea glass that time and waves had shaped into rough hearts. On yet another walkabout she brought back a piece of driftwood the size of her hand that looked exactly like a voluptuous naked woman.

The found objects always filled one of the four offering bowls that Neferet set out to sea in the deep of each night. She changed what was in the other bowls nightly, explaining to Lynette that the sprites were easily bored, and that she was attempting to intrigue and woo them.

And each night Neferet and her children took to the dark loch. The tendrils of Darkness carried the naked vampyre out onto the waters so that she could place her offerings on the surface. Each night some*thing* took the offerings—silently—and then disappeared.

Though Neferet did not require it of them, the house staff, all three of them, stood witness to the vampyre's nightly offering. They watched from the porch of Balmacara Mains and had even begun sending her off with whispered well-wishes. Goddess-like, Neferet would acknowledge each of them, nodding in appreciation of their devotion and even smiling kindly at the women. Lynette watched the staff change. They shifted from being terrified of the brollachan, which Lynette had researched and found out was basically a formless demon associated closely with the fey, kelpies, and water spirits in general. It can steal bodies and is particularly terrifying to children. By the end of the first full day at Balmacara, Neferet's good humor, her youthening, and her regal bearing had the staff changing their minds about her—or at least deciding that Herself was *their* brollachan. Instead of treating her with fear, they showed the vampyre respect—and Mrs. Muir even began mothering her, insisting Neferet wear wellies and take a shawl on her walkabouts.

Lynette waited for the vampyre to explode in random violence as she had in Tulsa, but it didn't happen. What happened instead was that Lynette believed with her whole heart and soul that she was glimpsing the kind of goddess Neferet could become—wise, strict, ruthless when need be, but ever loyal to those faithful to her.

Lynette was determined she would be her Goddess's first and most loyal subject—and she was also determined she would reap the rewards such loyalty would earn.

Lynette always joined her mistress, trekking across the damp, muddy bank and waiting there for her to return. Of course on subsequent nights she came prepared, carrying a towel to dry Neferet and a robe to wrap her in. On the third night, when nothing new happened except the same arm materialized from the depths to pull under the bowls which had been filled with fine chocolate, single malt scotch, fresh sliced apples, and seashells, Lynette could no longer remain silent.

"My lady, you appear pleased to be here and content with what happens out there." Lynette gestured at the black loch behind them as she and Neferet picked their way back across the rocky bank to the house. "But I don't understand.

It seems to be the same arm. It takes the offerings and then without saying a word goes away and nothing else happens. Are you waiting for something or someone?"

Neferet studied her, and Lynette felt a shiver of the fear she'd pushed aside the past few days as she'd become more and more accustomed to the vampyre and her unusual ways. Now she held her breath, relived the terrible scene of Ed's death, and hoped she hadn't accidentally committed an unforgivable breach of etiquette by questioning Neferet.

"Yes, my dear. I am waiting for something and someone. It is good that my handmaid understand what I am about." Neferet's tone was reasonable and she hooked her arm through Lynette's as they made their careful way back across the rocky bank. "There are four major groups of elementals—sprites that are made of air, fire, water, and earth magick, which is why I always leave four different offerings and why each of them symbolizes one of the elements. My intuition tells me that the sprites will not appear to me until the fifth night—after each group has been satisfied. And on that night, I shall make a special sacrifice."

Lynette's mouth felt dry. "Sacrifice?"

"Yes, sacrifice—offering—gift—libation—prasad—oblation. Different words for what is basically the same thing, which is what I have been doing here nightly."

"Do you need me to get you a special sacrifice for the fifth night?" she asked in a voice that sounded as if she was inquiring whether Neferet would like her to find a different breakfast tea and not what most probably would be something much more gruesome.

But Neferet smiled beatifically and shook her head. "No, dear Lynette. The special sacrifice must come from me, though you remind me that I will need a Sgian Dubh for the fifth night."

"A Sgian Dubh? I'm afraid you'll have to spell that for me, my lady. It sounds Gaelic and that language is hopelessly difficult."

"No need to trouble yourself. Call wee Denise to me. She'll procure the dagger."

"Dagger?" Lynette's stomach churned.

"Yes, a small ceremonial thing. Don't give it a thought, dear Lynette. Now, I am famished! Let us hope both of my feeders are here. You know how I hate waiting."

The next day Lynette unexpectedly found a Twitter thread online that brought her up short. It hadn't gained much traction. Seems few people back in Tulsa, neither humans nor vamps, were interested in pursuing a ghost story, and she would've hardly paid attention herself except that the posts kept disappearing.

At first Lynette thought it was a fluke or that she was imagining things. But after she counted three tweets and five Instagram posts that had been completely deleted—gone—and all had included either pictures or comments about what they were calling the TU vamp ghost, Lynette took notice. She also took screenshots. She had no idea if she was making too much of too little, but she would rather apologize for bothering Neferet than face the consequences of keeping something of importance from her, which meant she needed to bring it to Neferet's attention *before* the vampyre returned at midnight to begin preparing for her nightly ritual.

Following Neferet's lead, Lynette eschewed modern flash-lights for the flame of a newer version of the lantern Mrs. Muir had given the vampyre on the first night. Unlike Neferet, she wasn't impervious to the cold and wet, so she wrapped herself in a thick length of the plaid that Neferet had bought reams of—and she hadn't needed to be nagged by Muir to wear wellies. As she was leaving Balmacara, she literally ran into wee Denise, who was setting out bowls of cream and honey.

"Do cats like honey?" Lynette had asked.

The shy girl bobbed her blond head and giggled. "Och no, missus. They dinnae. I'm leavin' the offering for the gude fairies. From the Seelie Court—and hopin' they be keeping out the wicked wichts from Unseelie. And as ye can see it works fine. It brought us Herself."

"Huh. Well done, you." Lynette had no clue what else to say. Wee Denise tended to surprise her. She looked like a rather plain sixteen-year-old who was, as Mrs. Muir had first described her, not very smart. But something about her eyes said she knew things—older, darker things than a regular teenager knew. "Um, speaking of Herself—you didn't happen to see which direction she went tonight, did you?"

"Aye, missus. She went there—to the left. Good that yer goin' after Herself. Tis a dreich day. She should be home warmin' by the fire."

"Thanks, Denise. I tend to agree with you, but Neferet has a mind of her own. We'll be back by midnight. Please be sure the feeder is clean and—"

"Aye, get him—or her, blootered."

"If that means drunk, then yes, and thank you again."

Denise nodded, bobbed a curtsy, and went back into the house. Lynette wrapped the plaid shawl more closely around her shoulders and wished like hell for an umbrella as she headed down the bank and to the left.

It didn't take long to find Neferet. It was late, cold, dark, and the misting rain was almost freezing—Neferet's lantern was the only light on the beach. She'd put the lantern down near the waterline and was standing with the hem of her long plaid skirt hiked up and tucked into her waistband. Her bare feet were in the frigid water—her discarded wellies waited beside the lantern—while she tossed rocks into the loch.

Lynette approached her from behind, and Neferet didn't notice her, so focused was she on her rock throwing. Lynette could hear the vampyre cursing softly every time a stone plopped into the water and sank below the black waves, and she had to bite her cheek to keep from laughing. Neferet looked so young—so carefree—so completely approachable.

Lynette cleared her throat, but Neferet didn't acknowledge her.

"My lady, I do not mean to interrupt."

"Oh, I know you're there, Lynette. And you're not interrupting much. It seems skipping stones is the one thing I fail at."

"Skipping stones?" Lynette joined her, glancing at the pile of rocks Neferet held in a length of her voluminous plaid. "The problem isn't you, my lady." Lynette smiled kindly at Neferet. "The problem is there." She pointed to the pile of egg-shaped rocks. "They're not good for skipping."

"You know how to skip stones?" Neferet dropped the rocks and turned with keen attention to Lynette.

"Sure. Would you like me to teach you?"

"Oh, that would be lovely!"

"The most important thing is rock choice. It can't be too big or too little—about the size of your palm is best, and it must be flat. The flatter the better so it can skip." Lynette searched the beach, easily finding a suitable rock. "Like this one. See?"

"I do. It is very flat."

"Yes, and now you need to hold it like this." Lynette demonstrated holding it between her pointer finger and her thumb. "And then you throw it with a snap of your wrist—like this." She flicked her wrist and threw the stone. It skipped, but only twice before a wave covered it.

"Ooooh! You did it!"

"Well, not really. Two skips isn't great—four or five, that's excellent. But you need calm water to really get a good skip going."

"Truly?"

"Well, yes. It has to skip across the surface, and that's pretty much impossible with waves."

Neferet stared at Lynette for a long moment before turning to face the water again. She strode out into it until her calves were covered. She smiled and in the voice of a joyous girl said, "It would be so nice if the water calmed—just for a moment—so that I might learn to skip stones."

For a few breaths nothing happened. Then the wind stilled and the waves quieted, quieted, and finally the surface of the loch became glass.

Neferet clapped her hands joyfully and said, "Thank you!" before turning to Lynette. "Let's find more rocks."

A fast learner, the fourth stone Neferet threw skipped across the smooth surface of the loch three, four, five, six times.

"Six! Did you see, Lynette! Did you see! Oh, this is such fun!" Neferet laughed uninhibitedly.

Lynette couldn't help but stare. She found it difficult to

speak past the knot in her throat. The vampyre seemed not even the same being as the creature who had entered the Tulsa hangar alone, defeated, and angry.

"What is it, dear Lynette?" Neferet moved close to her side, studying her face.

Lynette shook herself. "It's just that this place has youthened you and when you laugh like that you look sixteen again."

Neferet's joy damped instantly. "I did not laugh like that when I was sixteen. Ever."

"I'm sorry." Lynette hesitated, and then touched Neferet's shoulder gently. "I know what it's like to have a terrible childhood."

"Do you? Do you truly?"

Lynette took Neferet's hand. "It started after my father left us when I was ten. My mother never recovered. Her entire identity was wrapped up in that man. Instead of learning to take care of herself, and of me, she clung to any man who would have her. Whenever one of them started making noises like he was going to leave, my mother, she used me to keep them interested. She told them that I was her property, so they could do whatever they wanted to me. Some raped me. Some did other things. When I begged her to protect me—to keep them from me—my mother told me I should thank her for preparing me for my future."

Even in the wan light of the flickering lanterns Lynette could see that Neferet's face had lost all color so that her sapphire tattoos stood out as if they were lit from within. She squeezed Lynette's hand and covered it with both of hers.

"Oh, dear Lynette. I understand. I was raped, though I haven't spoken of it for more than a century. I don't know how that child knew—the one pretending to be Zoey Redbird. But she was wrong about one thing. My father did not rape me. He had nothing to do with me after my mother died giving birth to the child he wanted—a son. He ignored me, keeping me a prisoner in my home until he could sell me to the highest bidder—which meant betrothing me to Arthur Simpton, heir to a very large family fortune. I was sixteen. Arthur raped me. The night of our betrothal—the night my father said to him what your mother said to the monsters who used you. *She is your property now. Do with her as you will.* And he did."

Lynette gripped Neferet's hands like a lifeline as tears leaked silently down the vampyre's pale cheeks. "What happened? How did you get away from him?"

"I was Marked, my dear. That very day. The House of Night accepted me—bloodied, beaten, and used." Neferet stared past Lynette out at the dark water to the hulking isle beyond. "I healed—strengthened—and then I stalked Arthur Simpton, trapped him, and killed him by using a strand of my mother's pearls as a garrote."

"Good! I'm glad you did."

"We are very alike, Lynette."

"I'm flattered you think so, my lady. And you just reminded me of why I came out here to find you." Lynette pulled her phone out of the folds of the plaid she'd wrapped around herself and tapped the surface to bring it alive. "First, the Tulsa House of Night has issued a notice that they are offering a one-hundred-thousand-dollar reward for your capture."

"Only one hundred thousand dollars?" Neferet scoffed. "How very frugal of them. My dear, I want you to search for something as you're combing through the internet. Look for even tiny mentions of discontent among vampyres from the Tulsa House of Night. Focus on males—young Warriors who were active soldiers during the war. I cannot believe all of them are happy to return to life under human tyranny."

"There seems to be a truce between vampyres and humans right now in the Midwest."

"It will not last. To be victorious over the humans, Anastasia Lankford would have to lead the House of Night into war." Neferet's laughter was cruel. "And that is something for which Anastasia is utterly unfit."

Lynette hastily made notes as she nodded. "Yes, my lady."

"What is the second thing you found?"

Lynette tapped the surface of the phone again. "I discovered something very strange going through some obscure Twitter feeds this evening. Your mention of Zoey Redbird is a coincidence, as that is a name being bandied about on these threads."

Neferet's green eyes narrowed dangerously. "Zoey Redbird? Show me. Now!"

13

Other Neferet

"That little bitch was no ghost!" Neferet was flipping through the screenshots with narrowed eyes. "And you say some of these posts have been deleted?"

"Not some—*all of them*. That's why you're only looking at screenshots. Every time one of these posts pops up, whether it's on Twitter or Instagram or Facebook, it disappears almost immediately. Every single time."

"That is odd. But what is odder is this person—this impostor. You did well in finding this, Lynette. I have been so focused on the future that I have totally blocked this horrid child and the bizarre things she said to me the night I was betrayed."

"So, she was there?"

"Oh, yes. She was the ringleader, which was unlike the Zoey Redbird I knew." Neferet paused and caught Lynette's gaze before she added, "That Zoey Redbird was a simpering know-it-all and no leader. I killed her." She watched her handmaid closely, judging her level of shock and fear, and was pleased that Lynette seemed completely unruffled.

"Some of the posts mentioned that the fledgling the People

of Faith killed—the act that started the war—was also named Zoey Redbird."

"Yes. That is correct. The fledgling's name was Zoey Redbird. I killed her and made it appear the People of Faith did it—and then I used that to declare war on humans. Does that change the way you feel about me, Lynette?"

Lynette's gaze didn't waiver. "No. I already knew that you're ruthless. You have to be. The world chews up and spits out weak women, and a weak woman would never be a goddess."

"You do understand."

"Yes. I do, and I always will. So, who is this ghost?"

"No ghost. I was face-to-face with her. She was no spirit or specter. She was absolutely not Zoey Redbird, though she somehow knew that I'd been the one to kill the real Redbird fledging.

"This was a fully Changed vampyre—confident and powerful—not a simpering child. But it is confusing. Along with knowing that I'd killed the fledgling, she knew obscure things about me that were *almost* correct. Like the fact that I was raped, but she named the wrong man as my rapist."

"Could it have been some kind of spell?" Lynette asked.

Neferet moved her shoulders restlessly. "Yes, that was my thought, but to create and maintain such an excellent Dissemble Spell the vampyre would have to be an extraordinarily powerful High Priestess, and one with centuries of experience. To give you an understanding of the power it would take I can tell you that I can cast a Dissemble Spell, but not even I could maintain one while dealing with sprites and holding a circle over an entire stadium. Add to that, the vampyre would have to be ancient, as for the past at *least* two hundred years, the out-of-touch crones on the High Council have frowned on using the Dissemble Spell, and refuse to allow it to be taught at any House of Night." Neferet shook her head. "So, my answer is yes and no. It could have been a Dissemble Spell, but it's highly unlikely."

"Could it be that someone who looked a little like Zoey Redbird was fixed up to look a lot like her? It would be a good way to sow fear and to smear your good name."

"That would be logical except why, then, is the Tulsa House of Night not spreading this ghost story across social media far and wide?" Neferet asked.

"It's the opposite. Someone is obviously trying to bury it. This is the fourth night since we left Tulsa. Every day I search the internet for news from home, and it is just today that I'm seeing any of this."

"And then it disappears as quickly as you find it."

"It does."

"There is more to this ghost story—a lot more. And I know who can tell it. That red vampyre who was with her—the lieutenant. He knew her well. Much of what they were saying was lost in the moment." Neferet sighed and shook her head in frustration. "I should have paid closer attention."

"You were being betrayed. You were focused on surviving," Lynette said.

"I was indeed. I will do better—when I return immortal and triumphant. I will have to remember to have that lieutenant questioned, *diligently*."

"I'll make a note to remind you."

"Oh, Lynette, you are the perfect handmaid."

"My only wish is to serve you, my lady, my goddess."

"What of your dream of living on the Amalfi Coast?" Neferet asked with a teasing smile.

"Only after you no longer require my services, my lady."

"You may be waiting quite a while then," said Neferet, again studying Lynette closely.

"*Come vuoi*," Lynette said with a shrug.

"As you wish." Neferet smiled as she translated the Italian and felt a knot within her release. "My dear, let us return to the house. It gets late and I would like to anoint myself specially tonight after the magick the lovely water sprites worked for me."

Lynette glanced back at the loch as they started back across the beach. "So, it was the sprites that did that?" she whispered to Neferet.

"Whom else, dear Lynette? Neferet paused and stared out at the silent loch. It had returned to being choppy and was, once again, dressed in white lace foam. "Whom else?"

Other Lynette

That night, as Neferet rode the waves with her children, she brought to Lynette's mind ancient warrior queens charging bare breasted into battle. Cloaked only in the thick fall of her hair and a fierceness that shimmered around her, Neferet's brightness turned the dark loch to smoky quartz.

Her offerings that fourth night were a bowl of honey mead, another filled with fine Medjool dates, a third brimmed with

Mrs. Muir's best traditional Hairst Bree—and into the final bowl Neferet dropped her favorite jeweled ring. It was shaped like a crown crusted with diamonds, and the fat square stone was an occluded sapphire, the exact color of the sea around Skye at midday.

Lynette watched loyally while the watery arm accepted the gifts as it had done the three previous nights. Neferet returned to her again, smelling of sea and wind, smoke and earth.

"My lady! I—I can smell the four elements all around you!" she exclaimed as she handed Neferet a thick terry bath sheet, helping her dry the saltwater from her naked body before wrapping her in a thick bathrobe.

"Of course you can, dear Lynette. The sprites recognize that I offer these gifts sincerely, with respect and reverence." Neferet spoke loudly, her voice carrying out across the tumultuous loch, but as they returned to the house she tilted her head to Lynette and whispered, "Wait until tomorrow night. I have them where I want them. They will come—air, fire, water, and earth. They will come, and they will be mine, whether they truly understand that now, or not."

"I never doubted it, my lady," Lynette lied. She tried to imagine what would happen the next night and her mind skittered away from the possibilities. Which Neferet would appear? The one who commands her children to devour others, or the one who skips stones with the innocence of a young girl?

Perhaps it will be a mixture of the two—goddess-like and magnificent—the vampyre who has become my protector, my mistress, and my future…

14

Zoey

"NO!" Aphrodite shrieked and stopped short, making Stevie Rae and me run smack into the back of her. "OMG, why are the two of you all up on me?"

"'Cause you stopped in the middle of the sidewalk, genius." Stevie Rae stated the obvious.

We'd exited the House of Night main school building through the covered side entrance because even though it was January and there was only a little weak light making its way through the winter clouds, I heart me some Stevie Rae and didn't want to see her fry like nasty overdone toast. At that moment, Aphrodite was standing, hands on hips, staring at the loaded school bus (with blackout windows, of course) that was waiting for us.

"Seriously? A bus? Isn't the point of being in-charge grown-ups that we do *not* ever have to ride in one of those tacky yellow things again?"

"Ooooh! Photo op!" Stevie Rae cheered as she pulled out her phone and then neatly turned Aphrodite and me around so that the bus was in the background of our selfie. "I always get more likes when I post a pic with you two. 'Specially when—"

"Oh, nuh-uh." Aphrodite flipped her hair and tried to walk away.

"—Aphrodite does something bitchy like that hair flip I just caught," continued Stevie Rae.

"OMG! *Finally!* We've been waiting out here *forever*." Other Jack stuck his head out of the open door to the bus. Then he saw that Stevie Rae was selfie-ing and he skipped down the bus steps to pose in the background, photobombing as Aphrodite glared and Stevie Rae quickly took a few more pictures.

"If you don't edit those before you post them I'm coming after you," Aphrodite said as she glared at Stevie Rae.

"Add a side-eye like that and I'll get more likes than a picture of a fluffy kitty in a teacup." Stevie Rae giggled and bumped Aphrodite with her hip. "Oh, loosen up. This is a big day for the House of Night and for Z in particular."

"Big day or not, I don't understand why we can't follow the damn bus in one of the school town cars."

"We're going on the bus like all the other teachers and kids from all the other *human* schools," Jack said firmly. "We're supposed to be *normal*, remember?"

"You know how I feel about normal," Aphrodite said. "It's overrated."

"Yeah, well, I'd usually agree with you about that, but not today. Not the very first time the House of Night has been included in a human high school swim meet in Tulsa's history," I said.

"If they *really* wanted to be inclusive, they'd hold it after sunset," grumbled Aphrodite, still not moving closer to the bus.

"The finals *are* at night, but we have to do the prelims during the day like everyone else," said Jack.

"Yeah, that supercool YWCA at 21st and Lewis even blacked out their windows for us. They're bein' real welcomin' even if it did practically take an act of God-*dess*." She wiggled her brows and giggled before continuing, "To make them relax enough to let us compete."

"Stevie Rae's right," I said. "I have jumped through every hoop they asked of me—" My words broke off as I smacked my forehead with my palm. "Ah, hell! I left the folder with those forms that we had to sign and notarize on my desk."

"No biggie. We can just send one of the kids back to get it. Aphrodite's takin' forever to get on the dang bus anyways." Stevie Rae hurried to the bus and stuck her head inside. I watched her look around before she targeted some kid named Kacie and told her to run back to my office and retrieve the file. A cute girl with a blue fledgling Mark, light-brown skin, and lots of thick hair expertly dyed Beychella blond hurried past us.

"Kacie? I don't recognize the name or the girl," I said as Stevie Rae rejoined us.

"That's Kacie Lockwood," said Jack. "She might just be the fastest swimmer on the team."

"Oh, is she the kid who just transferred in from the Chicago House of Night?" I asked Stevie Rae.

"Yeah, it's a kinda sweet story, really. She was newly Marked when Rephaim and I were at the Chicago House of Night, and she was the first kid I mentored. When she found out I was stayin' here and Kramisha was gonna take my place in Chicago, Kacie called me and asked if she could transfer down here. She's only been in Tulsa for a few days."

"That is nice," I said.

"What's wrong with her?" Aphrodite asked.

"Nothin'!" Stevie Rae said.

"Well, at least not much of anything," said Jack softly.

"Um-hum. That's what I thought," Aphrodite said.

"Is Kacie a problem?" I asked Stevie Rae.

"No, High Priestess, I am not."

The voice came from behind us and the four of us turned to see Kacie standing there offering my folder to me. Her eyes immediately caught my attention—big and dark, they seemed to hold secrets and a sparkle that said they also held a dose of humor (or attitude).

"High Priestess Zoey Redbird and Prophetess Aphrodite LaFont, this is Kacie Lockwood, formerly of the Chicago House of Night," Stevie Rae introduced.

"Are those Kate Spade's ice cream wedges from last season?" asked Aphrodite before I could say anything to the kid.

Kacie lifted one dark brow. "Good eye."

"I'm an expert. And in this particular case I approve of wearing leftovers in honor of our much-missed Ms. Spade."

"Leftovers?" Stevie Rae said.

"Things that were new last season," said Jack.

"Try to keep up," said Aphrodite.

"Welcome to the Tulsa House of Night, Kacie," I said.

"Thanks, High Priestess," she said.

"I want to know more of the answer to that question," said Aphrodite.

When we all just stared at Aphrodite, she rolled her eyes.

"Z asked if this kid is a problem," Aphrodite said.

"Oh, that's easy to answer," said Kacie. "I'm not a problem. School is. HP Stevie Rae gets that, so she also gets me. Most of the other priestesses and professors did not. That's why I transferred here."

"HP?" I asked.

Kacie shifted her attention from Aphrodite to me. "It's short for High Priestess."

"Ohmygoddess! I thought you were giving a nod to Stevie Rae's love for all things Harry Potter," said Jack. "But High Priestess makes a lot more sense."

"Jack, you make me smile." Stevie Rae put her arm around him.

Kacie's attention was still focused on me. She spoke up as she met and held my gaze—and, again, I was struck by the intelligence and humor I saw in her eyes—and this time I enjoyed the glint of attitude. "HP Zoey, I want you to know this place you've created here at this House of Night—it's the first time I've ever liked school."

"I get that," I said. "I wasn't a big fan of school, either. It can definitely suck—especially high school."

"High school in America is usually not much more than the institutionalization of a mind-numbing, racist, misogynistic shitshow. Even the Chicago House of Night was pretty much crap, though Stevie Rae was changing that. So, uh, thanks for running a better place here. And I'm not sorry for saying *shitshow*, even though I hear you don't cuss much. That is all." She flashed me a smile and turned to get on the bus.

Stevie Rae cleared her throat, which had Kacie pausing.

"Ooopsie," the kid came back to me. "Here's your folder."

Kacie handed it to me, but as she did it slipped from her fingers and like a flock of paper birds the carefully filled-out forms took flight on the afternoon breeze.

"Shit! I'll get them!" Kacie took off, grabbing each paper and shoving it back into the folder before she ran after another.

Stevie Rae sighed. "Kacie's too smart for her age."

"You mean too smart-*mouthed*." I grinned at my bestie.

"Yeah, that too," Stevie Rae nodded as we watched Kacie chase papers.

"She is a really talented swimmer, even if she does tend to intimidate the other kids because of how outspoken she is," said Jack.

"Smart mouth, excellent fashion sense, and good hair. I like her," said Aphrodite. "She's also gorgeous, which never hurts."

"When I first met her, I though she looked like what would happen if Beyoncé and JLo had a baby," said Stevie Rae.

"Bestie, you read my mind. I was thinking her hair is Beyoncé blond," I said.

"I have just happened to notice that she has a shoe collection that's right up there with Aphrodite and Kramisha," said Jack.

"Brains and beauty—a fantastic combo," agreed Aphrodite. "We'll need to keep an eye on her."

"Yep. That's a big part of why I said yes to her transfer," said Stevie Rae.

"I'll be sure the Dark Daughters welcome her," I said.

"That's real nice of you, Z. I was gonna ask you to introduce her next full moon ritual, but I was worried 'bout showing favoritism. This adulting stuff is confusin' sometimes."

"Right?" Jack said. "I volunteered to coach the swim team because before I was Marked, swim class was my personal high school nightmare. My young self was so, so shy about my body and my coach was a raging homophobe who lived for third-hour PE so he could humiliate me. Daily. I was that wretched man's target until the day I was Marked. I want to give kids a better experience than I had, but I also don't want to show favoritism or hurt a kid's feelings—but they still need discipline and guidance. It's really hard."

"You know, I've been thinking about teachers' pets and showing favoritism a lot, especially since I've been teaching that advanced spells and rituals class," I said. "And I've decided to hell with it. There's nothing wrong with picking out the kids who *are* super talented or smart or athletic— or whatever—and giving them extra attention, or even just extra encouragement. As long as we remember to give all the kids opportunities to shine. What do you guys think?"

Aphrodite shrugged. "It's a proven fact pretty kids get called on more."

"I'm so glad I was a cute kid. My childhood could've been *even worse.*" Jack shuddered.

"Yeah, I read a study on that and it made me call on the ugly kids on purpose," said Stevie Rae. Then she smacked her hand over her mouth and through it muttered. "Sorry. Callin' 'em ugly is so not cool."

"Not cool, but true," said Aphrodite.

I opened my mouth to say something profound, and stopped short as Kacie rushed up to me. Her cheeks were pink, and her full lips trembled slightly.

"Sorry about that," she said, obviously embarrassed. "I really can do things without messing up."

I smiled warmly at her. "It was just an accident." I liked that she spoke her mind. Too many fledglings, especially newly Marked fledglings, were either too timid to speak out or were content to be herd animals.

"I hate it when I do something stupid without meaning to," she said.

"Relax, Ice Cream Shoes," Aphrodite said. "Your sense of style has earned you a second chance."

"Hey, thanks, Aphrodite. You're not as horrible as people say you are." Kacie grinned and got on the bus.

I was trying not to laugh when I glanced at Aphrodite—who looked weird. Not mad. Not amused. Not annoyed. Just... weird.

"Hey, you okay?" I asked.

"Yeah. I'm fine." Aphrodite rubbed her forehead before flipping back her hair. "Are we going to go or what?"

"Yep! I'm ready now," I said.

"Oh, goodie! Stevie Rae, will you sit in the back with me?" Jack jumped up and down and clapped his hands.

"Ohmygood*ness*, 'course I will! The back seats are the bounciest!" Stevie Rae followed Jack onto the bus.

Before she stepped onto the bus, Aphrodite turned to look at me. "And I'm *not* sitting in the back seat—no matter how much the bumpkin whines and begs."

"Neither am I. Just don't look her in the eyes and sit in the front seat. Fast," I whispered—and we both laughed.

The Midtown Tulsa YWCA's parking lot was crammed with yellow buses whose black lettering proclaimed that there were teams here from Tulsa Public Schools as well as Broken Arrow, Jenks, Union, Bishop Kelley, and even Bixby and Coweta. The Y had arranged a special parking spot for our bus near a temporary tarp tunnel that led to the front of the building and was thoroughly covered so that we could all unload without worrying about the sun frying any of us.

"Ready for this?" Aphrodite asked me.

"Absolutely," I said while I shook my head *no*. I stood and faced the kids on the bus, who were all watching me expectantly. "Aphrodite, Stevie Rae, and I are going to go inside and be sure we're registered and whatever else we have to do. You guys wait here with Coach Jack."

"Remember, you're representing all fledglings *and* your High Priestesses. So act right," said Aphrodite.

"But most of all, have fun," said Stevie Rae as she joined us at the front of the bus.

"From what Coach Jack has told me, this team is talented and just plain awesome enough to do both—act right *and* have fun," I said, meeting the gaze of each of the kids. I saw nerves in their eyes, but also excitement—and I especially loved how their Marks blazed from their foreheads. No Tulsa House of Night fledgling was going to have to cover his or her Mark to mix with humans. Not ever again. "They're going to stare at you, but don't take it personally. There will be a lot of people here—kids and adults—who have never been this close to so many vampyres and fledglings. They're going to be curious."

"They might also be mean," said Jack from where he stood at the back of the bus.

"Because ignorance makes some folks real mean," said Stevie Rae.

"And, let's face facts—there's a lot of ignorance in Oklahoma," Aphrodite said.

"Aphrodite! Be nice!" Stevie Rae said.

"What? Okies keep voting in the same idiots who keep lining their own pockets and being apathetic about education and health care. Seriously. Don't get me started on

P. C. CAST & KRISTIN CAST

stupid Okie politics, 'cause you know I know what I'm talking about," said Aphrodite, one blond brow lifting into her hairline.

"But *we're* here to educate people about how we're all basically the same," I added.

"Yeah. Hold your heads high because even though we're all *basically the same* we're definitely superior to anyone ignorant enough to be mean just because of physical or religious differences," Aphrodite said. "Well, and, we're also literally superior, but we should probably keep that under-wraps for today."

"That's right!" Stevie Rae smiled and nodded enthusiastically. "We're not all hat and no cowboy!"

"What in the hell are you talking about?" Aphrodite said.

"Okay, let's go!" I turned Aphrodite by her shoulders and pushed her from the bus. "Coach Jack, someone will come back and get you and the team as soon as we're registered."

"No problem. I've planned a little minimeditation to get us ready. Just take your time." Jack waved us away.

"He's a real good coach," said Stevie Rae as we followed Aphrodite into the big brick building.

"He's a sweetheart," I said. "I don't even think of him as 'other' Jack anymore. He's just our Jack."

"Yeah, it's great having him back—even though technically it isn't actually really *him*," Stevie Rae said.

"It's nice seeing Damien so happy again," said Aphrodite. I noticed that her voice had gone somber and her eyes were suddenly a lot less sparkly.

"Yeah, it sure is. I wonder where Damien is today? It's not like him to miss Jack's first meet," I said.

"Jack said Damien had to be at the depot for a special

delivery of the velvet chairs that go with the reserved tables near the stage. He's tryin' to get the restaurant reopened by next month, and he's stressin' pretty hard over it," said Stevie Rae.

"Does he need more help?" I asked.

"I don't think so. Jack said everythin's handled, but Damien's a nervous mess."

"Queen Damien will be fine once his opus opens. Can you smell that?" Aphrodite paused and sniffed as we entered the building.

"Chlorine?" I said.

"Well, yeah, but I was talking about hormones. There must be thousands of kids in there." Aphrodite shuddered and jerked her perfect chin at the glass wall separating the lobby from the Olympic-sized pool and viewing stands that were currently crowded with a couple hundred kids, their parents, and coaches.

"Hundreds, not thousands. And when did you get so old?" I said.

"I was born old," said Aphrodite.

"OMG! Vampyres!" A squeal came from the registration desk a few yards in front of us. A young black girl with a neon-red ponytail dressed in an orange-and-black cheerleading uniform that proclaimed HORNETS across the front of it was literally clapping her hands and jumping up and down as she stared at us with dark eyes glistening excitedly.

"Cheerleaders… Jesus," Aphrodite muttered.

I ignored Aphrodite, planted what I hoped was a professional smile on my face, and went to stand in front of the cheerleader. "Hi, I'm Zoey Redbird, High Priestess of the House of—"

"OMG everyone knows who you are! It's so cool you're here! Everyone thinks so. Well, except for our parents. But whatever. They're all old and out of it. *They still vote Republican*," she scrunched up her face like she'd sucked a lemon.

"Exactly what I was just saying," agreed Aphrodite.

"It's cray, right?" said the cheerleader. "But y'all know better 'cause you're not old. You're *super* young. How old are you anyway?" the cheerleader babbled, suddenly reminding me of my old bestie, Kayla, and her nonstop high school word diarrhea (which I hadn't missed at all).

"I'm eighteen," I said. "Here's our paperwork. Everything is in order. Our team's waiting in the bus. Where should I tell them to change?"

"I'll show 'em to the locker rooms," said the cheerleader, beaming a big smile at me. "And welcome. My cousin was Marked five years ago. We were super close, but no one would let me call her or nothin' after she left for the House of Night, so I think what you're doin' is amazing—mixing fledglings with humans."

"If your cousin was Marked today you'd be able to stay in contact with her," said Stevie Rae. "That's 'cause of what High Priestess Zoey is doin' here in Tulsa."

"That's real brave of you," said the cheerleader. She stuck her hand out. "I'm Bridget, captain of Booker T. Washington's varsity cheer squad—*Go Hornets!* If y'all need anything just holler for me and I'll fix you right up."

"Thanks, Bridget." I smiled at the kid as I shook her hand. "Right now, all we need is a place for our team to change and for someone to let us know where we're supposed to sit."

"Oh, sure! Like I said, I'll show your team to the locker rooms. Do ya see that center front section of the bleachers?"

I followed her pointing finger to see an empty place in the middle of the section. It looked kinda like a missing tooth.

"I see it."

"We reserved it for House of Night fans. See ya inside and good luck." Bridget started to turn away and then added. "Hey, what's your school mascot?"

I stared at her. Ah, hell! The House of Night didn't have a school mascot!

Into the uncomfortably growing silence Stevie Rae spoke up. "We're the Ravens. Our colors are black and purple."

"Cool! See ya!" Bridget hurried past us and out the front doors. She jogged through the tunnel to our bus. The three of us watched her disappear inside—and reappear in a few seconds with Jack and the rest of the team following her in a neat line.

The team entered the building, staring around Bridget at me, looking like a flock of wide-eyed baby birds. I nodded encouragement and Jack made a shooing motion at them so that they followed Bridget, with him bringing up the rear.

"Good luck!" I called as Jack passed us.

"Yeah, good luck House of Night Ravens!" Stevie Rae cheered.

Coach Jack stopped like he'd run into a linebacker. "Go ahead guys! I'll catch you in a sec." Jack faced me with his hands on his slim hips. "Ravens? Since when?"

"It was a sudden inspiration. They asked and I was the only one with an answer. You don't mind, do ya?" Stevie Rae said.

"Well, I kinda thought the House of Night Swimming Seals would be nice," Jack said wistfully.

"Ssssswimming Ssssseals?" Aphrodite lisped.

"That's mean," said Jack. "You know I have a lisp some-times."

"Uh, yeah. That's why it's so funny," said Aphrodite.

Stevie Rae turned to me. "You're not mad about me naming us the Ravens, are you?"

"No! I'm glad you thought of something."

"Ravens." Aphrodite continued to laugh until she snorted.

"Everyone's staring at us," Stevie Rae said. "And not in a good way."

Aphrodite's laughter cut off like she'd thrown a switch.

Stevie Rae was right. Jack had caught us with the door to the swim meet area open just before we stepped through to head to our reserved seats, and every head that wasn't at least partially underwater was turned in our direction.

"Gotta go!" said Jack and he disappeared into the bowels of the building, hurrying after his team.

I straightened my spine, lifted my chin, and plastered a smile on my face. "Smile and look like none of this bothers you," I whispered between my teeth.

From my side vision I could see Aphrodite and Stevie Rae following my lead. They lifted their chins and smiled like they were oh-so-pleased to see all the gawking faces.

There were about a dozen seats with big black RESERVED FOR HON signs on them.

"Hell! We should've brought fans," I said as the three of us sat in the middle of the empty seats.

"It's okay. This is just the trials," said Stevie Rae.

"Yeah, we'll round up a bunch of 'fans,'" Aphrodite air quoted, "for the finals."

"Z, if the House of Night is gonna be participating in

sports with the human kids, I think we should start a pep club or whatnot," said Stevie Rae.

"I agree," I said. "You're in charge of that."

"Why me?"

"Your idea," I said.

"And your Raven." Aphrodite peered around me at Stevie Rae. "Don't think I didn't catch that you named our school mascot after your birdboy. Ya know, we coulda been the House of Night Warriors."

"Or the Ssswimming Ssseals." I couldn't help myself. "But I like Ravens," I added quickly before she and Stevie Rae could devolve into bickering.

"Thank you, Z," said Stevie Rae, sending Aphrodite a narrow-eyed look. "And I did think of Warriors. For 'bout two-point-five seconds, but it could be taken as Native American Warriors and that's cultural appropriation and racist—so no."

"Good point," I said. "Ooooo, here they come!"

Led by Coach Jack, our team entered the pool area and the gawkers shifted their attention from us to them. I stood and began to clap and cheer—Stevie Rae and Aphrodite instantly joining me—and I was happily surprised to see cheerleader Bridget and her entire squad stand and clap as well.

"Wow. They look really good," I said. "Where'd they get those uniforms?"

"Me, of course. Note the expensive material and the excellent mixture of our school colors," Aphrodite said smugly.

"They're gonna look great with a big raven and 'HoN' emblazoned on the back of those warm-ups!" said Stevie Rae.

Aphrodite snorted. Again.

I was glad to see that as our team warmed up, the gawkers relaxed. Sure, people still stared at us and the human kids were pretty much keeping their distance from our fledglings, but at least the main focus was the meet—or at least it mostly was.

Stevie Rae's sigh was bittersweet. "Rephaim would love to see this. He never got to play sports, 'cause, well—"

"He was a half-bird/half-boy monster?" Aphrodite offered with exaggerated innocence.

"Yes, but you coulda put it nicer," said Stevie Rae.

"Do you ever wish you and Rephaim had stayed in the Other World?" I heard the question blurt from my mouth before I could stop it. Aphrodite and Stevie Rae swiveled their heads to stare at me.

"That's harsh," said Aphrodite.

I held up my hands in surrender. "No, no! I didn't mean I wanted her to! I was only curious. It's just that Rephaim gets to be a boy all the time over there." I bumped Aphrodite with my shoulder. "Stop it."

"Oh, I know you didn't mean nothing, Z. To tell the truth, Rephaim and I talked 'bout it and we decided that this is our home—even if he is a bird half the time. Plus, Nyx made him stay a bird during the day because he needed to atone. Rephaim is too honorable to skip out on that," she said.

I felt a huge weight lift from my chest that I hadn't wanted to admit was there. "Is it selfish of me to say that I'm really glad?" I asked.

"Nah, Z. It's honest—that's all. Don't worry. Rephaim and I aren't goin' anywhere. *This* T-Town is our T-Town."

"I don't think I realized it until now, but I was worried," I said.

"Z, if Rephaim and I weren't happy here, I woulda said somethin' to you."

"You didn't tell me that you were miserably homesick in Chicago," I countered.

"True," Stevie Rae said. "But I learned my lesson 'bout that. I mess up, but I usually don't make the same mess twice."

"Would you two please make out later?" Aphrodite said, rolling her eyes.

"You know, Aphrodite, you've been super grumpy recently. Are you and Darius having issues? And that's a rhetorical question—so, don't answer. Just check your attitude." Stevie Rae crossed her arms and purposefully turned her back to Aphrodite.

"Darius and I are just fine!" Aphrodite said, a little too quickly.

I lowered my voice and leaned closer to my friend and prophetess. "Hey, she's right. My gut says there's something going on with you."

Aphrodite started to glare at me, but the glare changed to a sad sigh. Keeping her voice low, for my ears alone, she said, "I'm worried about him."

"Him?" I asked, even though I had a pretty good idea that she wasn't talking about Darius.

"Your other brother, of course. I just died over there. He just lost me. He must be utterly devastated. I'm worried. Aren't you?"

"I am. But he has a great support system over there. Other Anastasia and Other Grandma Redbird will help him."

She snorted and looked dubious.

"Aphrodite, there's nothing I can do from here, and believe me, I've thought about it a lot. I'd love to come and go between the worlds like there's a revolving door—but that's not reality. Reality is that to open the door to that world I have to use Old Magick, lots of it, and I honestly do not believe that's safe."

"I know all of that, but it doesn't stop me from worrying about him."

"Yeah, me either. I—"

"All swimmers line up for the four-by-one-hundred-meter freestyle relay!" the announcer interrupted me.

"Hey, look! There's our team!" Stevie Rae pointed and clapped enthusiastically.

The pool had cleared while Aphrodite and I had been talking. Teams were lined up behind their swim platforms—four kids deep. Coach Jack was standing beside our four kids clapping them on their backs and looking very coach-like and encouraging.

I shot Aphrodite a *let's talk about this later* look and then said, "I don't know anything about competitive swimming. How many laps do each of them have to swim?"

"Two," said Aphrodite.

"You know swimmin'?" asked Stevie Rae.

"Um, take a look at those tiny speedos and all that gorgeous naked male muscle. Of course I know swimming," said Aphrodite. "Four kids will each swim two laps. The first and the last kid are usually the fastest."

"Oh, look! Kacie's last in line. She *is* superfast! This is gonna be a great race!" Stevie Rae stood up and cheered. "Go House of Night Ravens! Woo-hoo!"

When the gawkers turned to gawk at Stevie Rae, I stood beside her and joined her cheer.

"Go Ravens! Swim fast! You can do it!" I yelled.

I heard Aphrodite sigh and say, "Okay, novices. Watch how it's done." She stood, cupped her hands around her mouth and expertly cheered, "GO IN HARD! COME OUT WET! R-A-V-E-N-S! RAVENS! RAVENS! RAVENS!"

Stevie Rae and I—as well as everyone around us—stared at her.

"What?" she said. "It's a legit cheer. And my personal fave from my human high school years."

I looked at Stevie Rae. She looked at me. I shrugged and grinned, and then the three of us shouted, "GO IN HARD! COME OUT WET! R-A-V-E-N-S! RAVENS! RAVENS! RAVENS!"

The starting pistol went off and the line of kids dove into the pool as the crowd cheered them on.

I'd never been to a swim meet before. I hate to admit it, but Heath's football obsession pretty much dictated my involvement in watching high school sports. In Broken Arrow, Oklahoma, football is a serious sport. Swimming—not so much. But as I watched our relay team cut through the water I decided that I'd been missing out.

"This is cool!" I yelled to Aphrodite over the cheering crowd.

"And it's climate-controlled," Aphrodite said. "Even though this humidity is terrible for my hair."

"Ooooh! Look! We're leading and Kacie's next on the platform! GO KACIE! GO RAVENS!" Stevie Rae shouted.

Maybe it was because I'm a swim meet novice, but I wasn't watching the kids who were swimming laps. I was watching Kacie—our anchor—as she stood on the platform. The other anchors were cheering their teammates on as the swimmers turned to start their return lap, but Kacie was just standing there. As I watched, she wiped her face, and I could see even from our seats that her hand trembled and she looked pale and was sweating like crazy.

"Hey, does Kacie get nervous at swim meets?" I asked Stevie Rae.

"Not in Chicago, she didn't. She was captain of the team, even though she was only a first-year fledgling." Stevie Rae's gaze went to Kacie on the platform and she frowned. "That's weird. She doesn't look good. Maybe she is nervous 'cause it's a human meet."

Aphrodite touched my leg, drawing my attention. Her blue eyes were somber and she kept her voice low for my ears alone. "I don't think that's it. Get ready to move."

"Huh?" I said, a terrible clenching beginning in my stomach. "What do you mean by *move*."

"If I'm right we're going to have to get down there to that pool. Fast. And then get outta here. Faster."

"What's Aphrodite sayin'?" asked Stevie Rae.

I met my bestie's gaze as Kacie half dove, half belly-flopped into the pool. "We think your kid's in trouble."

Stevie Rae's eyes got huge as her gaze went to the pool. "Oh, no…"

The first lap went okay. Kacie had been given the lead, thanks to a House of Night kid named Grayson who seemed to swim like the seal Jack wanted to name the team for, but she quickly fell back to second and then third. She was still in third place when she touched the far side of the pool and did that cool flippy turn thing swimmers do.

But she didn't push off from the pool like everyone else. Instead her head suddenly surfaced just a couple yards from the wall.

Kacie was coughing.

At first it seemed like she'd just messed up and swallowed a bunch of water, but the third time she coughed, scarlet burst from her lips, spraying the water around her. Kacie was treading water, but when she saw the blood I watched shock and fear collide across her face and she went under.

I was on my feet and running down the bleacher stairs two at a time. Stevie Rae and Aphrodite were on my heels.

That's when the human kids started screaming.

"Ah, hell. Ah, hell. *Ah, hell.*" I said over and over as I raced to the pool.

"I'll get her," Stevie Rae said. Then she dove into the blushing pool.

"What do you want me to do?" asked Aphrodite.

"Help Jack get the swimmers out of the pool and our team to the bus. I'll take care of the crowd," I said.

"Got it." Aphrodite hurried to the side of the pool that had the swimmers' platforms. All the competitors were milling around there—many were hysterical as they scrambled to get out of the pool while the blushing water turned a darker and darker tint of red. Jack was there with the rest of the coaches trying to calm the kids and help them from the water. "Everyone out of the pool! Find your team or your parent," Aphrodite shouted.

"And everyone else stay back and let the High Priestesses handle this!" Jack said.

I could hear Aphrodite and Jack directing people away from the pool, but my main attention was on Stevie Rae and Kacie as they surfaced. One look told me what I already knew, even though I was really hoping Kacie had been playing a practical joke of very poor taste on us.

Blood gushed from her eyes, nose, mouth, and ears. Kacie was gagging and retching. Her face had completely blanched of color and her beautiful brown eyes were pink-tinged and wide with fear as Stevie Rae pulled her to me at the side of the pool.

An attractive woman rushed up to me. Her calm gaze took in the pool and the dying fledgling. "May I help? My name is Sharon Griffin. I'm a doctor."

"Thank you, but there's nothing you can do for our fledgling. Take care of the humans. Some of them are pretty hysterical."

Doctor Griffin touched my shoulder gently. "I will. I am very sorry this happened here today." Then she hurried to the far side of the pool.

I drew a deep breath and quickly centered myself, reaching out to touch the element that filled the room.

"Water, I call you to me. Come, water!" The scent of chlorine was suddenly replaced with the comforting smell of salt and sea and sand.

"Fire, I call you to me. Come, fire!" I wasn't as good at this as Shaunee, but I do have an affinity for all five elements, so even though flames didn't burst to life around me I felt the air warm with the presence of fire. I continued. *"Fire and water—mix here and now. Shield this fledgling—gawking human eyes do not allow!"*

There was a great hissing sound as fire joined water in the pool and a wall of concealing mist lifted between the panicked crowd and us. Hidden from the watching humans,

I went to my knees at the side of the pool and gently took Kacie from Stevie Rae's arms.

Kacie was choking and sobbing. "It's okay. It's going to be okay," I told the dying fledgling over and over. I was glad my voice was calm—it was the only thing about me that was. My heart was beating so hard that it hurt my chest, and my stomach was so sick I was worried I might puke.

Stevie Rae slithered from the pool, shedding bloody water everywhere. Immediately she pulled Kacie onto her lap and wrapped her arms around the trembling girl.

"I'm here, Kacie. I'm right here. I'm not goin' anywhere," Stevie Rae spoke through the tears that cascaded down her smooth cheeks.

"I-I-I'm s-scared," Kacie managed to say before she coughed up a flood of blood and water.

I sat beside Stevie Rae and wrapped my arms around them both. "Spirit, please come to me. Fill this precious fledgling. Ease her pain. Ease her fear. Let her know Nyx is here. Surround her with love… always love."

Instantly I felt the familiar shiver of spirit as it manifested—and then the element I'm closest to left me and poured into Kacie Lockwood.

Her body stopped shaking.

Stevie Rae met my gaze and mouthed *thank you* before she continued to speak soothingly to her fledgling. "There's nothin' to be afraid of. I know Nyx. You're gonna love her—just like she already loves you."

Kacie looked up at her mentor.

"P-promise?"

"Absolutely, sweetie. Absolutely. And there's no school up there."

"*Good…*" Kacie spoke the word as her last breath left her. She turned her head into Stevie Rae's shoulder—sighed—and died.

Aphrodite rushed through the wall of mist—then stopped short and crouched beside us.

"Oh, crap. Well, I can't say that I'm surprised by this," she said.

I frowned at Aphrodite. "Hey, that's a shitty thing to say. This poor kid just died and Stevie Rae is super upset."

"Sorry. It'll help if you know *why* I'm not surprised."

"Nothin' will help. Kacie's dead and almost every damn human here is totally hysterical," said Stevie Rae, sniffing but keeping a tight hold on Kacie's slack body.

"You're upset, so I won't tell you that you're wrong. Again. I'll just tell you why. Remember before we got on the bus Kacie dropped Z's papers and was all embarrassed?" She didn't pause for an answer but continued while Stevie Rae and I stared at her like she was a crazy person. "Well, I made some offhand comment about her deserving a second chance, and when I said it I felt my forehead tingle."

"Aphrodite, have you lost your rabbit-ass mind? This fledgling is dead," Stevie Rae spoke through her sobs. "And you're talkin' about *yourself*?"

"Oh, for shit's sake! Not because I'm being selfish. When I felt my forehead tingle it meant a part of my tattoo disappeared."

I blinked. "You mean this kid—"

"Gets a second chance?" Stevie Rae blurted.

"Yes. That's exactly what I mean."

"Ohmygood*ness!* I'm so glad!" Stevie Rae hugged Kacie's still body close to her heart.

"So, let's get this soon-to-be red fledgling back to the House of Night—and then Z can deal with this publicity nightmare," said Aphrodite.

I nodded in agreement and thought, publicity nightmare is an understatement—ah, hell.

15

Zoey

Stark stood and opened his arms as Aphrodite and I joined him and Darius at our usual dinner booth. I stepped into his embrace, glad for the strength and comfort that always radiated from him.

"Hard day, huh?" he whispered into my ear.

I nodded, my head resting against his chest. "It sucked."

He kissed me thoroughly but quickly before we slid side by side into the booth across from Darius and Aphrodite.

"May I get you some brown pop to go with the spaghetti Stark already ordered for you?" asked the server who seemed to materialize beside our booth.

"Yes, absolutely," I said. "Only lace it with blood, please. And add an order of garlic bread—a really big order."

"Yes, High Priestess."

"Ditto for me," said Aphrodite. "Only make my spaghetti a giant Cobb salad and my brown pop champagne with a side carafe of blood."

"One bottle of Veuve Clicquot—rosé, correct?" the server asked as she wrote down the order.

"No, one glass of champagne is plenty. I'm a whole new me," said Aphrodite with only the slightest amount of sarcasm.

"Excellent. I'll be right back with your drinks. Gentlemen, would you like a refill?" The server glanced at Stark and Darius, who both nodded. "Beer and blood for Stark and red wine and blood for you, Darius?"

"That's it," said Stark, draining the last of his blood beer.

"Yes, and thank you," said Darius.

She smiled and hurried away.

"Hey, thanks for the psaghetti order," I said.

"Hey, you know I have your back," he said.

"So, how bad was it?" Darius asked.

"Awful," I said. "That poor kid. It's terrifying enough to reject the Change, but to do it in front of a crowd of humans in the middle of a public pool that turned into blood and chlorine soup." I shuddered. "Just effing awful."

"And of course every kid who is old enough to count has a damn phone, so the internet is currently flooded with images of that blood and chlorine soup. The parental hysteria is off the charts," said Aphrodite.

I shook my head. "I should've called fire and water and put that barrier up sooner."

Aphrodite touched my hand gently. "Z, don't do that to yourself. You did all you could. Your number one priority was to comfort that dying kid, which Stevie Rae and you did. I'm amazed you managed more than that. I wouldn't have thought to put up the barrier at all."

"Thanks. I appreciate you saying that. It's hard not to feel like a failure right now, though. The school phones are still clogged. Professor P and Lenobia are trying to handle them. Our House of Night servers crashed because they were flooded—mostly with 'righteous citizens defending the common decency of keeping demonic, Satan-worshipping

vampyres segregated from our good Christian children.'"
I air quoted. "And those are the nicer and less insane people.
I feel like I just managed to turn vampyre-human relations
back a century."

"It's crazy they don't ever see the irony of spewing hate
while they talk about what good Christians they are," said
Aphrodite.

"Seriously," I said, rolling my eyes.

"You've done nothing wrong, Zoey," Darius said. "The
difficult truth is there is always a chance a fledgling is going
to reject the Change. It cannot be predicted or stopped,
and with fledglings and humans mingling, logic dictates
that eventually humans are going to be witness to the death
of a fledgling. We live with that truth and I do not believe
it is a bad thing for humans to understand the reality
of it."

"Yep, that's what I was saying before you guys showed
up," said Stark. "What happened today was part of our
natural world. We aren't ashamed of it. We shouldn't have
to hide it from humans. Everyone knows not all fledglings
Change into adult vampyres, but because tradition and pre-
judice have segregated us from humans they have been able
to ignore it for generations—even though it has been their
brothers and sisters who have died. It's past time humans
pulled their entitled heads out of the sands."

"Or their asses," Aphrodite said.

"Yeah, I agree with both of you on that, but what about
our fledglings?" I asked the question that had been on my
mind since Kacie first coughed blood. "What is best for
them? To die surrounded by adult vampyres who understand
exactly what is happening and can help them transition to

Nyx in a peaceful, loving manner, or to be made a spectacle of by clueless, hysterical humans?"

"Well, as a vampyre who did reject the Change and die—and come back in a really crappy way—I vote to educate humanity. We are who we are," said Stark. "And we shouldn't apologize for it or hide from it. If that's uncomfortable for humans, then I can say that I have zero fucks to give about their issues."

"Yeah, humans are oh-so-quick to embrace vamps like Erik Night and a ton of other celebrities and artists, but they need to get some understanding of us beyond just 'ohmygod they are soooooo hawt!' Ugh. Just fucking ugh." Aphrodite scrunched up her face like something smelled bad.

Our conversation paused while the server brought our drinks, and then Stark asked, "What was the end result? Is the House of Night banned from all intramural sports with humans forever now?"

"They're undecided. I did mention that we're putting in an Olympic-size competition pool and that we would very much like to host big meets here on the House of Night campus—which totally stopped their arrogant tirade about pool safety," I said.

"*Pool safety?*" Aphrodite snorted. "Like anyone was in the least bit harmed except our fledgling *who died*?"

"Yeah, I started by pointing that out, but didn't get anywhere until I brought up the new facility."

"Humans are such greedy assholes," said Aphrodite.

"I wanted to tell them, 'Hey, I have a world I could send you to where vampyres have zero morals and they use all their powers to subjugate humans. How'd you like them apples?'" Stark, Aphrodite, and Darius were all staring at me like I'd soddenly kicked Nala. "Uh, I *didn't* say that to them."

"I kinda wish you had," said Stark.

"I more than kinda wish it," said Aphrodite.

"Well, I didn't have to say much of anything more after I mentioned the new pool we're building."

"We're seriously building an Olympic-size pool?" Stark asked.

I shrugged. "We have the money and the land. It's super hot here for, like, at least seven of the twelve months—so a pool sounds like a good idea. Plus, I realized something while we were sitting in those stands waiting for the meet to start. Well, before Kacie started coughing blood anyway. Our fledglings are missing out on their high school experience." I turned to Stark. "Think about Heath. What if he'd been Marked his sophomore year? His whole world was football. Sure, he could've funneled that into fencing or archery or hand-to-hand combat."

"Or knife training," Darius added.

"Yep, or that. And that would've been cool. Heath would've excelled—probably a lot like you have done, Stark."

"I wrestled before I was Marked. Placed third in State my freshman year. I was expected to be the first sophomore in my school to win State my sophomore year. Then I was Marked and that ended."

"How'd it make you feel?" I asked.

"At first I had too much to worry about what with becoming a vampyre and moving out of my home, having my family act like I was dead, and figuring out that I had this weird ability to literally always hit my mark with an arrow. But I missed wrestling. I've always been sorry that I didn't win State and have my name on that banner draped down the gym wall at my high school."

"Exactly!" I said. "Which is why I think the House of Night Ravens need sports teams that compete on a high school level with all the other teams in the area."

"You mean we'll actually have football, wrestling, track, and swimming?" Stark asked, unable to hide the teenage-boy excitement that spilled out of him.

"Yep," I grinned.

"And cheerleaders. That means cheerleaders too," Aphrodite said.

"Is that you volunteering to coach cheerleading?" I asked.

"Oh, hell no!"

"How about a dance squad?" I lifted my brows at her.

She opened and then closed her mouth. Sighed, and then mumbled, "Well, maybe. If I design the uniforms."

"Deal!" I said.

"Wait, I—"

The arrival of our food interrupted her and as we began to eat I asked, "So, I know Jack is hanging with the swim team and making sure they're okay, but from the absence of Damien I'm surmising that the depot is still stressing him out big time?"

Through a mouthful of tacos, Darius said, "I drove the red fledgling bus back to the tunnels after school and I saw him for just a moment. He was trying to decide between two shades of red for the linen tablecloths that I could detect absolutely no difference in. He asked me for my opinion. When I told him they looked the same to me it was like I'd said I couldn't tell the difference between a throwing dagger and an athame."

I glanced at Aphrodite and she mouthed: *big difference*.

"Huh. So yes, he's stressed."

"Yes," said Darius.

"Should I send help?" I asked.

Darius shrugged. "Honestly, I do not think so. It seems to be the kind of stress Damien thrives on, and he does have Toby Jenkins and that crew from the Equality Center working with him. It looks like chaos, but every time I go over there they have more and more done. I actually think he's going to open the restaurant on time."

"Well, I'll stay out of the way then," I said. "And it's a good thing everything is so peaceful right now. I mean except for our fledgling bleeding out in public today."

"Couldn't have been anticipated—couldn't have been prevented," Aphrodite said, and she nibbled her Cobb salad and sipped her flute of blood and champagne.

"Speaking of prevention," Stark began. "Detective Marx stopped by earlier today—"

"About the fledgling's death?" I felt my hackles rise. Marx was a cool human detective I'd worked with several times before, but if he'd come by to question us about Kacie's death we were going to have to have words.

"No. It was before that. He wanted to let us know that those freaks who worship Neferet have been sneaking into Woodward Park again and leaving offerings and notes for her."

"Wait—*notes*?" I said, almost choking on my spaghetti.

"Yeah. He brought one so I could pass it along to you." Stark pulled a small piece of paper from his jeans pocket. It was parchment colored and rolled up like a miniature scroll. It was even tied with a pretty black velvet ribbon. "They're all written in the same handwriting and they sound mostly like this. Marx said he'd email scanned copies of the rest of them to us."

I unrolled it. The note was written with what was obviously an old quill pen. I quickly read the elaborate handwriting. *"Hear our anger, mother Neferet, for your betrayal by the vampyres. We are here. We pray for your escape. We wait."*

"Who is *we*?" I asked

Stark shrugged. "Has to be humans. There are never any offerings or notes left from sunset to sunrise when the Sons of Erebus guard the tomb."

"Humans are fucking insane. Why do they have such short memories?" Aphrodite shook her head in frustration. "It was a year ago that Neferet took over the Mayo and declared herself Goddess of Tulsa. She killed almost everyone staying at that hotel."

"Not to mention the entire church full of people she and her disgusting snake children ate on the way there," Stark added.

"Seriously!" I said. "If Neferet escaped, the first thing she'd do would be to feed, and she sure as hell wouldn't be looking for vampyres to munch on."

"Right? Humans would be her avocado-toast appetizer to a main course of killing every vampyre she could get her claws into," Aphrodite said. "But still, *she'd eat them like toast* is the point they have somehow missed."

I was staring at the note and realized the quill had been dipped in ink that looked disturbingly like blood. Hesitantly I lifted it and sniffed it, wrinkling my nose. "What is that, squirrel blood?" I guessed.

"Marx had it analyzed. It's cat blood," Stark said somberly.

I gasped and almost dropped the note. "We need to notify the Sisters at Street Cats that someone is using cat blood as ink. It'd be tough to lure a House of Night feline away from here, but a stray could be captured."

"Or if they want to avoid the hassle they could just adopt from Street Cats," said Aphrodite, looking as sick as I felt. "I'll call them and leave a message, and then go by tomorrow. If they need extra help doing background checks is it okay that I volunteer a few fledglings to help out?"

"Of course," I said. "Stark, Darius, do either of you have any ideas about what we can do to stop this stupid romanticization of Neferet?"

"It's like those ridiculous women who still swoon about Ted Bundy," Aphrodite said. "Hello! Serial killer who bit, brutalized, and strangled women then had sex with their dead bodies. Reeeeal romantic." She shuddered. "Humans—just eew."

"Ted Bundy lived forever ago," said Stark.

"Bow Boy, watch a documentary or two. It's good for your brain."

"Do you have a suggestion about how to stop what's going on at Woodward Park?" I asked Aphrodite to shut her up.

"Short of declaring war on idiot humans like Other Neferet did? Sorry, but nope."

"I have an idea," said Stark. "We already have sunset to sunrise covered. What if, without telling even Marx and the TPD, we install some high-resolution cameras in the trees around the grotto? We'll get more of the kind we have here at the school. The ones that record continuously and broadcast the recording to our closed system."

"I like that idea. Sons of Erebus Warriors could take turns monitoring the cameras during the day, and when we see someone leaving notes like this we can dispatch a Warrior to track down the person."

"Then we check them out and decide if it's something the House of Night needs to handle," said Stark.

"Or something we turn over to Marx," I finished for him. "I like it. Get the cameras ordered and installed—secretly—ASAP. Anything else crazy going on?"

"That's about it. Shaunee and Erik returned to the NOLA House of Night just after sunset. She told me to tell you that she can be back in a flash if you need her," said Stark.

"Erik's back to filming something?"

"Yeah—that Superman thing," Stark said.

"Erik's still kinda douchey, but he does make one hell of a Superman," Aphrodite said.

"I think Shaunee is burning the douche out of him," I said.

Darius and Stark snorted together, which had Aphrodite and me laughing—until Stevie Rae rushed up to our booth. She was breathing hard and her cheeks were bright pink.

"Y'all need to come with me. Now."

"'Kay," I said. "What's up?" I wiped my mouth and gave my half-eaten plate of psaghetti one last longing look.

"It's Kacie. She's awake."

"Already? Doesn't it usually take a day or two for them to resuscitate?" Aphrodite said.

"Yeah. I've never known of a fledgling to come back in—" Stevie Rae glanced at the big bronze clock on the wall. "Less than eight hours. And that's not even the weirdest thing."

"What do you mean?" I asked as the four of us followed Stevie Rae to the infirmary.

"She woke up a fully Changed red vampyre," said Stevie Rae.

"That's crazy," I said.

"Oh, BFF, that's the least of the crazy. Just wait and see…"

Kacie was sitting up in her hospital bed watching the Netflix original *Northern Rescue* on her laptop when we knocked and then entered her room, leaving Stark and Darius to wait in the hallway. She glanced up at us and smiled as she recognized Aphrodite and me.

She still looked a little pale—but then I decided maybe it wasn't that she was unusually pale and instead the fact that her tattoo was so new that it looked almost neon against her light-brown skin. Stevie Rae hadn't been kidding (not that I'd expected that), but what I'd found hard to expect was what we were all staring at—a fully formed tattoo that was exquisitely beautiful. In the middle of Kacie's forehead was a crescent moon, the scarlet of fresh blood. From either side of the moon, her big dark eyes were framed by red bursts of waves that morphed into flames and back into waves again as they reached her cheekbones. It was fierce and gorgeous—a mask of magick as unique as the girl wearing it.

"Hi." Kacie sounded a lot more subdued than the girl who earlier that day had told me how much school sucked with endearing confidence.

I was trying to think of something profound to say when Aphrodite spoke.

"Hi, Ice Cream Shoes. Good to see you alive again."

"I have you to thank for that. So, thanks," Kacie said to Aphrodite.

At my side I felt Stevie Rae give a little startle of surprise, which made me glad of Aphrodite's next question.

"How did you know that?"

"You mean how did I know you gave me a second chance?"

"Yes," said Aphrodite, Stevie Rae, and me at the same time.

Kacie's eyes darted from Aphrodite to Stevie Rae and me, but she answered readily. "I'm not really sure. Trying to remember anything after Stevie Rae grabbed me in the pool is like trying to remember a dream. I get flashes, like the fact that I know you gave me a second chance and that's why I didn't stay dead."

"Accidentally," Aphrodite said.

I didn't chime in. I didn't tell Aphrodite to be nice. I trusted our Prophetess. There was an almost tangible sense of power in her voice—and I stayed silent to allow her to speak the truth.

Kacie's gaze slipped to the thick comforter stretched over her legs. "I'm sorry?"

"Don't be. Instead, live like your life is a gift from your Goddess, because it is."

Kacie's eyes filled with tears. "I will. I'll do my best to be sure my life makes a difference, and my best is damn good."

"I believe you, Ice Cream Shoes. And I expect you to prove me right."

"Show them what else," said Stevie Rae.

"Okay. I'm not super sure how," said Kacie.

"Just do what you did before," encouraged Stevie Rae.

"Okay. Here goes." Kacie sat up straighter, cleared her throat, and smoothed back her wild mass of curls. Then, in a steady, clear voice she said. "Man, I'm thirsty. I wish I had some water."

As soon as Kacie said the word *water* the room around us changed and for a moment it was hard to believe we weren't standing on the edge of the ocean, sandy beach beneath our feet and salty waves tickling them.

"Did she seriously just invoke water?" Aphrodite asked.

"She seriously did," I said.

Stark opened the door enough to poke his head inside the infirmary room. "What's up in there? We can smell the ocean."

"Our newly Changed red vampyre has a powerful affinity for water. Kacie, do you mind if Stark and Darius come in?" I asked the newly Changed fledgling.

"No, it's fine."

I motioned for Stark to come in, which he did with Darius following close behind. They remained nearer to the door than where Stevie Rae, Aphrodite, and I stood close to the hospital bed. We were all staring at Kacie. She'd picked up a full glass of water and sipped it—and I was 100 percent sure that glass had been empty before she said she was thirsty.

"So, I assume this is something new?" I asked Kacie.

"Totally," she said quickly.

"Show her the other one too," Stevie Rae said.

Other one?

"Okay, I'll just, er..." She fumbled with the bedspread nervously.

"Don't stress," soothed Stevie Rae. "Say what you did before. It'll be fine. Promise."

"All right." Kacie paused, gave a little shiver, rubbed her

arms and said, "Is it cold in here or am I still dead? Can we turn on some heat?"

Just like with water, the element's response was instantaneous. The room warmed by several degrees and was filled with the scent of a wood-burning fireplace.

"That's two," said Aphrodite. "What about the other three?"

Stevie Rae shook her head. "Nope. I invoked earth right away, and it didn't respond to Kacie at all."

"And I called to air and spirit, and nothing happened," added Kacie.

"So, fire and water. That's impressive," said Stark. "Congratulations."

"Thanks!" Kacie said, her cheeks starting to regain some pinkness.

"Did you have any premonition that you'd acquired an affinity for two elements when you woke up?" Aphrodite asked.

"You mean like the weird way I knew you'd given me a second chance?"

"Yeah, that's what I mean."

"Nope. I was as surprised as Stevie Rae," said Kacie. "But…" she began, then her face paled again and she closed her mouth so fast that her lips made a tight line across the bottom of her face.

"What is it?" I moved closer to her bed. "You can trust us, but if you'd rather just talk with Stevie Rae we'll—"

"No, we shouldn't leave," said Aphrodite. Then she shot me an apologetic look and spoke formally. "I'm sorry, High Priestess, but I shouldn't go. None of us should. Trust me."

"Always," I said. "Okay, Kacie, you heard our Prophetess. Tell us—she says we all need to hear it."

Kacie's fingers worried the comforter, but her voice was steady. "I felt different the second I woke up. At first, I thought it was normal, you know, for dying and then coming back, but the difference I feel isn't what Stevie Rae talked to me about—like it's normal to feel extra tired for a few days, and also I might be really hungry for, um, blood. Way worse than when I was a blue fledgling."

"What's the difference then? How do you feel?" I asked.

"Like she has a purpose."

Aphrodite's words caused Kacie's body to jerk in surprise.

"Yeah, that's it. How did you know?" Kacie said.

Aphrodite shrugged. "I *am* a Prophetess."

"Who usually gets visions. Did you have a vision about this?" I asked—already knowing the answer.

"If I had I would've told you right away—and I would've been blinded by blood and pain," said Aphrodite. "This is different. Something is happening here. Her fully formed tattoo—her powerful affinity for fire and water—all of it is a sign."

"Of what?" I asked.

Aphrodite shook her head. "I can't tell yet. I do have a superstrong premonition that something—"

"Is coming," Kacie interrupted. "Something... or some-*one*."

"With the strength of a tidal wave," Aphrodite said.

"And the force of an explosion," Kacie finished for her.

"Yes. That's it exactly," said Aphrodite.

"Ah, hell," I said.

16

Other Neferet

"Fire and water—my two favorite elements," said Neferet as she lifted the oil lantern and allowed its flame to play across the smooth loch. "What is stronger than a tidal wave and fiercer than an explosion?"

"You, my lady!" Lynette blurted.

Neferet's smile was a gift of beauty and warmth. "Dear Lynette, you have made these five nights so much more pleasant than I could've imagined. I will not forget your loyalty."

"But, my lady, that sounds like you're leaving. I—I don't understand. I thought you were making the sprites come to you."

"Shh!" Neferet turned so that her back was to the loch, and lowered her voice, putting her head close to Lynette's. "Oh, they will come to me. Of that I am quite certain. But, my dear, the point of all of this is that I gain entrance to that island behind us."

"But I assumed I would be going with you."

"That would not be wise, and I do not believe you would want to see what it is I must do there."

"You mean become immortal?" Lynette whispered. "Is it going to be bloody, or unattractive or frightening?"

"As I am not a goddess—yet—I cannot answer you, but it was not my immortality to which I was referring. The island is currently occupied by a queen who isn't courageous enough to become immortal, so I believe it is time to remove her from her throne and replace her with someone braver."

"You, of course, my lady."

"Of course. And that removal will most definitely be bloody and unattractive and quite possibly frightening—though not for me."

"Is that why you're not going out there naked tonight, because you're not coming back? I didn't realize. Are there other things I need to bring out here for you? Forgive me! I am not prepared."

"Oh, my dear, no. I do not believe for one moment the sprites will allow me entrance so easily—or at least not *secret* entrance so easily. I am going to take the advice of a—hum, let us call him a friend—and instead of offering to pay a sacrificial price to the sprites for access to the isle and for their secrecy, I am going to tell them that I will complete a quest for entrance."

"So, you'll come back tonight like the four other nights?"

Neferet studied her handmaid. It was clear that the woman was truly concerned. "It would upset you if I didn't?"

"Yes!"

Neferet touched her cheek softly. "Do not fear. I shall always return to my first and most favored handmaid. Now, it is time. How do I look?" She turned slowly for Lynette.

"You look like you have already attained immortality. It's hard to believe a mortal could be so beautiful. That dress is absolutely perfect."

"You made an excellent choice." Neferet smoothed the flawless black material down her body. The dress was simple —a floor-length black gown that hugged every curve and pooled with a long train at her feet. The neckline was high and the only skin visible was her left shoulder and arm, which the asymmetrical bodice left bare, and her long, graceful neck. Lynette had piled Neferet's thick auburn hair on top of her head so that every inch of her neck was visible. The only jewelry she wore that night was a large silver pentagram that rested just above her breasts. The effect was startlingly sensuous without being vulgar.

"I was shocked I found something adequate in Inverness. The town definitely has a shortage of couture shops." Lynette sniffed delicately, as if Inverness had left a bad smell with her.

"And it was your idea to coif my hair up tonight." Neferet patted the flattering updo.

"It is lovely. You should wear it up more. It makes your neck look like a swan's," Lynette assured her.

"Yes, I believe it does." Neferet's fingers stroked her skin. Then she became all business. "Now, give me the tray with my offerings."

Lynette had placed the tray near their feet while they'd been talking, and she bent to pick it up as Neferet lifted the lantern and began picking her now familiar way across the rocky beach to the waterline.

"Your offerings are different tonight than the other four nights," Lynette said as they reached the loch and Neferet took the tray from her that held four bowls.

"That is because each offering was found and collected by me. It is personal tonight and I want the mighty sprites to understand how serious I am about courting their affection." Neferet spoke in a clear, strong voice, signaling that she understood they were being overheard and was choosing her words carefully.

Lynette took her cue readily and asked, "I know each offering has a meaning, though I'm only a human and can't begin to understand what they are."

"Dear Lynette, I can easily explain. I shall begin with my two favorite elements, fire and water." Neferet pointed to the bowl that held a strangely shaped rock. "The dragon head symbolizes fire."

"Oh, I see it now! It does look like a dragon."

"Of course it does. And in this bowl is all the sea glass I've collected over the past five days. Sea glass symbolizes water and shows that element's power to mold and change things at will."

"The feathers must be for air," Lynette stroked one of the elegant white quills. "What bird is it from?"

"A swan. No other feather would do. And this gorgeous piece of Skye marble symbolizes earth." Neferet pointed at an almost perfectly round, fist-sized piece of white marble that glistened lazily whenever the light from Neferet's lantern touched it. "And, of course, this loaf of Mrs. Muir's freshly baked sourdough bread honors all the elements. Though I did not bake it I believe the sprites will appreciate that I offer it to them.

"It smells delicious," Lynette said. "Everything seems perfect." She glanced over her shoulder at Balmacara Mains where Mrs. Muir, Noreen, and wee Denise had taken up their nightly position on the porch to stand witness to Neferet's glory. "They're watching, as usual."

"Good. Though they live so close to the purest, most powerful form of magick in the world, these past nights they have witnessed more magick than during their lifetimes."

"They're really very lucky," said Lynette as she fussed with a stray strand of Neferet's auburn hair that had fallen loose.

"Yes, yes they are," Neferet said. "I shall return shortly, dear Lynette."

"Your feeder will be ready for you," Lynette assured her.

"Excellent. I have a feeling I will be ravenous." Neferet balanced the tray on her left hip and held the lantern aloft in her right hand. She turned to face the dark loch. "Children, make yourselves visible!"

The night around Neferet came alive as tar-colored tendrils of Darkness materialized. They slithered over one another, each vying to get closer to Neferet.

"Carry your mother to the center of the loch!"

The tendrils hurried to obey, forming a living raft that Neferet strode, barefoot, onto. They didn't have to be told on this fifth night to anchor her legs—to hold her tightly and safely. They glided out onto the surface of the loch, supporting her with loving care.

The loch was black glass. Dark and still, it appeared bottomless. Neferet ignored the creepiness of the night. Fear was for lesser beings and not a future goddess.

As on the four previous nights, Neferet motioned for her children to stop midway across the loch. Facing Skye, she placed the lantern at her feet gently, allowing her children time to properly secure it. Then she stood, holding the bowl filled with carefully gathered swan feathers.

"Sprites of olde! Spirits of earth, sea, fire, and air!
As is proper—as is right—I greet you on this
    magick fifth night.
I begin with air—bringing you offerings rare and fair!"

Neferet flicked her wrist, tossing the swan feathers above her. A sudden gust of wind caught them and lifted them up, up, up until they were completely out of sight. Satisfied, she took from the next bowl the rock that looked like a dragon's head with its mouth open, breathing fire.

"Fire, I honor your power at this dark hour!"

Neferet threw the rock as hard as she was able, like she was trying to reach the distant isle. With a sound like a lightning strike, the rock exploded in a burst of golden fire.

Neferet's full lips tilted up.

Next, she carefully poured the sea glass from the bowl into her hand.

"For water I offer this glass, once strong and still—
    now molded by your greater will!"

Neferet threw the handful of glass up and there was a shattering as it exploded and uncountable shards began to rain down on her. Neferet did not move. She did not cringe or command her children to shield her—and the shards fell all around her, missing her body completely as the water lapped them up.

She took the last bowl that held the oval of Skye marble in one hand and the loaf of fragrant bread in another. Then, as she bent and placed both gently on the surface of the loch, Neferet intoned,

> *"Ancient grains and marble perfect and white; I return*
> *both to blessed earth this night!"*

Instead of drifting away, the bowl holding the marble and the loaf of bread floated in front of the raft of tendrils like Neferet had placed them on a table. Suddenly they were sucked under the surface as if they had been tethered to the earth far below and someone had just pulled on that tether line. Neferet straightened and held her arms aloft, embracing the distant island.

> *"On this fifth night I seek one thing honest and true*
> *To meet air, fire, water, earth—each of you.*
> *I honor your traditions—old and wise,*
> *Ignored by mortals—forgotten, unrecognized.*
> *I ask with love and respect*
> *That my plea you do not neglect.*
> *I vow to cleave to olde ways; I shall never forget*
> *See me—hear me—greet me! I am Neferet!"*

Neferet had been determined to stand there in the middle of the loch, in the deep of the night, for as long as it took for the sprites to respond to her—even should that mean she waited until dawn. But her wait was less than the drawing of a deep breath. The night bloomed into life around her.

From the loch, water sprites broke the surface. They were brightly colored creatures—none bigger than Neferet's forearm—that looked like they were the product of miniature people mating with ocean creatures. Neferet didn't think she'd ever seen so many bizarrely placed fins and flippers.

Above her, more sprites burst into view and flitted around the sky on gossamer wings that framed humanoid bodies. With a crackle that reminded Neferet of the sound a log makes being consumed in a hearthfire, sprites that glowed joined the air fey so that the night around Neferet was lit by magickal fireflies the size of kittens.

Finally, there was a rush of wind that came directly from the island. It carried the scents of heather and newly plowed fields. The elementals that rode that wind swayed like leaves dancing in the breeze. They too were mostly humanoid with skin reminiscent of bark and hair formed from ferns and ivy. Leading them was a being larger and more fully humanoid than the others. Neferet felt a jolt of shock that she hid as she recognized Oak—the sprite that the vampyre calling herself Zoey Redbird had negotiated with at the stadium— the sprite who had led the others in returning humanity to the Red Army.

Neferet disliked her already and silently promised herself that one of her first acts as a goddess would be to repay this fey for her meddling.

But Neferet wasn't immortal yet, so she tilted her head in a slight bow of greeting.

"Merry meet, Oak. I did not expect to see you here."

"I see you Neferet and I greet you."

Then the sprite went silent, her big eyes trained on Neferet. The vampyre quickly decided that what she had intended to say to the sprites wouldn't be wise now. This sprite knew her—had already said that she knew Neferet had not followed Nyx for decades. So Neferet threw off the mantle of half lies and prevarications she had planned to use to coax the sprites into doing her will.

"I see you and happily greet you too, Oak. I am glad it is you speaking for the sprites."

"Why would seeing me again cause you gladness?"

"Because it was your actions that turned me to the path that led me here. When you called the Red Army an abomination and returned their humanity to them I understood my mistake, and I came here to correct it."

Again, Oak said nothing. She simply hovered silently as the other elementals flew around her, no longer gamboling playfully; the tension between the sprite and Neferet had acted like a mute button. The vampyre, now thoroughly annoyed by the sprite's behavior, kept a careful hold on her temper and continued.

"My mistake is the same one being made over and over again in the modern world." Then it was Neferet's turn to wait silently, patiently, while the sprite's indifference warred with her curiosity.

As Neferet had anticipated, Oak's curiosity won.

"And what mistake is that?"

"Being ignorant of the ancient ways."

Oak cocked her head, birdlike. "For many centuries the wielding of Old Magick has been discouraged."

"Yes, I know. That is the mistake I mean to correct. I present myself to you and the rest of the sprites as a student of the ancient ways. Old Magick has been shunned for far too long."

"You do this with the approval of Nyx?"

"Nyx gave no edict warning vampyres from using Old Magick, correct?" Neferet held her breath waiting for Oak's response. She was fairly certain the Goddess had not set forth any rules against Old Magick. Not that Neferet would've heeded or even paid attention to any such rules.

"*Correct. The taboo against Old Magick came from Sgiach many centuries ago when she formally declared herself Queen of Skye, the Great Taker of Heads, and Protectress of Old Magick.*"

Relief flooded Neferet. "Protectress or jailer?"

"*No one jails us!*" Oak's sharp teeth glistened.

"Well, it is true you come and go as you wish, but are you remembered? Understood? Honored?"

"*Here and there offerings are still left for us, especially in the Highlands.*"

"Bowls of cream like you are cats?" Neferet made a rude noise. "That is not the proper way to honor such as you. Would you not like more?"

All around Oak the sprites stopped their muted play and skewered Neferet with their sharp, intelligent eyes.

"*Humans do not like us—nor are we overly fond of them.*" Oak smiled fiercely, exposing more of her pointed fangs. "*And they infest the modern world.*"

"What if humans no longer had a say in whether you're liked or not? What if vampyres became your protectors—on and off Skye—and they were educated about Old Magick and the fey—how to honor both—how to remember both—how to wield both?"

"*Interesting... though the Great Taker of Heads would never agree.*"

"I wasn't aware that you had to obey Queen Sgiach."

Oak's dark eyes appeared to expand—as did her mouth and the razor-tipped fangs she bared at Neferet. "*Sprites are not ruled by queens!*"

"Then you also are not loyal to them," Neferet said. "If Sgiach no longer reigned there," gracefully, she gestured to the distant island, "what would that mean to you?"

"That a younger, stronger queen usurped her throne."

"And that would be fine with you?"

"We only interfere in mortal affairs when abominations exist." The sprite moved her moss-covered shoulders in dismissal. *"We care not who sits on the throne of Skye. So, that is what you ask of us—that you are allowed entrance to Skye to study us and to usurp Sgiach."*

"You're partially correct. I would study you elementals, but also Old Magick in general. As to Sgiach—I would prefer to avoid her completely while at my studies. Your queen and her people should not know I am on the island."

"Again, Neferet—fallen High Priestess of Nyx—sprites have no queen."

Neferet bowed her head, hiding her victorious smile. "Apologies. I will not make the same mistake again."

"You speak with power and guile, but what payment do you propose to make for entrance to our isle?"

Neferet felt a rush of emotion as the sprite's voice fell into the singsong cadence that signaled the fey's willingness to make a deal.

"For studying on the island in privacy—"

"Ssssecrecy." The sprite hissed the word ominously.

Neferet shrugged nonchalantly. "Semantics. For studying on the island secretly, I offer a favor."

"Favor? Payment that is not. Return when our price demand is not an afterthought."

Oak turned away, but Neferet's silky voice drew her back.

"Yes, favor—and that favor would be *more* than a simple payment of blood or jewels or even a hecatomb of cattle." Neferet loosed her own fierceness and she felt her children swell in response, causing her living raft to create waves in the loch. "In the future, when I have supplanted Sgiach and control vampyres and humans alike I will open Skye's gates and grant you freedom in *any* land I rule. I will make my own edict, and it will be that Old Magick is revered as it should be and wielded by those wise enough—brave enough—strong enough."

Neferet had every sprite's attention. They hovered around the raft, bathing it in preternatural brilliance.

"That is the favor I will grant should you agree to hide my presence from Sgiach. But to gain access to the isle itself I must, of course, pay—by amusing you."

At the words *amusing you* the demeanor of the sprites changed again. They wriggled around Oak, darting here and there, reminding Neferet of jubilant puppies.

Neferet had never particularly liked dogs of any type—especially not urinating, defecating puppies.

"Amusing? It cannot be seen what you could possibly mean."

Neferet wanted to shout her victory as Oak's words fell back into a rhyming pattern. Instead she smiled graciously and continued.

"Give me a task to complete—a quest to finish—a riddle to solve. I will do any and all simply to amuse you!"

The sprites rushed to Oak, swarming her as they chattered with trills and clicks and whistles. Neferet watched and waited—sure now of her success.

Oak lifted one hand and made a cutting motion. Every

sprite went silent. Then she met Neferet's gaze and spoke the binding words that meant the fey agreed to her terms.

"Here is what you must do
to be allowed entrance to our isle, secret and true.
Two tasks you must complete—
Difficult and bittersweet.
To move forward in the present as you ask
You must first kill your future and past.
Do you agree to this deal between thee and me?"

"I agree between thee and me," Neferet's voice filled the air around them.

"Then our deal is sealed—so mote it be!"

"So mote it be!" Neferet echoed.

With a sound like wind whipping through autumn leaves, the sprites dissipated, leaving Neferet alone with her children.

"Return me to land my darlings. We have much to do and much more to celebrate!"

As the living raft swung around Neferet reached up and loosed her hair so that it flew around her like flame—almost as bright and beguiling as the vampyre's victory smile.

Lynette's cheeks blazed bright pink as she rushed to Neferet, wrapping her in a cashmere robe and helping her into the slippers the vampyre preferred.

"They came!"

"Just as I knew they would." Neferet kept her voice low. She linked arms with Lynette as they started back across the deserted beach. "And now we have much to do. Dismiss my feeder for the night. I am entirely too busy to play with my food. Instead open one of his veins, fill a goblet and then pay him and send him on his way."

"Yes, my lady."

"I'm going to my room to change. Have Mrs. Muir lay out bread, wine, and cheese—and whatever you'd like to eat."

"If you agree I will insist Denise stays up, ready to serve you."

"Lynette, you think of everything. Yes, please do. And while I am changing I want you to begin puzzling this riddle. To move forward in the present, I must kill my past and my future."

"I thought they would send you on a quest. Like, perhaps, a dangerous scavenger hunt. This riddle seems mundane for creatures made from magick and the elements." Lynette sniffed delicately.

"I am inclined to agree with you. They are no more than sentient elements. How much of the world could they truly know?"

"Not as much as you, my lady."

"Exactly! Let us make short work of their riddle. But first, get me that goblet of blood. I am famished."

17

Other Lynette

"So, we need to think symbolically," Lynette said as she divided her attention between her laptop and her mistress.

"I cannot literally kill my past or my future because neither are tangible, nor do they exist in the present. It seems logical that I must find an individual who represents my past, and another who represents my future—and then deal with the literal part of the riddle and kill them."

Neferet sighed and sipped her goblet of mixed blood and wine. They were in the sitting room of Balmacara Mains that the vampyre had turned into her private space. Wee Denise came and went silently, making sure the fire burned cheerfully and their glasses were never empty. Even though they had been working at figuring out the riddle all night, and it was now well into midmorning, they were still at it.

Lynette didn't mind the late hours at all. She enjoyed her alone time with Neferet, especially *this* Neferet who could conjure the fey from a seemingly empty night and manipulate them into doing her bidding, and then curl up with her in front of the fire and work together like Lynette was no different—no less magical—than any other vampyre or High Priestess—or even goddess.

"It makes me wish I'd just brought a suitable sacrifice so we didn't have to deal with all of this." Neferet sighed again and waved her long, slender fingers at Lynette and her ever-present computer.

Lynette peeked up over the top of the laptop. "I know you're anxious to get to the island and begin your studies and we will figure this out—soon. But I hope you don't mind that I tell you I've enjoyed every moment of the time we've had together, with just the two of us. I—I don't mean to be impertinent." She cast her eyes down, afraid she'd been too familiar.

"Dear Lynette! It makes my heart lighter to hear you say that. I have enjoyed our time here too, and that is entirely due to you and your vast managerial skills. Do not fret. You will have many years by my side. There will be a very special place in my court for my original, and favorite, handmaid."

"Thank you, my lady. That gives me great comfort." And it also lets me know that I'm going to have to figure out a way to remind you that you've granted me a retirement of luxury on the Amalfi Coast.

But Lynette wouldn't worry about her endgame at that moment. For now, she was still in the game and playing it as she has played it her whole adult life—to win.

"So, where were we?"

"You must kill your past. That's where we started," said Lynette. She'd decided a few days ago that keeping Neferet on task took up more than half of her job. *It's a good thing I'm so highly organized*, she thought smugly as she searched the internet for symbolism examples—past and future.

"We know it's most likely *not* a place or Oak wouldn't have said that I need to kill it."

"Then that rules out doing something to the Tulsa House of Night—or the House of Night you went to after you were Marked," said Lynette.

"I agree, though it is a shame. I would very much enjoy watching either the Tulsa House of Night, or my alma mater, the Chicago House of Night, burn to the ground."

"Something you should consider after you become a goddess," said Lynette.

"Make a note of that in my to-do list, please," said Neferet.

"Of course, my lady." Lynette expertly opened her calendar and added another bizarre reminder. This one read: *Neferet wants to burn to the ground the Tulsa and Chicago HoNs. Remind her. Encourage her. It makes her happy.* Then, as Lynette returned to her research, she muttered, more to herself than to the vampyre, "I know how I'd kill *my* past. I'd get rid of each of my three useless ex-husbands. It'd kill the past—be enjoyable for me—*and* be a gift to society."

"Lynette! That is it!"

"You were married?"

"No, of course not. High Priestesses do not give away their power for social conventions, but I do take frequent lovers. So, if you could kill your past by getting rid of your three—" Neferet paused. Her brow lifted to her hairline. "You did say *three* husbands, did you not?"

"I did. I used to be a slow learner."

"I'm so glad you got over that."

"I also got over the notion that I needed a man to be successful," said Lynette.

Neferet scoffed. "It is quite the opposite. It is much easier for a strong, intelligent woman to find success if she is not shackled to a man—something human women seem to have a difficult time understanding."

"You should make educating human women part of your platform when you are Goddess of Night," said Lynette.

"You are correct. Think of how many men would simply be unable to function if they didn't have women orchestrating their lives and running their homes." The vampyre clapped her hands together gleefully. "Oh, do make a note of that idea, Lynette! And put yourself in charge of the education program."

"It is done—and thank you, my lady." That's right Lynette. Keep making yourself indispensable.

"Where were we?"

"You were talking about killing a lover from your past," Lynette said helpfully.

"Ah, right you are, but not any lover will do. I need someone who symbolizes my past as High Priestess of Tulsa's House of Night."

"What of your Sword Master? I believe his name is Artus."

"He would be perfect, but he was killed by Stark that terrible day at the stadium. His death has been entirely inconvenient," said Neferet.

I'm sure for him too, Lynette thought, but she said, "Did you have a special lover? Maybe someone who was important to the House of Night—or at least to Tulsa's House of Night."

"James Stark comes to mind, but we never had a true connection. His tedious sense of morality was a barrier between us."

"Okay, someone important like General Stark, but morally bankrupt—or at least morally ambiguous."

Neferet sat up straight. "Loren Blake! He and I have been lovers for the past several years. I even named him Vampyre Poet Laureate, a position that has been of traditional importance to the vampyre community for centuries!"

"My lady, he sounds perfect!" Lynette's fingers flew over the keyboard.

"He does, indeed. How shall I do it? Perhaps I could send him a gift. He really isn't very bright, especially not for a poet. He wouldn't think to be concerned if, say, his favorite dark roast coffee from Café du Monde suddenly was delivered as a gift with a basket of beignets. He'd devour all of it—immediately."

Lynette glanced up from her computer. "Poison?"

"That would be the easiest way. Of course, it could get messy, though Loren isn't known for his generosity, so I doubt that he would share." Neferet tapped her chin as she considered. "But would the sprites be bothered if a few other vampyres died with him?"

"It is hard to know for sure, my lady."

"True. Though it is a risk I am more than willing to take. Perhaps if I send only a couple beignets and a small sample of coffee he would not share at all."

Lynette's attention was suddenly caught by one of the responses from her search of Loren Blake's name and she clicked on it, bringing up Blake's Instagram account. As she read the last story she had to stop herself from jumping up and shouting in victory.

"Lynette? Lynette! Where is your mind? I asked you to express order from the Café du Monde site."

She met Neferet's gaze and saw the irritation there change as the vampyre recognized the excitement in Lynette's eyes.

"My dear? What is it?"

"What would you say if Loren Blake would come to you?"

"Here? I would say the last thing I need is the Tulsa House of Night knowing where I am. Have you become ill? How could you forget that?"

"Forgive me, my lady. I should not be coy about something of such import."

"Be clear, Lynette!"

"Yes, of course. I found Loren Blake's Instagram account, and from his last story it is obvious that he does not like the changes at the House of Night, *and* he misses you."

"Whatever do you mean?"

"Earlier today he posted this poem." Lynette read, "Silenced unfairly/Muted by cowardly fools/I miss her fierceness."

"Lynette! He speaks of me!"

"As well as the current House of Night administration. He calls them cowards. My lady, the poem received several thousand likes!"

"I knew it. I knew not all of my followers would betray me."

"Of course they wouldn't, my lady!"

"Give me your phone, dear Lynette. I need to make a call to Tulsa."

Lynette took her phone from the end table beside her and handed it to Neferet. "What are you going to do?"

"Simple. Thanks to your nimble brain I am going to lure Loren Blake to London, where I will kill him. Isn't it wonderful?"

"Yes, it is, my lady. I live to serve you." She curtsied low as Neferet began tapping in numbers.

Another win for me, she thought. And I will keep winning,

*especially now that I am allied with someone who under-
stands what is most important in life—power—and the safety
it affords. Choosing to follow this vampyre who will soon
be immortal and rule the world was the smartest decision I
ever made.*

Other Neferet

Loren answered on the third ring. "Loren Blake speaking."

Unbeknownst to him, Neferet put him on speaker so that
she and Lynette could hover around the phone and share
looks like the coconspirators they were. She pitched her
voice so that she sounded young, frightened, and terribly
needy—all the things the Vampyre Poet Laureate loved.
"Loren! Dearest! It is I! Are you alone? Can you speak without being overheard?"

There was a pause of several seconds—long enough for
Neferet to roll her eyes and begin tapping her fingernails
restlessly on the crystal goblet wee Denise had just refilled.
She almost hung up, but then Loren's voice whispered desperately back to her.

"Neferet? My one true love? It is really you?"

Relief washed over Neferet, and Lynette fist-pumped
silently in victory. "Yes! Can you talk? I need you desperately!"

"Yes, yes! I'm in Nyx's Temple. No one else is here right
now because everyone is doing something meaningful.
My love, that terrible bitch Anastasia kicked me out of the
school Council meeting, forced me to pray practically non-

stop in Nyx's Temple—you know how damp and boring this place is—*and she took away my title of Poet Laureate*."

Neferet smiled smoothly, though her voice did not reflect her pleasure. "No! She has no right! You were justly named Poet Laureate by me. I am the only High Priestess who can remove you."

"That's what I thought as well. I was just considering sending a strongly worded letter to the Vampyre High Council."

Neferet had to squelch the desire to tell him how utterly impotent and ridiculous he was. Instead she said, "The Vampyre High Council is a governing body as obsolete as flip phones and VHS tapes. It is past time those dinosaurs went extinct."

"My love, do you have a plan to get rid of them?"

"Don't I always have a plan?"

"Just hearing your voice is balm to my battered soul. It has been awful here since you left. Anastasia and her ilk want to make peace with the humans. Can you believe it?"

"I can. But that is something we can discuss when you get here."

"Where are you? I shall come immediately! 'I love you with so much of my heart that none is left to protest!'"

Neferet and Lynette shared disgusted looks. Neferet mouthed *Shakespeare quote*, and Lynette rolled her eyes.

"Here is what you must do. Leave the school immediately. Go straight to the Tulsa airport. Speak to no one. Tell no one where you are going. It would be best if no one sees you leave."

"My love, I can be as silent as the night!"

"I know you can, dearest. I am counting on your discretion and ability to blend with a crowd."

Lynette lifted her laptop and silently pointed at Loren's profile picture, which looked like a Hollywood headshot and was anything but discrete.

Neferet had to cover her mouth to hold back her laughter.

"My love, for you I would take on the world!"

"That means more to me than I can say, but today all I need you to take is the first available flight to London. When you arrive at Heathrow get a cab to the Covent Garden Hotel." Neferet motioned for Lynette to take notes, which she did swiftly and silently. "I will text you my suite number. Do not stop at the front desk. When you arrive, come directly to my chamber as I can hardly wait to be in your arms again."

"I shall! And I will text you my arrival time at Heathrow as soon as I book my flight."

"Dearest, please remember that you must travel with the utmost secrecy."

"I know! I know!" His voice dropped to a ridiculous whisper. "They've put out a reward for your capture—one hundred thousand dollars."

"Yes, dearest, I am aware of that. I am also insulted that the amount is so low."

"Well, there are many Warriors who would still follow you. Shall I tell them that you—"

"Loren! What did I just say about being discrete?"

Lynette put her face in her hands and shook her head in disgust.

"Oh, right. Sorry. I tend to be overexuberant."

Hastily Lynette typed, HE TENDS TO BE A BRAYING ASS! on her laptop and turned it to Neferet so she could see. Neferet hid her laughter with a cough.

"My love! Are you ill? Great Britain is so damp, especially this time of year. Are we remaining there, or are we, perhaps, traveling to a more hospitable climate?"

"We will definitely not be staying in London," Neferet prevaricated. "Now, I must go. Come swiftly, dearest! I await your embrace!"

"My own true darling, 'For your sweet love remembered such wealth brings, that then I scorn to change my state with kings!'"

Neferet couldn't bear anymore. She hung up before he could steal anything else from Shakespeare.

"Is he always like that?" Lynette asked.

"You mean a tedious bore who isn't entirely bright?"

"I do."

"Yes. But he is also exquisitely handsome and knows how to perform magick with his tongue."

"At least he has a purpose."

"Indeed. And right now, his purpose is to die, killing my past with him."

"I assume I am to book you into the Covent Garden Hotel?" Lynette asked.

"No, you are to book yourself into the hotel. You need not worry about getting caught. Humans do not care about vampyre deaths, so you won't have any issues from Scotland Yard."

"And very shortly you will be Goddess of Night, reigning over all vampyres, so I won't have to worry about issues from them, either."

"Exactly. But we will be cautious. I need time to become immortal, and it would not do to be caught before then. Get a regular suite. Nothing too expensive. Nothing to draw too much attention. You are a successful American business-woman who is in London for a short vacation."

"How short? How many nights should I reserve the suite?"

"Well, he'll probably be here sometime tomorrow. Book it for five nights, checking in tomorrow. We will not actually be staying for even one night."

"I assume we leave no trail from here to London and back?"

"Correct. Hire a car with cash. The same discrete service you used when we arrived."

"Yes, my lady."

"I wonder what will be the best way for me to do it? I won't use my children. London's House of Night will notify the Tulsa House of Night as soon as Loren's body is identified, and they would recognize the similarities in the kills from Tulsa. Lynette, I'm going to need a dagger. Something small, but lethal. And I will also need a small amount of poison in case that method will be easier than stabbing—" Neferet stopped speaking as Denise entered the parlor.

"Mistress, might I get ye anythin'?"

"I believe Lynette would take some coffee, wouldn't you, my dear?"

"Yes, please," Lynette said without looking up from her computer.

"And open another bottle of this excellent red. Also, call my feeder back. Lynette and I have a short journey to take, and I'd like to eat before we go."

"Aye, my lady." Denise curtsied, and then she hesitated, looking awkward and unsure of herself.

"What is it?" Neferet asked.

"I dinnae mean to be a bother, but I overheard ye. I can get ye as much poison as ye need from my auld grannie. Just tell me how you'd like the person to sicken or die."

"Your mistress didn't ask you for any such thing."

"Och no, of course Herself didnae." Denise curtsied again and began to hurry from the room.

"Wait." Neferet's voice stopped her. "You understand if you ever told anyone that you gave me poison I would deny it, and then I would kill you."

"Aye, mistress. I do."

"And yet you still offer."

"Aye. I ken you'd kill anyone who betrayed ye. I widnae. Ever."

"But can't the poison be traced back to your grandmother?" Lynette asked.

"Aye, and also aboot a thousand auld grannies in the Highlands."

"But why would you put yourself and your grandmother at risk at all for Neferet?"

Denise blinked in surprise. "Because I believe in her." She went to Neferet and stood nervously before the vampyre. "Mistress, I think you're pure dead brilliant. Whatever it is yer plannin'—whatever it is yer becommin'—take me with ye. I would serve you till the end of my days." Denise dropped to her knees and bowed her head.

Neferet gently lifted the girl to her feet and kissed her on each cheek and then softly on the mouth. "Henceforth, you shall be in my service. From now until the day you die. You are also under my protection. I take care of those loyal to me. And I shall take you up on your generous offer. I will need a lethal poison that dissolves easily in wine—champagne to be specific. It needs to be fast acting, but not *too* fast. Give the poison to Lynette. We'll be leaving for our short trip at dusk."

"Yes, my lady." Denise curtsied deeply and hurried from the room.

"You trust her?" Lynette asked.

"Strangely, I do. And whether her reasons for swearing herself to me are self-serving or altruistic, I trust that she fears me enough not to betray me," said Neferet. "Make the arrangements. I'll need mundane clothes, though I cannot look like a peasant in London, so nothing I wear here will do. I know. Get me *jeans*."

"Are you sure, my lady?"

Neferet shuddered. "It's a sacrifice I'm willing to make. But also get me an exquisite cashmere sweater. And, sadly, dark glasses and a hat. Oh, and I will need makeup to cover my Mark."

"Absolutely," Lynette said as she made notes.

"But first, call that feeder. Give him a couple shots of single malt and send him to my room. I am famished."

18

Other Kevin

Kevin was sitting on the bottom stair of the porch of the boys' dormitory, thinking how glad he was Dragon had asked him to hang around the dorm tonight, because he didn't think he could bear going back to his room, which wasn't really *his* room. It was hers, and she wasn't there anymore, which meant it wasn't a room at all. It was a reminder of what he'd lost—what he could never have again.

He felt guilty. Lots of vampyres would love to change places with him—to have been given permission to live in the professors' quarters of the House of Night without actually being a professor, and he was grateful. But the quarters he'd been given were Aphrodite's. They were haunted with her things—her scent, her clothes, her memories—the ghost of her love. And just then he felt too raw to deal with ghosts.

"I thought you had a big, fancy room over in the professors' quarters. Why you slummin' over here?"

Dallas kicked the bottom stair, narrowly missing Kevin's thigh.

"Dragon asked me to keep an eye on the red fledglings and vamps—and to be obvious about it. So, that's what I'm doing."

"Tell me somethin'—why shouldn't we let 'em fry themselves? And I'm not bein' a jerk. I'm serious. You're the only red vamp I know who is even close to normal, and I know a bunch of 'em. Isn't it meaner to keep them alive when they don't want to be than it is to just let nature take its course?"

"Like suicide is natural?" Kevin made no attempt to hide his disgust.

"No, but what I mean is we should just let them do what they want to do. *That's* natural."

"*That's* barbaric," said Kevin.

Dallas shrugged. "They say war is too, but we're in the middle of one."

"No, we're in the middle of a truce, trying to figure out a peaceful way to move forward."

"Yeah, that's what they keep sayin'. Whatever. Can you honestly tell me you like the way Tulsa is now better than when the war was going on?"

Kevin stared at Dallas. *This is exactly what Blake was talking about when he threw his fit in the Council meeting. It's people like Dallas who miss the war and want to keep it going.* "Yeah, I can honestly tell you that I like the Tulsa where rabid red vampyres *aren't* terrorizing the people and Neferet *isn't* leading us into an apocalypse."

Dallas snorted. "Apocalypse? Get real. Maybe for humans, but not for us. From where I stand, it was lots fucking better not to have to bow down to humans for a change. Even now, only about a third of the Utica Square businesses decided to stay open late for us—even though we sure as hell spend more money there than humans."

"Really? I didn't know you shopped at Saks and ate at

restaurants like the Wild Fork and Stonehorse Café," Kevin said sarcastically.

"Hey, how about you fuck yourself."

"Hey, how about you repeat that shit you just spouted to Stark, or better yet, Dragon and Anastasia."

Dallas started to swell up like one of those ugly fish that puff when they're pissed and Kevin, reluctantly, readied himself to punch the douchebag in the face, but the giggles of girls interrupted as two blue fledglings approached the dorm. One girl was a blond with striking blue eyes and boobs that jiggled freely under a skintight white crop top. She was arm in arm with a black girl who, Kevin thought, looked like a queen with her hair all free and curling around her head, making her appear tall and regal—like she could take on the world *and* have fun doing it. The girls had their heads tilted together as they whispered and laughed. Kevin knew they seemed familiar but couldn't quite remember their names. They stopped just before reaching Dallas and Kevin.

"Ladies, I see you got word about the party," Dallas said.

Dallas's smile was obviously a leer and Kevin did not understand why the white girl batted her eyes and gave him *that* smile—the one that said, *Come and get it!*

"We usually don't go to lame school parties that are actually *at* the school," said the white girl.

"Yeah, but what with the war and the—" the black girl began.

"The fucking awful inconveniences it causes, like having to stay on campus *all the time*, we decided to show up," the white girl finished.

"Yeah, war is definitely inconvenient," Kevin said.

"Especially for the people who die fighting so you can be safe here on this campus."

"Buzzkill," said the white girl, rolling her eyes. "Dallas, would you show me to the keg?"

"I'll show you anything you want to see, babe. And, get this—some of the art kids carved a double luge outta ice. They're pouring shots down it. You have to catch them with your mouth."

"Oooh, good thing my mouth is a professional!" The blond giggled and traded her friend's arm for Dallas's. The two headed up the stairs and she glanced over her shoulder. "Come on, Twin! A drink will make you less grumpy."

Twin! That's it! Man, my head is really messed up if it could forget Shaunee. And, of course her "twin" is Erin—the water to Shaunee's fire.

"Just because I don't agree with you about everything doesn't mean I'm grumpy," said Shaunee.

"Twin! We've been over this before. We're *twins*. That means we have to be together on this shit."

"Well, it does mean something, that's for sure. You go ahead. I'll catch up. I want to talk to Kevin for a sec."

"Don't know why. He's *definitely* not partying, but whatev." Erin pressed her boob into Dallas's arm. "What's taking you so long to get me to the vodka?"

"Girl, put yourself in my hands and I'll get you to the booze." He reached around and grabbed her ass as they headed up the stairs. Erin shrieked and laughed all the way into the dorm.

Kevin sighed miserably. That's what I'm supposed to be attracted to? No. Damn. Way. Not even with those boobs.

"I wanted to apologize to you."

Kevin pulled his attention from his internal annoyance to the girl standing in front of him.

"Apologize? What for?" Kevin's mind scrambled to think of what Shaunee could've possibly done to him and all his grief-exhausted mind could come up with was, *Wow, I don't remember Other Shaunee being so hot.*

"I'm pretty sure my feelings should be hurt that you don't remember me, but this once I'm cool with it. The only time you talked to me I was a bitch. That's what I'm apologizing for." She stuck out her hand. "Hi, I'm Shaunee. Erin—my twin, who went inside with Dallas—and I were super rude to the Prophetess Aphrodite about you. I was wrong and I'm sorry. And not just because the prophetess is dead. Because it was a childish, bitchy thing to do, and I'm not like that. Or, at least, I don't want to be like that. So, I'm sorry. For real."

"That's right! I can't believe I forgot."

"Well, in your defense you've had a lot going on."

"You two made fun of me—said I was Aphrodite's lover." Kevin barked a laugh. "Man, you pissed her off."

"Yeah, well, the joke was on us. You were her lover and you also helped save all of us, along with her sacrifice."

Kevin's smile turned bittersweet. "Not then. That night we were just getting to know each other. We hadn't fallen in love yet. Well, scratch that. I was probably already in love. She definitely wasn't."

"She was right, you know."

"Yeah, about a lot of things. Which do you mean?"

"She called Erin and me spineless little girls who only apologize about being bitches when we get caught and have to pay the consequences for being horrible. She made me think about how I was acting, and since then I've realized I don't like being horrible."

"I have a feeling your twin in there isn't in agreement with you," said Kevin.

"Yeah, I know. I'm not sure what to do about it. Erin and I have been inseparable since we both got Marked—on the same day—and ended up here. It used to be great that we were so close. We had each other's backs. We were never alone—or lonely. Then I guess I started to change, and she didn't. That's about it. But, hey, I didn't mean to dump that on you. I just wanted to tell you that I am honestly sorry that I made fun of you."

"Apology accepted. Wanta sit?" He motioned beside him on the stair.

"Sure, but I only have about five minutes before Erin comes back here to get me. That's the worst part. That I can't get her to understand that we can still be besties, even though we don't agree on everything and we're not together every damn second."

"You might want to rethink that," Kevin said. He scooted over so Shaunee had plenty of room to sit.

"Rethink trying to get her to understand?"

"Well, yeah, kinda. But I meant rethink her being your bestie. People change. And maybe now you two don't really have much—"

"Ohmyfuckinggod, what is taking you so long? The luge is the shit! Come on Twin! They're talking about a wet T-shirt contest, and you know how I like me some water!"

Shaunee sighed and muttered, "I am *not* getting my shirt wet so boys can stare at my boobs more than they do already." But in a louder voice she said, "Okay, coming," as she stood. "It was nice talking to you, Kev. Hope I see you around."

"Yeah, me too," said Kevin, surprised that he meant it.

Then Dallas stuck his head out of the door. "Hey, babe! There you are. They're setting up another double shot! Come on!"

"Oooo! Coming!" Erin grabbed Shaunee's hand and pulled her up the remaining stairs.

"Oh, hey, Kevin. Almost forgot. One of the computer nerds stuck his head out of their cave and told me to come get you. Figures you're friends with them." Dallas put an arm around Erin and tried to put one around Shaunee, but she easily sidestepped him and disappeared into the dorm.

Kevin sighed and got up, going inside much more slowly. There was almost no one in the common room, which didn't surprise Kevin. They'd all be in the movie room taking shots and playing video games. I'm going to say something to Anastasia. Not that I'm really a buzzkill, but someone has to get control of these fledglings, and the first step needs to be keeping fully Changed vampyres, like douchebag Dallas, away from them.

He was still grumbling internally when he opened the door to the dorm's media center. Even though every fledgling at the school had a laptop, a smart phone, and basically any other electronic device they desired, each dorm was also equipped with a high-tech media center where fledglings could research, run off any copies they needed to make (there was a 3-D printer in each dorm), and do almost anything they could do in the main media center of the school.

The row of computers was half full with three fledglings, sound-canceling headphones in place, fully concentrating on their screens. They were the students who had been tasked with looking for stories about ghost Zoey, and anything else that might cause Anastasia and the new House of Night regime issues. They were supposed to report whatever they found to either Kevin or Dragon, who would pass it along to the school's professional IT team.

"Oh, good. There you are." A fledgling named Santos took off his headphones and motioned for Kevin to come to him. "So, I was looking for those Zoey stories and going through Insta accounts, and I found this. I know you and Dragon didn't ask us to check him out, but when I read this and saw all the likes I thought I better show you." Santos pointed to the screen and the Instagram account he'd pulled up.

Ah, hell! It's Loren fucking Blake. Kevin read the poem and could feel his blood pressure spiking. "You have got to be kidding."

"Nope. I'm not making this shit up. At all."

"No, I didn't mean—" Kevin shook his head. "It's just that this is crazy." He reread the poem as he thought about what an asshole Blake must be to write something like that.

"Not as crazy as all the likes it got," said Santos.

Kevin's eyes widened as he saw the thousands of likes. "I want you to follow the like trail. Make a list—on one side, humans, and on the other, vampyres and fledglings. Email the list to Dragon and me." Kevin clapped him on the back. "Good job. Seriously."

"Will do."

"And keep this to yourself," Kevin added.

"No worries there. I'm not one of the idiots who think war is cool. I have friends who were killed in the war. A lot of them. I, um, used to be an equestrian."

"I'm sorry. Our High Priestess is working on getting horses back in the stables. Hey, you could let her know that you'd be willing to help."

Santos turned his gaze back to the computer. "I haven't been back to the stables since it happened. Since they were all killed. I'm—I'm not sure I can go there yet."

"I get it. No rush."

"It's a good idea, though."

"Keep at it. It'll get better," said Kevin.

"Do you mean the internet searching or missing the horses and everyone?"

"Both. I'll be back. And, again, good job."

Kevin cracked his knuckles as he hurried into what had been Neferet's over-the-top office—quickly refurbished by Anastasia, who was sitting behind an antique desk carved from rich walnut that gleamed in the soft light of the fat lavender-vanilla pillar candles that rested in simple but elegant marble holders—perfuming the room with soothing sweetness. Gone were the stiff velvet chairs and the huge photos of Neferet pretending to be Nyx. Instead Anastasia had added comfortable leather chairs before the antique desk and in the corners of the room, and the white walls were decorated with artist renditions of the real Goddess.

Dragon was pacing the width of the room and a very grim-looking Stark sat in one of the two chairs before Anastasia's desk.

Kevin hesitated at the door, not sure if he should've knocked or not, but Anastasia gestured for him to come in, saying, "Good, you're here. Please take a seat beside Stark. Our Sword Master is always more comfortable pacing when bad news is being delivered."

Dragon paused in his pacing long enough for Kevin to take a seat. Then he continued. "As I was saying, Blake is nowhere on campus. He's gone for sure. His room is a mess. He was obviously in a hurry to pack."

Stark crossed his arms over his chest and muttered, "Fucking traitorous asshole."

"I never liked him," said Dragon.

Anastasia was holding a piece of paper, which she stared at as she asked, "How long has he been gone?"

Kevin shifted his weight uncomfortably. "Well, I went to Nyx's Temple to look for him before I alerted Dragon to the fact that he could be missing, and the priestess there told me that he'd left the temple several hours ago."

Stark shook his head in disgust. "He could be anywhere."

"This haiku is truly despicable. What a terrible disappointment Loren Blake is." Anastasia sighed and then put down the paper and straightened her spine, her voice hardening. "Did any of our people see him at the airport?"

Dragon had begun pacing again. His hand rested on the pommel of the sword that sat in a leather scabbard strapped around his waist. Kevin thought he looked like an ancient Warrior come suddenly alive from the pages of a vampyre history book. His voice was deep and his words were clipped. "We don't have people there anymore. It's part of the truce. We agreed to reopen Tulsa International and let humans come and go as they will."

Stark leaned forward. "I contacted our private hangar. No one has seen him there."

Kevin snorted. "That doesn't mean he didn't hop on a regular human flight to almost anywhere."

"Oh, Goddess! You don't actually believe he could be in contact with Neferet?" Anastasia's usually serene face paled. "What does he know about the Other World? I should never have allowed anyone who was allied with Neferet onto our Council!"

Stark smoothed his hands down the sides of the chair's leather arms. "Well, then, that would have excluded me." His voice was rough with self-reproach.

Kevin didn't think about it—he simply acted on instinct. He reached out and rested his hand on Stark's shoulder. "Hey, that also would've meant Professor P and Professor Nolan would've been left out—and you know how awesome they are.

Dragon paced to Stark's side, nodding in agreement. "They remained here, doing their best to continue to educate fledglings, even though that meant they had to bow to Neferet. Do not torture yourself with blame, Stark. When you truly knew better, you did better." Dragon's gaze warmed and shifted to his mate. "And do not blame yourself either, my love. Now is not the time for that. Now is the time for action."

Kevin squeezed Stark's shoulder before dropping his hand back to his lap. "Dragon's right. Self-blame is what's destroying the red vampyres. We can't go down that path."

Anastasia smiled and some of the color returned to her smooth cheeks. "My Warriors are correct. I shall not waste my energy with self-blame."

Kevin thought her smile could lighten anyone's dark mood, and he grinned in return, saying, "Hey, we need to keep in mind that Blake doesn't know much. Remember that he tended to be too busy 'composing poetry'"—Kevin air quoted sarcastically—"to make most of our Council meetings."

Anastasia's bright expression turned somber. "But he does know that Zoey came from an alternate world much like ours. Correct?"

Dragon sighed and nodded. "He does. Though, like Kevin, I don't believe he knows many details."

Anastasia tapped the eraser end of a pencil against her desk. "Details or not, it would be very bad for Neferet to find out about the Other World."

"That's for sure," said Kevin. He leaned forward earnestly. "My offer still stands. I'll go to Zoey and warn her that our Neferet is still on the loose and might have found out about her world. And while I'm there I'll get as many details about Kalona as I can."

Anastasia shook her head, making a slicing motion with her slender hand. "No. Not yet. The risk is too great unless we have no choice." She turned to Stark. "Have you made any headway in finding Neferet?"

"You mean in the day since our last Council meeting? No. Nothing," Stark said. "And I have to say I agree with Kevin. Someone needs to go to the Other World."

Anastasia steepled her fingers as if she was preparing to pray. Her voice was serene steel. "Stark, I appreciate your insight. I appreciate that you found your way back to the Goddess and that you had a hand in stopping Neferet, but, like Kevin, your emotions are too involved. Your judgment is impaired when it comes to the Other World—so is yours, Kevin."

Dragon resumed his pacing. "Right now, we need to

focus on finding Blake and Neferet. Let's hope they're not together."

Kevin kept his frustration controlled, but he couldn't help the edge that crept into his voice. "And when we do finally find them, what do we do if they are together?"

Anastasia sighed. "Then, unless we capture or kill Neferet, you will, indeed, have to go to Zoey and warn her."

"I agree," said Dragon.

Kevin stood. "Okay, I'll go back to Blake's room and go through everything. Maybe he left something behind that'll give us an idea of where he's headed."

"I'll come with you," Stark said, standing beside Kevin.

They nodded respectfully to Anastasia and Dragon, then left the office quickly, heading toward the professors' quarters. The night was cold and the gaslights reminded Kevin of flitting ghosts under copper domes. He rubbed his hands together and realized his palms were sweaty.

He glanced sideways at Stark. "I have a bad feeling about this."

Stark's breath made misty puffs in the air. "Ditto. You're going to have to go to the Other World."

They'd reached the part of the sidewalk that passed the statue of Nyx, and the scent of the votive offerings left by fledglings filled the frigid air with a sweetness that had Kevin pausing before the Goddess. "Yeah, that's what I figure too," he said softly, staring up at Nyx. "I bet Blake heard from Neferet and he's going to meet her."

Stark seemed impervious to the presence of the Goddess. He grunted and rubbed his hands together to warm them. "That slimy bastard. I've always had a bad feeling about him. How much do you think he actually knows?"

Kevin opened himself to the soothing presence of Nyx, and was filled by a certainty that was echoed in his words. "I'm sure he knows that Zo came from another world, and I'd bet that he also knows that the Neferet over there is immortal and was defeated and entombed."

"Shit! That's bad," Stark said, shifting his weight from foot to foot restlessly.

Kevin let his gaze fall from the Goddess to Stark. "Yeah. I don't remember ever talking about how we actually got back and forth between worlds—at least not in front of anyone except Dragon and Anastasia."

"Well, that's a little good news," said Stark. "Blake is too stupid to figure out the hows of it by himself."

"Yeah, but Neferet isn't."

Stark ran a hand through his disheveled hair. "Shit. Bad. Again."

"Yep. I think Anastasia is going to have to let me go to Zo's world. I know she doesn't want to, but I really don't think we have any choice," said Kevin.

"I'm going with you."

Kevin shook his head. "Dude, I really don't think that's a good idea."

"Well, when has a bad idea ever stopped me? You go—I go. That's it."

Kevin shrugged and returned his gaze to Nyx. "Not up to me." He was filled with a rush of warmth that accompanied the certainty he already felt—and then he added silently, *Thanks, Nyx. Zo is definitely gonna need my help dealing with two Neferets as well as two Starks...*

19

Other Neferet

Neferet slipped by the front-desk staff easily as Lynette made a very loud, very American scene about needing a new key-card because hers kept not working. Keeping her head tilted down, and her hat and glasses on, Neferet chose the stairwell, avoiding the cameras in the elevator. They would, of course, record Lynette's face, as well as Loren Blake's, but with her hair piled up under her hat, her tattoos covered, and her face obscured by huge Jackie O sunglasses, Neferet could be any tall, willowy woman wearing jeans and a sweater.

The lock to Neferet's suite flashed green, and she slipped into the room unnoticed. The door closed behind her with a secure click and whir of the deadbolt. Neferet breathed a relieved sigh as she tossed her hat, sunglasses, and purse onto the plush couch. One of the things Neferet liked best about this hotel was that each suite had been decorated differently. This particular suite had a plush ivory carpet and a lovely terrace, and was decorated with gorgeous upholstery that featured exotic birds and flowers.

Neferet plucked the little sachet of sugar-like poison out of her emerald-green Manolo Blahnik clutch and shook it, noticing that the white powder glistened in the muted lamplight. Wee Denise had been so helpful in procuring the lethal dose. "Perhaps I *should* poison him." She rounded the couch, dragging her pointed nails along its high back as she considered her options. "It would be such a shame to stain any of this."

Neferet stilled as the door unlocked and Lynette breathlessly hurried into the suite. "The champagne service is on its way up." She paused, nervously smoothing out her cardigan. "I'll stay long enough to set it up for you. Is there anything else you need?"

Neferet frowned at Lynette. "Yes, handmaid, I need for you to not be so obviously nervous."

Lynette froze and then she sighed and fussed with her hair before she nodded and, sounding much more like herself, said, "You are absolutely right, as usual, my lady. All will be well. You simply will not tolerate failure."

Neferet sighed and slid the sachet back into her clutch. "Of course I won't, my dear, though I will be pleased when this tedious night is over. The drive here was unendingly long."

With her usual level of competence, Lynette fluffed the already perfect velvet throw pillows and moved Neferet's hat to the dresser top. "I know. But at least it stopped raining. I see a heater on the balcony. Do you want me to set up the champagne out there?"

Neferet sat on the love seat, lounging back against the down-filled upholstery. She glanced at the balcony, making her mind up instantly. "No, my dear. I do not want to chance being seen. I am extraordinarily memorable."

"Very true, my lady."

There were two knocks. "Room service." The muffled words drifted through the door.

Neferet stood and quickly stepped into the bathroom while Lynette opened the door. She waited impatiently, staring at her reflection in the antique mirror. Neferet grimaced, hating the fact that her exquisite Mark was hidden under thick makeup. "Never again," she promised herself.

Finally, Lynette called, "Okay, he's gone. Here, I poured you a glass. Thought you might need it." Lynette handed her the beautiful champagne flute filled with bubbly.

"You are such a dear." Neferet sipped appreciatively. "How much time do we have?"

Lynette checked her phone. "He landed thirty minutes ago, which is when he replied, acknowledging that he was at Heathrow and on his way here. It takes a little over an hour to get here from the airport."

"Excellent. That means I have time to change into nothing and drink most of this champagne before he arrives."

"Shall I order another bottle, my lady?" Lynette asked as she refilled Neferet's flute.

"Indeed. And I shall slip out of these awful jeans." Neferet paused and shuddered delicately.

"When I made the reservation I reminded them to have their highest quality bathrobe set out and ready in the suite." Lynette hurried past Neferet to open the expensive armoire that rested against the bedroom wall. "Oh, yes! Here it is."

Neferet glanced over the flute at it as she sipped champagne. "It will do. Put it in the bathroom for me, my dear."

Lynette disappeared into the luxurious bathroom. Returning she said, "I believe I should go get the extra bottle for you. I think it's best to keep people away from this suite as much as possible."

Neferet drained the glass before placing it back on its

silver tray. She pulled off her sweater and stepped out of her jeans, leaving them in a dark, discarded heap on the thick carpet. Naked, she refilled her flute. "I agree, dear Lynette."

Lynette quickly picked up her mistress's clothes, hanging them neatly in the armoire. "My lady," she glanced over her shoulder at Neferet. "Are you nervous?"

"Whatever for?"

"Well, you're getting ready to see an old love whom you're going to kill. That would make me really nervous."

Neferet laughed and waved her scarlet fingernails dismissively as she walked past Lynette, entering the bathroom to retrieve the thick bathrobe. "Dear Lynette, that is why I am the goddess and you are the handmaid. I am not nervous. I am anxious. Also, I can't seem to decide whether I should poison or stab him. It is such a conundrum."

"You should wait and decide when he's here. If he's just mildly annoying, you'll probably want to poison him." Lynette handed Neferet a refilled glass of champagne as she returned to lounge on the love seat. "Wee Denise did say whatever is in that little bag will make him pass out and then his heart will stop—painlessly and silently."

Neferet tapped her fingernail against the crystal flute. "But if he is entirely irritating and as whiny and clingy as he tends to be, it will probably be satisfying to stab him, even though he will bleed all over this deliciously plush carpet."

"That would be a shame," Lynette said as she gave the carpet an appreciative look.

"Exactly what I was thinking." Neferet shrugged nonchalantly. "Well, however I do it I shall make it quick. I want to get this annoying detail over with and return to Skye. We still need to figure out how to kill my future."

"That one's a lot harder than your past," Lynette said.

"Yes, I agree." Neferet made a shooing gesture at Lynette. "Quickly! Get that champagne. Then wait down the street at that exceptionally good Italian restaurant I pointed out on the way in. I do hope there will be time to have a delicious, leisurely meal when I'm finished with Loren. I adore their pasta."

"I could order something to go."

"No need. I'll simply take care of Loren quickly so that we can enjoy our dinner. I do hate takeout, don't you?"

"It's never as good as eating in the restaurant," Lynette said.

"Exactly."

"I'll return shortly." Lynette hurried out the door.

She was back with a second bottle of champagne just as Neferet finished loosening the intricate braid that had held her hair prisoner under the ridiculous hat she'd been forced to wear as a disguise.

"You look beautiful," said Lynette.

"I do, don't I? It'll be wasted on Loren because he will so shortly be dead, but at least I'll be spared the bad odes he would have written celebrating my beauty."

"That is a silver lining." Lynette glanced at her phone. "Oh! I have to go. He'll be here in about fifteen minutes. Not that you need it, but good luck."

"No, I don't, but I appreciate the sentiment."

Lynette hadn't been gone two minutes when there was a knock on the door. Loren was early. Neferet sighed in exasperation. She truly loathed people who were early. It was a

sign of a sense of pompous and unwarranted self-importance
—a description that accurately fit Loren Blake. Neferet
pressed her eye to the spy hole. Loren breathed into the palm
of his hand and sniffed. Neferet grimaced, sighed, and then
opened the door.

"Beloved!" She flung her arms wide, being sure her bathrobe also opened to reveal her nakedness.

"'She walks in beauty, like the night. Of cloudless climes
and starry skies. And all that's best of dark and bright, meets
in her aspect and her eyes,'" Blake quoted as he rushed into
the suite and took her in his arms, kissing her passionately.

Neferet returned the kiss. Briefly. Then she pushed away,
laughing coyly. "I have always so loved your eagerness."

"I have been without you for days and days, my own!
And look at you! You've covered your Mark!"

Neferet affected a trembling hand as she pressed it to
her forehead where heavy makeup completely covered her
elaborate tattoo. "I had to, dearest. I cannot let them catch
me and drag me back to Tulsa to be at the mercy of my
betrayers." With a choked sob, she collapsed into the plush
love seat before which Lynette had set up the champagne
service. "Do have a drink. You must be exhausted from
your flight."

Loren shuddered and dropped to the love seat beside her,
pouring himself a glass of champagne and refilling hers. "It
was a dreadful flight. I had to travel coach class."

Neferet gasped, not having to act to show horror. "That
is, indeed, dreadful. But, Loren, you made quite certain no
one at the House of Night knows you're here?"

"Absolutely, my own. I made sure of it. And anyway, the
new *leaders* of the House of Night don't care about me."

"Oh, dearest, do not underestimate your importance. For me, you symbolize a rich past."

"Yes, but for them I am only a deposed poet." He sighed melodramatically. Neferet thought for a moment that he would cry and swore to herself if he did she would pull the knife out of the deep pocket of her robe and slit his throat immediately. "Plus, they're too busy coddling the red vampyres and burying stories about that other Zoey to care about anything really important. I mean, come on. Who the hell cares that she was from another world that is a mirror of our own? Like that has anything to do with *our* world and *our* war?"

A stab of shock jolted through Neferet that was so strong, so surprising, that she almost dropped her champagne flute. She placed it carefully on the small table and turned to face Loren.

"What did you just say?"

He blinked stupidly at her ferocious expression. "About our war?"

"No, Loren. About the vampyre who ruined my life. About the *child* who caused my generals to betray me. About Zoey Redbird!"

"Ooooh, that's right! I forgot that you weren't there to find out about the mirror world."

Neferet waited, toying with the hilt of the dagger in her pocket, imagining sinking the blade into Loren's throat.

"Loren! Tell me everything you know about this mirror world. Now!"

"Of course. Sorry. I'm just breathless from being in your presence. I desire you so much, my own true love." He took the end of the cloth belt to her robe and playfully tugged it.

Neferet's hand snaked out and stopped him in a grip that had him yelping in pain.

"My love, that hurts!"

"Loren, you must remember that I am not only your love. I am also a High Priestess who has been unjustly usurped from her position. Now, tell me everything you know about Zoey and the world from which she came."

"That's easy because I don't know much. The Council kept having meetings without me. They never understand how busy I am. I just can't—"

"Loren! Now." He was close enough to her that she felt him tremble. Good, he's not too self-absorbed to completely forget that I am a powerful High Priestess.

"Well, you remember that red vampyre? The one named Kevin who Stark let into the blue section of the auditorium during your last assembly?"

"Yes, of course I remember him. He was with Stark when he and that bitch Aphrodite betrayed me."

"And you remember that his squadron, led by General Dominick, all just disappeared while he was on a separate mission?"

"Yes, vaguely. He said something about getting lost and not making his way back to them."

"Right. That's not what happened. Somehow this Zoey girl from the mirror world pulled General Dominick and all the missing vampyres to another version of our world—like I said, it's filled with people and places like us and ours, but different. Like over there some people are alive who are dead in our world, and the other way around too. Kevin got back his humanity over there because—get this craziness—Zoey Redbird is Kevin's sister. I'm sure that has something to do with why he's the only one who came back to our world. They probably killed Dominick and the other red vamps over there."

Neferet felt the pieces of the puzzle that had been plaguing her fall into place. "Zoey Redbird. I killed her in this world but couldn't possibly know that I would need to kill her in another world as well."

"What? *You* killed her? I thought the People of Faith killed her."

"Loren, dear, try not to think. Just tell me what else you know about this mirror world—like, how did Kevin and his should-be-dead sister go back and forth between there and here?"

Loren shrugged. "I have no idea. But she's powerful. Oh, and so is Kevin. Did you know both of them have affinities for all five elements?"

"No, but now I do. What else don't I know?"

"You're going to love this—in Zoey's world there's another one of you!"

Neferet felt herself go very still. "Explain that."

"I don't know much. Those simpletons were always done with the bulk of Council business when I joined them. Now that I think about it, it's almost like they somehow *knew* I was still loyal to you."

"Imagine that," Neferet said. "Remember for me, dearest. What all did you hear about that other Neferet? How did she allow Zoey to come to our world?"

"Zoey's in charge in her world. Oh! I remember! The Neferet over there is walled up in some kind of immortal jail."

"What? Why would they do that?"

"Apparently she became immortal. Isn't that insane?

Their Neferet named herself Goddess of Tulsa, so they got a magickal being to help them defeat her—someone with wings. I can't remember his name. Anyway, since they couldn't kill her, they walled her up in a tomb." He shuddered. "It's a good thing you don't live in that world."

As Loren poured himself a second glass of champagne, Neferet kept herself under strict control, though her heart was beating so hard and fast that she felt slightly dizzy. Now the strange things Zoey said make complete sense. She was speaking of another version of me—the me she knew and defeated in her world. And in Zoey Redbird's world I am immortal! I'm ambitious enough to have become immortal, but I only wanted to rule over Tulsa? That does not seem accurate. Loren probably got that detail incorrect. But, then again, a child defeated that other version of me, so perhaps she is an immortal-yet-weaker, flawed version, which is sad. So very sad.

"Dearest one, you didn't happen to overhear where they are keeping that poor, unfortunate Neferet, did you?"

"Sure. Woodward Park. She's walled into the grotto. Isn't it strange that there's another world like ours with another park called Woodward?"

"Can you think of any other detail you know that you may have forgotten?"

Loren sighed. "No. Forgive me, my own true love. I didn't know I would be seeing you again so soon—or at all."

Neferet sat up straighter and returned her flute of champagne to the silver tray that rested on the little gilded table before them. "They do not know that I am alive?"

"In every meeting I was in they were trying to figure out whether you are or not."

Neferet smiled and smoothed back her hair. "That is very, *very* good."

Loren returned her smile with his own, which was as charming as it was vapid. "Where have you been, my love? Not in Tulsa, that's for sure."

Why not tell him? He's not going to live to betray me. "Well, coincidentally, I have been wooing the sprites on the Isle of Skye so that I can use Old Magick to become immortal. Only *this* Neferet will never be satisfied with simply being Goddess of Tulsa."

"That's brilliant! If that other Neferet figured out how to become immortal—you will too, for sure! Hey, if you could figure out how to get to that mirror world, you could just release her from her tomb and ask her yourself!"

"Yes, Loren. I am aware of that."

Loren laughed. "Anastasia will *never* think to look for you on Skye. As far as I know they think you're hiding somewhere in Tulsa licking your wounds." His grin turned seductive. "Speaking of licking…"

"You're quite sure you can remember nothing more? Especially about the spell that was used to move Kevin and Zoey between worlds?"

"The only thing I ever heard was that Old Magick and those tedious sprites were involved. You know, the creatures who restored the humanity to the Red Army—which was a truly stupid thing to do because now we have red vampyres hurling themselves off rooftops and walking into the sun and setting themselves ablaze." He shuddered. "But, enough of that unpleasantness. Let us go back to the licking."

Neferet smiled, slid both of her hands into the pockets of her robe, and then parted it, revealing herself completely to

Loren. As expected, he discarded his champagne flute and leaned forward eagerly, his eyes riveted on her bare breasts.

Neferet pushed him back against the love seat and with a quick motion straddled him.

"Oooh! I like this. A little rough play is fun." Loren spread his arms wide. "I am all yours. Take me any way you desire."

"Oh, I shall." Neferet bent and pressed her lips to Loren's throat. He moaned and titled his head back, giving her better access to his neck. His hands slid inside her robe and he cupped her hips, holding her firmly against him.

Neferet's fingers caressed a line down the side of Loren's neck. He moaned again. Fast as a striking viper, Neferet pressed the tip of her fingernail against the softest part of his neck—just under his chin—and she sliced, easily cutting a gash in his skin. Before he had time to respond she covered the gash with her lips and began feeding from him.

He grunted as the pain hit his brain. "My own! I haven't fed since I left the House of Night. A sip will be fine, but more than that will leave me too—"

"Oh, Loren. Do shut up." Neferet bared her teeth and bit him, tearing open the gash in his neck so that blood poured from the wound as she drank from him. Before he could struggle—before he truly realized her lethal intent, Neferet put her hand in the pocket of her robe and drove the dagger deep into his chest, sliding it between two ribs and burying it to the hilt.

Loren's eyes went huge and round. He made a mewing sound. Red spittle foamed his lips. "Why?" he gasped as he crumpled into her, clutching at her bathrobe.

Neferet stood, pulling the dagger out of his chest and moving off him so that he fell onto the floor with the bathrobe still balled in his fists. She let it slide off her too, so that it went with Loren, covering him so she didn't have to look at his dying face nor view his final convulsions. Before she answered him Neferet licked the blade clean of his blood.

"Why? That's simple." Neferet strode into the bathroom and took a hand towel from the sink, wetting it quickly before she returned to stand over Loren's swathed, but still twitching body. As she wiped the blood from her face and chest she spoke, allowing her voice to be filled with all the disdain he deserved. "So, so many reasons—not the least of which are that you're self-absorbed, vapid, and annoying. But mostly because you are my past—and my past must die." She dropped the bloody towel on him and went to the armoire, dressing in the clothes Lynette had so recently hung there. Then she washed her hands and checked her reflection in the mirror. Discovering that there was still some blood on her lips, she licked it off with a contented sigh before returning to the main room of the suite and donning her hat and dark glasses.

Lastly, she retrieved her emerald clutch from the corner of the love seat, breathing a sigh of relief that it had escaped any blood spatter. She paused before leaving. "Goodbye, Loren. I cannot imagine Nyx is going to greet someone like you happily. Isn't it a shame you've been worshiping the wrong goddess? Oh, and that question was rhetorical. Don't feel the need to answer as I know you're busy dying."

With new purpose, Neferet closed the door to the suite behind her and hurried down the hallway to the elevator, and as she appreciated her reflection in the mirrored wall she realized something that was as pleasing as it was significant. She smiled as the empty elevator arrived, and she stepped in.

Though her Mark was still covered by the thick, waterproof makeup, she took off the dark glasses and discarded the hat, letting it drop to the floor of the elevator. The doors closed, and she punched the bronze button to the lobby. Then she turned her gaze to the camera and said, "Do your best, simpletons. I will not be in this world to find."

Other Lynette

Lynette chose a table for two in the corner of the quaint Italian restaurant and took the seat that faced the door so that she could sip her glass of the excellent house red and nibble bread and cheese while she waited for Neferet to appear. She pondered whether or not she had become morally bankrupt—especially as it didn't bother her at all that she was waiting for her employer to murder someone.

Somewhere between her first and second goblet of wine, Lynette decided that she was morally fine. Neferet was going to become a goddess, and goddesses made life and death decisions all the time, didn't they?

Lynette was toying with the thought of ordering some marinated olives to go with her bread and wine when she was shocked to see Neferet enter the restaurant. She stood, waving at Neferet, who smiled and joined her.

Lynette picked up her purse and looked for her waitress. "I'll get the check right away, my lady."

Neferet sat, sweeping her long hair back so that the

auburn mass cascaded down her back. "Oh, no need to rush, my dear. Loren will *not* be joining us." The server arrived, and the vampyre—Mark still discreetly covered—smiled and ordered. "Do you still carry Giuseppe Quintarelli Valpolicella? The Classico Riserva is my preference."

"Yes, madam! You have exquisite taste."

"I do. Bring us a bottle. Also, your divine antipasto plate, two insalatonas, and your incredible penne all'arrabbiata—for two."

"Immediately, madam!"

Then Neferet added, "Oh, but first—we're celebrating, so we require two glasses of your best prosecco."

"Very good, madam!"

The server hurried away. Neferet sighed and smiled, putting her chin in her hand and leaning forward to chat with Lynette like a happy girl. "Oh, Lynette, so many of our obstacles have just been removed."

"My lady," Lynette pitched her voice low. "Where are your glasses and your hat? You are much too beautiful to be forgettable. These people will *all* remember you, even though your Mark is still covered."

Neferet's laughter drew appreciative glances. "I no longer need that disguise. If I hadn't been so ravenous I would have taken the extra time to scrub this terrible concealment from my face."

Lynette tried not to worry, but she had to clasp her hands together under the table to keep from fidgeting with her linen napkin. "So, it went well, my lady?"

"Better than well!" Neferet lowered her voice. "He gave me some spectacularly important information. We do not need to kill my future. I do not need to spend a tedious amount of time on Skye trying to coax Old Magick to make me immortal."

"That is fantastic!" Lynette felt flushed with relief.

The server returned with their glasses of prosecco and Neferet remained silent until she was out of hearing range, then she lifted her glass.

"To the trip we are going to take!"

Lynette was confused, but she raised her glass as well, clinking it against Neferet's.

"Where are we going, my lady?"

"Dear Lynette, I just discovered who our ghost Zoey is and why the House of Night is burying all mentions of her on the internet."

"I knew it was them!"

"Yes, they should have also buried Loren Blake. Had they done that I would be heading to the desolation of Skye, where it could be months and months before I discover the power and knowledge I need." She sipped her prosecco and then laughed softly. "It's ironic that they *will* be burying Loren."

"You did kill him?" Lynette whispered.

"Of course."

"Poison or dagger?"

"Dagger and my teeth. He was too tiresome. I simply could not wait the thirty minutes wee Denise said it would take for the poison to work. I had to shut him up immediately. His vapidness earned him a painful, though quick, death. I am not a monster, dear Lynette. I am *fairly* certain he did not suffer—much—in the short time it took for him to die."

Lynette had to squelch the urge to reach out and touch Neferet's hand—the hand that had just minutes before driven a dagger into a man's body and killed him. Just the thought of it gave her a little shudder of exited pleasure, which should have worried her, but Lynette didn't allow it to. Very soon she would be the handmaid, and the most beloved human, to a *goddess*. Why should the normal rules of society apply to her? They certainly didn't apply to Neferet.

And then she realized that something big must have just gone down. Neferet was relaxed, happy, and showing her face—though with her Mark covered, which wasn't surprising. Vampyres kept to themselves in Europe. If any of the other patrons here, or even at the Covent Garden Hotel, were vampyres, they too had their tattoos covered, if for no other reason than to save themselves from unwanted attention.

Still, as she'd said, Neferet was unforgettably beautiful, whether people recognized her as a vampyre or not. If Scotland Yard questioned any of the wait staff or any of the diners later, they would undoubtedly remember her.

"My lady," Lynette leaned forward and lowered her voice again. "But if he's dead shouldn't we be discreet? They will, eventually, find his body."

"Yes, they certainly will, but by that time we will be beyond their reach."

"On our trip?"

"Oh, I haven't told you! Yes, my dear. We are going on a trip—to the world where that *ghostly* Zoey Redbird came from, and in that world, there is a version of me who has been entombed by that vile child."

Lynette couldn't say anything for several long breaths. She hid her shock by sipping prosecco and then had a further reprieve while the waitress brought their antipasto platter and opened the bottle of expensive red wine. By the time they were alone again, Lynette could make herself speak without sounding as breathless and panicked as she felt.

"My lady," she began slowly, reasonably. "Do you mean a *literal* other world?"

"I do. One that is a mirror to our own." Neferet kept her voice pitched low and for Lynette's ears alone, but her excitement was almost tangible. "And the sprites I've become so familiar with hold the key to the door between this world and that."

"So, we're going to a different version of our world where you'll somehow rule?"

"Oh my, no! I would not usurp myself, but I understand your confusion. I have not been clear. The children who are running the Tulsa House of Night in the mirror world have entombed the other version of me because they could not kill her. Can you guess why, my dear?"

"Because they're afraid?"

"That is partially very correct. They definitely fear her, but it's the *why* that is so important." Neferet leaned closer and whispered conspiratorially. "The Neferet in their world became immortal."

Lynette felt a sizzle of delight. "She did it!"

"She certainly did. All I need do is to release her from what I am quite certain is an atrocious confinement. She will, of course, be happy to return the favor by sharing with me her path to immortality. I shall become a goddess and then we will return here, to our world, where I will reign in my proper position."

"As Goddess of the House of Night?"

"As Goddess of Night. I will not limit myself to Tulsa. Nor

will I limit myself to only reign over vampyres. You have taught me that, dear Lynette. Because of your importance to me I want you to accompany me to mirror Tulsa. I cannot possibly do without my handmaid there."

"Go with you to another world?" Lynette tried, and failed, to wrap her mind around something that seemed utterly mad and completely impossible.

"Yes, yes, yes. That's all I've been talking about since I arrived."

"It—it is a lot to take in."

"Well, I cannot imagine it being a difficult thing to move between worlds. Zoey is a child—barely eighteen. If she can do it, I should also be able to do it."

"But, what about me? I'm not a vampyre. I'm just a human."

"A human who is dear to me and under my protection." Neferet shrugged. "I shall simply pay the sprites something extra. Perhaps they would like me to lure a lovely stag and then sacrifice the creature to them. I do remember that sprites are bloodthirsty."

The excellent wine turned to vinegar in her mouth and the scrumptious food to chalk. A terrible premonition seized Lynette. Her intuition—which had led her from the miserable trailer park life her mother had settled for to a life of opulence and importance—screamed, *This is a bad idea!*

"What is it, my dear? You look like you might be ill."

"My lady, I'm terrified. I'm not a magickal being like you. Just thinking about moving from this world to another makes me feel sick. Can't I stay at Balmacara Mains and be sure things are perfect for your return?"

Neferet stared at her without speaking for so long that

Lynette's fear, which started as a reaction to a possible future event, shifted to a fear of the present. Had she just pushed the vampyre too far? Did Neferet believe she was being disloyal?

Finally, Neferet reached across and covered one of Lynette's hands with hers. "I understand your fear. Truly, I do. But I need you. You must come with me on this journey to my immortality to remind me."

"Of what, my lady?"

"Of the importance of our humanity."

Lynette stared down at their joined hands. Hers was so much more elegant than Lynette's, who at forty-five was already showing age spots and more wrinkles than she would've thought possible just a few years before. She looked up and met Neferet's gaze and saw only concern there. *Is this my destiny? To help a goddess remember her humanity?*

"Humanity is something that's very important for a goddess to remember," Lynette said slowly.

"There! You do understand! You *must* accompany me. I feel sure of it. And I shall keep you safe, dear Lynette. Trust me."

"I've put *all* of my trust in you, my lady, my goddess."

"Excellent! Excellent! Now, let us feast and discuss the future!"

Though it was decided that she would join Neferet in the Other World, Lynette felt rather numb, but she nodded and agreed with the vampyre—and that was what she continued to do throughout their leisurely dinner. Neferet chattered about immortality and how much she was looking forward to freeing another version of herself in the mirror-world's Tulsa. She even spoke about the fun she might have aiding that Neferet in taking vengeance on Zoey Redbird.

Lynette said little—though Neferet was too filled with excitement to notice. It took everything in her not to excuse herself to use the ladies' room. Her fear was still shrieking at her to go! Sneak out the back! Disappear into London! Neferet wouldn't have time to look for her now, and if Lynette was smart, reinvented herself, kept a low profile and drew no attention, it was possible Neferet would never find her—even if she managed to gain immortality and return to this world.

But Lynette didn't want a low-profile life. She'd had a taste of magick and of the wealth and power it brought, and she wanted it—wanted it badly. Badly enough that by the time Neferet asked for the bill and had her call their car, Lynette had decided that she was going to ignore the fear that had taken up residence in the pit of her stomach. *It is my destiny to aid this vampyre in becoming a goddess. I will remain by her side and keep reminding her that humanity—and humans in particular—are important.*

Neferet was leaving a wad of cash with their bill when the vampyre suddenly exclaimed, "Oh, I have been foolish!"

Lynette shook herself from the introspection that had silenced her for most of their dinner. "Surely not, my lady. You have an excellent plan."

"It's not that. I just realized that I do not believe I put the DO NOT DISTURB sign on the door of the suite."

"Well, that's not a big problem. I have the room key in my purse. You go ahead and get in the car. I'll slip into the hotel and be sure the sign is on the door." Lynette swallowed past the dryness in her throat that was more excitement at the possibility of seeing Loren's dead body than fear, and whispered, "I'll even make a quick call to the front desk and tell them that I'm sleeping late to get over jet lag, so they should hold all calls and all service until I remove the DO NOT DISTURB."

"That is very wise of you! We will not be here to be harassed about Loren's death, but if we know that we have at least a full day more or so before anyone will discover him we can take our time—perhaps even visit Inverness for another lovely meal and some shopping before we travel to free my other self." Neferet sighed. "I wonder if money is interchangeable between worlds. Poverty is such an inconvenience, though I am quite certain the other version of me will be wealthy."

"Money makes everything easier," agreed Lynette. Her phone bleeped with a text message. "The driver is just outside."

They exited the restaurant and headed for the black limo parked at the curb, waiting for them. Lynette turned to the right to walk the half a block back to the hotel—and she froze.

Police cars filled the street in front of the Covent Garden Hotel.

"In the car. Now!" Neferet commanded.

Lynette's legs unfroze, and she joined Neferet in the back seat.

"Driver, avoid that mess in front of the hotel."

"Yes, ma'am."

"Oh, and before you put the privacy window up, which I want you to do immediately, do you know the cause of all the excitement over there?" Neferet fluttered her fingers nonchalantly at the police presence.

The skinny driver, whose teeth were very bad, caught Neferet's gaze in the rearview mirror. "Me bloke's been textin'. He says there's been a murder at the hotel."

"A murder! How dreadful. Who died?"

"They haven't released a name yet, ma'am. Would ya like me to let you know if they do?"

"Oh, don't trouble yourself. I was just curious. We shall be sleeping most of the way back."

"Very good, ma'am. Anythin' else?"

"No. We'll let you know when we need to stop, but we are in a hurry, so let us make this return trip as swift as possible.

The driver touched the brim of his black hat, nodding respectfully to her. "Yes, ma'am." He flipped a switch that raised the privacy partition and then backed down the narrow street until he could turn around and head away from the hotel.

"Well, my dear, it appears we will not be having another leisurely dinner before we leave, nor will we be shopping in Inverness." Neferet sighed with annoyance.

Lynette couldn't speak. All she could think of was her credit card—the one that had reserved the suite in which a dead man had just been found.

"Lynette, my dear, we need clothes to travel in."

Neferet was speaking, and Lynette heard her words, but she couldn't make her mind hold their meaning. There are traffic cameras all over this city—and on the highways taking us north. Neferet walked out of that hotel with her hair and face uncovered. She is too beautiful to be forgettable—and she met me just down the street. They're going to find me. They're going to lock me up!

"Contact Mrs. Muir." Neferet continued to drone on and on as Lynette tried not to hyperventilate. "Have her send wee Denise to Inverness. I'll need black slacks and a dark—but tasteful—cashmere sweater. I shall also need some lovely black leather boots. Something flat, though. I have no idea how much walking we will have to do, but I would be prepared. You should have her get travel wear for you too. You definitely cannot go in one of your stylish suits. Those heels you wear are quite attractive but are not good for the out-of-doors."

"I'm sorry, my lady. What did you say?"

"Lynette, I gave you explicit instructions to pass along to Mrs. Muir. Whatever is wrong with you?"

"My lady," she turned to face Neferet, "I'm worried. It's my room they found Loren's body in. They'll be looking for me." Lynette thought she might be sick all over the limo.

Neferet's smile was a cat licking cream. "Then it is a very good thing that you won't be in this world to find. Now, listen carefully this time. This is what we shall need for our lovely trip…"

20

Other Kevin

"Kev! Wake up! Kev!"

Kevin shot up and stumbled to the door. He'd fallen asleep on the couch in Aphrodite's room, which was now his room, thanks to the generosity of Anastasia. But Kevin still hadn't been able to make himself sleep in the bed—*her* bed.

The truth was he rarely slept at all these days.

"Yeah, I'm coming!" He pulled on a sweatshirt and sweatpants before opening the door.

"Blake is dead," Stark said with no preamble as he tucked his laptop under his arm and brushed past Kevin into the opulent room. "I know it's not sunset yet, and it's tough for you to be really awake until then. But this is important."

"Dead? Seriously?" Kevin yawned, rubbed his eyes, and headed to the minikitchen for some coffee. "Don't worry about waking me up. I don't sleep much anymore."

Stark glanced around with open curiosity. "Damn. This is nice." He plopped onto the couch and immediately opened his laptop and started typing.

"So, what happened to Blake?" Kevin returned with two mugs of black coffee.

"Anastasia got an emergency call from the London House of Night." Stark took a drink before setting the mug on the coffee table. "Seems our Poet Laureate was discovered at the Covent Garden Hotel with a gash in his neck and a dagger between his ribs."

Kevin stopped midsip and set his mug on the arm of the couch. "What the hell?"

Stark passed him the computer. "They sent crime-scene photos."

"Damn, that's a lot of blood." Kevin grimaced as he scrolled through the photos.

"Keep going until you get to the close-up."

Kevin scrolled until he saw it. Blood filled the frame; its bizarre pattern blazed scarlet against the brilliant ivory carpet. "What is that?"

"Flip it horizontally."

With a few clicks, the image turned right side up. Shocked, Kevin sucked in a breath. "Does that say 'Skye'?"

"We think Blake wrote the word in his own blood before he died. Pretty impressive, actually, for as big a douchebag as he was. I'm surprised he thought to leave us any kind of clue."

Kevin looked up from the picture. "It was Neferet."

Stark nodded. "Scotland Yard gave the London House of Night all the video surveillance and info from the hotel. The suite was booked by Lynette Witherspoon, and the video clearly shows that she's the same person who used to be our flight concierge."

"She's with Neferet?"

"Definitely. Going into the suite we just get a brief glimpse of a tall woman coming up through the stairwell and entering the room. The woman keeps her face averted from the cameras and has dark glasses and a hat on, but it definitely looks like Neferet. Lynette joins her. Champagne is delivered. Lynette even brings more up."

"So, she's not Neferet's prisoner."

"It sure doesn't look like it. She comes and goes freely. The video shows Lynette leaving the room and the hotel just a few minutes before Blake gets there."

"Neferet is still in the room?"

"Yeah. But she's only in there for a little while with Blake—twenty-two minutes exactly. And when she comes out of the room, she takes the elevator and definitely isn't hiding anymore." Stark scrolled down until he got to the still shots from the video.

"Holy crap. That *is* her. She's hiding her Mark."

"Yeah, but that's the *only thing* she's hiding after she kills him."

"Do you think he told her about the Other World before she killed him?" Kevin's gut roiled.

"Oh, definitely. There's audio from the elevator. Check it out." Stark tapped the link and Neferet's distinctive voice lifted to them.

"*Do your best, simpletons. I will not be in this world to find.*"

"Fuck!" said Kevin.

"Yeah, but on the positive side, Blake didn't make enough of the Council meetings to know hardly anything about Zoey's world, or about how you got to and from it. Well, except that Old Magick was involved," Stark said.

"Yeah, Neferet's gotta be scrambling to put two and two together with what little information Blake had."

"It's good for us that he wasn't the brightest Crayola in the pack," Stark said.

"True, but Neferet's smart as hell. She'd have asked the right questions, so he had to have told her that Old Magick was responsible. That's gotta be why she's heading to the Isle of Skye. All vampyres know the biggest concentration of Old Magick in this world is on Skye." Kevin stood. "So, what are we waiting for? Shouldn't we be heading there?"

"Yep we should, and I'm just waiting for you to pack. Anastasia gave us permission to go to the Isle of Skye. Today. The jet is already on its way here to get us."

Kevin hurried to Aphrodite's bedroom where he quickly changed into jeans and a sweatshirt. As he threw clothes into one of Aphrodite's giant leather bags, he called out to Stark, "Hey, you know, I could conjure Oak and ask her what she knows about our Neferet—if she's seen her or whatever."

"Anastasia thought of that and rejected the idea. She said we need to remember that Old Magick is dangerous—the more you use it the more it infects you."

"Yeah, but this really is an emergency," Kevin said, grabbing his shaving kit and tossing it into the bag.

"That's true, which is what I pointed out, but she also said that it's not wise to let the sprites know we're on to Neferet. They don't take sides, and if Neferet asks them the right questions and gives them the right payment—"

"Crap! I didn't think of that. She's right," Kevin interrupted. "Oak would tell her anything for the right payment."

"Literally. Every damn thing. And we know that Neferet would make whatever sacrifice the sprites require—no matter who or what it is."

"We need to grab Neferet before she figures out the right questions to ask," said Kevin, emerging from the bedroom, bag in hand. "Hey, you understand we'll either be coming right back here with Neferet, or heading to the Other World after her," said Kevin.

"Yep," said Stark. "And if you go—I go with you."

Kevin shrugged. "Whatever. It's your funeral."

"I hope you didn't mean that literally," Stark said.

"Me too, dude. Me too."

Zoey

I decided that the Gathering Place was the coolest thing to happen to T-Town since *The Outsiders* was filmed here—and that was about a zillion years ago. The place stretched for miles and miles along the Arkansas River, and was filled with parks and nature trails, awesome stuff for little kids to play on—like a literal castle—and restaurants and such for those of us not so little anymore. It even had a lake in the center of it (which was currently where Stevie Rae, Aphrodite, and I were). The whole place was still so new that it smelled like cedar mulch and possibilities.

Stevie Rae spread out her arms and twirled around on the dock. "I love these kind of days. You know, when it's the middle of the winter, but it feels like spring. And this place is awesomesauce!"

Aphrodite grabbed Stevie Rae's arm, stopping her

twirl—and also keeping her from tipping off the dock and into the water. "Careful, bumpkin. Don't fall in and miss the one time I agree with you. And, Z, I'm glad you approved giving the city money to help finish the Gathering Place," Aphrodite said. "It turned out way cooler than I thought it was going to be."

"Right?" I said. "I mean, the drawings for it made it look great, but the real thing is even better. Hey, you guys want to know what I like best about it?"

"Totally," said Jack as he and Damien strolled up to us. "Do tell!"

I grinned at Jack. He was hand in hand with Damien. Both of them almost glowed with happiness—even though Damien was perpetually stressed about the pending opening of the new Depot Restaurant.

"I like best that this giant river park is basically in the backyard of one of the richest parts of T-Town—as in, there's pretty much only one kind of person who can afford to live just a few steps east of here—but this park is open to everyone. It's *filled* with all different colors and kinds of people."

"And fledglings and vampyres," added Stevie Rae. "With almost no issues from humans."

Aphrodite snorted. "Don't get too starry-eyed. It hasn't been open long. Give it a year or so without some upper-middle-class white woman making a hysterical call to the TPD because fledglings are being fledglings." She rolled her eyes. "Goddess forbid a different type of person is having fun."

"Maybe the TPD will be cool enough to fine anyone asshole-ish enough to do that," said Jack.

"One can hope," I said.

Stevie Rae sighed. "People can be a pain in the butt."

"Speaking of pains in the butt, how's Ice Cream Shoes doing tonight?" asked Aphrodite.

"She's not a pain in the butt; she's unique," Stevie Rae said firmly. "And she's good. I'm workin' with her to deal with her new affinities. Kacie is super powerful—especially for a newly Changed vampyre. And that power's gonna take some gettin' used to."

"I totally get that," I said.

Stevie Rae turned to face me. "Z, would you maybe spend some time with Kacie? I think it'd really help her."

"Sure. I'd be happy to help."

Stark called from the booth at the end of the dock. "Hey! Four boats are finally available! Let's hurry. They're going to set off the fireworks in just a few minutes and the view from the lake is the best."

I waved and yelled, "Coming!" We'd been waiting for about thirty minutes for enough paddleboats so we could all paddle around the man-made lake that was at the heart of the enormous park and watch the latter of the two nightly fireworks displays. Because I'd sent a hunk of House of Night cash to Tulsa specially for the completion of the park, the city had very nicely added a second and later fireworks show to the schedule. They had also approved my request that the park be open until 3 a.m. Tonight it was filled with vampyres and fledglings. Some were at the skateboard park, zooming up and down things that looked like giant empty swimming pools. Others were playing basketball or checking out the many trails. And still others—especially the youngest, newly Marked fledglings, were exploring the forts and bridges and crazy slides that filled a huge, rambling jungle-gym type area. Basically, fun was being had by everyone—even the young humans who braved the late-night hours to mingle with fledglings. I'd been sure the Sons of Erebus Warriors were visible to discourage any hazing by humans—as well as any biting by fledglings. So far—so good…

"Z! Come on!" Stevie Rae's voice broke through my train of thought.

"Okay! Okay!" I quit gathering wool, as Grandma would say, and followed Stevie Rae, Aphrodite, and Jack to the paddleboat loading dock. Our guys—Rephaim, Darius, Damien, and Stark were already standing beside the little boats waiting to help us climb aboard.

"Rephaim, did you get popcorn? I love watchin' the fireworks with popcorn!" Stevie Rae squealed happily as Rephaim helped her into their little boat and then handed her a big bag of visibly buttery popcorn.

Stark took my hand and I hopped into our boat. "Did you get me popcorn?"

"Nope. Better. I got you this." Stark grinned and handed me a giant pickle wrapped up like a corn dog.

Before I snatched it from his hand I kissed him—long and hard. "You are my hero."

"That's right. I am. And I know my Z hearts her some giant pickles," Stark laughed as we began pedaling out on the lake.

"Hey, wait for us! You know how I feel about physical exertion," Aphrodite called from somewhere behind us.

"Work those legs, girl!" Stevie Rae yelled back.

"Come on, Aphrodite!" Jack called. "We're just gonna paddle to the fireworks platform. Then we'll stop and watch the sparkles!"

I heard Aphrodite mutter, "Sparkles. Goddess, he's just like Jack," making me almost spew pickle out of my nose.

Jack and Damien's boat was in place first, and the rest of us fell in beside them, stopping our boats and facing the fireworks platform. It was easy to stay together. There was almost no wind on this strangely warm January night.

"It'll probably snow tomorrow," said Stark, tilting back his head and staring up at the star-filled Oklahoma sky.

"Or ice. We haven't had an icepocalypse in a year. We're due," I said around a mouthful of pickle.

"You look ridiculously cute eating that." Stark reached across the small space between us to tuck an escaping piece of hair behind my ear.

"Is that a phallic comment?" I waggled my eyebrows at him.

Stark laughed. "Um, no. Your lips look all pickled and your breath is not great when you eat those things."

"So, not dead sexy?"

"Will you settle for dead cute?"

"If you kiss me I will," I teased.

"I'll take that challenge!" Stark leaned over and tried to give me a gentle, sweet peck on the cheek and I turned my head, meeting his mouth with my pickle lips and kissing him thoroughly—*with my pickle tongue.*

He sputtered and wiped his mouth, but he also took my hand in his and kissed it, grinning at me. "I love you—pickle mouth and all."

"Well, if I didn't believe it before, I definitely do now that you've passed the pickle test."

"Oh, good. I've passed. Does that mean I don't have to take this particular test again?"

"Only if you get super lucky."

"Ooooh! It's going to start! It's going to start!" Jack cheered from the boat to our right, clapping happily.

"I like this part of paddleboating," Aphrodite said.

I glanced to my left where she and Darius sat still beside us. "You mean because you're doing no paddling?"

"Exactly," she said. "And my Warrior brought my fave snack." She lifted a champagne flute and the minibottle that Darius had brought for her that held about a glass and a half of champagne.

"Hey," I caught her attention so I didn't have to shout what I wanted to say. "You're doing a real good job of watching your drinking. I just wanted you to know I noticed."

"It's weird. After Nyx gave me this special Mark," she pointed to her intricate tattoo of red and blue—the only mixed red and blue tattoo in vampyre history, "I realized I could drink as much booze and take as many pills as I want, and neither one would hardly affect me. But I didn't want to anymore. A glass—maybe two—is enough. And pills? Now that I'm responsible for giving people second chances I don't think it's very smart to mess up my mind. And I *am* smart. Time I act like it."

I nodded. "You're being a good Prophetess."

She tilted her head as she looked at me. "Thanks, Z. I appreciate you saying that." Aphrodite leaned to her right so that she and I were closer, and she lowered her voice. "I wanted to talk to you about my visions—or, more accurately, my *lack* of visions."

"It hasn't been that long since you've had one. Has it?"

"Well, no. But since the other day when I talked to Ice Cream Shoes and we had that weird double premonition about her new abilities and something coming, I've started to wonder if maybe Nyx is going to give me a different kind of vision now."

"You mean visions that don't involve your eyes bleeding, crushing headaches, and being inside the body of whoever is being murdered?"

"Yeah. Exactly. It'd be a super nice change to not ever feel—" Aphrodite's words broke off in a gasp and a small shriek. "Goddess! Snake!"

Darius and I looked down at where she was pointing and, sure enough, I caught the sinuous reflection of the dark water rolling gently around the thick body of an even darker snake as it slithered past us.

"You know snakes are nothing to be afraid of," I said.

"That is a water moccasin. We should be afraid—*very* afraid. They're poisonous and mean." Aphrodite shuddered. "And they remind me of those disgusting tendrils of Darkness Neferet called her children. It's just so damn gross that I can't even see a snake without thinking about—"

Then, right in the middle of her sentence, it happened. Aphrodite began to tremble—at first it was just a slight shaking of her hand. Just enough for her champagne to slosh over the sides of the glass and into the lake. She looked up from frowning at her hand, obviously confused. Her trembling increased, and she dropped the flute into the water.

"Oh, shit!" she said. "Not here!"

And then her eyes filled with blood before they rolled into the back of her head as she sagged against her seat. It happened so fast that Darius had to scramble to catch her so she didn't follow her champagne glass into the lake.

"I'm coming!" I dropped my half-eaten pickle and stood.

Balancing precariously, I quickly told Stark, "She's having a vision! Get me closer to their boat."

"Will do. Hang tight just a sec, Darius, Z's coming!"

"Damien! Stevie Rae!" I shouted as Stark expertly paddled our boat so that it brushed the side of Aphrodite's. "Aphrodite! Vision!"

As I scrambled over to join Aphrodite and Darius, I saw Stevie Rae and Damien understand instantly what was happening. While the fireworks exploded overhead, I held Aphrodite tight as Darius's powerful legs propelled us back to the dock.

Zoey

"Goddess, that was embarrassing." Aphrodite was reclining on the couch in her suite with a wet washcloth pressed against her eyes.

"I don't think hardly anyone noticed," Stevie Rae said. "What, with all the fireworks goin' off and everythin'."

"You are a Prophetess of Nyx. Anyone who witnesses one of your visions should count themselves blessed," said Darius.

He was sitting beside Aphrodite on the couch with her bare feet in his lap—grounding her, comforting her. I thought, not for the first time, what a great couple they made—though somehow it made me feel a little disloyal to my brother from another world to think it.

"Can you talk about your vision yet?" Jack was hovering

around Aphrodite. He'd brewed her some ginger tea that'd he'd brought from the suite he and Damien shared. He said it would help settle her stomach, and her hands had finally stopped trembling enough to hold the mug.

Aphrodite nodded shakily. "Yeah. I can talk now. Could I have more of this tea, though? It is really helping my stomach settle."

"Oh goodie! I'll brew you some more." Jack took her porcelain teacup and hurried back to the kitchenette.

I sat on the coffee table and scooted close to her. Stevie Rae was standing beside me. Stark and Rephaim were sitting on the two chairs in front of the fireplace. Everyone had done their part to help Aphrodite recover—by now the Nerd Herd was a well-oiled machine when it came to her visions and the painful aftermath. But Aphrodite was always the same. She sifted through the pain and the horror of each vision as quickly as possible.

"Is it any of us?" I asked as Damien pulled out his phone and got ready to take notes.

"No. The vision was strange. I don't know who I was. It was a woman. I know that for sure, but she was so panicked that I could barely get her to glance down at her body. When she did I could tell it wasn't any of us, and that she was older, like probably in her forties, but that's it. And then I did manage to catch a quick glimpse of her reflection, but it was weird—like she was looking into a mirror that was distorted and dark. I still didn't recognize her, but she seemed familiar."

"A mirror?" I asked. "So, you were inside a house?"

Aphrodite grimaced and rearranged the washcloth so that it covered her light-sensitive eyes more completely. "No. I was outside and it was dark, but I was able to recognize where

I was." She drew a deep breath before finishing in one quick burst of words. "The vision took place at Woodward Park."

"Was Neferet in it?" Stevie Rae's voice sounded as trembly as I felt.

"Definitely." Aphrodite paused as a shudder pulsed through her body. "She was so damn gross. Well, part of the time she was. When she was killing that poor woman, she was *disgusting*."

"Do you mean literally, as in physically disgusting? Or just her normal sociopathic level of disgusting?" I asked.

"Both. Here's what happened. Remember the water moccasin I saw?"

"Yeah," I said.

"And how I said it reminded me of Neferet's tendrils of Darkness?"

"Yeah, for sure."

"Well, that's how the vision started. The snake suddenly changed and became a whole nest of writhing tendrils that came slithering out of Neferet's tomb. They looked different than last time we saw them. Remember how they were really big and thick, like huge, eyeless black snakes?"

"Yeah, I do." I shivered. "They were all teeth."

"Really gross," Stevie Rae said.

"Yeah, but in my vision, even though there were a lot of them, they were small. Like no bigger than the length of my hand, and about the width of a finger. But they were still every bit as destructive. They came from everywhere—through the cracks in the rocks, up out of that brackish water—they even seemed to be slithering from Neferet's body. And she was covered in them, like they were living clothes." She shuddered. "It was super disgusting."

"She broke out of her tomb? How?" I'm not sure how I managed to keep my voice steady because my insides were totally in revolt and I felt sick with fear.

"I didn't see that part. Probably because the woman's death didn't happen as Neferet broke out. It was like she had already escaped. So, at first, Neferet was completely naked except for the nauseating, slithering worm clothes. Her body was emaciated. Remember how she looked that night? Like her arms and legs were too long?"

Stevie Rae's voice shook. "I-I'll never forget how she looked."

Damien's face was the color of spoiled milk. "It was terrible," he said.

"None of us will ever forget," said Stark, wiping an unsteady hand across his face like he wished he could wipe away the memory.

"Well, that's how she looked in my vision. Only worse. Then I blinked, and she looked normal, dressed all in black—boots, slacks, and a black sweater, cashmere, I think—which was weird because I can't remember the last time I've seen her in anything but Silver Screen movie-star glam dresses. Oh, and she had her hair piled on top of her head in an exquisite updo.

"Then, it was like she kept shifting back and forth. And the woman whose body I was in wasn't always terrified. In the beginning, she was just hanging out drinking red wine with Neferet. They were at the park, but the woman wasn't afraid of her at all. It was really strange. I got the distinct feeling that they were friends. Maybe even more than friends."

"You mean the woman and Neferet were lovers?" I was

amazed at even the thought of Neferet taking a middle-aged human as her lover—be it a man or a woman.

"No, not lovers either. I wasn't with the good part long enough to understand it, but I can say for sure the woman and Neferet are close—really close. Then I got this weird flash and the scene changed and Neferet changed. I watched her hover above her broken tomb with her tendrils writhing all around her. That's when the woman I was in panicked, and things got super confusing. Neferet kept flickering back and forth from normal to nightmare. Then the woman died." Aphrodite's chin trembled as she spoke. "Horribly—and it took awhile."

"How?" I really didn't want to know, but like Aphrodite—it was my duty. I had to know. I had to help. I had to try to stop whatever awful thing was going to happen.

"The normal Neferet was nowhere to be seen and the disgusting snakelike Neferet sent her tiny, revolting tendrils to burrow into the woman's body and basically eat her from the inside out. It was really, *really* nasty. She was absolutely hysterical, and in an incredible amount of pain. It took a long time for her to die." Aphrodite swallowed. "And that was the good part of the vision."

"The *good* part?" Like her legs could no longer hold her, Stevie Rae sat heavily beside me on the coffee table.

"Yeah. The instant she died, Neferet stopped shifting back and forth between looking like herself and looking like a giant spidery nightmare. She was all nightmare. Darkness poured from her body. Like a tsunami, it crashed into Tulsa, completely enveloping the House of Night and Utica Square—and it kept spreading like an unstoppable virus. I saw it cover all of Tulsa, then Oklahoma, and then the entire country."

"And you're sure it was *our* House of Night and *our* world? You didn't see Other Kevin or anything that might've made you think you were getting a vision from the Other World?" I tried not to hold my breath as I waited for her reply.

"It was our world for sure. It was our grotto—exactly how it looks now. Unless it was walled up in the Other World?"

"Nope," I shook my head. "Their Woodward Park looks like ours *before* we trapped Neferet. And I'm pretty sure you'd realize it if it had been a vision from Kev's world. It's darker there. Less people are walking around. It's gloomy."

"No. It wasn't like that. It was all familiar. I'm sure it was a vision from this world."

Stark stood and went to the fireplace. Steadier now, he ran his hand through his hair and said, "So, Neferet escapes. And she can shift between looking normal and looking like a monster. The escape part is surprising, but the fact that she can change her appearance really isn't. She's immortal. Who the hell knows the extent of her powers?"

"Did you get any clue about a time frame for her escape?" I asked.

"Yes," Darius said. "Did you see any trees? Try to remember if there were leaves on the trees at the park or not."

Thinking, Aphrodite paused and then shook her head, which made her suck in her breath in pain. She pressed the washcloth against her burning eyes and said, "There were definitely no leaves on the trees, but there may have been buds."

Damien continued to take notes as he spoke. "So, she's either going to escape in the next couple months—or some other winter or early spring."

"My visions usually happen within weeks—tops a month or two."

"I suppose there's no chance Nyx is givin' us a year or so warnin'?" Stevie Rae asked hopefully.

"That'd be nice, but my intuition says this vision will happen sooner rather than later. I did get a sense of one thing very strongly. The focus of the vision was *not* Neferet. It was the woman her tendrils attacked. If that woman dies, we're doomed. I have zero clue why—I do not know who she is and I do not know how the death of one human could make such a difference to Neferet. All I know is that I am completely sure that if Neferet kills her, our world is going to be covered in Darkness."

"Then we have to figure out who she is," I said. "Once we do that all we need to do is keep her away from Neferet."

Darius sat up straighter, meeting my gaze. "We can stop the whole thing by being sure Neferet doesn't escape from her tomb."

"That's going to happen. I have no doubt about that at all," said Aphrodite.

Jack returned from the kitchenette and put the fresh cup of tea on the coffee table beside Aphrodite. "Honey, let this cool for a little while." He went to Damien and sat on the arm of his chair, looking as pale as his lover. "But Neferet doesn't have to escape, right? Your visions are warnings. They *can* be stopped. Damien told me you guys have stopped them a bunch of times. You even saw me killing him in one, and that definitely did not happen." He took Damien's hand and held it like he had no intention of ever letting it go.

"Yes, we can stop her visions from coming true. If we couldn't I'd have died more times than Buffy," I said firmly.

"Z, how old are you, thirty? You gotta update your bingeing," said Aphrodite.

"*Buffy* is a classic," I said.

"Imagine me rolling my eyes," Aphrodite said. "And, Jack, you're right. We have stopped my visions from coming true many times, but Neferet's escape happened *before* my vision. If that was stoppable, it would've happened *during* the vision."

"Maybe your vision isn't to keep us from changing the fact that Neferet gets free, and instead it's warning us that we need to be prepared," I said.

"Yeah, and we need to protect that woman from Neferet once she does get free," added Stevie Rae.

"So let's start by tripling the guard at Woodward Park," I said.

"Immediately," Darius said.

"I'll let the Sons of Erebus Warriors know," said Stark. "You go ahead and stay here with Aphrodite until she falls asleep."

"Thank you." Darius nodded gratefully.

"Stark, how are those cameras coming?" I asked.

"I'm pretty sure they'll be delivered in the morning. At least that's what the tracking info said. I was going to get them installed tomorrow after sunset."

"If they aren't delivered in the morning go get something —anything," I said. "Just put temporary cameras up if you have to. We need eyes out there during daylight. I'll notify Detective Marx about Aphrodite's vision right away."

Rephaim spoke up, sounding uncharacteristically defeated. "There isn't much the TPD can do against an insane immortal vampyre."

"True," I said. "But they can be prepared to evacuate people who live by the park should anything weird start happening."

Aphrodite yawned and shivered. "Is it cold in here? I'm freezing."

"No, my beauty. This happens every time you have a vision. You will be yourself again after you sleep," Darius said.

"Okay, that's our cue," I said. "I'll call Marx."

"I'll take care of tripling the Warrior guards at the park," said Stark. "And I'll also double-check the tracking on the cameras and have the IT vamps ready to install them the instant they arrive." Then he added, "And if they aren't arriving in the morning, I'll be sure we buy some temp cameras and get those set up."

"Just text me," said Damien. "I can go get the cameras after sunrise if need be. And I have a thought. Z, I know the last time we tried to cast a protective spell over the grotto it went awry."

"Understatement of the century," Aphrodite mumbled.

"But I think you should consider casting some kind of protection over the grotto—or maybe all of Woodward Park, even if it's just an early warning system," Damien finished.

"I hear you," I said. "And I don't disagree, but we have to be careful about what kind of spell we cast."

"Yeah, it can't be tied to Zoey," said Stark. "We all know what happened to Thanatos when Neferet broke the protective spell she'd cast over the Mayo."

"It was terrible." Stevie Rae shuddered. "We can't take a chance on losing you like that, Z."

"I'm all about not dying," I assured my BFF and everyone else. "But I also agree with Damien."

"How about I take a break from the depot renovation— move back the opening to, say, Valentine's Day, and instead research protection spells?" Damien offered.

"I hate to have your opening messed up," I said.

Rephaim rested his hands on Stevie Rae's shoulders. "It won't matter when the restaurant opens if Neferet destroys our world," he said.

"Rephaim makes an excellent point," said Damien.

Jack looked like he was going to burst into tears. "I really don't want this world destroyed. It's my fave."

"Neferet isn't going to destroy this world," said Aphrodite. "I'm given visions so that *we can change things*."

"That's right. We can stop this," I said. "We have to."

"We're never lettin' Neferet win," said Stevie Rae.

"Never," Stark echoed.

"We stopped her once. We can do it again," said Darius.

"Together," I said firmly. "That's the key. We can stand together against anything."

"Should you call Shaunee and Shaylin back here?" Stark asked.

"Yes," Aphrodite said.

"It's that urgent?" I asked her.

She turned her head so that she faced me. I could see the bloody tear trails left on her cheeks and her shirt. She was so deathly pale that her red and blue tattoo looked neon.

"It is. I feel like things are moving already. Small things, though. But they're picking up energy—like the beginnings of an avalanche."

I made my decision instantly. "Stevie Rae, call Shaunee and Shaylin. Update them and tell them to come home as soon as they can."

"Sure thing, Z."

"I wonder if we should also call Kramisha," I said. "She usually gives us a heads-up about—"

My phone's text notification chimed.

I took my phone out of my jeans pocket. Kramisha's name glared up at me, and, with a terrible sense of foreboding, I clicked on the text.

> Shit's going down. I just wrote this. Knew I had to send it 2 you. I'm coming home ASAP. XO, K

Her text included a simple haiku that had chills skittering up and down my spine and lifting the tiny hairs on my arms. I read the rest of the text aloud:

> *"Her life is a key,*
> *Humanity locked within.*
> *Open at your peril."*

"Shit," Aphrodite said. "I seriously hate prophetic poems with all their figurative language and symbolism, but even I know that the 'her' has to be the woman I saw. Like I said— she dies and we're fucked. And I'm using the global *we're*."

Jack sounded out of breath as he blurted, "But that only happens if we don't stop Neferet from killing one human woman. Right? Right you guys?"

"Right." I put on my best High Priestess–in–charge voice. "And we're going to stop her."

Aphrodite snorted.

In silent agreement, my mind shouted, *Ah hell, ah HELL, AH HELL!*

21

Other Neferet

Neferet sat quietly while Lynette finished her coiffure. She'd decided to wear it up. A new look for a new world and a new life. They'd arrived at Balmacara Mains in the early afternoon and Neferet had fed and then slept—not stirring until well after sunset. She'd needed the time alone.

Loren's death hadn't been initially difficult for her, but when she put it into perspective as killing her past it gave her pause. She'd been attached to her past. She was Neferet, High Priestess of the Tulsa House of Night. That title had defined her for decades and now that it was as dead as Loren, she had to decide who she was.

Neferet wasn't a High Priestess.

Neferet wasn't a goddess.

Neferet wasn't a normal vampyre. She never had been, and she never would be normal.

And with that realization, the final piece of the riddle Oak had tasked her with completing slid into place.

"That's it! I know how to kill my future!"

That realization opened the dam, and Neferet was washed with sudden insight.

Over the past week, she'd discovered things about herself

that had been a surprise—like how she'd come to rely on *humans* to aid and succor her. And that she truly considered Lynette a friend.

The last time Neferet had a true friend she'd been a powerless child named Emily Wheiler. Strange that it seemed she had somehow come full circle here on the outskirts of an island that was filled with unimaginable power as she took her final steps toward immortality.

Neferet had summoned Lynette to her suite to help her dress. She hadn't done that before, but this day was special, and Neferet felt there was a ritual-like importance to everything about it.

Lynette had understood. Not wasting any time with chatter, she dressed Neferet slowly, carefully, with focused attention to detail. Neferet had Lynette clasp the silver pentagram around her neck. Then she slipped large diamond stud earrings into her lobes. With her hair up, they twinkled with cold fire and framed her face with starlight.

Lynette stepped back and studied Neferet from head to toe. "You look fierce."

"As do you. You know how I feel about jeans, so I was hesitant when you told me what you planned to wear, but now I see the wisdom of it. You would blend in anywhere."

"That's what I thought. I'm trying to be as unmemorable as possible."

"Temporarily, Lynette. Once I am a goddess and we return, this world will acknowledge you as my handmaid *and dearest friend.*"

Lynette's face flushed. Her hand went to her throat. "My lady! That's how I feel too. It seems like I've known you my whole life but had to wait to meet you."

"And now that we have met I cannot do without you."

"I'll always be here for you. That's what being a friend is all about." Lynette looked down and when she met Neferet's gaze again the vampyre saw tears pooling in her eyes. "I have a confession to make. Before you I didn't have any friends. Not really. I met women for brunch. I went to galas and mingled. I was always invited to restaurant openings and gallery shows—but not because I had friends. They invited me because I had money and business connections. They didn't actually like me."

"I actually like you." As Neferet said the words aloud she realized how true they were, and her own eyes filled with tears.

"I actually like you too. I'm still frightened about tonight, though."

Neferet took both of her hands. "I give you my oath. As long as I draw breath, I will protect you. You have nothing to fear—not if you are at my side."

"That's where I'll be. I give you my own promise on that. Like Denise, I believe in you."

"When you say that, you make me want to be the best goddess I can possibly be—beloved by all, even humans."

"Maybe most especially humans. Many of us who aren't magickal have craved that special something vampyres have—that could be why humans find it so hard to accept vampyres."

"Because they're jealous?" said Neferet.

"Yes, but it's more than that. More like, because all of us want to be as special as vampyres and we can't—*that's* why we're jealous. But being beloved by a benevolent goddess, one who cares for us *as much as she cares for those who are special* would be as close to a miracle as most humans will ever get."

"There is great wisdom to what you say. And I can tell you that during this past week I have felt more cared for and supported than during my entire reign as High Priestess in Tulsa—and that is solely because of humans."

"And remember this, my lady. There are *a lot* more humans than vampyres in the world. Think of the power you would wield if they all worshipped the Goddess of Night."

Neferet felt a rush of emotion that brought with it a happiness that bloomed within her breast. She embraced Lynette and held her close. The two women clung to one another as they finally understood how it felt to be accepted.

"You are wise beyond your years, my dearest friend. I will do it. I will be Goddess of Night to *all* humans, and any vampyre who is wise enough to worship me."

"And if they choose not to worship you? The vampyres, I mean. Humans will—I feel quite sure of it."

"Well, I shall follow the wisdom of a vampyre named Darwin. He wrote that only the fittest and most intelligent of a species should survive. The others—" Neferet shrugged, "—should be culled from the herd for the good of the many."

"Very wise, my lady."

"Is the travel bag ready?" Neferet asked.

"I have packed it with everything you requested." Lynette picked up a large leather backpack and slid it onto her shoulders.

"Excellent." Neferet went to her makeup table, and from one of the small drawers she scooped up what was left of the jewelry that she'd brought from the travel collection she kept on her jet. "And now let us go. Let us not keep the sprites, and our future, waiting."

Mrs. Muir, Noreen, and wee Denise waited in the parlor Neferet had claimed as her own. As she and Lynette entered the room, the three women curtsied low, bowing their heads respectfully.

"Please rise," Neferet said.

"I finished the bread ye asked me ta bake," said Mrs. Muir. "Shall I ready it for the fey?"

"Yes. Please add a bowl of honey and of wine. I will gift it to the sprites."

"Aye, Mistress."

Mrs. Muir disappeared into the kitchen to return shortly with a tray laden with fragrant, fresh bread still warm from the oven, local honey, and a big bowl of wine so rich and red it looked like blood.

"Tonight, I ask the three of you to accompany me to the shore of the loch, but it is only a request. I do not demand it. I will never demand the worship of humans, but I will appreciate it and remember it for an eternity should you choose to follow me." Neferet strode to the door. When she reached it, she turned to see who would follow.

Lynette paused with her. When no one spoke, she held out her arms and said, "Mrs. Muir, shall I carry that try or will you be joining us?"

The old woman hesitated, but finally muttered, "I'm gaunnae join Herself."

Lynette's gaze took in Noreen and wee Denise.

"I chose Herself before. I'll be choosin' her again and again." Denise joined them at the door.

"And you, Noreen?"

"I'm afraid—my legs are all shoogly."

"I know just how you feel," Lynette said. "I used to be afraid, but not anymore. Not after I swore to Neferet's service. She is my protector. *She commands the sprites.*" She met Neferet's gaze. "You'll protect them, won't you?"

"You have the word of a goddess on it," Neferet said.

"'Tis good enough for me." Noreen hurried to the door.

Neferet smiled. "Excellent. Dear Lynette, please give me my dagger."

From within the backpack Lynette drew the dagger that had ended Loren Blake's life.

"Please place it on the tray Mrs. Muir carries."

Lynette did as she was told. Neferet watched Mrs. Muir give the sgian dubh a wary look. Noreen paled as the foyer light caught the blade and shimmered dangerously. Only wee Denise's expression did not change. Neferet was not surprised.

"Come with me, my dearest subjects." Neferet lit the lantern that waited nightly beside the door and walked out into the still, dark night.

A calm certainty filled Neferet as she picked her way across the rocks and driftwood of the empty, night-cloaked beach. She could feel the supportive presence of Lynette and the three servants as if it was as tangible as the tentacles of Darkness that swarmed to her, unseen by anyone except their mother.

"You know what is about to happen, don't you, children?" she whispered to the tentacles as they slithered around her, wrapping up her legs and coiling around her arms like the rarest of jewels. "Remain with me. Do not leave my side. I will not enter a world bereft of my children."

The night was cloudy, but as they reached the waterline the

wind shifted, blowing from the island that crouched on the horizon. It brought to them the scent of the earth, rich with groves and moss and hidden places. It also blew away the low clouds to reveal a fat, shining crescent that turned the black water silver and made the damp rocks sparkle with mischief.

Neferet turned her back to the loch to face the four humans. "I have something for each of you—a token of my appreciation and fidelity. Know that even though I shall be out of sight, you shall never be far from my thoughts. Keep my tokens as proof of my promise to return—and with my return I shall bring with me power beyond your imaginings."

Neferet opened her hand to reveal precious gemstones set in platinum.

"Mrs. Muir, you may give the tray to Lynette and approach me."

The tray changed hands and then Mrs. Muir stood before the vampyre. She clasped her hands before her and Neferet thought she looked as if she might be praying—which she found highly appropriate.

Neferet lifted a slim silver chain from the pile of jewels. Dangling from the end of it was a large freshwater pearl the color of a blushing sunset, set in a circle of pink tourmalines.

"This is for you. And with it you have my thanks and my promise of return."

Mrs. Muir looked utterly shocked. She snatched the necklace from Neferet, her eyes wide as they reflected the fire of the stones. "Thank ye, Mistress." She bobbed a curtsy.

"Noreen, I have something for you next."

Noreen stumbled as she approached Neferet and then stood in front of her, chewing her lip and fidgeting.

"This is for you, Noreen." Neferet chose a brooch that

was shaped like the fat crescent above them. It was flecked with rubies so that it glistened like fresh blood. "Wear it in remembrance of me."

Noreen's hand shook as Neferet dropped it into her palm. She curtsied awkwardly. "Th-thank you, Mistress."

Neferet turned her attention to Denise. The girl didn't wait to be summoned. With eager steps she hurried to stand in front of Neferet, and when she looked up at the vampyre, passion blazed from her eyes.

"Dear wee Denise, I have saved the best for last. The first night I gave gifts to the sprites, I chose a ring made of an occluded sapphire the exact color of the water surrounding Skye. This pendant is its mate—the only match to my ring there will ever be." Neferet held up the platinum chain from which hung a single sapphire—cut in a square like the ring. Its setting was encrusted with diamonds. It caught the flickering flame of Neferet's lantern and shinned with a light that seemed otherworldly. "I give it to you along with my promise that this is just the beginning of the rewards you will reap for your loyalty. I shall never forget that you and my dearest Lynette were the first to swear into my service."

"Och, my lady. Ye leave me speechless." Denise curtsied and bowed as Neferet placed the necklace over her head so that it dropped heavily between her breasts to rest near her heart.

"Now I would ask that the three of you wait and watch from there." Neferet pointed a short way back on the beach.

They moved away. Mrs. Muir and Noreen were still staring at their gifts, but wee Denise's gaze was riveted on the vampyre.

"Ready?" Neferet asked Lynette.

"If you are—I am."

"Today truly begins my journey to a new future—a new eternity."

"I believe in you, my lady. I know you can do this."

Neferet squeezed her hand and then went to the edge of the loch and stopped just short of the water lapping her boots. She placed the lantern beside her. "Lynette, remain by my side, but take a step back. I do not want the sprites to focus on you."

Lynette moved back a step. Neferet turned and took the dagger from the tray and slid it carefully into the pocket of her slacks. Then she raised the tray above her head. As she spoke, her voice echoed eerily across the water like a restless ghost.

"Sprites of air, fire, water, and earth! I, Neferet, summon you! My quest complete, I bear gifts and come to claim my reward! Appear to me one and all—come as promised, answer my call!" Neferet placed the tray on the loch. "Children, reveal yourselves and carry these gifts to them."

Tendrils manifested fully, writhing over one another in eagerness to obey their mother. They carried the tray of bread and honey and wine out onto the loch, leaving it to float on the surface.

The night sizzled into life. Sprites lifted from the water to engulf the tray and pull it under. At the same time, hundreds of fey appeared. Dazzling in their infinite array of colors and shapes, they filled the night with their whispering voices as they flitted about erratically, not settling until Oak appeared in the middle of them. As before, she was larger and more humanoid than the others. She raised one slender hand and the sprites went silent.

"Neferet, why is it that tonight we meet—
though the death of your future you have yet to
complete."

"I thought you would like to witness the end of my quest—the death of my future."

"That is true. It will amuse me to observe you."

"I killed Loren Blake and with him destroyed my past, and after doing so I understood how to rid myself of my old destiny—my old future—so that I may embrace the new. I do that now and ask that you and these special humans, in service to me, serve as my witnesses." Neferet spread wide her arms. "From this night forth, I renounce my title of High Priestess of Nyx. I reject the service of the Goddess. I reject the Vampyre High Council. I no longer belong to any House of Night. From this night forth, I choose to take the path unblazed in this world—neither vampyre nor human and not yet divine, with a new destiny I will myself align. So I have spoken—and for eternity so mote it be!"

Oak nodded her head, causing the maidenhair fern that cascaded around her shoulders to sway gracefully.

"My test you have passed.
So we shall do as you asked.
Access to the isle from which
all others are banned
you now do command!"

The sprite waved her hand and a narrow stretch of the

loch below her solidified into a magickal bridge that led from the bank of the mainland directly to the Isle of Skye.

Neferet did not move.

"I appreciate your fidelity to your word. I hope that you will appreciate that my plans have changed, and it is entrance to a different place that I require."

> *"Our deal was made.*
> *The price was paid.*
> *Enter the isle or remain*
> *To us it is all the same."*

"Then what if I say that the payment for my entrance to Skye is simply another gift to amuse, which means that for my new future I will pay a new price."

"This is highly unusual. We only accept payment for a task agreed upon."

Neferet knew that Oak's shift from poetic singsong to regular speech signaled that the sprite was not in negotiation mode, but she steeled herself and continued.

"I know that you brought Zoey Redbird here from another world."

The sprite's sharp gaze narrowed on Neferet. "Know what you will. Answers only come with payment."

"I am aware of that, but you misunderstand. I do not want answers from you. I can discover them for myself. I only want you to open the door to her world and allow me entrance."

Neferet saw the flash of surprise that lit the sprite's face and felt her first thrill of victory.

"And I am willing to pay whatever new price you ask for that entrance."

"We have, indeed, allowed entrance to and from
    Other Worlds before
but now we are bored and wish to do so no more."

Neferet took the sgian dubh from her pocket. She lifted her forearm and rested the blade against her skin.

"I am no longer High Priestess. I have rejected my future to forge a new destiny. Have you ever had a blood sacrifice from someone who is no longer one thing and yet to become another?"

Birdlike, Oak tilted her head.

"You are a creature truly unique
But a sip of blood is not enough payment for what you
    seek."

"Then name your price."

Oak's long finger pointed at Lynette, who had been standing as silent as the stones around them watching the exchange between Neferet and the sprite.

"To pass from world to world with the power we lend
I demand the sacrifice of the life of your only true friend."

Neferet felt rather than saw Lynette's body jolt in shock, and anger began to brew within her.

"I should have mentioned this earlier. I apologize for my oversight. Dear Lynette must accompany me to the world that is a mirror of this one. She is not merely my only friend. She is my handmaid, and I cannot do without her. Choose another sacrifice and I will give it to you."

"Only the exchange of a life will do.
Return when your need
is more important than friendship to you."

"No. Lynette has been faithful and true. You want me to sacrifice her? That I will not do!" Neferet blazed with anger. "Let's not play games like we're gibbering fools. I want something. You require sacrifice. I know the rules. Stop this charade. Tell me the true price you demand to be paid."

There was a great and overwhelming silence, and then Oak began to laugh. It was a terrible sound picked up by the other sprites. From hundreds of fang-filled mouths, the eerie noise lifted and reverberated around them like a choir of competing specters.

Neferet stood there without speaking, without reacting at all. Instead she waited with endless patience until Oak finally raised her hand, silencing the fey.

"I have grown bored of the comings and goings
*   between worlds—that I readily do say.*
But you—you deviate from the norm and pique
*   my interest today.*
So I offer you one last chance.
Let us stop this teasing dance.
There is a single payment I will take.
My patience is gone—make no mistake.
A dear life sacrificed you need,
So, for you, whom shall bleed and bleed and
*   bleed?"*

Neferet wanted to explode with fury. How dare this

creature demand anything of her! She was nothing but the reflection of the earth. Mundane. Ordinary. Most people didn't even believe in the fey anymore and Neferet was giving the ungrateful bitch the opportunity to be important—to be of the world again, honored and respected and paid tribute to. It was ridiculous that she—

"I will give my life as payment fair, and do so freely out of love as if answering a prayer."

Neferet whirled to see that wee Denise was walking forward, her gaze riveted on the hovering sprite.

"Wee Denise! No, I do not ask this of you."

Denise smiled as she reached Neferet. "It is because you widnae ask it that I do it. Go to the other world, my lady, my goddess. But dinnae forget your wee Denise and that she were faithful to you till her last breath and beyond."

Neferet took her face between her hands. "Wee Denise, you have the word of a goddess. Your name will be honored for eternity." Neferet kissed her.

Denise smiled. "It woulda been a bonnie thing to see—you returnin' divine." Then her gaze lifted to the sprite and she began to walk into the loch as she said, "But maybe I will see it—from wherever I'll be."

Before wee Denise could walk to the sprites, Neferet caught her slim wrist, halting her. Neferet met Oak's gaze and said firmly, "A payment this great means when we are ready to return we shall not wait."

Irritation crossed the sprite's expressive face, but Neferet could see that greed and bloodlust superseded it.

"I accept this payment dear.
Fey! Bring her near."

"And when it is time for Lynette and me to return?" Neferet said, still holding on to Denise's wrist.

"When you wish to return use your own blood to call.
I will respond when the scarlet drops fall."

"You must let me go now, my Goddess," wee Denise said, smiling up at her.

Neferet could not find the words to speak, so she simply lifted Denise's hand to her lips so she could kiss her once more before she let her go. She had to force herself not to rush after the girl and pull her back onto the shore. She felt powerless as the glowing sprites surrounded Denise, lifting her out of the water and carrying her up to Oak as if she rode on a magick carpet made of light.

"How interesting. From you I feel no fear," Oak said to Denise.

"Och, well, I've been leavin' gifts for yer kind most my life. I cannot be afeared of somethin' I find so dear."

"Your courage does you credit, wee Denise
And now through death you shall find release!"

The sprites descended on Denise. They covered her body so that even Neferet had to turn her eyes away because of the brightness. There was an explosion of light and then all of the sprites except Oak disappeared. Neferet blinked, trying hard to clear her sight—and she was surprised to see that one other sprite remained—a small water elemental only about the size of her fist. The little creature hovered above Neferet, looking like a large dragonfly with a woman's torso from which dangled *a long platinum chain that held an occluded sapphire set in diamonds.*

Beside her, Lynette gasped. "Denise?"

"Aye, well, sorta!" Denise's voice drifted down to them just before, with a little popping sound, she disappeared with the rest of the water fey.

*"Your price has been paid.
I have opened the door."*

Oak's voice echoed around them as a glistening oval materialized directly in front of Neferet and the sprite faded from view. *"Enter at your own risk, and begin the future for which you paid."*

Neferet reached out and Lynette took her hand.

"Are you ready, dear Lynette?"

"Yes, but don't let go of my hand."

Neferet gripped her friend's hand tighter. "Never. Deep breath."

"Deep breath," Lynette repeated.

Together, the vampyre and the human entered the portal—forever altering their future and the futures of both worlds.

With the sound of a giant's sigh, the portal closed. The wind returned and the clouds continued to drift back to obscure the moon. One enormous cloud churned and billowed high and mighty. Two massive white horns took shape—followed by a huge head and the body of an impossibly large bull.

From the darkening night sky a deep voice reverberated. *"Ah, my heartless one, you have surprised me. Again."*

The bull's laughter quaked through the clouds, releasing torrents of freezing rain that blanketed the highlands of Scotland in the cold darkness of an evil amused but not yet satisfied.

THE END... FOR NOW

Acknowledgments

Kristin always is a wonderful editor and partner, but she deserves a special acknowledgment for her work on this book. Thank you, Ja! You heppa-ed, Mama. Love yousees!

Thank you to our wonderful Blackstone Publishing team: Josh Stanton, Josie Woodbridge, Anne Fonteneau, Greg Boguslawski, Jeff Yamaguchi, and Lauren Maturo. Team Cast rocks! Special mention to Courtney Vatis for the fantastic brainstorming sessions and editorial eye! And an extra-special *"OMGoddess you're awesome"* to Kathryn English who created this spectacular cover, which is our favorite of all the HoN and HoNOW covers!

To my agent, Ginger Clark—thank you for helping me juggle an insane amount of work while I was finishing this book. Here's to many, many more years together.

Thank you to Teresa Miller and Theo LeGuin who led me to Ginger!

Steven Salpeter—I appreciate you!

A very special thank-you to my amazing assistant, Sabine Stangenberg. Thank you for making my world run smoothly so that I can disappear into my cave and write. I appreciate you so very much.

Thiago Marques—thank you for the fast and accurate research help. I know I can always count on you! XXXOOO

To our loyal, loving fans—we adore you. Please never forget: you are strong, beautiful, and worthy of love... always love.

On Grief and Loss: First Steps

There is a thematic element of grief and loss that runs through the plot of *Forgotten*. I found it interesting how the different characters in their different worlds dealt with survivor sadness and the sacrificial acts of others.

To begin with, I love the words of Mother Earth early in the book when she and Kalona discussed despair and anger:

> *"Yes, despair is more in your brother's nature—anger is more in yours... You should know that both emotions are allies of Darkness. Both will eventually destroy Light if left unchecked."*

It is vastly important that people, especially young people, understand that sadness and anger are often closely linked. Think about how you feel when you're filled with sorrow. It's like a weight pressing on your body, your soul, your mind. It's debilitating and isolating. Now, consider how anger makes you feel. Find the subtle similarities: the heaviness, the powerlessness, the crippling way it can isolate you.

Both emotions rob life of joy. They are soul-suckers and dream-stealers, destroyers of Light and love.

But loss is part of the circle of life, and anger after loss is a normal reaction. Its numbing effect feels almost good. It shifts our focus from our internal grief so that we can shove it aside temporarily—but for some people that temporary compartmentalization turns into a lifetime of rage and misery, which is exactly what happened to our world's Neferet.

How do we *not* do that? How do we choose love and Light when rage and Darkness feel so seductive?

I believe a big part of combating the lure of dark emotions is to step into the Light—and by that I mean to not allow ourselves to be isolated. Did our Neferet open up to anyone after she was brutalized? No, not truly. Instead she withdrew, and when she did, Darkness engulfed her and altered the course of her life.

I understand Neferet's choice. I've felt the pull of isolating despair. I have a good friend who told me once, during a time in my life when I experienced great loss and also was physically injured, that I "went dark." And I did. Without even realizing it I withdrew from friends and family. It felt safer, easier, less painful to fold in on myself—much like what Other Kevin experienced after his loss of Other Aphrodite.

Thankfully, my tribe of friends and family refused to leave me in the Darkness. One particular friend, the intuition teacher and animal communicator Bridget Pilloud*, put me on a path out of my miserable isolation with a simple and beautiful exercise that I then shared with Grandma Redbird, who used it to help Other Kevin through his grief. Here it is, in easy steps. It is something you can do alone— or something you can guide someone through. I've found

* Bridget Pilloud can be reached via her website, www.PetsAreTalking.com

that it works particularly well if you're outside—especially if you have access to wooded land.

Bring with you matches and a smudge stick (I prefer white sage, but there are many different versions of smudge sticks and herbs that can be used: sage, lavender, sweetgrass, Palo Santo, etc.).

1. Light your smudge stick, and as you smudge yourself, concentrate on the cause of your grief. Speak aloud the name of the person or animal or aspect of your life that you have lost (ex: if you have had to relocate and are deeply grieving the loss of your home). Allow yourself to grieve! Just as names are powerful, tears are cleansing—something especially important for young men to know in a society that tells them it isn't manly to show their emotions. But Grandma Redbird said it much better than I:

"No, my sweet boy. Do not hide your grief. There is no shame in showing your tears. Kevin, being a man means claiming all your power. Strength without honest emotion is toxic—to yourself, and eventually it makes you toxic to others. How can you truly love without showing sadness, acknowledging loss, dealing openly with despair?"

2. We see this every day in a patriarchal society that has raised so many men who are utterly out of touch with their emotions and toxic to themselves and others. Mothers, grandmothers, and sisters—let us all do better raising our male children.

3. When you feel able, carefully set aside the smudge stick on a rock or something nonflammable. Then breathe in

deeply to a count of four—in and out, in and out—four times.

4. With your next inhale, send your breath to a specific part of your body that hurts and when you exhale, imagine your breath carrying the pain from you (ex: the night Bridget guided me through this exercise I had a terrible grief headache, so my first inhale went to my head).

5. Then, aloud, ask for help from whatever is causing you grief. It can be as simple as saying, "Please help me to stop being so sad that you're gone that I can't go on with my life." Or as complex as Kevin's request of Aphrodite:

"I feel like I lost myself when you died, and I can't find myself again without you… If you could help I'd appreciate it. This pain is so bad, Aphrodite. Mind-numbing and soul-sucking. But I'm afraid to let it go because if I do, I'm afraid that means I'm letting you go too. And if I had my choice, I would never, ever let you go… Please, help me. Please."

6. And finally—the most magical part—*expect a response!* When I did this exercise, my grief was caused by months of injury and loss, culminating in the very unexpected, sudden death of my warrior canine, Badger. He collapsed in front of me and died in minutes—which was more than I thought my already battered heart could bear. When I asked for a sign, what I was gifted with, later that night, was the sound of him barking outside my door—so clearly, so loudly, that I actually rushed outside calling his name. He was there, of course, but only in spirit.

After your cleansing and releasing exercise, be sure you nourish yourself. Have a healthy meal, soak in a soothing tub—whatever helps you ground. And remember, no one is ever really gone. We are all joined by spirit and, if you open yourself, love… always love.

Know that this exercise is not meant as a solution to grief, depression, and/or anger. It is simply a first step. The rest of the journey to healing is up to you. Remember—you are strong, brave, and worthy of love. I believe in you.

Fan Q&A

You have questions? P. C. & Kristin have answers for you!

Do you have any news on the movie/TV series? We've been waiting FOREVER! Is it ever going to happen? (Too many of you asked this question for me to attribute it to one or a few readers, so let's say this one is from everyone!)

  P. C.: We've been waiting forever, too! Which makes us very, very happy to be able to tell you that our producers, Davis Films, have teamed up with Academy Award–winning producer Don Carmody and International Emmy-nominated producer David Cormican through their DCTV to adapt House of Night to a live-action television series! Kristin and I are absolutely 100 percent behind this adaptation. We adore the team and are confident that they will respect our books while bringing our beloved characters alive on the TV screen. Stay tuned for more announcements soon!

What was the first book you read that put you on the path to being an author, and when did you first start putting together the House of Night stories? —*Rachel Ann Miller*

P. C.: When I was thirteen years old I discovered Anne McCaffrey's brilliant series, the Dragonriders of Pern. It was the first time I understood that a female could write and star in a fantasy/science fiction series. I told myself right then that I was going to be an author and populate my worlds with strong women.

In 2005 Meredith Bernstein, who was then my agent, and I were having dinner at a Romance Writers of America national convention and she said she would love for me to write a series "set at a vampyre finishing school." I was teaching high school at the time, and my mind immediately went to YA. The rest is history…

When you're writing, do you and Kristin still have the same level of excitement for these characters in the HoN Other World series compared to when you two first started writing the House of Night series? Has your love for these characters changed over the years? —*Jennifer Smith*

P. C.: I'll always love the HoN universe. Writing in it feels like coming home. I adore the characters, and because they started so young and so immature it's still exciting to help them grow and evolve. My love for them has changed over the years—just like your love changes for friends and family. I've grown closer to some, like Kevin in both of his incarnations, and some just fade out of the story and the HoN life, like Drew or Venus.

K. C.: My love for the HoN world grows with each novel because my writing and editorial skills improve with each. It's like playing a sport—it becomes more and more fun as I hone my skills. Plus, in the Other World novels, it's so exciting to see how different some of my favorite characters are from the original HoN books.

What was one of the most surprising things you learned in creating the House of Night world? What about the Other World? —*Bri'ann Piguet*

P. C.: In both worlds I have been surprised about how many real-life events creep into the fictional worlds. Some are planned—like highlighting the hypocrisy of the Bible Belt and the type of people who attend church constantly and carry around their Bibles but are the first to judge and condemn anyone who doesn't look, act, or believe as they do. But often real-world themes that I do *not* plan to insert into the fictional HoN world become mirrored through the attitudes of my characters and the events that happen to them, like what happened between Aphrodite and her mother. I didn't plan for her mother to play such a significant role in *Lost* but the level of racism, entitlement, and toxicity that I was, and still am, seeing in too many upper-middle-class white women informed the characters and the plot. When that happens, I think of it as a very special kind of magick.

What draws you to writing about vampires? Are you a vampire yourself because you really have all the ins and outs figured out of this amazing society? And which character are you most like?

—*Lee Ryder*

P. C.: That's a good question! I was never drawn to writing about vampires. I was drawn to writing about teenagers and the issues they deal with on a daily basis. The House of Night is simply a vehicle to tell a larger story—one that highlights the struggles and joys young people face daily. I don't think of the characters as vampires. I think of them as real kids (and adults), and then I put those "real" people in a paranormal setting.

I could be a vampire! I write at night and rarely wake up before noon. When I'm near deadline I usually go to bed about the time the sun is rising. But I'm a vegan, so that blood stuff is not for me.

There are pieces of me in many of the characters. The easiest character for me to write is Aphrodite. I feel a huge affinity with Lenobia—and she has several of my horses. I'm also very close to Grandma Redbird, though she is wiser than I.

I know that Neferet had bad influences in her life that led her down the wrong roads. We know that she was power hungry. Was there ever a chance in either book that she could have turned out good, like Aphrodite, if she'd had friends like the Nerd Herd? —*Denise Hapner*

P. C.: That's an interesting question and really the basis of the Other World. If you've just finished *Forgotten*, you'll already understand that because Other Neferet's past differed from our Neferet's past *she* is different. I rely a lot on the nurture versus nature belief when I write the Other World characters.

With every character developed and their lives evolving or devolving in both series, did either of you consider the duality of Stevie Rae's complex experiences and life and have her revert to the mind-set of the original red vampire? Where in the process did Rephaim become the choice (perfect choice BTW) to be her soul mate? —*Michelle Landron*

P. C.: Aphrodite's sacrifice enabled Stevie Rae, and the rest of the red vamps and fledglings in her world, to regain their humanity. Then it was just a matter of choice, and Stevie Rae (along with Stark) clearly chose love over hate—Light over Darkness. She will not revert because of that choice, and neither will Stark. Some characters won't be as firm in their choice, which is why we could see others reverting—and have seen it.

I love the Rephaim question! His relationship with Stevie Rae was a total surprise to me! I planned that Stark would fall in love with Stevie Rae! Obviously, Stark had another plan—which happens frequently with my characters. I did *not* know that they were going to be a thing until the moment in *Tempted* when he speaks to her, and the humanity in his voice won't let her kill him. Had I known that they were going to fall in love I wouldn't have made Raven Mockers so hideous! You'll notice as you read through *Tempted* and beyond that I stop describing Rephaim, except for his voice and his hands, because *he is a hideous beast!* Sheesh. Talk about making my writing life difficult!

K. C.: Since I edit and brainstorm as opposed to write any books in the HoN series, this is one of the character development aspects that I leave to P. C., because she can see into Stevie Rae's future. Stevie Rae lives in P. C.'s head (as weird as that might sound) and she connects with her in a way that I'll never be able to.

Grandma Redbird is such a constant balance within the chaos, is she modeled after someone in particular?
—*Stacey Dhom*

P. C.: Grandma Redbird is modeled after and inspired by the third face of the Goddess, the Crone. She is a blessing to write.

Did you already know at the conclusion of the first series that Aphrodite would be a vampyre again? What gave you the idea to make her both blue and red?
—*Logan Kiner*

P. C.: No! I only knew that Aphrodite would be a being like none other. At the end of the original series she was a Prophetess of Nyx—not entirely human, but also definitely not a vampyre.

Aphrodite gave me the idea for her dual tattoos when she pulled herself out of her downward spiral and chose to give *herself* another chance. When she did that—I realized the full extent of who she was, and that's when Nyx gifted her with her unique tattoo and new power.

Did you originally intend for Kalona to turn good? Or was he supposed to just be a bad guy that the Nerd Herd defeats

and that was that? I've always been fascinated by Kalona even after he "died."

—*Rachael Hillis*

P. C.: From his very first scene I intended to redeem him and have him reunite with Nyx, but I had no clue how it was going to happen. I only knew he would have to work hard to earn his Goddess's forgiveness, which he did. He is one of my all-time favorite characters, and I have loved revisiting him in the form of Other Kalona.

Did you intend for Aphrodite to be such a huge influence in the beginning of it all? She's such a dear character now. Do you ever have any second guesses whether you guys made the right decision on her mark? (I love her so much!)

—*Heaven Leigh Wallace*

P. C.: I always intended that Aphrodite's character would grow and evolve and end up being very tight with Zoey and the rest of the Nerd Herd. You can see that as early as the last scene she's in with Z at the end of *Marked*. No, I've never second-guessed my decision to take away her Mark, and then to gift her with one that is unique to the HoN world. I love her exactly as she is.

Would you ever change Grandma Redbird to vampire as she can't live forever?

—*Kilah Gooding*

P. C.: Grandma Redbird won't be a vampyre, but I can

promise you that I have figured out a way for her to live forever! I couldn't bear it if anything happened to her.

Zoey's birth father is never mentioned... Will he be brought up or end up being someone powerful?

—*Cynthia Hobbs*

P. C.: Absolutely not. Zoey's birth father abandoned his children when he and his wife divorced. He isn't powerful. He's a deadbeat dad and completely irrelevant in Z's life and in the HoN world.

Have you ever regretted a plot point in any story? Have you looked at a character and felt sad about where they have ended up?

—*Carrina North*

P. C.: No, I don't regret plot points, but often characters and their choices make me sad. I snot cried when Jack died. I didn't know Heath was going to die until that terrible moment, and then along with Zoey I was shattered. I hated that Erin Bates made such bad choices. But I'm also pleasantly surprised by characters! Shaunee's evolution was lovely. Stark's loyalty makes my heart happy. And Other Neferet has been a delightful discovery.

Who was your most difficult character to build, looks- and personality-wise?

—*Kilah Gooding*

P. C.: The most difficult character to write in the original House of Night books was Neferet. Her descent into Darkness and madness was a terrible journey to experience with her, especially because it began with a rape. I was raped when I was thirteen (NOT BY MY FATHER), and I understand all too well the lure of revenge and the self-loathing that kind of violence can create. Writing the novella *Neferet's Curse* was one of the most difficult exercises of my life, but it was also cathartic. I'm glad I chose love and healing over anger and Darkness.

How have you found writing this alternative universe version of House of Night? Did you find it creatively freeing or challenging to rewrite the narrative and flip it on its head?
—*Ted Ryan*

P. C.: I've found it challenging, but also very satisfying. I have to continually remind myself that even though the characters have the same personality traits they also have had much different life experiences, and those experiences inform their actions and their emotions. It's a little like recreating the characters from scratch. I have to know everything about their pasts in the Other World, and then allow them to show me their natures. I always know I've gotten it right when the writing comes easily. If I'm stuck or try to force a choice on a character everything stops and I have to go back to that character's past. Again. This happened often with Other Neferet. She surprised me more than any character has in a long time. I think she'll surprise you, too!

What kind of research do you do, and how long do you spend researching before beginning a book? Also, what is your writing outline process like?

—*Bri'Ann piguet*

P. C.: I like to old-school research! I have a huge library. I love to pore through texts, marking up pages and writing notes to myself. As I read, ideas begin to form and characters start speaking to me. It is also important that I visit the places I write about, which is why the majority of my books are set wherever I'm living (or have lived or visited). I believe it is important to ground fantasy in reality. Even my books that are pure fantasy, like the Divine Series, have huge pieces of the real world in them.

How long I spend researching depends on how long it takes me to start seeing the world and the people who will populate it, but the truth is I continue my research as long as I'm writing.

I hate outlining. Kristin is so much better at it than I am. When I outline alone, I basically just write notes that I turn into paragraphs. I usually have the beginning and the end of a book when I start writing—and maybe a few scenes in between. Then, thankfully, my characters take over!

K. C.: I love outlining so much! It's impossible for me to start writing until I've outlined, especially because I don't write sequentially, so I need that map to help keep track of where I am and where I'm going. First, I write a general Act I, Act II, Act III outline which serves as an overview of the beginning, climax, and resolution of the novel. Then, I'll go back and do a chapter by chapter outline that connects the three acts. As I'm writing, I consistently remind myself that my outline is just a jumping-off point and that I can always change it as the story evolves.

What compels you to take locations from places you have visited and add them to your stories? (e.g. the catacombs and the buildings of the HoN setting?)
—*Rhiannon "Rhinny" Rickets*

P. C.: Part of my research process is to go to the places I'm using as settings. I need to be there to really understand how it feels, looks, smells, etc. I've always loved writing fantasy or using paranormal elements, and because of that genre choice I think it's important to ground my readers in reality so that they'll come with me when I add the magick!

I would love to know—did you always see this series evolving into what it is now? Did Kristin? Do you still feel that sense of attachment, like there's more story to tell in this world, or do you feel that after *Forgotten* it will be time to part with Tulsa for a while?
—*Rhiannon Storm*

P. C.: In 2005, I sold three books to St. Martin's Press—*Marked*, *Betrayed*, and *Chosen*. I'd only written three chapters of *Marked* at that time, and I had zero clue the series would evolve the way it did. But by the time I was working on *Chosen*, the series had begun to take off, so my wonderful publisher and hero, Matthew Shear, said the words to me that every author dreams of hearing from their publisher: "P. C., write whatever you want! Do whatever you want to do with this world! We want more, more, more!" At that time, I brought in an additional mythology and began expanding the world and the characters, which is why the books shifted from Zoey's first-person point of view to include other characters in third person—except when Z is the focus on a scene. Then she still carries the POV.

K. C.: I was nineteen when we first started writing the series and, for some reason, I assumed it would be a crazy, enormous success. Now, as a much older adult human, I'm blown away by its success!

P. C.: At this time, I don't have any more books planned, but that doesn't mean much. When I finished *Redeemed* I didn't think I'd revisit the HoN world for at least a decade, and you see how that worked out.,.

K. C.: Currently, *Found* is the final book in the Other World series. Like P. C., I didn't see returning to the HoN world for quite some time. In 2014 I had the idea to do an anniversary novel, (which ended up being *Loved*), but I never anticipated it would become its own series and breathe fresh life into the HoN. It's all very exciting!

How do you create the spells/poetry/rhymes?

—Jessica Blaine

P. C.: The spells, etc., are really just poetry, so what I do is think of the scene as a poem—and then write it. I'm Pagan, so the spells and rituals come easily to me—writing them is my personal devotion to the Goddess.

How did you create the lore for HoN? —*Evie Lynne*

P. C.: I began with biology, which means I called my dad! He taught biology for a zillion years and has always been my reference for science-based things. He makes sure my ecosystems work in all my books, and I don't mix up stuff like meiosis and mitosis. After he answered a bunch of questions, I created the foundation of how my vampyres Changed from human to vamp. Then I delved into the sociology of the HoN world. I made the decision quickly that mine would be a Pagan matriarch, and that informed many of my world's details. Next came the creation of my heroine, Zoey Redbird. I based her very loosely on Kristin when she was a teenager, and Kristin is of mixed heritage, which I mimicked in Z. For the rest of the lore, I went back to my Celtic roots, added a dash of Wicca and a dose of fantasy—and the House of Night was created!

When you two write a book together, do you send it back and forth or do you sit down and bounce plot ideas off of each other? —*Patricia Darlene Morales*

P. C.: Kristin and I don't write the HoN novels together. I do all the writing and Kristin is my editor. We do co-write the Dysasters, another YA series. We outline the books together and divide up the characters, choosing which characters each of us can envision the best, or has the best automatic connection with. Then when we start writing, whomever's character is the focus of a chapter writes that chapter. At the conclusion we do physically sit together and pass the laptop back and forth, though, because there are so many characters and so many points of view going on.

Have you two ever gotten to that point where one of you does not want to work with the other for a while? If you have, how have you worked past that?

—*Victoria Morrison*

P. C.: I'll answer from the mom point of view. I had a toxic mother. Not only did she constantly pick at and demean me, but she and her mother couldn't be in a room together without sniping and bickering. Years before I was pregnant with Kristin I vowed to break that cycle. Kristin and I do not fight. When she was a child I made the rules and enforced them, but I also listened to Kristin—and tried to see things from her point of view—to really understand her. I made mistakes, all parents do, but I acknowledged them and apologized and tried to do better. I have always respected, as well as liked and loved, Kristin. So, when we began working together we already had a strong, healthy relationship. I am proud to say that relationship has continued into her adulthood. She is wonderful to work with. I know I can count on her honesty, her intelligence, and her talent. I appreciate her. If she or I ever have an issue with a project we're working on all we do is talk about it—just like any other problem we've had. Kristin is my best friend. I wouldn't fight with my bestie.

K. C.: P. C. is fantastic to work with! She's telling the truth when she says that we don't fight. If I don't agree with something that's happening in one of the books, she listens when I voice my opinion and we come up with a solution together. It really helps that we had such a strong relationship prior to working together and that we continue to have a strong relationship separate from writing.

Out of the elements, which one do you and Kristin connect with the most?
—Ande Gullickson

P. C.: I'm an earth girl!

K. C.: I totally connect with the tranquil and also destructive power of water!

There is a running theme of elemental affinity in your work. What research led you to finding that particular theme, and what goal(s) have you both in giving such descriptive language for the feeling of being attached to them? I have an affinity with air and water, and I honestly fell in love with these books and the Goddess Summoning series for the familiarity and kinship I feel with the language used!
—Elizabeth Fontenot

P. C.: Thank you, Elizabeth! I'm Pagan and respecting and honoring the elements is an important part of that tradition. I prefer to keep the magick in my books element-based because of my belief system—though I do add a nice dose of fantasy and fiction to the mix. Being descriptive is simply part of good writing!

A lot of a story involving a hero or heroine requires progression (feats, new powers, love, loss, etc.). Have you given any of your characters any power or feat that you regret? I imagine it's difficult to constantly be trying to best your previous climaxes and gains over and over.

—*Byron Cox*

P. C.: I don't have an issue with this because my characters are so much more than their paranormal abilities. They're living, breathing people first—paranormal beings second. I don't try to best their abilities book after book. I simply allow them to mature (or not—depending on the character's choices), so that becoming decent human beings, or vampyres or whatever, is their superpower. The rest is just icing.

Being a part of the LGBTQ+ community, I've always loved and appreciated the representation in your books. Why has it been important to both of you to have that representation present? Would you ever consider having one of the characters' Other World counterparts be a different gender or identify differently?

—*Daniel Jackson*

Would you ever include a transgender or gender nonconforming vampyre/character in any of your books?

—*Mina Baptista*

P. C.: As these two questions are very similar and very important I'm going to include both and answer them together.

I taught secondary school for fifteen years in Broken Arrow, Oklahoma (Go Tigers!). When I began writing HoN, I made a commitment to populate my world with characters who truly reflected the teens I interacted with on a daily basis, so it was completely natural for me to include the LGBTQ+ community. Beyond that I have long been an advocate for marginalized peoples. I am a successful, educated, upper-middle-class cis white woman. I have a powerful voice. I will always use it to protect, empower, and advocate for those whose voices have been drowned out by racism, homophobia, religious hypocrisy, and misogyny. Think of how much could change—how much true *good* could be done in the world— if all white women metaphorically linked arms and refused to allow the voices of hatred and ignorance to have a platform. Women *are* powerful. We *are* wise. We *should* be joining to nurture one another and make our country and our world a place of love and Light and acceptance. What can you do to make the world better?

I do have an awesome transgender female character, Charlotte, in the Dysasters, the YA series Kristin and I write together. And in my fantasy series, Tales of a New World, I introduce River, who identifies as gender neutral. I absolutely would add a trans or gender nonconforming character to HoN should she/he/they speak to me.

When I say the answer is "love… always love," I'm not being hyperbolic or clichéd. I'm being real. Love has no gender.

K. C.: The reason why I feel it's important to include LGBTQ+ representation in my novels is simple—I write stories about humans. Our species is so unique and complex. To write a book that ignores the beauty and challenges of our uniqueness and complexities wouldn't be true to who we are as a people.

Will you continue to write about the characters into adulthood (whole new series) and make it into more of an adult series? Hope to see the characters live on in more series and spin-offs to come! PS, how's life being a grandma/mom?

—*LeAnna Herstowski*

Do you think that we might get more books after the conclusion of this series? I absolutely adore your books and would love for new stories all the time from this book universe!

—*Shelly Harris*

Will there be more novellas on some of the characters?

—*Ande Gullickson*

I asked this on the last post but for good measure (because I really want this): Have you ever considered a novella about Sgiach and Seoras?

—*Niki Rangnow*

Will you and Kristin make anymore novellas? If so, will they be about what the whole Nerd Herd has been up to/doing since graduation? I'd really like to know their side stories!

—*Ashley Munoz*

Will this series be as long as the original HON series? I hope so, I love this universe and these characters. I wish it would never end. —*Alyssa Hawk*

P. C.: So many of you asked questions similar to these that I grouped several together and will answer them all at once. Okay, here's what's up with more books—and this goes for all your favorite authors who write the books and series you love:

Career authors, like Kristin and me, who make their living writing books, write what our publishers contract us to write—it's how we pay our bills, buy groceries, and support our families. If you want more books from them all you have to do is *buy their books—encourage friends and family to buy their books—gift people with their books—spread the word and get a buzz going about their books!* Publishers will only contract authors for books that sell. So, if you say you're going to wait around until the series is completed to "binge" it, like you're watching Netflix, chances are very good that the series won't be completed. It has happened to me, and I've been a bestselling author for more than a decade. Imagine how devastating it can be for new authors! Also, never, *ever* download a book illegally. Not only is it stealing and creating some seriously awful karma, but you're dooming that author to career failure.

As to whether I want to write more books in the HoN world—of course! I love this world. I've always wanted to tell Grandma Redbird's story. I would love to write a book set after the first vampyre was created (you can find that creation story in *Kalona's Fall*). I love Sgiach and would definitely tell the story of the Great Taker of Heads. It would be fun to write an anthology with short stories that tell about how each of the Nerd Herd was Marked. I could go on and on, but whether I do depends on whether I'm contracted to write more, and that depends on you. So, the end… for now?

PS In answer specifically to LeAnna—I absolutely love being a grandma!

Who are your personal top-three favorite characters and your top-three least favorite characters, and why?
—*Josie Buckner*

P. C.: FAVES: 1) Aphrodite—she has always been very easy for me to write and I love the evolution of her character, 2) Grandma Redbird—she is the incarnation of the Crone, the third face of the Goddess, so writing her feels like a blessing, and 3) Lenobia—she has my horses!

LEAST FAVES: 1) Zoey's mom—she represents all those moms who used to sit across the table from me at parent-teacher conferences trying to justify why their teen was failing or acting out, when it was obvious that their child was screaming to be heard—to be a priority, 2) Aphrodite's mom —she's an entitled racist person who deserved the end she got, and 3) Neferet—I don't actually dislike Neferet, but she is a difficult character to write because of her descent into Darkness.

K. C.: My absolute favorite characters are 1) Heath— he's such a squishy lovebug and I absolutely adore him, 2) Aphrodite—she's so sassy and fabulous and has grown so much. I'd love it if she was my friend, and 3) Jack—I AM SO GLAD HE'S BACK! (Still mad at P. C. for killing him.)

My least favorite characters are 1) Loren Blake—he was a total predator. And then he was murdered… twice, 2) Dallas —he turned into such an ass. Yuck! And 3) the White Bull— because, well, *evil*.

1) There are many inspiring and powerful quotes in all of your books. As an author, how does this part of creation work? Do you create those quotes and then insert them into the story or are they something that comes naturally during the writing process? 2) How do you feel knowing that there are so many fans around the world who are inspired and passionate about your work? 3) You and Kristin always keep in touch with all of your fans and that's something we don't see coming from other authors or known people. How did it start? —*T. J. Marques*

P. C.: (Waving at Thiago and all our Brazilian "Nighters"!)

1. The quotes come naturally from the characters as I write them. If I try to be clever or to insert myself too much in what my characters say I fail miserably.
2. The worldwide love for the House of Night is one of the greatest joys of my life, and will be until the day I go to frolic with the Goddess.
3. I love connecting with my readers! It started because I can (literally) talk to moss about my books. Ask Kristin. Seriously. So, when readers actually *talked back to me* it was fantastic! My only regret is that sometimes it's difficult to keep up and get my writing done.

If you could bring alive one person from the book (from either world) who would it be and why? (A question for both P. C. and Kristin.)

—*Randy Shewmaker*

P. C.: Grandma Redbird because the world needs more kindness and wisdom.

K. C.: Definitely Aphrodite. We would have so much fun!

What does a real Okie twang sound like? Will you ever come to Jacksonville, Florida, for a book signing? It's beautiful (and will still be lovely weather) in the fall!

—*Sara Rennard*

P. C.: Well, those of you listenin' to the audio will hear an Okie twang right now! Ha!

Thanks for asking about book signings! Many readers don't know that authors don't set their tours—publishers do that. If you want to try to get your favorite authors touring near you the best things you can do are to 1) buy their books locally and encourage friends and family to buy their books, and 2) ask your local bookstore management to request, via the authors publisher(s) that their store be added to a tour stop list. Publishers listen to bookseller requests—and they also look at sales numbers when deciding where to tour their authors.

Fans always have a way of showing support for their favorite books/authors (I have a tattoo that was inspired by the cover of *Untamed*). What is the strangest thing anyone has given you or shown you that was inspired by your books?

—*Maureen Gurney*

P. C.: Oooh! I love this question! (And please share a pic of your tattoo with me online!) Fans have gifted me with so, so many fantastic things! Right now I have a hand-knitted shawl wrapped around my shoulders that a fan gifted to me almost twenty years ago after my first book was released. It's decorated with symbols from my Partholon books and I adore it. But the weirdest thing *by far* was when a woman asked Kristin and me to take a picture with her "babies" that she had created based on HoN characters. I was confused because we were at a signing and she had no babies with her, but I said, "Sure!" She took off her fanny pack, opened it, and pulled out little babies that represented the Nerd Herd *and they were made of hair!* Kristin almost lost it. Our editor was standing behind us and (after the woman left) she said that was the strangest thing she'd ever had happen at a signing.

  K. C.: The hair babies!!! I just cannot...